A CLEAR BLUE SKY

Also by Barbara Whitnell

Charmed Circle
Freedom Street
Loveday
The Ring of Bells
The Salt Rakers
The Song of the Rainbird
The View from the Summerhouse

A CLEAR BLUE SKY

SKY

Barbara Whitnell

ST. MARTIN'S PRESS ✿ NEW YORK

Library of Congress Cataloging-in-Publication Data

Whitnell, Barbara.
A clear blue sky / by Barbara Whitnell.
      p.   cm.
"Thomas Dunne Book."
ISBN 0-312-13945-4
1. Married people—England—Cornwall (County)—
Fiction.   2. Family—England—Cornwall (County)—
Fiction.   3. Cornwall (England : County)—Fiction.
I. Title.
PR6073.H653C58   1996
823'.914—dc20   95-43713   CIP

First published in Great Britain by BCA.

First U.S. Edition: January 1996
10 9 8 7 6 5 4 3 2 1

For Stan and Bess,
with much love.

A CLEAR BLUE SKY

1

"I thought," Oliver Sheridan said to his daughter, surveying the collection of suitcases, plastic bags and sundry other receptacles that stood at the bottom of the front steps, "that we were about to spend a fortnight's holiday by the sea, not embark on a trans-Africa safari."

"You know Mum," Emma said, thrusting a pair of Doc Martens into a Sainsbury's bag already overflowing with assorted shoes.

"I do. Indeed I do," Oliver said. "Where is she, anyway? She can't still be defrosting the fridge or cleaning the stove."

It was a well-worn family joke that Kate was never ready to leave until everything had been spring-cleaned. She hated, she said, to come home to a dirty house after a good holiday, but Oliver maintained the truth was that she couldn't bear to think of a chance burglar running a pernickety finger along the mantelpiece to check for dust, or shaking his head over an unvacuumed carpet.

"I think she's making sure that all the windows are locked," Emma said.

"I've done that!"

"You know Mum," Emma said again, with amused resignation.

"Emma," her mother called from the open front door. "Did you bring the cake tin out? The round one with the pink flowers? I can't see it anywhere."

"I did." Oliver, having heaved the largest suitcase into the boot, paused in his labours for a moment. "I put it inside, under the passenger seat. Do you want the cold bag somewhere accessible?"

"Not necessarily." Slowly Kate came down the steps, checking a list as she did so, looking up sharply as she took in the full impact of his words. "Careful, Oliver – it must go upright. There's a casserole inside full of chicken Provençale for tonight's dinner."

"I'll wedge it in the corner. It'll be fine there."

"I think that's everything." Kate was still frowning over the list. "I did put knives in, didn't I?"

"Knives?" Emma, feverishly checking the contents of a holdall, paused for a moment and looked up at her mother in bewilderment. "Why knives? I thought the house was furnished."

"It's in case you get out of line," Oliver said, baring his teeth and making a menacing gesture towards her. "Spare the knife and spoil the child, I always say."

Kate ignored this nonsense.

"Rented houses never have any implement capable of cutting through anything more substantial than butter," she said. "It's a well-established fact. Actually, I've a good mind to take the salad spinner, too. They do make life easier, and I'm willing to bet there won't be one provided."

"Why not the kitchen sink?" Oliver enquired mildly.

"Mum, have you seen my address book?" Emma had returned to her task of rummaging through the holdall. "I must take it. I've promised to send cards to absolutely everybody."

Kate opened her mouth to reply, but instead cocked her head on one side and stayed silent. The telephone was ringing inside the house.

"I'll get it," Emma said, leaping up the steps. "I expect it's for me. Clare said she'd call to say goodbye."

"But—" Kate bit back her words, knowing that the fact that Clare, Emma's best friend, had been on the phone the previous evening for a full hour meant nothing. Fourteen-year-old girls, she knew from experience, never ran out of urgent things to communicate to each other. Anyway, she hoped it was Clare, and not word of some vital emergency that would prevent Oliver leaving London in roughly ten minutes' time. They had a long drive ahead of them.

"It's for you, Dad." Emma, more slowly, was coming down the steps once more. "Fish-features," she added in Kate's direction, as her father went inside.

"Em!" Kate did her best to utter a note of reproof, but found it impossible not to look amused. "Anna's a very attractive woman."

Damn her, she added silently. Anna Vincent had taken over as locum when Dr Harker, one of the older members of the firm at the Health Centre where Oliver had his practice, had suffered a heart attack, followed by complicated surgery. She was slim, attractive, blonde, immaculately made-up at all times, and never – or so it seemed to Kate – suffered the slightest pang of self-doubt or feeling of inadequacy; an example, in short, to all aspiring career women everywhere. Still, it had to be said that if one were hell-bent on being bitchy, there was something undeniably piscatorial about her rather wide round eyes and flattened lips.

From the very beginning, her supreme self-satisfaction had grated on Kate. The impression she gave of a woman who could deal competently and crisply with any problem set before her somehow implied that others constantly fell short – especially others such as Kate who worked part-time as a counsellor for Relate. Five minutes of Anna's company made her feel no more than a bumbling do-gooder – a well-meaning but ultimately inefficient amateur.

This would have been aggravating on its own, but it was made worse by the undeniable fact that despite Anna's apparent efficiency, the demands of the Health Centre – its economic problems and the paperwork associated with its new fund-holding status – seemed to fall a great deal more heavily on Oliver since her arrival than it had ever done before. This, of course, was understandable at first, but as the weeks went by, Kate began to suspect that the latest member of the firm was relying on her feminine wiles to get away with murder in such matters as night calls, weekend duties and many other matters; in other words, she was a fraud, playing the role of a career woman while at heart she was nothing more than a bimbo.

Kate began to enquire more assiduously than ever about Brian Harker's health, and was disappointed, if understanding, when after his convalescence was over he took three months' leave to visit a daughter in Australia. They were not, it seemed, to be relieved of Anna for some time to come.

Still, she was a good doctor, Oliver said. A good diagnostician; which, Kate thought, must be why she had diagnosed him as being such an easy touch.

"This call better not be something serious," she said to Emma, pushing ancient beach towels into a crevice among the cases. "If That

3

Woman has dreamed up something to drag your father back to the Centre . . ." She left the sentence unfinished, but the fierceness with which she gave the last towel an extra shove betrayed her feelings. "Really, we must get off soon."

Emma wasn't listening. Instead her attention was on a figure on a bicycle approaching the house, her expression one of amused disdain.

"Look what the cat's dragged in," she remarked, sotto voce.

"Hi, Em." A lanky youth with round spectacles and hair so short that it looked as if someone had run a lawn mower over it, swerved into the small space outside the house and came to a halt.

"Well!" Emma could hardly have sounded less enthusiastic. "What brings you here?"

The youth scuffed the drive with the toe of his disreputable trainers. "I just thought – well, I knew you were going away today, so I came to say goodbye and have a good time."

"Thanks," said Emma shortly.

"How kind of you!" Kate, feeling that her daughter's response was lamentably lacking in social grace, smiled at him. "It's Adam, isn't it?"

"Damien," said the boy. He was wearing a strained expression and was blinking nervously, a prominent Adam's apple leaping around in his throat like a caged animal. Perhaps, thought Kate, that's why I thought—

"I'm sorry. Yes, Damien, of course. Well, we're almost off, Damien."

"Absolutely any minute," added Emma.

"Yes, well . . ." he laughed nervously. "I mustn't hold you up."

"No." Emma smiled frostily.

"You're – you're going to Cornwall?"

"That's right."

"I've been there. Once."

"Oh? Where did you stay?" Kate was still being bright and sociable, despite a glare from her daughter.

Damien looked hunted.

"I – er – I can't actually remember. It was quite a few years ago. It was definitely Cornwall, though." He paused for a moment. "Or Devon," he added uncertainly. "Maybe it was Devon."

Kate adopted an expression of interest, but Emma looked at him coldly.

4

"It obviously made a lasting impression," she said.

He took the remark at its face value, and grinned widely.

"Yeah, it was great."

Emma turned away from him.

"Well," she said, a note of finality in her voice. "I'd better get on. There are still some last minute things—"

"I hope you have a good time."

"So you said. I'm sure I shall."

"You could send me a card." Damien laughed nervously once more, as if to show he was only joking.

"I could, couldn't I?"

"Yes – well – " Damien lingered for a moment longer, but since Emma merely looked at him and said nothing, he seemed, finally, to grasp the fact that there was little left to stay for. After expressing, once more, the pious hope that she would have a good time, he wheeled his bicycle round and rode off, stopping as he reached the road to look round and remind her not to forget the card.

"In his dreams," she said scornfully to Kate. "Honestly, megawet or *what*?"

"You weren't very nice to him, darling."

"Well, look at him! He's *gross*, Mum. A total dweeb. Everybody knows it. You shouldn't have encouraged him."

"I was only treating the poor lad with common politeness."

"He's the last person I want hanging around. Oh, Mum, when are we going? I can't wait to get started."

Emma had been enthusiastically in favour of this holiday ever since it had been suggested. It would be fun, she'd said. Clare had been to Porthallic the year before and had come back singing its praises. It was, it seemed, a cool kind of place.

"Clare says it's brilliant," Emma had reported. "Loads of people have holiday homes there. Some people even let their kids stay on, even when they've come home themselves. It sounds really wicked."

Kate, unfazed, knew that wicked didn't mean *wicked*, but everything that was good and wonderful and likely to appeal to the average fourteen-going-on-fifteen-year-old with a taste for whatever was – in her own, out-of-date terminology – with it.

"I wish Clare would phone," Emma went on. "I thought of some last-minute things I wanted to ask her. She *said* she would. She's probably trying right this minute but can't get through, not with old Fish-features rabbiting on—"

"Not any more," Kate said, as Oliver re-emerged from the house. He was frowning, she noted, her heart sinking.

"You haven't got to go, have you?" she asked anxiously.

He shook his head and appeared to force a smile, as if determined to put all the cares of the surgery behind him.

"No, it was nothing like that. Anna wanted a bit of clarification about the computerised records on mental health. Remember – I told you about them?"

"I remember," Kate said flatly. Oliver had recently written an article in the *British Medical Journal* entitled "Mind and Body: A Family Practitioner's View of Psychosomatic Illness", and as a result the Health Centre had been asked by University College Hospital to cooperate in a long-term study. She had thought at the time, and still did so, that it was one more straw that could yet break the camel's back; however, Oliver had always been interested in this area and the other doctors had been willing, so she had kept her doubts to herself.

"She couldn't possibly have asked Tom or Derek, of course?"

Tom Farland and Derek Nicholls were the two other doctors in the partnership. Oliver shrugged and smiled.

"They were probably busy," he said.

While you, Kate thought as he picked up the last remaining bags, have only to attend to the small matter of taking your family on holiday. She managed, however, to remain silent.

"Have I got time to phone Clare?" Emma asked.

"You're absolutely sure you've brought everything down you want to take with you? What about the flippers?"

"They're in that blue bag."

"Do you really need those Doc Martens? You'll be on the beach most of the time."

"Mu-u-um! Of *course* I need them! If you think I'm going to wear *sandals*—"

"Silly of me," Kate said dryly. "I somehow thought that sandals might be more appropriate for a holiday by the sea—"

"Get *real*," said Emma, as she made for the house once more.

6

"Two minutes," Kate said, calling after her. "Not a second more. Then we're leaving, with or without you."

"Ha ha," Emma said mirthlessly, knowing she lied.

"I don't think I've forgotten anything."

Kate was still pouring over her list as they drove away from the tree-lined avenue in the direction of the M4.

"Mmm?" Oliver's attention was engaged elsewhere as he watched for his opportunity to accelerate into the stream of cars racing around the Chiswick roundabout.

"Lynn said she'd bring the salad for tonight." Kate continued to look worried. "I wonder if she's remembered? I meant to ring and remind her—"

"She'll have remembered." Oliver was soothing but still a little distracted, as a space opened up and the car's engine roared into life. "Don't fuss, darling."

"I'm not *fussing*."

"Well, it doesn't matter, does it? We can always eat out."

"Eat out?" Kate turned to look at him. "Eat *out*? Haven't you listened to a word I've said over the past few weeks? The house is virtually on the beach. There's nothing there, Oliver, nothing at all, except the farm at the end of the lane where we can buy eggs and vegetables. I told you! You said it sounded like Paradise."

"What, no Chinese takeaway? No M & S? How can we support life?"

"Only by being thoroughly organised."

"Well, then, we're home and dry." There was a note of ironic amusement in his voice. "Being thoroughly organised is your forte, isn't it?"

"There's no need to be so snide about it!"

"I'm not being snide." Oliver took a hand off the wheel and patted her knee in a mollifying kind of way, but Kate remained slightly piqued.

"How you imagine any woman juggles a house and children and a job *without* being—"

"I don't imagine. No such heinous thought ever entered my tiny mind."

"If I had five pounds for every couple I see whose problems stem from a husband's sheer insensitivity—"

"So help me, I'm sensitive! Listen," Oliver went on after a moment. "Let's agree a kind of truce. I won't talk about the National Health Service or psychosomatic illness or dissociative states for the next two weeks, if you preserve the silence of a Trappist monk about Relate."

Softening a little, Kate laughed.

"OK, it's a deal. I'll eat my new straw hat if you keep to it, though."

"I'll try, I promise, if you do the same. For two glorious weeks I'd welcome a break from other people's problems."

"Sorry I'm such a bore."

"I meant patients, idiot."

For a few more miles Kate was silent, though Oliver was too well acquainted with her to think it was the scenery that occupied her attention. She would, he knew, be going over the arrangements in her mind – checking this, worrying about that. Trying, in short, to think of all eventualities, all in the best of causes. This holiday meant so much to her, and she was determined that it would, for everyone involved, be as perfect as any holiday could be.

"I wonder why we haven't done this before?" she mused. "It seems the obvious thing."

"Well, Leo and Lynn have always gone abroad with those friends of theirs, haven't they?"

"Yes, of course." Kate sighed and shook her head. "The Marshalls. Geoff and Jane. And now Geoff's lost his job they won't be having a holiday at all. Lynn and Leo feel terrible about it."

"Why should they?"

"Of course they feel terrible! It was Leo who encouraged Geoff to apply for the vacancy at Pangbourne's last year. And now Leo's hung on to his job, but Geoff's been made redundant."

"Hmm." Oliver drove in silence for a moment. "Leo was lucky," he said at last.

"He's good at what he does. Anyway, he's worked for Pangbourne's for ages. I expect it was a matter of last in, first out."

Emma, jerking to the silent beat of her Walkman, took out her earpiece to join in the conversation.

"Wouldn't it be great if Caroline was with us?" she said.

8

"Oh, it would." Kate's agreement was heartfelt.

"I'd like her to be here too," Oliver said, a little defensively. "But really she's OK where she is. Mark my words, she'll thank us for making her go through with it."

"Oh, sure," Emma said sarcastically. "I bet she's loving every minute of being a slave to those foul kids and putting up with that awful Frau Ulbricht and terrible German food."

"Well, she's sounding a lot more settled than when she first went out," Kate pointed out, clinging to the comfort this thought afforded her. "Summer in the Ulbrichts' villa on the Italian Lakes doesn't sound too much of a hardship to me – and she says herself her German has improved out of all recognition."

"The whole experience will do her the world of good, mark my words."

"Well, you'd better not try it with me," Emma said fiercely.

"I would point out," said Kate patiently, "that nobody made her go. The whole thing was Caroline's idea. It was only after she got to Munich that it all seemed a bit too much like hard work."

She suffered the familiar pang, however, remembering the early phone calls made by her elder daughter when first she had gone au pairing – that tremulous, tear-filled voice speaking of homesickness and exploitation. Her immediate reaction was to drop everything and fly to Germany to bring her back on the instant, but Oliver had restrained her. Had, in fact, put his foot down, which was strange when one considered how he had always indulged the girls. Normally her complaint was that he was too busy being top of the ratings with them to back up any disciplinary restrictions she might impose, but on this occasion he had insisted on standing firm.

The Ulbrichts, he said, were a respectable family, vouched for by friends. The work they expected Caroline to do sounded reasonable, and her time off in line with other au pairs. It would do her no good at all if, having put her hand to the wheel, she was allowed to turn back at the first hint of homesickness. After all, next year she would be at university, and this period of standing on her own feet would do her the world of good. The homesickness, he assured Kate, wouldn't last long, and the benefits of being able to speak fluent German in this communal age would be immeasurable.

It had seemed hard and unfeeling at the time, but Kate had now to admit that he had apparently been right. Caroline had made friends and seemed to be enjoying life – which was no comfort to Emma, who missed her badly. As did Kate herself.

Deliberately she switched her thoughts away from her absent daughter and mentally checked her holiday list once more. She hoped nothing was forgotten, and that the whole enterprise would be a success. She felt so responsible.

It had all been her idea, right from the beginning, born one night when worry about Caroline had effectively banished sleep.

Her latest piteous phone call had sparked off a row with Oliver that even now it was painful to recall. Conscious of Emma's presence they had preserved a kind of armed truce during the evening, but the argument had flared again just before they went to bed and harsh words were spoken, issues raised, that ranged far beyond the immediate problem. Kate had said he was remote and uncaring and had in turn been accused of being overemotional and overprotective – wanting, said Oliver, to run everyone's lives for them. Including his. And if she wanted to know the truth, he was heartily sick of it.

It had ended, much to Kate's fury, with tears of rage and frustration on her part – rage because it was all so unjust, she only wanted people to be happy, and frustration because she could never think of all she wanted to say until after Oliver had fallen asleep, which on this occasion, as on all similar ones, was immediately his head touched the pillow.

She, on the other hand, had found it impossible to do the same and had, eventually, gone down to the kitchen where she made tea, sitting to drink it at the breakfast bar she had always hated. She felt it compared unfavourably to the scrubbed table that had stood four-square at the very centre of her childhood. Sipping reflectively, she reviewed her life.

The feeling that somehow, somewhere, it had failed to live up to expectations was hardly a new one. She thought, as she often did, about her own childhood – hers and Lynn's – when everything seemed full of promise. There must have been childhood squabbles between them, she supposed; they weren't angels, after all – but she couldn't remember them and certainly she'd never been aware of any tension between her mother and father. When had either uttered a hint of criticism of the other? When had her father ever treated her mother with less than love and admiration and tenderness and respect?

Never would they have indulged in the kind of slanging match that had so recently set the rafters ringing in the Sheridan household. Her mother – dear, sweet, gentle Rose – would have been devastated had it been any different. Tranquillity and good manners and the warmth of approval had wrapped them all in a secure and delightful cocoon.

Kate had met Oliver at someone's birthday party, and had fallen in love on the instant. She had been twenty-one, a nurse in training at St Thomas's, and he six years older – newly qualified, self-confident, handsome and funny, with a touch of arrogance that merely added to the glamour of his dark good looks.

She knew herself to be reasonably pretty; maybe not as pretty as her sister Lynn, but not at all bad. Even so, she had never expected such a gorgeous creature as Oliver Sheridan to fall in love with her in return. When, however, it became clear that he had done so, she came to accept it as a logical continuance of her happy, favoured childhood, confidently expecting the uncritical type of approval she had enjoyed from her parents to extend into her marriage. For her part, she was determined to do everything to be the perfect wife that Oliver deserved.

She became pregnant almost immediately and was glad to give up her job so that she could give all her energies to creating the same kind of gracious, well-ordered home that she had known all her life; the kind of home where a man could relax in a calm, strife-free atmosphere, shrugging off all his workaday troubles the moment he crossed the threshold. A home where friends were welcomed, where flavoursome meals were served amid spotless napery and prettily arranged flowers. A setting, in short, worthy of the hard-working, idealistic young doctor that she knew Oliver to be.

That he came to show signs of irritation at her struggle for perfection had been a puzzling blow to her. She had not allowed for shortage of money in those early days, or the fact that his own childhood home had been untidy – even chaotic, with a coldly intellectual mother devoted only to her medical career and a father who had more interest in the life cycle of obscure invertebrates than the supply of clean shirts or an immaculate house. Neither had she taken into consideration Oliver's

11

mercurial nature or the long hours he was forced to work, or broken nights, or dinner parties interrupted or never attended, or children less biddable than she and Lynn had been. Even after nineteen years of marriage, she was still unable to come to terms with the fact that she always seemed to fall short of her own exacting standards, formed and nurtured so long ago.

A montage of good times from her own childhood floated before her as glumly she sat sipping her tea, to the accompaniment of the whirring of the fridge. Mealtimes, full of discussion and jokes and laughter; these days they were often no more than an opportunity for Emma to wrangle about the time she was expected to come home at night, just as Caroline had done before her.

Then there was Christmas. It had always been a magical time, with its secrets and excitement and silly games, and Dad reading bits of Dickens by the fire. It was years since either of the girls had taken pleasure in anything like that. It was all TV these days, with some trashy film on Christmas night that no one could possibly bear to miss.

And holidays. Year after year, the family had taken that house in Cornwall, near St Mawes – always the same time, always the same house – never wanting anything more exotic, never minding the rain or the chilly temperature of the sea. Even when they were quite grown up none of them would have dreamed of missing it. It had been a time, somehow, for re-establishing the ties that bound them, underpinning the relationship that was so important to all of them. Even after marriage the tradition continued, for a year or two. It was only with the arrival of babies and the eventual death of her father that things had changed, other arrangements had been made, and now it was – how long? Oh, years and years since she and Lynn had spent any length of time together. She and Oliver had taken the girls up to Brascombe, the small Worcestershire market town where the Bryants had their home, for the occasional holiday weekend, and sometimes Leo came to London for a conference or exhibition or something of the sort, and then he and the family would stay for a few days – but somehow the time was always filled with shopping or appointments or going to a concert or play, and there was never time to relax in each other's company.

Now, sitting alone in the kitchen at dead of night, thinking about the

12

past and the fun they used to have, she resolved to ring Lynn the very next morning to suggest that they should come to stay – and it was in that moment that inspiration struck. Why not recreate those wonderful summers of their youth? Why not suggest a joint holiday? A house by the sea, big enough to cope with them all – in Cornwall, where else?

She sat up straighter, happier now that she had plans to make, and the more she thought about it, the more desirable her idea became. The children, she felt sure, would love it; in fact it was surely the sisters' solemn duty to introduce this new generation to the kind of holiday that they had so much enjoyed when they were young. Granted, it was already May and late in the year to book, but not too late, surely? Inevitably there would be cancellations.

Lynn and Leo hadn't made any plans, she knew that. The last time she'd phoned Lynn she had asked, simply by way of conversation, if they were going to France with the Marshalls as usual. It was then that she'd been told the news of Geoff Marshall's redundancy. He had lost his job at Pangbourne's – just one among many, but no less upsetting for that in view of Leo's role in bringing the vacancy to his notice, less than a year before.

It was, in fact, only recently that Leo had known for certain that his own job was safe. He had gone to Pangbourne's, the pharmaceutical manufacturers, direct from university and had worked his way up to a senior management position in the finance division. The takeover of the company by Reitz-Keppel, the German-based multinational, had long been rumoured and was eventually thought to be inevitable. When this came to pass, everyone expected a shake-up and knew that inevitably heads would roll – but which heads would do the rolling was the subject of wild surmise. Leo believed that the entire finance division would be moved to Cologne and what would happen to him was anybody's guess.

In the event, and despite the takeover, his job proved to be safe, but not before he and Lynn had spent weeks of uncertainty and dread. Holidays, Lynn had told Kate, had been the last thing on their minds.

A real family holiday would be a *wonderful* idea, Kate thought, her eyes brightening. She felt sure Oliver would agree. He and Leo were as unlike as any two men could be, but they always got on well.

Everyone got on with Leo. He was just the nicest, most easy-going

13

man in the world. A bit straight-laced, maybe; a bit earnest and conventional. You tended to know what his opinions were before he stated them – but he was a lovely man just the same. (And undoubtedly, thought Kate in parenthesis, a lot easier to live with than Oliver.)

And who could tell? Maybe, under the influence of all that wonderful scenery and a slower tempo of life with more time to spend together, she and Oliver might recapture some of the delight that had lately disappeared from their marriage. Maybe she herself would be able to relax, become less tense, more laid-back about everything. Not feel it necessary to *try* quite so hard. That remark from Oliver about being sick to death of being organised had lingered on in the memory, returning at intervals to haunt her. He had a point, she knew, but what he didn't realise was that without her efforts, their life would be chaotic. There were so many things to accommodate: his job, her job, Emma to ferry here, there and everywhere. Not to mention meals and shopping and a full social calendar. How did he otherwise explain the appearance of food on the table, clean shirts in his drawer? True, she had Mrs Parsons to clean twice a week, but this still left a lot to do.

And even if she did concede that she was too preoccupied with these mundane matters, in all fairness some of the blame for the recent staleness in their marriage must surely be laid at Oliver's door. He had been so remote lately, so impossible to talk to. She knew his work was important to him and that it was right it should be so, but it was wrong that their relationship should suffer because of it, and it would do them both good to get right away.

Oliver, next day, had been in a conciliatory mood, regretful about the row and only too ready to make amends, so that an agreement to the idea in principle was quickly forthcoming. Lynn, too, was enthusiastic. It was just what they needed, she said. The tension of the past weeks had been frightful.

Immediately Kate set enquiries in motion. Every agent she rang assured her that no such accommodation was still available for the period she required, but a casual conversation with a fellow worker at Relate had supplied her with the telephone number of a friend of a friend who had, at once and with great relief, offered her the tenancy of a large house practically on the beach.

"We've had a cancellation," the friend said. "The same family have it for those same two weeks every year, but suddenly a daughter's getting married in America and they're dashing off – you know how it is. I'll put the details in the post right away."

Oliver whistled in horrified astonishment when he saw the size of the rent demanded, but Kate persuaded him that set against what they usually spent when they took the car across to the Continent, it wasn't too bad.

"The ferry alone always costs a bomb," she said persuasively. "And this will be split down the middle, after all. Do look at these photographs, darling – doesn't it look gorgeous? Porthlenter, it's called. Mrs Dawson, the owner, says it means 'shining cove' in Cornish – isn't that lovely? She says it's only a stone's throw from the beach, surrounded by the most gorgeous country. I wonder why it is that landladies always think you're going to want to throw stones? Anyway, it's well furnished, she said. Nothing grand, but very comfortable. Apparently it was once a farmhouse and all this land around belonged to it, but her father-in-law was a builder and thought he'd buy it and modernise it and make a killing. He sold the land to the farmer next door, but he loved the situation so much he couldn't bear to sell the house after all, so he lived in it himself until he was carried out feet first. The Dawsons inherited it."

"Lucky sods," said Oliver, looking with envy at the pictures. "Why don't we have relations like that?"

"They go down a lot themselves, but always let it during August."

"I can see why, if they can charge a rent like this. I should think they'll be retiring in unimaginable luxury to the French Riviera at any moment. Is it big enough for all of us, though? Where's Rose going to sleep?"

Kate frowned, still a little perplexed by her mother's refusal to come with them. She had expected her to seize the opportunity of a holiday with her children and grandchildren with both hands.

"Well, she's arranged to go away with that funny friend of hers – the one she goes to art classes with. Amy Binns-Taylor, you know the one. They're going to Provence on a painting and pottery-making holiday. They booked it months ago."

"Pottery, eh? She is branching out."

"Yes – who'd have thought it? Poor love! Ever since Dad died I get

15

the feeling she's just rushing around in circles, trying to find things to fill in the time."

"But she doesn't want to fill it in with us."

"Apparently not. So four bedrooms are perfectly adequate."

"Who's going to have the one with the *en-suite* bathroom?" Oliver asked.

"We'll toss for it when we get there. It doesn't matter a lot, does it? There's another bathroom on that floor, *and* a shower in the downstairs cloakroom. Oh Oliver, doesn't it look perfect? I'm sure it was *meant* to be!"

"Maybe it was." Oliver reached out and pulled her close, and for a few moments she lay with her head on his shoulder, excited and happy, all dissension forgotten.

"So you do agree?" she asked, twisting her head to look up at him.

"If it's OK with Lynn and Leo—"

"Oh, it will be! I know it will."

She reached up to kiss him, and he kissed her back. The magic of Cornwall was working already, she thought. It was all going to be wonderful.

Now, three months later, she couldn't help worrying, just a little. Everything had been her idea, and it would be her fault if the holiday was less than perfect – if the house failed to come up to their expectations, if it turned out to be so isolated that shopping was difficult and the provision of meals an awful chore. And would the children find enough to do? She did so want everyone to have a wonderful time.

"Calm down and stop worrying," Oliver said, fully aware of the direction of her thoughts though his eyes were on the road ahead. "It'll be fun."

"I hope so." She looked at him gratefully, not even surprised, after nineteen years of marriage, that he knew her well enough to divine her unspoken feelings. "At least the weather's set fair."

"Not a cloud in the sky," Oliver said. "Mr Fish opines that we're in for a heat wave."

"Well, I hope you packed an umbrella then," said Emma, dourly.

"Seat belts fastened?"

From outside the car, Leo Bryant looked through the window at his family, corralled on the back seat.

16

"Yes," said Lucy, answering for all of them.

"No," said James at the same time. "At least, I have, but I'm unfastening it again because I want to go to the loo—"

"You can't do, idiot," said William. "You've just been. I'm not letting you out."

"Yes, you are," Leo said in a voice that, though pleasant, brooked no denial. "Come on, Wills. Get out of the car and let James get past."

"What a pest," William grumbled, obeying his father. "It's always the same, wherever we go—"

"He gets nervous," Lucy said, leaping to the defence of her younger brother, even now scooting back into the house. She always did leap to his defence, particularly where William was concerned. William was a robust ten-year-old, full of bounce and energy, whereas James was shy and rather small for his seven years. From the moment of his birth she had been filled with tenderness for him. "He can't help dreading car journeys. You know that, Wills."

"Well, if he's going to be sick, bags he sits by the window."

"He wanted to! It was you who wouldn't let him."

"Well, I don't see why I should be the one to sit all squished up in the middle. Why don't you?"

"Why should I? My legs are longer than yours—"

"Better sit in the middle, Wills," Leo said firmly. "To start with, anyway."

"*Da – ad*!"

"You'll have to take it in turns. Where's your mother? I thought she was ready!"

"She just dashed next door to have a last word with Mrs Nelson about feeding Moggity."

Leo, who was large and sandy-haired and had the appearance of an oversized and amiable teddy bear, folded his arms on the roof of the car just above the driving seat and rested his head on them. Guiltily, the words "Give me strength" sprang to his mind, but he pushed them away. Lynn had a lot to think about, he reminded himself. She'd been at that wretched bookshop until late yesterday and had been up till almost midnight doing last-minute washing and ironing. She tried to do too much, that was the truth of it. He'd be glad when the shop was a thing of the past—

His thoughts swerved away; he hadn't mentioned the possibility of change to Lynn. It was hard to do so when she was still basking in euphoria over the fact that he still had his job. She was a marvellous wife, no doubt about it, the best; but would even the best of wives see his point of view?

Where was she? He lifted his head and stared, frowning, at the house next door. Why was it they could never get off on time?

Lucy, conscious of his feelings, hoped very much that her mother would come soon. Going on holiday nearly always produced this kind of stress. Dad liked to set a time to leave and keep to it, while Mum treated it as something to be aimed at, but happily ignored if necessary.

Normally life proceeded on its tranquil way, with few – if any – cross words between her parents; they weren't the sort of people to whom cross words came naturally. Going on holiday, combining as it did her father's meticulous time-keeping and her mother's easy-going, laid-back temperament was always something of a strain, however, and she was always glad when they were at last on the road. Then, she knew from experience, despite the odd spat with William who hated to sit still for more than five minutes, peace and friendship would be restored. It was just this early bit that was so traumatic.

"She's coming," she said now with relief. "They both are."

"Thank heaven." Leo, forgetting his momentary annoyance, as he always did at the sight of his wife, turned to smile at Lynn. "Everything fixed?"

"Sorry, darling." Lynn's expression was strained. "I wanted to make sure Mrs Nelson had the back-door key. I gave it to Alan – you know, the youngest boy – to give to her yesterday with instructions about cat food, but I suddenly had a dreadful feeling he might have forgotten to remind her about the gerbils. It's all right, though. He hadn't."

"So everybody has got everything they want, and I can now lock the house?"

"I think so. Last check, everyone—"

"Where's my Game Boy?"

"*Here*, you twit—"

"I want to sit next to Lucy—"

"Why can't we *take* Moggity?"

"You did put the picnic basket in, didn't you?"

"Mum, Mum, I think my stick insects are going to be too hot on the back shelf—"

"Belts done up? Right, we're off," Leo said, fastening his own safety belt. "What's forgotten, stays forgotten."

"Wait – did I cancel the papers, Leo?"

"You said you did."

"Then I expect I did." Lynn looked over her shoulder towards the children in the back of the car and smiled at them. "Everything all right in the back?"

She looked normal again, Lucy noted thankfully. That awful tight, strained, unsmiling sort of smile that had been in evidence for ages and ages seemed to have gone at last, now Dad's job was safe – in fact she looked better than ever, really, because worry had made her lose weight, which was something Lucy had been advising her to do for ages.

They were among the lucky ones. Debbie Marshall, her best friend, wasn't, which made her feel sad and guilty, even though she knew that it wasn't her fault – or her parents', really, although she knew they felt that it was. Dad had only meant to be kind and helpful when he told Geoff about the vacancy at Pangbourne's – now Reitz-Keppel, and a different place altogether.

Still, the result was the same. Geoff was now out of a job, in common with numerous other people in their small, Midlands town, and it was difficult to know what to say, how to act, except to assure Debbie that they'd still be best friends, no matter if the family moved away or if she had to go to a different school.

She'd gone back to tea with Debbie the other day and they'd found Jane crying in the kitchen, which had, perhaps, been the most embarrassing moment of her life to date. So now, beneath the natural excitement caused by going on holiday, was the relief that she was leaving all the awkwardness behind.

She was looking forward to seeing Emma, too. Emma was – well, different. Glamorous. Sophisticated, with all kinds of unconventional, off-the-wall views about things. What, Lucy wondered, would she think of her younger cousin now? Would she feel that she had almost caught up?

Lucy had been encouraged lately by the number of people who had said she looked like her mother. She couldn't see it herself. Her hair was darker and she had a different sort of nose – but there had to be something in it, because people as widely divergent as Debbie and the vicar had remarked on it. Of course, her mother's blonde hair was not entirely natural these days, but it had been once; in fact, she had always been something of a beauty. There were photographs going back years that proved the point, beyond any doubt. The thought that she was even remotely like her was one that Lucy found pleasing in the extreme. Would Emma notice?

Dad always said that he'd never been able to understand why a girl like Mum should ever have looked at him, but Lucy thought it was perfectly obvious. Mum had seen how kind and nice and funny and cuddly he was, and who could ask for more? When the time came to get married, Lucy thought, she would look for someone exactly the same.

"Lucy, let's play something," James said (except that this emerged as "Luthy, letth play thomething" on account of the fact that he had only half a large, new tooth in the front of his mouth, plus a space where the other would come in time). He was peering at his sister round William who, reluctantly, had taken his place in the middle between them.

Lucy made an effort to rise to the occasion.

"I Spy?"

"Too boring!"

"What then?"

"How about 'Sing the Sig'? Oh, shut *up*, Wills!" William, who had begun to hum the *Neighbours* signature tune in a loud falsetto, merely continued, at increased volume, bouncing up and down in time to the music. "Shut *up*! That's not the way we do it. It's the other way round. You say the programme and the other person has to sing the tune. Anyway, we don't allow *Neighbours*, it's too easy. You're just going to spoil it if you go on."

Lucy once more weighed in on James's side.

"Yes, shut up, Wills. You're only doing that to make him mad."

"Well, bags first go then."

"Only if you play properly."

"The Bryant family is on its way." All irritation forgotten, Leo smiled sideways at Lynn, and she smiled back.

"May God have mercy on our souls," she said.

2

The Sheridans had left the main road and turned into a lane which seemed to get narrower the further they progressed along it. Kate was certain it couldn't possibly lead anywhere – that Oliver must have mistaken the turning three miles back; but Oliver, putting his faith in his detailed map of the area together with the instructions issued by Mrs Dawson, insisted on pushing ahead.

He gave a cry of triumph as they came to crossroads and a hamlet consisting of a scattering of cottages. A notice beside the road proclaimed this to be Sproull's Corner, and it was shortly after this, they had been told, that they would find Brook Farm beside a narrow track that would, given persistence, take them to Porthlenter.

The track, when located, was indeed narrow and full of potholes. Furthermore it twisted first this way then that with other small tracks leading off it, so that not only persistence but a certain amount of clairvoyance appeared to be needed. Oliver drove at little more than walking pace over its uneven surface, bracken and blackberry bushes brushing each side of the car. To the right of them were fields, with woodland beyond. Ahead of them and below, the sea dazzled and enticed in the sunlight.

"What do we do if we meet anyone coming up?" Emma asked.

"Back," said her father, succinctly.

"I can see a roof down there." Kate was leaning forward, peering anxiously through the windscreen. "Maybe that's it."

"It sure is away from it all," murmured Oliver.

"Paradise, you said—"

"And meant! Don't bite my head off!"

"Look at the sea," Emma said. "And smell the bracken!"

"Mrs Dawson never said the house was quite so inaccessible."
Already Kate was worrying about what Leo and Lynn would think.
Would they even find the place? Had her instructions been clear
enough?

"We've only gone three miles from the main road," Oliver pointed
out. They were by this time drawing level with the house they had seen
from above. "It just seems longer because we've gone so slowly. And
this really must be it. Any further and we'll be right in the sea. Can you
see a name anywhere?"

"There – look! Porthlenter." Emma, leaning out of the window,
pointed excitedly. "It's painted on that round stone by the gate. This is
it!"

Already she was out of the car, looking around her, opening the gate.
She looked unaffectedly happy and eager; a child again, pleased to be
on holiday. It did Kate's heart good to see it. It seemed to prove that
beneath all the strenuous efforts to be cool and hip, there still lurked the
same, likable Emma she had always been. Heaven send, Kate thought
piously, that this version would emerge more frequently as the years
went by.

Cautiously, Oliver drove over an old stone cattle grid into what had
clearly once been a farmyard. A barn still stood on the far side of it.

The main building was long and low, grey stone under a slate roof,
the porch over the back doorway smothered in purple clematis tangled
with tiny, crimson roses. Kate began to experience a premonition of
relief – a feeling that perhaps, after all, nobody was going to find
anything to blame her for.

"Oh Oliver, it is rather lovely, isn't it?" she said softly, looking at the
house through the car window – just savouring it for a moment, not
moving. "It looks as if it's grown there."

"Come on," Emma called. "Who's got the key? Let's go and look at
the inside."

Unhurriedly, as if the diminished tempo of life had already affected
them, her parents got out of the car.

"Listen to that silence," Oliver said, standing motionless.

"Come on, Dad."

It wasn't total silence, Oliver realised as slowly he followed his wife
and daughter towards the house. Bees were humming and somewhere,

at some distance, he could hear the bleating of sheep.

The house seemed held in a small hollow filled with warmth and sunshine and the scents of high summer. Maybe, after all, despite all his secret fears about a family holiday and all the pressures and worries he knew he would be unable to forget, this had been a pretty good move of Kate's.

It wasn't the sharing with Leo and Lynn that worried him. He and Leo had always got on well, notwithstanding their differences in character and political orientation. Not that they had ever spent two whole weeks together. Tact would undoubtedly need to be employed if discussion arose – as it surely would – about the doings of the government and the future of the National Health Service about which he held the gravest fears.

No, it was the thought of hours of leisure spent with Kate that filled him with disquiet. She understood him too well. She would know there was something on his mind, would pluck out of the ether that it was something more than the usual, general problems associated with his job, like having too much to do and not enough time and money to do it.

Kate and Emma were chattering like starlings beside the door, fitting the key into the lock, finding it difficult to turn, it seemed; but he left them to it, pausing for a moment, hands in pockets, to turn his back on them and look once more on the valley that surrounded them.

What a place, he thought. What a view. What peace! Just to look at it felt like a cool and soothing hand placed upon his feverish brow. Surely here he would be able to get some order back into his life, sort out his priorities. Everything had been in such turmoil recently, his emotions as wayward as those of any teenager. Male menopause? Perhaps. Or was he just making excuses? Either way, he was conscious of a lessening of tension, as if a tight band somewhere in the region of his midriff had suddenly been loosened.

He turned round at the cry of triumph that announced the door had at last been opened, and hands in pockets, strolled towards his wife and daughter.

"It's going to be OK," he said, smiling.

Kate returned the smile briefly, still anxious, not quite ready to relax.

"We haven't seen the inside yet," she said.

They were not disappointed. The initial tour of inspection took them through the big, farm kitchen (with its square, scrubbed table, Kate noted delightedly, almost a replica of the one she remembered from her childhood home) into the back hall where they found the cloakroom with the shower, and thence into the flagged hall where a heavy oak door presumably led to the front garden. On the left was the sitting room, full of faded chintz, with an open fireplace flanked by bookcases.

They barely noticed the furnishings, however, but were stopped in their tracks by the view that was revealed outside its windows. A small area of garden – rough grass, dotted with shrubs – lay between them and a low stone wall in which was an arched gateway. Beyond it was the sea, so close that Mrs Dawson's stone's throw suddenly seemed a practical possibility should anyone be so inclined.

To the left, a track wound over the fields.

"That must be the footpath to Porthallic," Kate said. "Mrs Dawson said it was only a fifteen-minute walk."

"Those cliffs look pretty lethal. I hope they're fenced."

"Oh, bound to be, surely? It's all National Trust land."

Emma, who had wandered off, called from the dining room at the other side of the hall.

"There are French windows here, and you can see the way down to the beach. It's terribly near. And look, there's a sort of terrace with a table where we can eat outside."

"That must have been one of the renovations," said Oliver. "I bet the original house didn't have French windows. Or a terrace."

"It'll be nice, though, won't it, having meals out there? Oh, I hope this weather keeps up!" Kate's imagination had taken a leap beyond the pleasures of dining *al fresco* to the horrifying possibility of howling winds and slanting rain. What on earth would they do with the children then?

"It's going to be all right," Oliver assured her, taking her by the shoulders and shaking her gently. "Put your faith in Mr Fish. Come on, let's go and see what upstairs has to offer."

From the main bedroom, the view was even more spectacular. Oliver went straight to the window and gazed in silence for a moment or two.

"I hope we win the toss," he said softly. "This is magnificent."

"Well, we'll have to give in with good grace if we don't," said Kate,

26

briskly practical. She left him contemplating the view while she performed a quick inspection of the other rooms. "Whoever loses," she said, returning to join him, "it isn't going to be a disaster. There's another lovely big room along the passage with the same view."

"But no bathroom."

"It's only across the passage."

"I'll take this one," Oliver said, implacably, not moving.

"We'll have to take our chance, the same as the others."

"D'you think they'd be open to a bribe?"

Emma, scurrying around from one bedroom to another, yelled from some distant place.

"Mum, bags Lucy and I have this room at the end."

"When do you expect the others?" Oliver asked.

"Any minute, I imagine – that is if they can find the place at all. I'd better put the kettle on."

"And I'd better start unloading." Oliver moved from the window, raised his voice to reach the unseen Emma. "Come on, Em, I could do with a hand."

"Just coming," said Emma.

She made no move to join him, however, but stayed exactly where she was, leaning on the wide sill studying the view, conscious of a slight lessening of excitement.

As a view, you couldn't fault it. There was a beach, and cliffs, and fields and hills; all very rural, all very reminiscent of a Daphne du Maurier novel. She could hear the waves throwing themselves on the beach and gulls crying. You could almost expect a pirate ship or a preventive man to hove into sight at any moment, or a swashbuckling hero in doublet and hose. Which maybe, Emma thought, was what she should have expected, instead of the in crowd of which Clare had spoken so enthusiastically. The fact was that in or out, there was no crowd at all. No *people*, even. She hadn't, she had to admit, expected something quite so isolated. Trust oldies to think this was a perfect place to spend a holiday!

Still, it was very beautiful. Even she had to admit that. And this room was OK. The two beds were fairly close together, but that didn't matter too much.

Her thoughts turned to Lucy. Secretly, she had always rather enjoyed the open admiration with which her cousin had regarded her. She wasn't a bad kid. A bit wet, but given her upbringing, you couldn't really blame her for that. What would she be like to share with? She'd be – what? – thirteen now? Growing up. At thirteen, Emma thought, *she'd* been quite civilised, but Lucy might be different.

Her younger cousin had always trailed her, a few steps behind in her development – still riding a tricycle when Emma had a bike, still using armbands when her cousin could swim unaided. They'd always got on quite well, but the last time they'd had anything to do with each other, which was almost a year ago, Emma had been conscious of a greater gulf dividing them than had been apparent before, as if she had already stepped over the chasm into adulthood while her cousin still lingered on the other side. The gulf would be even greater now. She, after all, would be fifteen in only two months' time.

She recognised that in many ways Lucy was intelligent – in fact she had grown rather weary of hearing reports of how well Lucy was doing at school and what high marks she achieved. Ninety per cent for maths in her last exams, if you please! It wasn't natural! Emma frequently achieved high marks in English, but maths had always been a closed book to her.

It had to be said, however, that in other ways Lucy seemed almost retarded – a fact which Emma put down entirely to the fact that she went to an all-girls school. She had pictures of Jason Donovan and Take That on her bedroom wall. Well, honestly!

The Bryants, as a family, tended to be a bit – well – naive, Emma thought. It wasn't that she didn't like them. Auntie Lynn and Uncle Leo were great, really. Kind and funny and altogether nice. But it had to be said that they were old-fashioned in some ways. Maybe that's what came of not living in London – still, you'd think with television and films and everything that they'd be just like everyone else. They weren't, though. They were the sort of people one imagined those politicians had in mind when they went banging on about Family Values. The sort of people who went for jolly picnics and bike rides together, pedalling, earnest but happy, along country lanes in a strung-out line, wearing matching helmets, returning home to make models out of sticky-backed plastic and the middle bits of loo rolls.

Uncle Leo ran some kind of youth club at the church, too. Emma tried, and failed, to picture her own father engaged in this kind of activity. There wasn't, she thought, struggling to be fair, anything actually *wrong* in it – presumably someone had to do it. It just seemed a bit – well – uncool. She could never imagine even wanting to attend a youth club, let alone run one.

Auntie Lynn was really fantastic to look at – or at least, she had been until she began to put on too much weight. The last time Emma had seen her, she'd looked, in her view, decidedly mumsie. And as for fashion – well, she didn't know the meaning of the word!

It was her own mother who had style. Emma was always proud of her when she came to events at school. Mum always said that Auntie Lynn lacked organisation and method when it came to planning her wardrobe. She was, Emma had heard her telling her sister once, just plain lazy when it came to clothes – buying the first thing that came to hand, snapping up things in sales just because they were cheap, sending away for things by mail order and wearing them even if they didn't fit, simply because she couldn't be bothered to send them back.

But Auntie Lynn had just laughed. She didn't mind being told off. Didn't mind looking as if she had no idea what was stylish and what wasn't.

With parents like that, Emma thought magnanimously, you couldn't really blame poor Lucy for being behind the times when it came to music and dress and all that stuff. It was only because she and Caroline – mostly Caroline, to be honest – had educated her mother that she was remotely tuned to their wavelength. It was, she conceded, much harder for Lucy than it had been for her. Lucy didn't have a Caroline to pave the way. Maybe it was her solemn duty to take an older sister's place, show Lucy that there was a life beyond sticky-backed plastic and Jason Donovan.

She remembered, suddenly, that she was supposed to be helping her father unload the car, and without undue haste, hoping that he had perhaps completed the task unaided by this time, she turned to go downstairs.

In the silence of the passage where thick walls shut out the sound of the sea, she heard voices raised in welcome and laughter, the sounds floating up the stairwell. The Bryants, it seemed, had arrived. Not hurrying – too much eagerness was, after all, uncool – she continued on her way. Maybe it would be all right, and maybe it wouldn't, she thought. Time would tell. For the moment, she'd reserve judgment.

The train was crowded. Ruth Kernow was thankful that she'd booked a seat, and grateful to Hannah for suggesting it because she never would have thought of it for herself.

She was grateful, too, for the lift to the station; but that having been said, she wished that Hannah would now go away and leave her to it. Anyone would imagine, she thought with sardonic amusement as she looked at the thin, rather untidy girl on the platform below her, that she was incapable of getting herself to Cornwall. All she had to do, after all, was sit in the seat that had her number on it. What did Hannah think she would do? Leap off the train the moment her back was turned? Create some sort of a disturbance?

"I shouldn't stay, dear," she said, standing up to speak through the narrow aperture of the window. "I'm ever so grateful for what you've done, but there's no point in hanging about."

"Oh, I'll see you on your way." Hannah was looking up at her with the sort of expression that seemed to say she was determined to do her duty, come what may. "By the way, I've checked on the buffet car. It's only two carriages along."

"I've got my sandwiches."

"You might need a drink."

"And my thermos. And the chocolate you gave me."

"There's still time if you want anything else."

Hannah's eyes were palely intense under the lank, tow-coloured hair. No doubt that she was kind and meant well, but why didn't she just *go*? Why didn't the train start? All Ruth wanted to do was to sit in silence and contemplate the incredible fact that this long-awaited journey was about to begin.

She was going back. Going home. She'd thought of this moment for so many years with a mixture of fear and longing, not believing it would ever come to pass. But she was free now – free to do what she wanted to do for a change, instead of having to come and go at someone else's behest. If Hannah would only leave her alone it would seem more real.

An engine began to throb and the train gave an anticipatory quiver.

"I think you're off at last," Hannah said, a smile which must surely be one of relief on her face. "Take care of yourself, and have a lovely time."

"I'll send you a card, dear. And thanks again."

Thanks, thanks, thanks, thought Ruth dourly as the train drew away from the platform and she was able, at last, to take her seat. I'm sick of thanking people for what I don't want. Sick of doing what I'm told. Sick of others making my decisions.

Say what you will, she thought, the world may have changed for the worse in many ways, but this wonderful freedom was one change that was for the better.

"Your daughter?" said the plump and pleasant-faced woman in the seat that faced her. "She seemed a really nice girl – so concerned for you."

"No," said Ruth. "She's just – just a friend."

"Oh, really? Well, some friends are as good as family, aren't they? Not that I've got anything to complain about. My daughter's a lovely girl. I'm on my way to stay with her, actually. Exeter, she lives."

She wants to talk, Ruth thought in dismay. She wants to tell me about her daughter. And grandchildren, probably. But I don't want to hear about them. I haven't room for them.

She found her heart beginning to pound in the way it always did when others tried to invade her space. Now more than ever she had no wish to converse; neither did she have the social skills to withdraw from such overtures with a good grace.

She turned away coldly and took a magazine out of the bag that also held her sandwiches and her thermos, and opening it at random, fixed her eyes on an article within it about the needs of pre-school children. "Does Mother Know Best?" the headline demanded. She neither knew nor cared. Children frightened her. They always had, even when she was a child herself. They were so uncontrolled, so unpredictable. Cruel, too.

She didn't even want to think about them and she read nothing beyond those first four words, conscious only of an excitement that was growing minute by minute.

Nothing could stop her now. She had taken her first footsteps back to her youth. At last she was going home.

"Porthlenter." Lynn lingered over the sound, dreamy and full of contentment. "I love these Cornish names, don't you? Lostwithiel – Mevagissey – Tintagel," she rolled the words round her tongue.

"And a thousand more. They're magic, aren't they?"

"The sound of St Just-in-Roseland has always appealed to me," Leo said. "Though I've never been there."

"There's a lovely church by the water's edge. It's not far away. We could go."

"For now," Oliver said, refilling his glass from the wine bottle on the table, "I'm content to stay right here."

Dinner was over and they were sitting outside. The summer evening was warm, the sky above them still cloudless, but a little paler now, throwing leaves and flowers into sharp relief.

Earlier, with the sun still high, they had dropped everything and had all gone down to the beach to swim and explore, united in agreement that nowhere could they have found a more perfect place to spend a holiday. Even Emma had seemed charmed by it. Semicharmed, anyway, though the clear lack of any social life was still a worry.

The beach was wide and clean, with fine pale sand, only sparsely populated by other families, for it was a long and hilly walk to the nearest car park. Granite cliffs provided rocks for climbing and caves for exploring, high to right and left, but dwindling as the land dipped towards the valley – *their* valley – where a small, icy stream dug itself a channel on its way to the sea.

William lost no time in joining forces to make a dam with two other boys, already on the beach but without the handicap of attendant adults. James, however, wandered off on his own, fascinated by all the life he could find in the rock pools. Lynn nodded towards his thin, intense little body.

"There you have my two sons," she said to Kate. "As different as they could be."

"Both very self-sufficient."

"Well, up to a point. James doesn't really like to be left out of things, but he's shy with strangers, particularly noisy ones like those two. He prefers his creepy-crawlies. Wills has to have company, the noisier the better. I wonder where those two hang out? Are they locals, do you think?"

"They don't sound it."

"Well, let's hope they're around for a bit. It'll be wonderful if he's found a couple of mates in the first five minutes."

"Pity there's not another brother of James's age."

"Yes. Well – he'll get used to them, I expect."

"It's good to see Emma and Lucy getting on so well."

"They always have done, haven't they?"

"Yes, thank heaven."

"This was an awfully good idea, Kate."

Kate smiled uncertainly, but said nothing. It's early days, she was thinking. But oh, I do hope she's right! I want everyone to have a marvellous time – a holiday they'll remember for always.

Back at the house, rooms were allocated, beds made. Oliver, to his well-concealed delight, had won the toss, and the room with the bathroom was his and Kate's, but not before Kate had gone through agonies of conscience.

"No, you two have it," she said to Lynn and Leo. "I want you to have it. I'd feel awful—"

"It's OK," Lynn assured her. "Honestly, you are an idiot, Kate. What was the point in tossing for it if you immediately give it up? Besides, you ought to have it. You've done all the arranging and the writing of letters. It's only fair."

"You're absolutely sure? We could have it for a week each, turn and turn about."

"I don't think that's at all a good idea. Truly, Leo and I are perfectly happy with the other room. Tell you the truth, I'd be a bit worried about that corn dolly thing over the bed in your room. I've got a sneaking suspicion it's some sort of ancient Cornish fertility charm."

"Say no more," Leo said firmly. "The room is yours, Kate. I'm about to unpack."

"Well, if you're sure . . ."

It would take more than a corn dolly to have any effect on her fertility, Kate thought with grim humour. A certain amount of cooperation from Oliver seemed a *sine qua non* – however, this was not a reflection she shared with the general company and the matter was declared settled. Later, they had sat at the table on the terrace over-looking the sea and had eaten Kate's chicken Provençale and Lynn's salad and had all but demolished the chocolate gateau which had been in the round cake tin with the pink flowers on it. Now they sat in comatose bliss, only William and James showing signs of restiveness.

"I agree with Lynn," Leo said to Kate. "This was definitely one of your better inspirations."

"So people keep telling me." Surreptitiously, Kate touched wood. The omens, she thought, did appear to be good. Emma had been charming and natural throughout dinner and when it was suggested that she and Lucy might like to make coffee, they had both responded with good grace.

"Why do we go abroad?" Lynn, eyes closed, lifted her face to the still-warm sun. Kate laughed at her.

"Don't say you've forgotten all those British summers spent cowering behind windbreaks! I do have to admit, though, that belting down the Autoroute du Soleil loses its appeal when the weather's like this at home. Oh, here comes coffee. Thanks, darling." She took a cup from the tray that Emma had brought outside. "However," she went on when everyone was similarly served. "We must get a bit organised, mustn't we?"

Oliver groaned. "Give us a break, Kate!"

"But it'll be far less trouble if we work out a kind of roster. You agree, Lynn, don't you?"

"Yes, I suppose so." Well-accustomed to her sister, she exchanged a grin of amused complicity with Oliver. "We must take things in turns. I'll do supper tomorrow night."

"And I," said Leo, "will rustle something up on Monday."

William turned a stricken face towards his mother.

"Mu-um! Can't we get fish and chips from somewhere?"

"Hey!" Leo bristled with mock outrage. "I can do a mean chilli con carne, as well you know."

"If you have the right packets," Lucy said cheekily.

"*And* fish fingers," her father continued indignantly. "And beefburgers. With or without oven chips. Come on, admit it! There's a gastronomic reputation at stake here."

"I see there's a barbecue," Oliver said. "We must remember to pick up some charcoal when we go shopping."

"It's a pity Grandma Rose didn't come," said Emma. "She never minds cooking. And she's jolly good."

"Why didn't she?" asked William.

"Because," said his mother, "she's being all artful and crafty in Provence."

"Throwing pots, to be exact," added Kate.

William, who was drinking a glass of orange juice, snorted with amusement, earning a kick on the shin from Lucy.

"Shut up, Luce! It's funny! Can't you see Grandma throwing pots? Ker-pow – here comes a cup. Splat – there goes a plate—"

"Simmer down, Wills," warned Lynn.

"It means *making* pots," James said, his half-tooth in some obscure way adding to his earnestness. "Even I know that."

"So do I, twit. But it sounds funny, doesn't it?"

"I can't imagine Rose ever being mad enough to throw anything, can you?" remarked Lynn. "Or any of us, come to that."

"Which might not be a good thing," Oliver said. "A little bit of ker-pow splat probably does a lot to relieve the feelings."

"Mm." Lynn considered the matter. "I suppose it might be cathartic, for some people. But for good or ill, if it's not in your nature, then it's not in your nature."

"You're just too lazy to want to clear up the pieces afterwards," said Kate. "You'd rather just agree with people."

Lynn accepted this with equanimity.

"You're probably right. I don't say I haven't got mad from time to time, for one reason or another, but I couldn't imagine actually wanting to *break* anything."

I could, Kate thought. I have. There are times when Oliver makes me so angry—

She looked up and found his eyes upon her; not humorously knowing as she might have expected, but troubled. He smiled at her vaguely, almost as if she were a stranger, and looked away; but not before she had seen a puzzling look in his eyes. Was it – could it be – *sadness*? If so, why? It made her feel apprehensive, as if something was about to happen that she hadn't expected. Hadn't even *thought* of worrying about.

"Are we just going to sit here?" William asked. "I want to go down to the beach again."

"Have a heart, Wills!"

"Don't you ever get tired?"

"Never," William said emphatically. "I've never been tired in my life."

"How very enviable." His mother's voice was mildly sceptical. "May I suggest, then, that you make a start on washing the dishes?"

"*Mu-um!*"

"Why do all children utter that particular heart-rending, two-note cry of protest when they feel their rights are being infringed?" Oliver asked.

"It's to distinguish it from the three-note, querying cry that goes up at the end," said Lynn. "As in 'Mu-u-um? Where are my clean pants?' and 'Mu-u-um? When's dinner?' "

Kate joined in the laughter. She must, she thought, have been imagining things. Oliver looked quite happy and relaxed now. It was going to be all right, she was almost sure of it. And it was lovely to see Lynn again. There was no one like a sister – no one with whom she shared so much of the past, no one to whom she could talk so freely. The weather forecast had once again been excellent, a heat wave definitely on its way, so perhaps there was no need to worry about that particular aspect of the holiday, either. But she still, mentally, touched wood, just in case.

"Shall we do the dishes, Emma?" Lucy asked.

Emma looked taken aback, and her response was guarded.

"OK. Just for tonight."

"The boys can help."

"Bags wash."

"Do we *have* to, Mum?"

"Yes, Wills, you do. Go on – many hands make light work, and all that. It's everyone's holiday, you know, not just yours."

"Lucy's grown into a lovely girl," Kate said warmly, watching the children as they disappeared into the house. "She looks just like you did at the same age. And she's growing up so fast."

"Aren't they all? Your Emma's a cracker, too. She's going to turn a few heads any moment now."

36

"She already has an admirer," Kate said. "Whom she treats abominably. He came round to say goodbye before we left this morning, and she was perfectly beastly to him. I felt so sorry for him, poor lad. He looked so woebegone."

"Serves him right," Oliver said lazily. "He's not nearly good enough for my daughter."

"You didn't even see him!"

"I'm making an educated guess. Anyway, the experience will do the lad good, whoever he is. It's a rite of passage. We all go through it."

"That's right. Make a man of him," Leo said with exaggerated heartiness. Kate greeted this reproachfully.

"You wouldn't be so flippant if you'd seen his face," she said. "The pangs of love are just as bad at fourteen as they are at any other time. Worse, maybe."

"For heaven's sake!" Oliver looked sardonically amused. "What way is there to treat the pangs of love, other than flippantly? Love makes fools of us all, at some time or another. It's one of nature's big jokes. You of all people, with your never-diminishing line of couples in need of counselling, must know that. No doubt they were all" – he sketched quotation marks in the air – " 'in love', at some time or another. Not for nothing do we say that so-and-so is crazy about someone. That describes it absolutely. We all go slightly crazy from time to time."

"You're a cynic, Oliver," Leo said. "If love didn't last, there'd be no happy marriages. And I'm here to tell you that's a false assumption."

"I'm not saying that. Of course love lasts and of course there are happy marriages – but you're not seriously telling me, surely, that the couples involved in them actually continue to suffer these much-vaunted pangs? Life would be insupportable!"

Leo laughed, finding that, after all, he was in agreement.

"You're right, of course." He was speaking to Oliver, but smiling at his wife as he spoke. "On the other hand, I still experience a *frisson* of pleasure when my wife comes into a room."

"Leo!" Lynn was smiling back at him, a little embarrassed.

"It's true." He reached out and took her hand. "If I didn't know what a jewel I had before, then these past weeks have proved it beyond doubt. She's one in a million, Kate, this sister of yours."

37

"And you're a sentimental idiot," Lynn said, leaning forward to kiss him lightly.

"More coffee, anyone?" Kate, suddenly, felt an urgent need to change the mood. "Tell me, has anyone any plans for tomorrow?"

"We'll have to lay down a few ground rules," Leo said, coming back to earth a little. "None of the children are going to want to stick around with us all the time."

"I'm sure there's no need to worry. After all, they're sensible kids—"

"The girls may be, but Wills can't see a cliff without wanting to climb it. I'm going to have to convince him they're out of bounds."

"I'm not mad about them going into the sea without one of us around, either."

"Emma's a strong swimmer."

"This area is said to be very safe."

"Even so—"

"You're right, of course," Oliver said. "They've got to know the risks – but on the other hand I can't help thinking that a certain amount of freedom will do them the world of good. It's almost impossible to allow it at home, but here—" he waved an arm, indicating the empty countryside and the blue sea. "My instinct is to let them run moderately wild."

"Like we used to, Lynn," Kate said. "Remember?"

"Mm. It was heaven, wasn't it?"

"That," said Leo, "was a long time ago, before muggers were ever heard of, and no one knew what a paedophile was."

"They can't be very thick on the ground around here, surely?"

"I confess it's the cliffs that worry me more."

"Actually," Kate said, "Mrs Dawson did mention that there's the odd disused mineshaft that we ought to be wary about. They're marked, she said, and wired off, but even so the boys ought to be made aware of the dangers. Apparently they lost a dog down one once."

"The thing to do," said Lynn, "is for you to take the boys climbing, Leo. Show them the dangers, tell them about the mineshafts, and threaten Wills with a fate worse than death if he dares to go on his own. James won't be a problem – he's much too timid."

"There are disused tin mines all over Cornwall," Oliver said.

"Wasn't there something in the news not long ago about someone's house disappearing into one? Without any warning at all, if I remember rightly?"

"It's being so cheerful that keeps you going," said Kate, glaring at him. Any minute, she thought, they'd all be blaming her for choosing a house in such a danger spot.

Lynn, knowing the direction of her thoughts, grinned at her.

"Don't worry so, Kate. You're as bad as Leo. Hey, Oliver – any more wine in that bottle?"

Oliver lifted it and pulled a face.

"Not a lot," he said. "Reinforcements are called for." He poured what remained into her glass and went inside for more.

Lynn took a sip from her replenished glass.

"Kate, weren't you astonished when Rose turned us down in favour of Amy Binns-Taylor? I thought she'd think this was just like old times – all of us, all together in Cornwall."

"Maybe the memories would have been too much for her," Leo suggested. "She's carved out a new life for herself now. It doesn't always do to wallow in the past."

"Leo, that sounds terrible! We're not wallowing in the past," Kate protested indignantly. "Just reliving happy times. And they were happy, weren't they, Lynn? I'm not just seeing it all through a rosy, nostalgic mist, am I?" She held up her glass for Oliver, now returned, to fill for her.

Lynn shook her head.

"It was lovely," she said. "D'you remember, Kate, sitting outside just like this with music from that old wind-up gramophone coming through the windows? Those terrible records!"

" 'In a Monastery Garden'," said Kate.

"And 'Rustle of Spring'."

"And 'The Laughing Policeman'. They were so awful they were almost beautiful. In the end we became almost obsessive about them, didn't we, Lynn? We rushed to wind up the gramophone and put them on the minute we got there."

" 'Rustle of Spring' was the favourite. We used to swoop about dramatically like a pair of Isidora Duncans."

"Do you remember that day the vicar's wife called when we were in the middle of it and we got the giggles and couldn't speak?"

"Daddy was furious, wasn't he? He said it was the height of bad manners – and of course, he was right. But what's one to do in that state?"

"Speaking of getting the giggles, there was that other awful time – do you remember? When that terrible man from Daddy's office was on holiday somewhere near and dropped in for tea?"

"He had wobbly teeth and sprayed everyone within a half-mile area when he talked."

"And we didn't dare look at each other because we knew we'd set each other off. And then you had to hand round the scones."

"And he said, 'Ah – sconessss', and you leapt backwards and they all went flying."

Oliver and Leo exchanged a glance and a grin, and angled their chairs closer as their wives continued reminiscing.

"I wonder what the chances are of hiring a boat to go out fishing," Leo said. "William's terribly keen."

"Sounds like fun," Oliver agreed. "There'll surely be one available in the village. I understand there are other activities in Porthallic itself. Water-skiing, and so on."

"William would enjoy that. I intend to spend as much time with the boys as possible. There's been so much going on recently, I feel I've neglected them."

Oliver reached for the bottle, hesitated, then filled his glass once more.

"What the hell," he said. "We're on holiday." He grinned, indicating Kate and Lynn with a jerk of his head. "The girls are happy, aren't they, with their little stroll down memory lane?"

"It's nice for them to be together. Lynn doesn't see nearly as much of Kate as she'd like."

"Yes. I'm constantly amazed by them. My brother and I haven't a word to say to each other when we meet. But then that's hardly surprising, the way we were brought up. My parents didn't have much to say to each other, either."

"Lynn and Kate had such a happy childhood."

"Yes." Oliver's smile was more a sceptical twist of the lips as he looked into his glass. "A blissful childhood," he said, cocking an eyebrow at Leo, "leads to a contented maturity. Discuss."

Leo looked at him, half-amused, half-puzzled.

"You mean it might not?"

"It could be downhill all the way."

"You're a cynic."

"So you keep telling me. But surely you agree that it could raise expectations that were impossible to fulfil. Maybe an angst-ridden youth might give rise to a more philosophical attitude in later life."

"Well, it's a point of view," Leo said. "I suppose all youth is angst-ridden to a certain extent."

"Yeah," said Oliver. He was silent for a moment, and then he sighed and gave a brief, rueful laugh. "Isn't maturity?" he asked.

The bus came to a halt in the little square beside the harbour. Only a handful of passengers had made the journey from Truro to Porthallic and Ruth was more than content to sit and wait until the last had alighted, especially as the driver had kindly agreed to help her down with her luggage.

"Where you off to, my handsome?" he asked her, when she was standing in the square with the case beside her. "Thass a bravish weight to carry."

"I can manage," she said.

The driver grinned to himself, thinking she was possibly right for she was a big woman, no one could say different, standing head and shoulders taller than him, with a face on her that would turn the milk sour. If she'd been like that little blonde dolly bird who was even now heading up the hill, he might have persisted with his enquiries, offered to carry the case for her – provided, that was, she was going somewhere handy. He had his schedule to think of, after all. But as things were—

"You'm sure?" he asked.

"I'm not going far. Only Chapel Street."

She stared at him coldly, willing him to go, to leave her alone now that he had performed the only action she desired of him – to deposit her and her case in the middle of Porthallic.

She wanted to stand and enjoy the moment. Her memories of the place had always been elusive. Sometimes she felt she could see it all

41

perfectly, remember every physical detail of the place; like the way the pillar box was set into the harbour wall, and the blueish sheen of the slate on the low roof of the cottage that stood on the corner.

Yet at other times the picture in her mind was shrouded in a strange and impenetrable fog so that the memories were as inaccessible as those of the events that had led up to the leaving of Porthlenter Farm.

There were nights when she would return there in her dreams – when she would be walking in the fields or on the beach. And somehow it would seem to her in those dreams that the darkness had lifted and she was about to remember everything, and she would be calm and happy, full of assurance because she knew that all was well. Nothing frightening had happened.

On those occasions she would awake with a feeling of relief, but all too quickly harsh reality would dispel the dream. There was no assurance, no happiness, only the darkness and the dread and the clinging fog.

But she was here now. This wasn't a dream. She was actually standing in the little square, with the shops on one side and the harbour on the other.

She picked up the case. The driver was right; it was a bravish weight. It was good to hear all those forgotten words again. And when had anyone last called her "my handsome"?

Chapel Street was over there – through the square and to the left, up the hill a little way, turn right. The chapel itself was on the corner.

She stopped in astonishment when she reached it. The chapel had gone – at least in any recognisable form. It was all different. There was an extension at the side, another storey, a new roof, a different door. And over the door a large painted sign saying "Porthallic Holiday Apartments".

The wonderful feeling of excited expectancy seemed to drain away leaving her strangely disorientated. She put out a hand to clutch the railings, staring up at the building in dismay. She stood there, trancelike, for several minutes, until she became conscious that someone was addressing her.

"Are you looking for somebody?" The questioner, a plump young woman in shorts and a suntop, sounded suspicious. She had emerged from the front door and had paused on the pavement to look at the woman who stood and stared blankly upwards. When Ruth failed to answer, she took a step nearer and looked more closely.

"Is anything wrong? Are you ill, or something?" She had moderated her tone, concern taking the place of suspicion. Ruth shook her head in reply, but still the woman hovered near.

"Are you sure?" she persisted. "You wouldn't like a glass of water?"

"I'm all right," said Ruth, embarrassment making her sound gruff – even angry, which in turn caused the woman to look affronted and flounce away down the street without a backward glance.

Vaguely regretful, Ruth glanced after her retreating figure. It wasn't her fault, she thought; but oh, this was a travesty, a wreck of the chapel she had known. She took a deep breath as if mustering her strength and looked along the street. Number 12, the address was. Rest-a-While Guest House. She'd got it out of *Dalton's Weekly*, just one among many addresses in Cornwall. She'd been attracted to it because it was in Chapel Street, along which she had walked so many times in the past. And now she found there was no chapel! Who could have allowed such a thing to happen?

Slowly, conscious now of a deep weariness that seemed to sap all her energy, she continued along the road. Rest-a-While was a little larger than most of the other houses, though, like the others, its front door opened directly on to the street.

The landlady's name was Mrs Cornthwaite. She had written in a painstaking hand giving details as to price of accommodation and times of buses from Truro.

Cornthwaite wasn't a Cornish name. Ruth had been pleased about that; had hoped it meant that the landlady was a newcomer to the village. She wanted to see the place once more and hopefully to find her own answers to the questions that had plagued her for years, but she had no wish or intention to talk to old acquaintances. If enlightenment came, then she would be pleased, but the last thing she needed was to be forced to talk about the past or enter into explanations. It would feel too much like taking off her clothes in public, leaving herself exposed and helpless.

She rang the bell, heard footsteps from within. Mrs Cornthwaite proved to be short and stout and middle-aged, with a bright flowered dress, even brighter lipstick, and hair an unnatural shade of mahogany.

Dyed, of course. The kind of woman, in short, whom Ruth felt least at ease with. She swallowed convulsively and flicked her tongue over her lips, nerving herself to speak.

"Mrs Cornthwaite?" she enquired.

The landlady smiled and nodded.

"That's right – and you're Miss Ruth Kernow. Come in, do. You're very welcome. You don't mind if I call you Ruth, do you? And you must call me Beryl. We don't believe in standing on ceremony. As my Arthur always says, we're one big happy family here at Rest-a-While. People come as clients and leave as friends."

The air inside was redolent of past meals, and unseen in some inner room, a television set at full volume vibrated with gales of canned laughter.

"I'm afraid you've missed supper," Beryl Cornthwaite continued. "But I can get you some sandwiches and a pot of tea, if you didn't manage to have anything on the train. Leave the case, dear – I'll get my husband to bring it up in just a mo. Up we go! You're in our sweet little single room at the back. The Rosebud Room, my husband calls it – just in fun, you know! There's nothing high-falutin' about us, we like people to feel at home, but it's all done out in pink with roses on the wallpaper. He does love a joke, does Arthur. You'll get used to him.

"Bathroom and loo just here. Couldn't be more convenient, could it? You have to share with the two couples on this floor and the gentleman in the room next door. It's another single, just like yours, only blue." She gave Ruth a little push. "Pink for a girl, blue for a boy! He's a nice man – very quiet. Sharing a bathroom shouldn't be a problem. We've got a really good crowd here at the moment." She paused a moment and indicated another, narrow staircase leading to the next floor. "There's only the one double up there, and that's en suite. Arthur put a little shower room in last winter. He's good like that – ever so handy, and it makes a big difference. Here he is with the case now – *not* on the bedspread, Arthur!" Exasperated, she rolled her eyes in Ruth's direction. "Honestly, what can you do with them? That pink satin shows every mark, but it's pretty, isn't it? I do like things nice. There we are, then. I hope you'll be comfortable."

"Thank you."

"What about the sandwiches? Egg, cheese or fish paste?"

44

"Oh . . ." Ruth felt unready for such decisions. "Just a cup of tea, please."

"Really? You're sure? Well, nothing like a cuppa, is there? Go down and put the kettle on, Arthur, while I tell Ruth the rules of the house. One—" She held up her hand and ticked each item off on her fingers as she spoke. "No electrical appliances in rooms. Two – no laundry to be done in the bathroom. Three – no noise before seven or after eleven at night. Breakfast is served at eight thirty, optional dinner at seven p.m. You can let me know at breakfast if you want it or not." She broke off and looked a little more closely at her guest. "You look tired, dear. I expect the journey was a strain. First time in Cornwall, is it?"

"No."

Ruth let the monosyllable stand, without any elaboration. Not the chatty sort, Mrs Cornthwaite noted. No beauty, either, and strange with it. Shy, perhaps, with the strangest way of pulling her neck into her shoulders so that her chin disappeared. One thing about this job, she thought; you do meet all sorts.

"Oh?" she said. "You've been before, then?"

Ruth gave a sudden trill of laughter, quickly curtailed. It was an incongruously girlish sound, but the list of rules had unnerved her, though there wasn't one that she was in danger of breaking. "I – I – " Anxiety tended to make her stammer. "I – I lived here as a child."

"In Porthallic? Well, I never! Did you really? There aren't any Kernows about now, are there? I've never heard the name, anyway."

"No . . ." Ruth got no further.

"I'm a Londoner myself," Beryl confided. "Arthur comes from Yorkshire, but I'm from Balham." She leaned against the door jamb and folded her arms across her ample bosom, settling down for a bit of a gossip. "We've only been down here six years, but we love it – wouldn't go back for anything. Quiet, sometimes, in the winter, and a long way from the family, but there you are, you can't have everything, can you?"

Ruth stood twisting her hands together, barely listening.

"The chapel," she said, the words bursting out of her in an uncomfortable rush. "How long has it been like that?"

"The chapel?" This sudden change of subject caused Beryl Cornthwaite's face to go blank for a moment. Then she pursed her lips, shook her head. "I can't really say. Before we came, anyway. I heard it was empty for years and years before they made it into flats. Falling down, apparently. I suppose it was full enough years ago, but there isn't the call for it now. The population's smaller than it was, you see, even if people went to church like they used to – which they don't. You'd be surprised, there's hardly any young people here now – not all year round, I mean. In the summer, of course, it's different, we get plenty then, but there's not the all-year-round work any more. And half the houses are holiday homes, empty most of the time. The school was closed the year after we came. What children there are are bussed into Truro. It'll be the post office to go next, mark my words, and then what will the old people do about collecting their pensions?"

She paused, suddenly recollecting that Ruth had completed a long journey and was still without so much as a cup of tea to revive her.

"Well, hark at me going on and on when all you want is a wash and brush up and a bit of a rest!" She pushed herself away from the door jamb. "I'll go and see to the tea. Come down when you're ready."

Ruth, expressionless, waited for her to go. Once alone, she sank down on the bed, her face falling into grim lines of despair.

No call for the chapel? How could anyone say such a thing when godlessness was everywhere? But oh, how right Mrs Cornthwaite – Beryl – had been when she spoke of the chapel being full in the days gone by! Those Sunday services had lived on in her memory when so much else was forgotten. How could she ever forget the singing and the sermons? She had listened open-mouthed to them. Full of hellfire and damnation, they were, giving the congregation guidance, a moral framework.

Of course it had changed after the war; she remembered that, too, but only hazily, the way she remembered so many things. Father had fallen out with the minister about the way things were done, had insisted on leaving and setting up his own breakaway sect. The Brethren, they called themselves, though they were nothing to do with the Plymouth Brethren who had their meeting the other side of the village. Her father, Ruth remembered, thought them misguided and had fallen out with them too. She hadn't minded a bit about that, but she had always been sorry about the chapel; had imagined that one day she would go back there.

46

Where would the people get guidance from now? No wonder the world was in such a mess, nothing but wickedness and immorality on the telly and in the papers. Young people today, they had no standards, no one to look up to.

Had she been wrong to come, after all? She was beginning to think so. Perhaps she wasn't ready for it – should have given it more time. It felt so strange, being in this room, in this house. She didn't know how she was expected to behave. All those rules, and having to make decisions about what to eat. Why didn't the woman (Beryl! She would never be able to bring herself to call her that!) just give her something? Anything would do.

She'd had no preparation for this. For over forty years others had told her what to do and when to do it, and though she had at first been excited at the thought of having her freedom, of living in her little council flat so close to the park, nothing had worked out quite like she expected. How could she have foreseen that freedom meant sharing a block of flats with other tenants who were noisy and uncouth – even violent, at times? Especially the children. There was a gang of boys who shouted after her and played tricks on her. They hid around corners, watching for her approach so that they could open the lift gates on another floor, thus preventing her using it. They mocked her West-Country accent too, just as if their Cockney was anything to brag about. Once they pushed a dead mouse through her letter box, and once something much worse.

She'd complained to Hannah who'd got on to the Council, but all they'd done was put extra locks on her doors which didn't do anything to stop the boys bothering her; so she didn't, after all, go out very much for all her freedom, not to the park or to anywhere else. She did her necessary shopping at the parade opposite, and was taken to the chapel in Putney. Someone came to pick her up for Sunday service and for the Women's Bright Hour on Wednesday. They had a rota for that kind of thing. The services were all right, but nothing to write home about. Not nearly as good as Mr Pavey and the Porthallic Wesleyan.

It had been Mrs Roper, one of the women from the chapel, who had asked her if she was taking a holiday. There was a holiday home on the Isle of Wight run by the Fellowship, that would be just right, Mrs Roper said. Some of the other women were going there in August.

At first Ruth had demurred, but somehow she'd found herself pushed into it. It was only when she'd taken the money out of the post office to cover the cost that she began to have doubts. Why should she pay good money to go to the Isle of Wight when it was Cornwall that still obsessed her – still lay in wait in her dreams, a place uniquely beautiful and mysterious, for ever beckoning her back to childhood?

She had hesitated for some time; it was a momentous step, after all. A risk. There were moments when she felt she would give anything to remember the truth; to know what really happened all those years ago. Suppose seeing her childhood haunts again caused the curtain that had shrouded her memories to lift; suppose the fog was blown away. And suppose – just suppose – that what was revealed was too frightening to bear? It was a possibility. On the other hand, the longing to see it all again was a long-felt ache in her heart.

Hannah had backed her up.

"It's your money and your holiday," she'd said. "You do whatever you like."

So here she was, a paying guest in Mrs Cornthwaite's guest house, just as entitled as anyone else to fish-paste sandwiches or anything else that was going. Still it was hard to believe, hard to feel right.

"Funny woman," Beryl said to Arthur downstairs in the kitchen as she waited for the kettle to boil. "The nervy type, I'd say. Looks as if a smile would crack her face. Still, I expect she'll come round. What sort of age, would you say?"

Arthur dragged his eyes from the television screen.

"God knows," he said. "You can never tell these days."

Idly, Beryl looked in the mirror on the wall beside the sink, patting her hair.

"Well, she's as nature made her, that's for certain. I can never understand these people who don't make the best of themselves, can you? And those trousers – did you see? They were *flares*! She must have had them for donkey's years!"

Arthur made no reply, the TV show having claimed his attention once more. The kettle boiled and Beryl moved to make the tea.

"Funny woman," she mused again. "You can tell she's getting on by her figure, but there's something – I dunno – kind of girlish about her, as if she doesn't quite know what to say or where to put herself.

Know what I mean? She's sort of shy. Mousy."

Arthur's eyes were still on the screen, his expression lugubrious despite the studio laughter.

"Make us a cup, love, while you're at it," he said. He continued to stare at the antics of a panel of celebrities engaged in a fatuous guessing game. Laughter and applause swelled and the celebrities grinned, full of self-satisfaction. Arthur pressed the "off" button on his remote control.

For a moment he sat still, his gaze still fixed on the blank screen, then he gave a mirthless heave of laughter.

"Bloody big mouse," he said.

"What's he like?" Lucy asked, propping herself up on one elbow.

"Well—" Emma put down her hairbrush and lifted her dark, shoulder-length hair to the top of her head in an experimental kind of way, twisting this way and that to see the effect. "Well, he's sort of quite tall," she said. "With *amazing* eyes. Kind of greenish." No need, she thought, to mention the glasses or the Adam's apple. No need whatsoever.

"And he came round to say goodbye?"

"That's right. I was really surprised."

"You didn't know how he felt?"

"No. Well—" Emma let the hair drop again and turned to face her cousin. "I sort of guessed. Everywhere I went, he was sort of *there*, right?"

"And is he awfully good-looking?"

Emma struggled for honesty.

"Well, I wouldn't exactly say that," she said. "But there's a lot of character in his face – and that's the most important thing. You know. Personality, and all that sort of stuff."

"Charisma," suggested Lucy.

Emma turned back to the mirror, feeling that she'd gone just about as far as she could go with Damien and rather wishing that she'd ignored the impulse to impress Lucy.

"What about you?" she asked, intent on changing the subject. "Have you been out with anyone yet?"

"No. Well, not really. I mean, there's a boy at Sunday School who

49

took me on the bumper cars at the fair, but I think it was only because there wasn't anyone else."

"Actually," Emma said, "I haven't really been out with Damien, either. We just go around with the same crowd, that's all."

"Parties, and discos and things?" Lucy's eyes were bright with longing and admiration.

"Yes. Well, sometimes. More often we hang around in Dino's Diner and drink coffee. Or go round to someone's place to watch a video. That sort of stuff."

"Fabulous," sighed Lucy.

"Last Saturday it was Clare's birthday party. She had a disco and we all slept over – girls in one room and boys in the other, to save parents having to come and collect us."

"Was Damien there?"

"He's *always* there – I told you."

"It must have been awful, leaving him and coming away. Still, he'll be there when you get back, right?"

"Right."

Why did I start this? Emma thought as she got into bed and lay back on her pillow. She could see it was going to be more trouble than it was worth.

"Listen to the sea," she said after a short silence. "You can hear it whoosh-whooshing on to the beach. It must be high tide."

"This is a super place, isn't it?" Lucy said.

"A bit far from civilisation, if you ask me."

This aspect hadn't struck Lucy, but if Emma said so then she supposed it must be.

"Good thing we've got each other," she said. In the darkness, Emma rolled her eyes. "What shall we do tomorrow?" Lucy went on eagerly. "Shall we have a swim and then go and explore?"

"Why not? Let's go to Porthallic. That's where it's all happening. My friend Clare says it's brilliant. She says there's a café there that absolutely everyone goes to in the evening."

"The oldies won't say we have to stick around with everyone else, will they?"

Emma laughed derisively.

"They'd better not," she said. "I say, Luce," she said, after a moment. "You'd look fabulous with a bit of eye make-up. Shall we have a go tomorrow?"

"Oh, Mum would never—"

"I'll be awfully discreet. She probably wouldn't notice."

"Well, OK, then. Thanks."

"'Night, Luce."

"'Night, Em. Hey, you know what I'd really like?"

"No – what?"

"I'd like to have my hair in one of those fancy plaits, like Jacky."

"Who's Jacky?"

"You know. Jacky Marshall – my friend Debbie's sister. She's a model. I've told you about her. She always looks fabulous."

"I can do that for you tomorrow, too."

"*Can* you? Honestly?" Mention of Debbie had reminded her of the Marshalls' misfortunes, but all was dispelled in the excitement caused by this offer from Emma.

"It's easy. Clare showed me how. She's good at things like that. She wants to be a hairdresser."

"Oh, wicked," breathed Lucy, sinking back again. "Thanks, Em. You're great."

"Do something for me in return, then."

"What? Anything!"

"Just count to ten before you volunteer for any more washing up. Deal?"

"Deal," said Lucy.

"And shut up now," said Emma. "I've got things to think about."

"Damien?"

Emma pulled a face in the darkness.

"That'd be telling," she said.

"OK." Lucy's voice was almost reverent. "'Night, then."

"'Night, Luce."

Emma stayed silent. She had just realised that perhaps now she would have to send a card to Damien after all, or Lucy would wonder why.

What a waste of a stamp, she thought.

3

Kate and Lynn were lying on their sun loungers beneath an umbrella, dutifully carried down to the beach for them by Leo and William. Oliver had gone off in the car on his own with the aim of arranging a fishing trip on some future occasion, but had also been persuaded to take a shopping list with him just in case the village shop in Porthallic proved able to meet their more urgent needs. Emma and Lucy, having been in for a swim, had now sauntered far down the beach.

"Exploring," they said to their mothers. "Shan't be long."

"No hurry," the mothers murmured in response, revelling in the unaccustomed state of total indolence, Kate rousing herself sufficiently to call after them to put shirts on over their swimsuits, and not to forget their hats.

Somewhat closer, but at a sufficient distance not to be a hazard, Leo, William and William's lately acquired friends were playing cricket, with James an unenthusiastic part of the outfield. The boys were now known as Paul and Daniel, and, it was reported, were staying with their grandparents.

"How good Leo is with those boys," Kate said, lifting her head a few inches to witness him bowling enthusiastically to Paul, the elder of the two.

"He enjoys it," Lynn said. "He should have been a teacher." She laughed softly as, like Kate, she watched the scene before her. "He enjoys it a lot more than James does, poor darling," she said after a few moments. "Look at him! He's a bit like me. He hates all the hearty activities that Leo and William love so much, but he refuses to be left out. Leo makes sure that he has a ball thrown his way every now and again."

"He's a nice man, your Leo."

"Mm. He is." Lynn looked at her sister and grinned. "I hope he didn't embarrass you when he waxed so sentimental last night."

"Not in the least. I thought it was rather endearing," Kate said. "Anyway, it's no news to us that he's as crazy about you as he ever was. I was rather jealous as a matter of fact."

"What nonsense! I'm sure you've no need to be. Leo," Lynn went on after a moment when Kate made no comment, "has become kind of . . ." she paused, lost for words, then made an encircling, drawing-in gesture. " . . . He's almost defensive about all of us, as if he saw his role as provider threatened and he's determined not to let it happen again. That's how I read it, anyway. He seems to have become – I don't know – quieter since then. More solemn, somehow."

"He's never been a man to take his responsibilities lightly. And it must have been an awful shock for him. For all of you."

"Oh, Kate, it was! In the world of finance, anyone over forty seems to be regarded as a has-been, and I'm sure he thought if he lost this job he'd never get another anywhere near as good – and we've got so many commitments! The mortgage, Leo's mother, insurance policies – you name it. And of course, as far as the house is concerned, we owe much more than we could get back on it if we tried to sell at the moment. We bought right at the peak. I honestly think that when I die, I shall have 'negative equity' carved on my heart, like Queen Mary had 'Calais'."

"Well, thank God it's all over."

"Yes, thank God," Lynn echoed fervently. "I don't think, though, that I'll ever take happiness for granted again. When something like that comes at you out of a clear blue sky, you become a little nervous – a little less confident that it won't happen a second time. How I would have survived at all without Magda and the bookshop, I don't know. The job was a lifeline."

Kate turned her head to look at her with sympathy.

"Poor darling," she said. "I'm so sorry. It must have been hell."

Lynn laughed ruefully.

"At least I lost weight," she said. "There's always a silver lining."

"And it suits you. You're looking great. But any more would be too much, so make sure you stop right there."

Lynn, lying back with her eyes closed, smiled.

"You're jealous."

"No, it's not that, really. I'm just thinking of you."

"Pull the other one. Hey – did I detect a hint of make-up on my daughter's face this morning? Am I to assume that Emma has taken her in hand?"

"Oh Lor' – I didn't notice. I wouldn't rule it out, though. Do you mind?"

Lynn sighed, then laughed.

"No, I suppose not. It's only a lark, isn't it? And bound to happen sooner or later. Do you remember Hilary Kendall and all the trouble we got into when she pinched her mother's make-up and we plastered our faces with it?"

"And we all appeared at some stuffy Kendall family gathering looking like a trio of tarts?" Kate laughed at the memory. "I can see the faces of those Kendall aunts now."

"Hilary's mum was fairly puce with rage, as I recall – and who can blame her? It was Lizzy Arden, after all. We must have used up a year's supply between us. At least Emma was more discreet. She seems . . ." Lynn hesitated – "awfully grown-up for fourteen," she finished after a moment.

"Well," Kate sighed, "she's nearly fifteen. And whatever we might think, fourteen is quite grown-up these days. We didn't accept it quite so readily with Caroline, I have to admit, but she blazed the trail and we're far more laid-back with Emma when it comes to clothes and make-up and her social activities. I've finally come to terms with the fact that teenagers would rather be dead than be different and no good can come from making one's daughter feel like a social pariah."

"But don't you worry—?"

Kate laughed.

"You know me! I worry all the time. I never sleep if she's out and I have to bite my tongue all the time when I see some of the awful clothes she wears. But we've laid down certain rules of behaviour and Oliver's put the fear of God into her about drugs and sexually transmitted disease and all that, and thereafter we feel we have to trust to her good sense. As a matter of fact, she surprises me sometimes. She's more puritanical than one might imagine – it's amazing how many kids are, despite all you hear."

"Really?" Lynn sounded doubtful. "That's good to hear. You see, Lucy's always looked up to her so much. She'd put her head in a gas oven if Emma told her to."

"Hmm." Kate looked apprehensive. "I'll have a tactful word."

"Don't get me wrong," Lynn said hastily. "Emma's a lovely girl, I've always thought so. Caroline, too."

"Hmm," Kate said again. "Actually," she went on after a short silence, "it's thanks to Caroline that we're here at all. I had such a row with Oliver about whether we should let her come home or not! He turned out to be right, of course, blast him – but that was the night I got to thinking about our youth. How happy we were. How marvellous those holidays were. How serene Mummy was. Rose. It's still an effort to think of her as Rose, isn't it?"

"I'm just about used to it. It's sort of emblematic of a new phase in her life, don't you think?"

"The painting and throwing pots phase. She was so lost when Daddy died. They were all-in-all to each other, weren't they?"

"He wouldn't something the winds of heaven to something her face too roughly. Or whatever the quotation is."

"Well, your Leo's the same. He wouldn't want anything to something your face too roughly. Sometimes I think that Oliver would say the rougher the better."

"Nonsense. Oliver's a dear."

"He can be, I'll allow. Just recently . . ." Kate sighed. "I mustn't whinge. He's had a lot on his mind, and he works terribly hard."

"This holiday will do him good."

"I hope it will do us all good." Silence fell for a few moments. "Anyway," Kate said at last, reverting to the subject before last in a way that anyone but Lynn would have found baffling. "I don't suppose there'll be much left on either of their faces after that swim. They were diving through the waves like a couple of young porpoises."

"Where are they now?" Lynn half sat up and shaded her eyes with her hand. "I can't see hide nor hair of them."

"Relax," Kate said lazily, her eyes closed once more. "What harm can they come to down here?"

"Has it all gone?" Lucy asked anxiously, turning her face towards

Emma as they walked over the warm sand towards the rocks at the far side of the cove.

"Just about. But it doesn't matter – that was only a preliminary experiment. I'll do it properly before we go into the village this evening. And I'll do your hair, too."

"Will we be allowed?"

"Why not? It certainly isn't *our* turn to do the dishes, is it?"

"No, but—"

"We're only going for a *walk*, Lucy, not a pub-crawl! The oldies can't object to that, can they?"

"No – no, I suppose not."

"What do you do in the evenings at home?"

"Oh, lots of things."

"Like?"

"Well, there's always homework, of course. Then on Tuesdays there's my music lesson, and Wednesdays there's Guides and on Friday nights I go to a gym class—"

"Wow," breathed Emma in simulated awe. "Mind-blowing, or *what*?"

"Don't be horrible! I'm not as old as you. Anyway, I bet you do those things too."

"I don't go to Guides," Emma said, in tones of disgust. "Never have! I couldn't bear to have to smile and sing under all difficulties – I much prefer to scream and shout. And anyway, I wouldn't be seen dead dressing up in those poxy uniforms. They're *gross*!"

"It's good fun, actually." Lucy was on her dignity, ready to be hurt. Emma put a casually conciliatory arm around her shoulders and gave her a brief squeeze.

"Oh Luce, don't be cross. I was only teasing, right? I'm sure it's lots of fun, if you like that sort of thing. I say—" She was looking around her as they walked. The beach was far from populated, but there were isolated pockets of families with children. She seemed, to Lucy, to be regarding them all with a jaundiced eye. "I can't see much sign of all these terribly cool people Clare was telling me about, can you?"

Lucy giggled.

"Not unless they're heavily disguised as mums and dads and squalling brats," she said.

Emma laughed too. Lucy wasn't bad, really, in spite of her unsophistication. She came out with the odd mildly amusing remark now and again.

"Porthallic is where it's all happening, of course."

"I bet you wish Damien was here," Lucy said.

Emma was silent for a moment, contemplating another flight of fancy regarding Damien's biceps, swimming prowess, tanned torso and – possibly – heroic rescue of a drowning child. Then she sighed.

"Not really," she said, wearying of the whole deception. "Look, Luce, I'm not that mad about Damien, actually. It's true he dogs my footsteps, but I'd just as soon you didn't go on about him, if you don't mind."

Lucy stared at her in astonishment.

"But you said—"

"I know what I said!" Emma sounded irritated, but whether it was with Lucy, or Damien, or perhaps even with herself, wasn't at all clear. "Just shut up about him, OK?"

"OK."

Lucy felt bewildered and out of her depth, but Emma's contrariness did nothing to diminish her standing in her cousin's eyes. It merely seemed to hint at hidden depths and mysterious currents that were as yet unknown; just one more instance of Emma's grown-upness, something more to be admired, along with Emma's hat, which Lucy had coveted from the moment she had first seen it, feeling hopelessly outdone in her neat, linen number bought for Guide Camp the previous year. Emma's hat, by contrast, was a huge, floppy straw, pinned up at the front by a large pink rose, and Lucy had already decided to petition for one exactly the same – and while she was about it, dark glasses like Emma's, too. They were, she thought enviously, seriously cool.

They had reached the rocks at the far end of the cove by this time. There were no families here. The beach was stony, and utterly deserted.

"Come on," Emma said, beginning to climb. "Let's see what's on the other side. There might be a secret smuggler's cove or something, full of pieces of eight and kegs of rum."

The climb was not a difficult one; many feet had gone before, but the rock stretched far further than they had imagined, one set of mini-Alps followed by another. Emma forged ahead, anxious only to see what lay beyond, but Lucy stopped several times to peer into the pools that were held in crevices in the rock.

"James would love this," she called out. "Better than cricket, poor old James."

Emma was waiting for her to catch up.

"He loves all sorts of creepie-crawlies, doesn't he?" Emma said. "Those stick insects he brought down give me the shivers."

"Be thankful he didn't bring his wormery, then. He's given it to a friend to look after."

"I wonder if he'll turn into a kind of David Attenborough?" Emma adopted a crouching position. " 'And here,' " she said, in a portentous whisper, " 'we find the barnacle in its native habitat, about to mate with another barnacle—' "

"Hey – who's the king of the castle?"

A voice from below caused them to look down, and Emma straightened rapidly, conscious of looking foolish. A boy of about their own age was standing beyond and below them, hands on his hips, looking up at them with a grin on his face. He was wearing nothing but a pair of tattered denim shorts and Emma looked with envy at the expanse of brown skin thus revealed, wishing, not for the first time, that her parents weren't so set against sunbathing. Having a doctor for a father could be a definite disadvantage sometimes. She fancied herself with a tan, but couldn't see how she would ever be able to achieve one.

Was he, Emma wondered as she returned his regard, part of the hip Porthallic social scene described by Clare? It was possible. At least he was someone of their own age group, and while she would normally have been aloof when accosted by a total stranger – an attitude, in her opinion, rather more fitting the sophisticated woman of the world she yearned to become – she felt it behoved her to behave in a friendly manner on this occasion, just in case.

"Hi! How far is it to the next cove?" she asked him.

"No distance." He jerked his head behind him. "It's just beyond that next lot of rocks."

"Is it worth seeing?" Emma was rapidly losing her enthusiasm for rock climbing. It had been going on too long. On the other hand – did she or did she not want a social life?

"Come on and see for yourself," he said. "It's great."

59

He still looked amused, however, and there was something in his expression that made Emma almost sure that he was having them on. Maybe the rocks went on for miles and miles, and they'd end up in some distant place they'd never heard of.

He had an open, friendly kind of face – white teeth, blue eyes, blond hair – but Emma knew from experience that appearances meant little. He looked pleased with himself, she thought. Cocky. Well, weren't they all?

"Mind the seaweed," he warned as they approached. "It's slippery just here."

Lucy, overwhelmed with shyness, failed to look where she was putting her feet and momentarily lost her balance, giving a little scream as she did so.

"Here, take my hand," said the unknown boy, reaching up to her.

"It's all right. I can manage." She spoke in a strange, clipped voice quite unlike her own.

"Please yourself." He turned and swiftly made his own way across the next small barrier, the girls picking their way more slowly.

When they finally jumped down on to the shingly little beach they found it was more of an inlet than a cove, and not nearly so attractive as the bay they had left behind them. It was littered with all kinds of detritus blown onshore by the prevailing wind. There were plastic bottles, cartons, cans, old tyres, frayed bits of rope – even a torn length of flowered material, weighed down with sand, its colours faded. Emma wrinkled her nose.

"It's foul," she said disgustedly. "Nothing but a junk heap. What a mess."

The boy laughed.

"You'd be surprised what you find here," he said.

"Like what?" Emma was resolutely unimpressed.

"Some things you wouldn't want to know about. But believe it or not, I found a message in a bottle last week."

"You didn't!"

"I did. It was from some Marine Institute in America, studying currents and stuff, saying would anyone who found it write back."

"And did you?"

"Sure. I sent them a postcard. I know my civic duty."

"What's over there?" Emma asked, indicating the next jumble of rocks.

"Just other little beaches like this one. Then Porthallic beach, and Porthallic itself. We came from that direction."

"We?"

"Jacko. My mate."

"Do you live here?"

"Thass right, my 'andsome." The boy adopted a broad Cornish accent for their benefit, grinning widely. As he spoke, Emma caught a movement out of the corner of her eye. She turned her head to see another youth emerging from behind a rock. He had dark, straight hair falling past his cheekbones like a curtain and a face that was thin and bony, as pale as the other boy was tanned. He wore a misshapen T-shirt over his jeans and despite the heat, a waistcoat that had once been striped in red and yellow but had faded until the stripes were almost indiscernible.

He stood in silence, watching them, unsmiling, and for the first time Emma felt a twinge of fear. She and Lucy had, she realised, done what her parents had always insisted was foolish and to be avoided at all costs; they had isolated themselves with strangers, far out of earshot of any other living person.

"I see we've got company," the second boy said. "Friends of yours, Eddy?"

The moment she heard him speak she felt, illogically, slightly less afraid. His voice had been recognisably educated. Even now, with public school pupils adopting the glottal stop and dropped "h" to prove themselves no more privileged than the rest, she could tell that he came from the same social class as herself – that he wasn't a thug or a street fighter or a football hooligan.

Unhurriedly, he sauntered over to them. There was a calm self-confidence about him that she found impressive though she still regarded him with caution.

"Smoke?" he asked her, pulling a crumpled packet of Marlboro out of his back pocket and holding it out towards her.

For a moment Emma hesitated. She'd tried smoking, of course, as had most of the girls she knew; but unlike many of them who had taken to it like ducks to water, she hadn't liked it at all – which was, on the whole, a cause of mild regret. There was no doubt in her mind that, unhealthy and antisocial as the activity might be, there was something supercool about it. She was beguiled by the mental picture of herself, in hat and glasses and swimsuit, leaning against a rock, cigarette in hand. The fact that smoking, like sunbathing, was a practice strongly deplored by her parents added enormously to its appeal; but there it was – she didn't like it, and there was nothing to be done.

"No thanks," she said. "We're not stopping. This is a foul kind of place."

"But interesting," said Jacko, taking out a cigarette for himself and holding it between long, bony fingers. "You never know what – or who – is going to show up."

He looked faintly amused – by her? Emma, irritated by him, had no idea. Under his sardonic and leisurely scrutiny she found herself growing self-conscious, uncomfortably and most uncharacteristically aware of her near nudity, the brevity of her swimsuit that the cotton shirt did little to cover; aware, too, that she wasn't nearly as worldly-wise as she liked to pretend and hoped profoundly to become. He had none of the obvious attractions of his friend, but despite her irritation she could not help admiring his composure and confidence as he drew on his cigarette, watching her through narrowed eyes. Talk about cool, she thought. This guy was beyond cool – beyond supercool, beyond megacool.

"Come on, Em, let's go," Lucy said, already beginning her ascent. "Mum will be wondering where we are."

Emma could have killed her.

"Tootle-pip, then," said Jacko in an exaggerated upper-class accent. "We mustn't keep Mummy waiting, must we?"

The girls didn't speak until they were over the first hump of the rocks, well out of sight of the two boys.

"He was horrible," Lucy said, whispering as if he could still hear her.

"Mm." Emma was noncommittal and still a little tight-lipped about Lucy's lack of nous, conscious that their street cred, probably low to begin with, had now dwindled to nothing. She had to agree with her, though. Jacko was undoubtedly odd-looking, and he certainly hadn't been particularly pleasant. Clearly he had regarded them as two children, hardly worthy of his notice – which was something she found hard to take since she had looked at herself for a long time in the mirror wearing her hat and her glasses and had been impressed by her cool and enigmatic appearance. On the other hand, there was definitely something about him—

"I don't know," she said at last. "I didn't think he was so bad, really."

"He gave me the shivers," Lucy said, and didn't speak again until she jumped down into their own, familiar cove. Then she looked up at Emma as she was about to do the same. "The other one was quite nice, though," she said diffidently. "Eddy. I thought he looked a bit like Jason Donovan."

Emma groaned.

"Say no more," she said, turning her eyes to heaven. And for a while Lucy obeyed her. Her thoughts, however, were still on the boys as they made their way along the beach.

"What do you think they were doing there, Em?" she asked at last. "Didn't you think that the other one, Jacko, looked sort of shifty when he came from behind the rock?"

"How should I know what they were doing? Maybe Jacko was having a quiet pee." Being Emma, however, she was unable to leave it at that. She lowered her voice to a dramatic whisper. "Or maybe he was up to no good. Maybe they're smugglers, waiting for a boat to come in full of contraband."

Lucy turned wide eyes upon her.

"What sort of contraband?"

"I don't know, do I? I don't suppose it's wine or that sort of stuff any more, 'cos these days you can just go across to France and more or less fill the boot up, can't you?"

"What, then?"

"Well—" Emma shrugged her shoulders. "I don't know," she said again. "Drugs, maybe. That's what people smuggle now, isn't it?"

"Oh, Em!" Lucy stopped walking and stared at her. "Should we tell the police?"

Emma laughed so much she almost fell over.

"Honestly, Luce, you are an idiot! Tell them what? I was only kidding. I don't suppose they were doing anything wrong."

Lucy looked put out and continued walking in silence for a moment or two.

"I don't care what you say," she said at last, her tone defensive. "There was something really peculiar about that Jacko chap. I wouldn't put anything past him."

Emma laughed again.

"You're probably right," she said; but far from finding the thought abhorrent, she was intrigued by it and rather hoped that their paths would cross again.

Porthallic, at eleven o'clock on a summer Sunday morning, was as busy as it was ever likely to be. There were two coaches parked alongside the quay, and people everywhere – milling about the road and forcing cars to edge their way through at a snail's pace.

The car park beside the quay was almost full, but Oliver managed to find an empty corner, for which he had to pay an exorbitant amount. He did so reasonably philosophically, thinking to himself that there was little doubt that the inhabitants of Porthallic had a lean time all winter and had no option but to make the most of this summer bonanza.

It was low tide, and from the harbour where boats were beached, high and dry, there rose the pungent odour of fish and sewage – a factor which seemed to be no deterrent to the tourists who strolled unconcernedly about the quay.

You had to call it quaint. Oliver despised his inability to conjure up a more original word, but he could think of none that described it better. Quaintness was its profession, its *raison d'être*. It was not, truly, a working fishing port any more, but had the appearance of a stage set – a make-believe harbour, prettied up for the season, its shops selling only souvenirs, closed, as likely as not, for half the year. Maybe, Oliver thought, they just rang a curtain down in October; but then was ashamed of his thoughts, aware of condescension. What right had he to patronise the people of Porthallic for scratching a living as best they could, when they could? Wasn't he part of the urban exodus that made it all possible?

Amid the gift shops and the art shops and the pottery shops and the shops selling picture postcards and buckets and spades, he found a small supermarket, surprisingly well stocked. He commented on this to the man behind the cash register when he was paying for the contents of his basket.

"Well, Porthallic's full of holiday houses," the owner said. "In the season we get people from all over." He looked at Oliver, a bland and innocent expression on his face. "Even sophisticated people like yourself, sir."

"OK, OK!" A little shame-faced, Oliver grinned at him. "Point taken. It must be very strange here in winter. Like a ghost town."

The man smiled, but said nothing. It struck Oliver that it was probably totally wonderful in winter, but the man was too polite to say so, and he felt ashamed all over again. Maybe the local inhabitants raised a cheer and held a festival when the last tourist drove away and they had the place to themselves once more. At that moment there was an influx of mothers with small children, all clamouring with noisy insistence for sweets and ice-cream, and this suddenly seemed less a fantasy than a racing certainty.

Oliver raised his voice over the racket to ask where he should go to arrange a fishing trip, and was directed to someone by the name of Cap'n Tamblyn.

"You'll find him down on the quay," said the shopkeeper. "A big chap in a striped shirt. White hair. Seaman's cap on the back of his head."

Having first put the groceries into the car, including a large bag of charcoal for future barbecues, Oliver followed instructions and located Cap'n Tamblyn without any trouble.

"Tuesday," the big man said, consulting a clipboard and removing a pencil from behind his ear. "If that suits you, sir? I'm booked up tomorrow. Tide'll be right around midday."

"That's fine. Tuesday at twelve, then."

"No more than six in the party, sir, if you don't mind."

"We'll have to draw lots."

"Name, sir? Sheridan?" Laboriously Cap'n Tamblyn wrote it down. "That's fixed, then, sir. There's just the small matter of the deposit."

This paid, Oliver's business in Porthallic was completed and there was no reason why he shouldn't go back immediately to join his wife and family; every reason why he should, in fact. The sooner he got the milk into the fridge, the better it would be. He lingered on the quay, however, sitting on a ledge with a wall at his back to watch all the activity. The tide was going out and many of the boats were

65

immobilised by the mud left by the receding water.

People-watching was an occupation that had always fascinated him. He never minded being the first to arrive at a restaurant, or having to wait for a train; seeing the profusion of shapes and sizes and types in which the human race was constructed was a constant source of interest to him. How was it possible that the basic equipment of two eyes, a nose and a mouth could be arranged in so many different ways?

It wouldn't hurt to sit for a while. Indolence, surely, was what this holiday was all about. It would, he told himself, enhance the slowing-down process that he had been aware of from the moment of his arrival in Cornwall. It would give his nerve ends time to heal, give him a chance to relax and draw breath.

Then he smiled, briefly and ruefully.

Who was he kidding? As always when he thought there was nothing in his mind, he found Anna there, waiting for him. Nothing had healed, nothing had changed.

He jerked himself out of his lethargy, pushing the thought of her away, and standing up, he thrust his hands in his pockets and strode to the end of the quay, giving himself the pep talk he had delivered many times before.

This infatuation – for really, there was no other word for it – would soon pass. It wasn't love. Not really. Why, there were times when he didn't even like the woman!

He believed utterly what he said the night before; it was a kind of madness, no less – in his case, middle-aged madness, something hormonal, from which he would recover.

Kate was his wife, and he loved her. End of story. It was true, it was true, he assured himself. He *did* love her, in spite of the fact that there were times when she irritated him beyond bearing.

In the days when they had first met she had reminded him of a small, engaging, furry animal, lively and full of fun and anxious to please. He had not, at the time, realised how infuriating this would become. Now, on occasions, he had to hold himself back from shouting at her to stop fussing, to let him be.

He recognised this as unfair and tried, not always successfully, to hide it. Over the Caroline business, the fussing had got to him in a big way and he had said things that were undoubtedly better left unsaid, things that he regretted and had apologised for, yet which still somehow hung in the air between them.

Kate had to give Caroline room to grow, he'd said. To be miserable, if necessary, just so she learned to stand on her own two feet. In fact – if he were to be honest – she needed to give them all room. She meant well, worrying over his heavy workload and his health and whether he was getting the recognition he deserved; but didn't she see that it was demeaning? That he was big enough and old enough to do his own worrying, if and when necessary? That he really didn't need to come home and defend to her his decision to take on this extra study or that additional duty? Couldn't she *see* how mad it made him?

It really hadn't been fair of him to flare up like that. He'd been tired and frustrated and overworked, it was true, but even so, he should have exercised more diplomacy. There was really no excuse. She had such good intentions; couldn't bear to think of any of them being unhappy. Couldn't bear, really, to think of anyone being unhappy – which was, when one thought about it, as unlike Anna's coolly calculating nature as it was possible to imagine.

She gave so unstintingly of herself. No one appealed to her in vain, either for moral support or more tangible gifts. How often had he implored her to say "no" to some of the demands that were made upon her? Requests for cakes to be made for church bazaars, talks to be given to women's groups, hospitality to visiting foreigners? All were acceded to with her own brand of mildly flustered, good-natured competence that charmed even as it irritated.

She could still surprise him, too, still make him laugh – still turn him on, for God's sake. Those were the important things, not trembling hands and a dry throat and all the other small madnesses that were the outward and visible signs of inner turmoil.

He turned and retraced his steps more slowly. He would go back now, back to Kate. And he would behave well, be nice to her, play the model husband, just as she deserved. But even as these resolutions formed in his mind, his eye fell upon the telephone box that stood at the other end of the quay, just where it joined the road, and his steps slowed.

It wouldn't really hurt, would it? He'd said that he would ring if ever he got the chance, and with the family several miles away he was scarcely likely to get a better chance than this.

From this distance his view of the box was obstructed and he was unable to see if it was in use. If it is, he thought, I'll walk straight on. I won't wait. I'll take it as a sign. But if it's not—

It was empty. He could see it clearly now. He hastened his steps a little, suddenly anxious that no one should occupy it before him. But as he reached it and put his hand out to pull the door open, he was struck by a sudden revulsion at his own weakness and for a moment he paused, undecided.

"Excuse me," a voice said at his elbow. "Are you going to use the phone? Because if you're not—"

Blankly he looked round. There was a youth behind him – young, fresh-faced, at the beginning of life.

"Er – no. It's all yours. I've changed my mind."

He felt hollow with loss as he walked towards the car, as if he had given up far more than an exchange of words, and as he put the key in the lock he remembered an antidrug poster that hung in the waiting room at the Health Centre. "Just Say No", it directed sternly.

Oliver laughed shortly, then sighed.

"No one said it would be easy," he said aloud.

4

Ruth had hardly slept a wink. The so-called Rosebud Room might be a poem in pink to its fond designer, but it possessed unseen pipes that gurgled all night. It was well after two in the morning before she fell asleep, and only shortly after three thirty that the gulls began their piercing dawn chorus. She had forgotten how, on summer mornings as soon as it was light, they perched on the rooftops and shrieked and shrieked like lost souls.

She'd never really liked gulls. They were, in her opinion, nasty, predatory creatures, with wicked eyes and beaks. She'd argued with her brother about them. Eric wouldn't hear a word against them. He envied them. They knew what they wanted, he said. They were beautiful and strong and free – you only had to see them wheeling in flight to know that. So what if they did dart after anything edible with those fierce beaks of theirs? They were as God made them, doing what they had to do to survive.

He was right, of course, but she still couldn't find it in her heart to like the creatures. Especially when they were shrieking at three thirty in the morning, with a cry that would waken the dead.

She must have dropped off once more, because suddenly she woke with a start and the sun was streaming through her window, making her afraid that she was late and would have missed breakfast. In the event, she only just managed to make it on time, the last of the other visitors was just leaving the dining room as she arrived, and so she sat and ate in solitary splendour.

She had thought of mentioning the pipes; but Mrs Cornthwaite, who bobbed in and out with orange juice, toast and marmalade, bacon and eggs, was as loquacious as ever, telling her of the unexpected arrival late last night of a young couple who'd come down on spec and been sent to her, just in case she had room, by Mrs Penberthy down the road.

"Just imagine," Mrs Cornthwaite said, re-enacting her astonishment, "the foolhardiness of coming to a place like this in the height of the season without a booking! I ask you! 'Well,' I said, 'you just happen to be in luck,' I said. 'There's a tiny attic room I can let you have if you're not too fussy.' Arthur hasn't got around to finishing it, you see, and it's not what you'd call up to our usual standard. That's going to be a job for next winter. Still, these two young things were glad to have it. It's only for a couple of nights." She came a little closer and lowered her voice confidentially, sucking in her cheeks and mouthing her words in an exaggerated kind of way. "Not married, of course. The cheek of it, really, when you think – two youngsters like that asking for a double room. Can you imagine anyone doing such a thing in our day? But that's life today, isn't it? Nobody cares about that sort of thing any more. Anyway, it means we're full up to the rafters. Not an inch of room anywhere."

Clearly Ruth was stuck with the Rosebud Room – and lucky to get it, it seemed, gurgling pipes notwithstanding. She ate her way through her breakfast in silence, and felt a little restored by the end of it.

"Got any plans for today, then, dear?" Mrs Cornthwaite asked, just before she disappeared into the kitchen bearing a tray of dirty dishes.

"Just – just to look round," Ruth replied hesitantly.

"Yes, of course, you'll want to see all your old haunts, won't you? You'll find a few changes, I expect."

"I expect I will."

"You know the school? Well, it's a Craft Centre now. Ever such lovely things they've got there. Pricey, of course – well, isn't everything? – but worth having a look at."

"Craft Centre." Ruth repeated the words tonelessly, as if they had no meaning.

"I suppose you went there when you was a girl."

"Yes," said Ruth.

Craft Centre, she said to herself once more as Mrs Cornthwaite disappeared. She was conscious of a chill of apprehension. Would she find everything changed? If so, was her intention of revisiting the past doomed before it even started?

"I almost forgot," said Mrs Cornthwaite, coming back into the room. "Will you be in for supper tonight? It'll be roast chicken and three veg and a nice fruit trifle."

The matter was agreed. Ruth was to eat at Rest-a-While that night, but the moment Mrs Cornthwaite had left her she found herself regretting the decision. The other guests would be there. They might talk to her, try to be sociable. Would Mrs Cornthwaite put her at a table on her own? Or would she put her with the lone gentleman in the blue room next door? She might do. She would probably think she was doing Ruth a favour.

For some moments she sat on in the dining room, worrying. She could always knock on the kitchen door, say she'd changed her mind – but that was as distressing a prospect as the other. In the end she decided to leave things as they were. She'd get through it somehow, just this once, and if it was too bad, she need never do it again. She was, after all, a free agent. She could do just what she wanted to.

The two young people whom she assumed must be the ones Mrs Cornthwaite was talking about, the ones who were sharing a room even though they weren't married, were coming down the stairs as she went up, looking as if they were making for the beach. They smiled at her and wished her good morning, but her only reply was an uneasy glance out of the corner of her eye, as if she hadn't heard them. It wasn't right, what they were doing. She couldn't condone it, no matter what others did. There were standards, after all. On the other hand, let he who is without sin . . .

At the top of the stairs she looked back, but they had already disappeared, laughing, into the street.

Once upstairs, she looked at her unmade bed and wondered what she ought to do about it. Make it? Leave it for someone else? She'd encountered an enormously fat, cheerful-looking woman with a Hoover on the landing, and it occurred to her that making beds might be part of her job, too; but really, she had no way of knowing. The rules governing the subject were unknown to her, but in the end she decided it was less trouble to make it than to worry about it. What she really wanted to do, she decided while engaged in this activity, was to go in search of her old home. She'd take a stroll round the harbour, just for old times' sake, then go up the hill and approach it over the cliffs. There was a place where the path began its descent into the valley where you could see it all spread out in front of you. That was one of the things she had always remembered.

She liked walking. At first, before the unwelcome attentions of her neighbours, she'd walked all over London, and she missed doing so since she had been forced to stay indoors. It would be nice, she told herself, to stretch her legs again – get a really good breath of fresh air.

However, once she had walked only a short way, she realised that the journey and the sleepless night and her uncertainty about how to behave had taken more out of her than she had imagined. She felt exhausted, her limbs heavy. Her head ached a little and she felt daunted by the thought of the hill that she would have to climb if she were to make the journey to Porthlenter.

She'd take things easy for today, she thought. She would just sit on the quay, get herself rested, so that she could undertake the more strenuous walk to the farmhouse tomorrow. There was, after all, no immediate hurry. She had waited over forty years to see it again. It wouldn't matter if she had to wait another day or two.

But oh, it hurt her to see what had become of Porthallic! She found a seat on the quay and sat looking at the scene with pain and outrage.

Sunday morning. In the old days, everything would have been quiet, all the inhabitants enjoying the Sabbath calm. No fishing was allowed on Sunday then, and no swimming off the quay. Instead people went to chapel. Well – she corrected herself – not everybody, of course. There were plenty of godless folk, even in those days. Wasn't Father always talking about the old days when every pew was full, even the ones in the gallery? He used to bemoan the fact that Sunday by Sunday the chapel was half-empty, but even so, there was a sizeable congregation each week by today's standards. Now there was none, and no chapel either, and what the future would be for all these poor children she hated to think. There was a hymn they used to sing: "Will your anchor hold in the storms of life?" The words of it came back to her as she sat and looked at the iniquitous place that Porthallic had become.

Today all the shops were open, Sunday or no Sunday, and doing a brisk trade by the look of it. And the place was thronged with half-naked heathens sucking ice lollies and screaming at their children – children who, by rights, should be singing hymns in their Sunday best,

72

with shining faces and polished shoes, not racing up and down here, undisciplined, with no direction to their lives. What anchor, she asked herself, would they have when the storms blew?

If she lifted her eyes away from the village she could see the hill down which they had walked to chapel every week all those years ago; and as she looked at it, the present with its noise and bustle and godless throng seemed to dissolve and disappear, its place taken by a quieter, more ordered world. Some might call it harsh; Ruth, however, preferred to think of it as disciplined.

Her shoes were hurting. Mother had taken her into Truro last market day, and they'd bought them then. They were sensible-looking shoes – lace-ups, like a boy's – and had seemed comfortable enough in the shop, but this walk up the field and across the cliff and down the hill into Porthallic had proved too great a test for them. She could feel them rubbing a blister on her heel and she didn't know how on earth she would bear to keep them on all the way to chapel. And back again.

Every step was an agony, but there was nothing she could do about it. She could hardly arrive at chapel without shoes on her feet; besides, Father always got cross if she made a fuss about aches and pains of any description.

She'd learned that long ago, when she was only tiny. It didn't matter how tired she was, or how long the way, or how much she cried with weariness and begged to be carried, Father had always insisted that she kept on walking. Now that she was nine years old, he would be even less forbearing. Hardship, he said, built character and made you strong, and, of course, he was right because she could walk for miles now without getting tired.

In days gone by, when she was very small, Mother would plead for her, and protest that she didn't mind, she would carry her; but the most she was allowed was to squeeze her hand and smile down at her encouragingly. Sometimes she would tell stories to take Ruth's mind off her tiredness – stories from the Bible, of course, for Father allowed no others, not on a Sunday, and always, for the rest of her life, Ruth associated the story of the infant Samuel with toiling up the hill after evening chapel.

"Speak Lord, for Thy servant heareth," Samuel had said. And he was only four! It seemed to Ruth unfair that she had reached the age of nine without hearing, directly, a word from God's lips. Now, limping along, trying to keep up, she prayed for relief; but there was no response, spoken or unspoken. The agony was just getting worse. Even so, she supposed she was luckier than Eric.

He was walking in front with Father. His back view looked sober and dejected. As well as no games and no secular stories to be told on Sunday, Father forbade any songs but hymns. Just before they'd set out for chapel, however, he'd caught Eric whistling "Red Sails in the Sunset" while he polished his shoes. There had been no time to punish him then; Father had shouted and thundered, of course, but the real punishment – the beating with the belt that Father wore on weekdays – was to be carried out later, after their return from chapel. Ruth could see the justice of it for Eric knew the rules as well as she did. He'd said that he hadn't realised he was whistling at all, he was just being absent-minded, but Ruth, primly, thought that a poor excuse. Sunday was Sunday, after all.

She looked at him, walking in front of her, and in spite of knowing him to have sinned, in spite of her own troubles, she felt her heart melting with love for him and sorrow at the thought of the pain he would suffer. At times like this she couldn't help wishing that sometimes Father wasn't so strict. It wasn't, she knew, that he enjoyed punishing them; he told them that often enough. He only did it for their own good – but even so, it would be so much more comfortable if he could let things slide sometimes. She didn't expect it, however, in this case, or, really, in any other. He wasn't one for letting things slide, especially where Eric was concerned.

Eric was wearing his best suit, navy blue and just like Father's, except that his trousers finished at his knee. Below the knee, his legs were encased in thick, home-knitted, knee-length stockings held up with black garters. Because it was Sunday and he had been especially careful about his toilet, his hair was plastered down with water and lay close to his head except for the little tuft on top that always refused to lie down no matter what he did to it. Ruth often teased him about it, but now she found it didn't make her want to laugh. It made her want to put her arms around Eric and protect him – which she knew was silly because he was older than she was and really ought to be doing any protecting that was necessary.

Before they turned the last corner and came down the hill into the village, the sound of a bell floated up towards them; two bells, actually. A high ding-ding-ding from the tiny church of St Peter's on the far edge of the village and a lower dong-dong from the chapel. Their chapel.

It was nothing like the cascade of sound that she once heard when they went to Truro. She had thought it the most wonderful thing she had ever known, that magical melodic confusion of bells that went up and down the scale, mingling and parting and mingling again. She had demanded to know why they couldn't have bells like that too, but Mother explained that only the Church of England bothered with such things. Being Chapel, they had no need of bells to bring them closer to God. Why? Ruth had asked, but she hadn't really listened to the answer, for she knew already, because Father said so, that the C of Es had all kinds of silly ways like reading prayers out of a book instead of making them up as they went along, and were only slightly less wicked than Roman Catholics. St Peter's was Church of England, but it didn't have proper bells because it was too small and too poor. What it was like inside, she had no idea, for Father would never dream of entering it, or permitting any of his family to do so.

Even after they were seated in their pew, their bell went on for some time. Mother, after bending her head to pray, always lifted it and looked around her a little anxiously. Ruth knew it was because she hoped to see her brother. Uncle Ben. Sometimes he was there, but more often he wasn't. Usually she had to content herself with smiling and nodding to others in the congregation, but on the mornings he was there, her face lit up and she gave the lovely warm smile that made her look beautiful.

Fortunately, Father always prayed for a long time, his head buried in his hands. He disapproved of Uncle Ben – had forbidden him, in fact, to come to the farm at all, which was why Uncle Ben sometimes came all the way over from Truro on a Sunday morning to see his sister. This fleeting glimpse in chapel was all that Mother ever saw of him. Ruth tried to imagine what it would be like if sometime in the future someone prevented her from seeing Eric, and she decided that she couldn't think of anything worse. But Father had his reasons, even if, as far as the children were concerned, they were shrouded in secrecy.

Uncle Ben, Father said, had thrown in his lot with the devil. More he would not say.

It hadn't always been like that. When Ruth was very small, she could remember looking forward to Uncle Ben's visits to the farm. He was funny, and made them laugh; and he brought presents – little ones, like a tiny celluloid doll for her and a Matchbox toy for Eric. Once he had given her a necklace of red and blue glass beads that he'd bought in a church bazaar; and another time, a yo-yo with a mirror inset on each side, so that when she worked it up and down the string it flashed like a jewel. Ruth loved the necklace even though she was never allowed to wear it, Father being against such adornment, but she thought the yo-yo the most exciting present she had ever had.

The visits and the presents had stopped quite suddenly. Ruth knew her mother was sad. She had seen her crying once, and had heard her pleading with Father in a low voice; but it made no difference. Uncle Ben was never allowed to visit the farm again and so it was only in chapel that Mother was able to exchange smiles and glances with him, for even Father, though he held high office, couldn't stop him going to the chapel if he chose to do so.

For her part, Ruth always passed the time before Mr Pavey began the service by looking up the hymns they were going to sing, the numbers of which were displayed on a wooden board at the side of the pulpit. She liked the jolly ones best, the ones that everyone sang loudly and with zest – not that there were often many like that. Sometimes, as if by mistake, the odd one would creep in on an ordinary Sunday, but for what she termed to herself a Good Sing it was necessary to wait for the Sunday School Anniversary. They always had special hymns then – hymns that the children had to learn for weeks beforehand. Then, on the great day, they all sat together in the front of the chapel and sang their hearts out. Ruth always had a new dress for Anniversary, and to her it was the most important day of the year – better, even, than birthdays. At least, it always had been so until the previous year, when Ella Kitto had told her that she was so ugly she ought to sit where no one could see her. All the other children had laughed. She'd looked in the yellowed mirror in her mother's bedroom for a long time after she'd come home, and she saw that Ella was right. She *was* ugly, with a kind of heavy, drooping face, and her hatred of mirrors was born in that moment.

On most Sundays the tunes were dirge-like, for Mr Pavey favoured hymns about sin and suffering and being washed in the Blood of the Lamb and crucified with Christ. The words of them were so well known to her that the images they conjured up were not shocking, but merely familiar and comforting, as were the Bible readings, the words of which washed over her, burning themselves into her conscious and subconscious mind so that they were with her for ever, through all her trials and tribulations, never forgotten no matter what else might be.

Drowsing on the seat in the sunshine, Ruth remembered the past so clearly that it seemed it had happened that day, that hour. She could see herself, wearing a brown coat and round hat; could see Eric, scrubbed, pale-faced, apprehensive. Waking, she blinked and looked around her, gathering her wits, her excitement growing.

It was going to be all right. Coming back here would bring everything back, despite the changes. She had wanted to fill in the gaps in her memory, and that was exactly what was happening. Just fancy dredging up all that about the shoes, and Eric being in such trouble for whistling on a Sunday! The fog would lift, by and by, and everything would become clear.

Bathed in unaccustomed optimism, she sat and smiled and felt contented; but as the moments passed she found the relief ebbing away and uneasiness taking its place. Her smile died and she felt afraid without knowing why, shrinking into herself once more, certain that something bad and frightening was about to happen.

It was tiredness, she told herself. Just tiredness. She needed to rest, that was all.

Conversation had died between Kate and Lynn – which was, Kate thought, the really nice thing about being here with her. One could talk or not talk.

Lynn had taken a paperback out of her beach bag, and pulling the chair to almost upright, had begun to read. Kate, contemplating doing the same, was overcome with lethargy; too lazy, for the moment, to rummage for her book. She was enjoying the luxury of doing absolutely nothing, she told herself; but the prolonged silence began, eventually, to irk her.

77

"You know, Lynn," she said at last. "I was thinking . . ."

"Mm?" Lynn wasn't really listening, Kate knew.

"About you, actually. About the new, slimmed-down you."

"Gee, thanks."

"Listen to me! I was wondering if you'd thought about buying some new clothes. You must have gone down a size . . ."

"Two, actually."

"Well, there you are. You dress too old, d'you know that?"

"That's what Lucy says."

"Well, she's right. If you had your hair cut shorter and bought some trendy clothes, you'd look years younger. Why don't we go into Truro one day, just you and me, and do some shopping?"

"Why don't we?" Lynn spoke as if she were considering the matter. Then she laughed. "Because I can't be bothered, that's why. Leave me alone, Kate. I'm perfectly happy the way I am. Going shopping is no way to spend a holiday."

Kate looked disappointed.

"It seems such a waste. I'd *enjoy* taking ten years off your age."

"It's a pleasure you'll have to postpone. Maybe I'll come down to London for a day or two after we get back. Anyway, if I go on eating like I did last night, the pounds will soon go on again."

"Honestly, you're so undisciplined!"

Lynn laughed again. "Aren't I, though? What is to be done with me?"

And unperturbed, she picked up her novel again and continued, serenely, to read.

After an early supper, the girls removed themselves to prepare for their assault on Porthallic, reappearing on the terrace some time later to say their goodbyes.

"Cor," said William, hooting with laughter. "Get Lucy! She's got stuff round her eyes."

Lucy went pink, glaring at him before casting an anxious look at her mother.

"It's only the tiniest bit."

"It looks lovely, darling," her mother said. "For this kind of occasion, I mean." She looked sternly at Leo as if daring him to add anything further.

Dutifully, he smiled at his daughter, swallowing his disquiet.

"Lovely, darling," he said.

"I like the new hairstyle," Kate said.

"Emma did it."

"You're just copying Jacky," William said derisively.

"What if I am?" Lucy was immediately on the defensive.

"Exactly," Lynn said pacifically. "That merely shows how very fashionable it is. Don't show your ignorance, my lad."

"If I was a girl," William said, "I'd want to look absolutely *not* like anyone else."

"I'll remember that when you're agitating for expensive trainers, just because everyone else in the form's got them," Lynn said. "Take no notice, Luce. Have a wonderful time."

"What, exactly, are you aiming to do in Porthallic?" Oliver asked. "I would imagine the possibilities are limited."

"They're going to see and be seen," Kate told him. "What else?"

"We just want to check it out," Emma said. She peered at him through a straggly fringe of hair with a touch of defiance, daring him to raise objections or laugh at her. It was, she knew, the sort of thing he might do. He was so dreadfully old-fashioned, and never seemed to realise that the clothes she wore – in this case, descending layers of limp cotton reaching to her ankles, an embroidered waistcoat and a round hat with an upturned brim set straight on her head and pulled down over her brow – represented the height of teenage fashion. Gravely, Oliver lifted his glass to her.

"Happy checking, then," he said. "You'll knock 'em dead."

His amusement, however, spilled over once the girls were out of earshot, and he dropped his head in his hands.

"Kate, what *is* she wearing? She looks like the Little Match Girl!"

"Is that what they call grunge?" Leo asked.

"Lord, no! Grunge was the craze before the craze before last." Kate smiled at him sympathetically. "Lucy really did look lovely, didn't she?"

"She's only thirteen." Leo, at last, ventured a protest.

"Very nearly fourteen," Lynn pointed out. "You can't expect her to stay a baby for ever. Naturally she wants to do what all her friends do."

"They grow up so early these days. I think it's rather sad."

"Dad, when are we *going*?" William, almost dancing with impatience, was anxious to be off on an expedition across the cliffs during which Leo intended to point out those areas that were strictly off-limits.

"Are you girls sure you don't want to come?" Oliver asked.

Kate looked at Lynn, and they both laughed, as if the question was too foolish to merit an answer.

"You don't have to go if you don't want to, Oliver," Lynn said.

"It's in the interests of masculine solidarity," he explained.

I hope it's that, Kate thought, as she listened to the diminishing sounds of their departure. Of course it's that! It was ridiculous to think that he was avoiding her – had, in fact, been avoiding her all day. He was giving her space to talk to Lynn, that was all.

"Such peace!" Lynn sighed with appreciation. "I've never felt so lazy. I feel as if all my works are slowing down and grinding to a halt."

Kate dismissed her foolish disquiet and stretched like a cat.

"In a minute," she said, "when I've summoned the energy, I'm going to move my chair to that patch of sun by the hedge."

"Good idea," Lynn said, not moving. "Me, too. While you're at it, you could get another bottle of wine from the kitchen."

"So I could," said Kate. And leaning back, gave a deep sigh of pleasure.

"Look," said Emma. "That must be Porthallic Beach that the boy mentioned. Clare told me about it, too. She said it was a great place – always something going on."

The girls had walked over the cliffs and now stood at their highest point. Behind them was the valley and their own beach, wide and pale and deserted; ahead they could look down on the village and the harbour, and the stretch of sand that lay beside it. It caught the full evening sun and even now there seemed plenty of activity down there.

"It's a lot different from our beach," Lucy said. "Is that where this café is?"

"Near the harbour, Clare said."

"Come on, then." Lucy, excited by the look of the place, set off at a brisk pace. Even from this distance it was clear there were cafés and shops – that there were sailboards for hire, that people were water-skiing.

"God, I wish we were staying here," Emma breathed enviously.

"It doesn't look such a nice beach."

"Who cares? It's got people, and things to do."

"Well, it's not too far if we want to come—"

"Are you kidding?" Emma's Doc Martens were proving not quite as comfortable as she had thought. "It's *miles!*"

"We're nearly there now."

They found the café recommended by Clare without difficulty. Neptune's Cavern, it was called. Though there were many others, it was the only one that seemed entirely occupied by teenagers, the only one that, even from afar, seemed to vibrate with the thumping beat of loud rock music. Inside, it was small and dark, hung about with lobster pots and glass floats.

"It's awfully crowded, isn't it?" Lucy said, peering in at the throng. "There's nowhere to sit."

"Oh, we'll find somewhere." Confidently, Emma led the way inside, but was forced, ultimately, to concede that there didn't seem to be a spare inch. "We'll have to wait a bit," she said, looking coolly around her, as if willing someone to get up and leave.

No one did. Instead, others arrived, crowding in at the door, some giving up hope and leaving, others showing more persistence.

"Well, there's no doubt it's the in place," she said approvingly. "We'd better hang on for a bit."

"Emma, look," Lucy hissed urgently. "It's them. Those boys. Over in the corner."

"Too bad. They needn't think I'm going to notice them." Emma, having looked, turned her head away, chin lifted. But then she had second thoughts and looked in their direction once more. She and Lucy were, she felt, in no position to be choosy. The two boys were with a number of friends of both sexes, the entire group looking more like a cool in crowd than anything she had seen to date. She took a breath, rehearsed a number of introductory remarks, but instead exhaled again and smiled widely as Eddy scraped his chair back and came over to speak to them.

"Hey – yo," he said, as smiling and friendly as ever. "Great to see you. You're just in time."

"Oh?" Emma looked at him haughtily, anxious not to let him run away with the idea that they were seeking him out. "In time for what?"

"To hear me play." He jerked his head towards the bar where, now that she looked, Emma could see a guitar leaning against the wall in the corner. "Come on – you can squeeze round our table now that I'm leaving it. Come and meet the gang. Jacko'll introduce you."

Jacko inclined his head and raised his eyebrows as they joined the table. Equally unsmiling, Emma looked back at him, daring him to make some remark about how kind it was of Mummy to let them come; he didn't, much to her relief, but instead, indicated his companions with a bony finger, one by one, naming them as he did so.

"Sophie, Stig, Jaffa, Jenny, Karen, Billy, Poppy, Bonzo."

They all seemed friendly and duly squeezed up as instructed by Eddy. Emma took his chair and an extra stool was produced from nowhere for Lucy.

The loud music died and a comparative hush settled on the café as Eddy went over to pick up the guitar. Emma glanced over at Lucy. Her lips were parted in a smile and her eyes were big as saucers. She's in heaven, Emma thought, with a small, superior smile of her own.

Eddy, sitting in the only available space on a high stool just beside the door to the kitchen, began to play, and Emma's smile threatened to become wider. I might have known, she thought.

Three hours later, at home and in bed, Lucy was reliving every moment of it, sighing with remembered delight.

"Oh, wasn't it *fun*?" she breathed. "I'm so glad we're on holiday together, Em. I'd never have been able to go to a place like that on my own. Hey—" Aware suddenly of silence from the direction of Emma's bed, she lifted her head from the pillow to look towards her cousin, now an indistinct shape in the darkness. "You liked it too, didn't you? Eddy's great, isn't he? I think he even *sings* like Jason Donovan!"

"Yeah," Emma drawled. "Maybe he'll get over it."

"What do you *mean*? He was brilliant."

"If you say so." She grinned to herself in the darkness. As Eddy's recital had proceeded, her initial reaction had been confirmed. His kind of music went out with the Ark. It was, in her view, more suitable for wrinklies or for babes like Lucy than for actual *people*.

"Well, I thought he was fabulous." Lucy had detected the smile despite the darkness, and her tone was defiant.

"You don't say! I never would have guessed!" Emma laughed softly. "He's good-looking, I'll admit. In a clean-cut sort of way."

This, in her eyes, was less than no recommendation at all, but clean-cut was fine by Lucy who had been wrestling with divided loyalties. Now she relaxed and smiled again.

"He is, isn't he? Not like Jacko. Now he's what I call weird."

Emma said nothing. She still didn't know what to think about Jacko. He *was* a little weird – she couldn't deny it, but it was a weirdness she found attractive. He had something the others didn't have – Stig and Jaffa and Eddy and all that lot.

He didn't say a great deal, but they all looked up to him, that much was obvious. He seemed older, more mature than the others, though it was clear that they were all much of an age, the boys all in the same form at Truro School, all weekly boarders. He had seemed a little detached from the group, Emma thought. He watched and listened, smiling faintly at their fooling, but would then produce a one-liner that was wittier than all the rest of them put together.

He made her strangely shy, made her feel that he saw through her pretence of coolness. They'd exchanged only a few words, but these were enough to make her think that he could be nice if he wanted to be. Enough, certainly, to make her want to see him again.

"Do you still think Eddy and Jacko are smugglers?" Lucy asked.

"I never thought they were."

"Drugs, you said—"

"Oh Luce, I told you I was only having you on. You're so gullible!"

"No, I'm not. I didn't really believe it."

"Sez you," said Emma sleepily. "Shut up now, Luce. I'm going to sleep."

Mendaciously, she yawned. She wasn't really as tired as all that. In fact she felt very far from sleep. She just didn't want to go on talking.

Lucy was OK; uncool to the nth degree, of course, but better, in some ways, than she remembered. Even so, it was hard spending all day every day with the same person because it left no space at all for tuning in to your own thoughts. And right now, Emma said to herself, she had a lot of thoughts to tune in to.

5

After all, Ruth had not been able to resist walking over the cliffs towards her old home.

In the cool of the evening after the early dinner provided by Mrs Cornthwaite – at which, to her great relief, she was allowed to remain at her table for one – she toiled up the hill from the village and along the footpath, her intention to go all the way down to the valley – even, perhaps, bring herself to knock at the door of the farm and announce herself to the present inhabitants. In the event, however, she got no further than the highest point of the cliff where she could look down and see the house beneath her, for suddenly, with no warning, she was gripped by such a feeling of terror that she found herself fighting for breath. It was beyond her comprehension. One minute, it seemed, she was looking at it with fond recognition; the next she was cowering away from it, hiding her face as if the sight of it was more than she could bear.

A reawakening of long-buried memories she had expected – even hoped for; wasn't that the main purpose of this visit to the scenes of her childhood? She had faced the possibility that her memories, when awakened, would not be happy ones, but she was unprepared for fear of this paralysing magnitude.

Her instinct was to turn and run, but there was no strength in her and she could do nothing but sink down on the grass and, hands still covering her eyes, shudder in horror. Finally the worst of it passed and slowly, as if terrified of what she might see down below her in the valley, she took her hands from her face.

All was quiet. The sea was glassy and still, stained yellow and pink and palest green in the evening light. Even the birds were silent, the only movement being that of a yacht with tan-coloured sails beating its way back towards harbour.

She could see the differing texture of the fields – the humps and bumps that gave them light and shade, and the darker growth that marked the passage of the stream to the sea. Inland a little, Brook Farm looked exactly as it had always done, and the woodland clothing the hills to the east, with the trees in full leaf, were as she remembered them.

Pedlar's Woods. As if the fear had brought with it a sharper perception, the name, long forgotten, suddenly snapped into her mind with the suddenness of a gunshot. It had been their playground, hers and Eric's, their land of fantasy where they could sometimes escape their father's harsh regime. There, in the woods, she had been as happy as she had ever been. Why then did the sight of them now make her shake with dread?

The house itself seemed to crouch ominously in the valley. Waiting. But for what? Looking down, it seemed to her that time after all had not passed, but that all that had been was still in existence and that it would be for ever and ever as if the evil lurked in the ground, like gas, ready to seep out and finish its foul work. Here her parents had died, with violence. She knew that, because she had been told; she herself could tell nothing.

The differences that she could see were superficial; two shiny cars in the yard. A tidier garden. Other changes, if there were any, were not visible from here. And as she continued to fix her eyes on it, some semblance of calm returned, her vision seemed to clear and she saw that it was not, after all, threatening, but looked as lovely, as secure, as ever. She felt she could walk down the hill and find Mother in the kitchen making pastry, looking up with a smile to greet her as she came home from school, Father clumping in from the barn in his muddy boots, and Eric—

Oh, Eric! The thought of him brought such pain that she bowed her head as if with the weight of it, and it was only gradually that she was able to lift it again, to look once again at the farm below her. And as she stared, transfixed, the terror came back and her heartbeat quickened. Her breath rasped in her throat and she covered her mouth with both hands, her eyes wide and staring, conscious only it was happening again – that awful thing that had not taken place for so long that she had thought it a thing of the past – the big black wings beating, louder and louder, the darkness coming nearer. And now it was upon her, so horrible that she covered her eyes and moaned in fear, pleading with God to leave her in peace, to let this cup pass. To make everything as it was before.

Was it minutes or hours that went by before it left her? She had no idea. She only knew that when at last the world returned to normal she felt exhausted, yet at the same time at peace, wanting only to sleep. It had always been the same. After one of these visitations – one of my turns, she called them to herself – she felt bone-tired, but at the same time strangely purified. Why? She didn't know, and had no idea why they happened. As far as she knew, no particular memory had returned to trigger it on this occasion – unless, perhaps, the house had done so? But what had happened there? And why, if what had happened was so terrible, would she fear it without remembering it? It made no sense, and brought no memory in its wake, just the old, familiar blank. The empty space. The dread.

For a moment she could find no energy to move, but at last, shakily, she stood, and without a backward glance towards her old home she stumblingly retraced her steps to the village, where, to her great relief, she managed to reach her room without meeting Mrs Cornthwaite or any of the other guests. She undressed quickly, leaving her clothes littering the room in unusual disorder. She felt too tired, too weak to put them away, too weak, even, to read her Bible and say her prayers.

"Forgive me, Lord," she whispered aloud. "Forgive me, forgive me."

She wanted only to sleep; was sure that she would, once her head was on the pillow. And yet she found, despite the near euphoria she had known on the cliff, she was not to be allowed such quick relief. Behind her closed eyelids, she saw it all once more – the sea, the valley, the farm below. Still there were no answers to her questions, but just a teasing remnant of memory as if a curtain had been momentarily twitched aside. Herself – a little older now – and Eric, on their way home from school.

Coming over the brow of the clifftop, looking down, she had seen the van parked in the yard, and she recognised it at once. It was old and battered, and it belonged to Uncle Ben.

Eric was trailing behind her – slower, as always, because he had stopped to look at the gulls and the shags and the guillemots.

"Look," she shouted to him. "Come and see. Uncle Ben's there."

He looked more frightened than pleased. She saw his eyes widen, his mouth fall open.

"What'll Father say?"

"'Tis market day. He'm over to Truro."

Still looking scared, Eric quickened his steps and joined her.

"He'll be back any time now," he said. "Then there'll be some row. I ent going down."

"Well, I am. I want to see un."

Ruth took to her heels, racing down the hill, swinging her school satchel in jubilation. Uncle Ben! How long was it since he'd been to the house? Years and years. She must have been six that last time – she'd still been in the Infants, anyway, because he'd brought her a colouring book of *Children of Other Nations* and she'd taken it to school to show Miss Jordan, the infants teacher. Eric had *Birds of Britain* and had kept it for ages. Now she was eleven, in the top class of the Juniors.

At the bottom she looked round, but Eric was nowhere to be seen. He was, she thought, going the wrong way about it if he wanted to avoid a row. If Father came home and found he hadn't done his chores, then there'd be trouble.

But oh – Uncle Ben! She realised now how much she had missed him. Seeing him once every few months at chapel wasn't enough, because he wasn't allowed to speak to them, though he winked and smiled and looked just as nice as ever. He was the only person in the whole wide world who had ever paid her compliments.

"Hallo, my handsome. How's my favourite niece, then?" he used to say, enfolding her in a bear hug. It didn't matter that she was his *only* niece; it still made her feel as if she was someone special. "She'm growing away lovely, ent she Thora?" he'd say, holding her at arm's length and smiling at her. "See they eyes! Dark as coals, they are, just like her gran."

Jollity was rare in their household, but where Uncle Ben was present, there was always joking and laughter. Somewhere between the bottom of the hill and the back door, she resolved to play a joke on her own account. She would creep up quietly to the kitchen door, then burst in and surprise him so that he fell back in his chair clasping his heart and gasping like a fish as if about to expire with the shock, just like he used to do. He was a great play-actor, was Uncle Ben.

Silently she approached the back door which stood half-open. She reached towards it, then froze. Her mother was crying.

"I can't do it, Ben," she was saying, stifling her sobs. "Tidn't no use. I'd lose the children for sure."

"That bastard's made your life a misery for long enough. And theirs—"

"That's as may be, but I can't leave them. You know that. What would their life be?"

"We could take him to court—"

"What good would that do? 'Tis my duty to stay, no court would say different."

"You've got yourself to think of. Look at you! You'm just a shadow of what you used to be. Come with me, maid—"

"I can't!"

"Think about it, then."

Ruth pushed the door open so fiercely that it banged against the wall. If she had wanted to shock, then she had achieved her purpose, for both her mother and Uncle Ben looked up with an expression of sheer panic on both their faces.

"Go away, Uncle Ben," she shouted. "Go away. You can't have my mother."

"Ruthie – little Ruthie—" Uncle Ben was coming towards her, arms stretched out, but she swung out at him with her satchel.

"Get away from me. Get away from here. I'll tell Father."

"You'd better go, Ben," her mother said. "Like I said, tidn't no use. There's nothing can be done. I'm not leaving the children." She, in turn, held out her arms to Ruth who ran to her, crying. She felt Uncle Ben's hand on her head, stroking her gently.

"I didn't want for you to be upset, Ruthie," he said. "'Tis hard for me, seeing your ma so unhappy. Don't tell your father, there's a good girl – that'd do no good to any of you."

But she cried and cried, and couldn't reply.

89

"Just go, Ben," her mother said. And after a few moments Ruth heard the van start up and drive off.

Ruth lifted her skirt and removing a handkerchief from under the elastic of her knickers, she blew her nose and wiped her eyes.

"He might meet Father up the lane," she said indistinctly.

"I pray not."

"'Tis all he deserves."

"He meant well, Ruthie. He wants me to be happy."

Ruth looked up into her mother's face. A shadow of herself, Uncle Ben had said; well, her face was thin, and there were dark shadows under her eyes, but they'd always been there, hadn't they? She was old, after all. Thirty next birthday. In spite of which, when she smiled, as she was smiling now, she looked lovely.

"Why ent you happy with us, Mother?" she asked.

For a moment her mother said nothing, just looked at her and stroked the hair away from her face in silence.

"I am happy, dearie," she said. "'Tis just that sometimes your father's not the easiest of men. Still, he means well." She sighed then, and straightening her shoulders, looked at the clock on the shelf over the range. "Look at the time! I must get on. He'll be home soon."

"Uncle Ben better not try to get you away again."

"I don't suppose he will," she said. She bent down to open the door of the range, lifting out a casserole. "You won't say anything to Father, though, will you? 'Twould only upset him for no good reason."

Ruth left the room without making any promises. Let her worry, she thought. Let her think I might, it'd do her good. Do them both good. And for the first time she began to understand why her father disliked Uncle Ben. Upstairs, in her own room, she cried again because now she disliked him, too, and this was a thought that made her so sad, she didn't know how she would bear it.

Lynn woke to the sound of a large and heavy male attempting to move stealthily around the bedroom. A wardrobe door creaked loudly.

"What's going on?" she asked drowsily, not opening her eyes.

"Sorry." Leo came and sat down on the bed beside her, bending to kiss her cheek. "I didn't mean to wake you."

She grunted, yawned, and rubbed her eyes.

"What time is it?"

"Early. Go back to sleep."

"What are you doing?"

"I thought I'd go for a walk. I've been awake for hours and it's another wonderful morning. Shall I get you a cup of tea now you're awake?"

"Uh-uh." Eyes closed again, Lynn shook her head. "I intend to sleep for another couple of hours. At least."

Leo laughed and kissed her again.

"See you later then, darling."

Once outside, he stood for a moment, in front of the house with his hands in the pockets of his shorts, blinking lazily like a large marmalade cat. The sea was pinkly pearlescent and a fine, impermanent summer haze blurred the outlines of the cliffs and paled the colour of the sky which showed every sign of becoming, a little later on, as blue as it had been the day before, and the day before that.

The best time of the day, he thought, as he turned towards the footpath that went over the fields towards the clifftop. The world was cool and fresh and newly made, and spiders' webs were still spangled with dew.

At this point the path was steep, but even if it had not been, he would still have stopped frequently to look at the valley which lay in all its glory behind him. It was harvest time, and a tractor was already at work in a distant field. That, he knew, would be Mr Penrose of Brook Farm at the top of the lane, the farm where William's friends Daniel and Paul's grandparents, Mr and Mrs Barstow, had converted a barn for their retirement. They used to live in the West Indies, William had said, adding – without attempting to say if these items of news were in any way related – that Mrs Barstow talked a lot and painted and always made Paul and Daniel go to bed early.

William had further reported that Mr Penrose was a nice man, but he had the reddest face in the whole wide world. He and James had been introduced to the Penroses and to Brook Farm only yesterday when they were taken up by Paul and Daniel to be shown a new litter of kittens by the two boys and given a Jammy Dodger by Mrs Penrose.

What a place! What a view! What a *life*! Did the Penroses appreciate it? Or did they spend their days worrying about quotas and subsidies?

Everyone has problems, he thought, his happiness in the beauty of the morning leaching away as he remembered his own. This reflection, however, proved to be of little consolation. His, many would say, were of his own making. He still hadn't talked to Lynn, but had sworn to himself that he would do so before the holiday was over.

He didn't know, really, why he dreaded laying his plans before her. She'd always been understanding and easy-going; she'd know what was driving him to this decision, and she would back him up, just as she always had.

At the highest point he stood and gazed out to sea. Already the haze was lifting. He could see a large container ship on the horizon, and two small boats close at hand chugging purposefully out to the fishing grounds. The day was beginning.

And what did his day hold? Time spent with his family whom he adored; maybe a day on the beach or perhaps a sentimental journey to some local beauty spot for which Kate and Lynn had cherished a special affection, ever since those idyllic childhood holidays he had heard so much about; sunshine, and laughter, and pleasant company. Was it too much to hope that it might also give him an opportunity to lay his plans before Lynn in such a way that she would be as enthusiastic about them as he was?

He gave a brief, rueful laugh. Yes, he told himself resignedly. Far too much, in all probability. But still, on such a day as this, it was impossible not to feel optimistic. Lynn would surely see it was all for the best.

Some time during her second night in the Rosebud Room Ruth woke to find her face wet with tears. She put it down to exhaustion – exhaustion and unhappy memories. The pipes were banging and gurgling again, but she slept once more, surfacing every now and again to the sound of them.

She felt less than refreshed in the morning, and more embarrassed than she had thought possible when both she and the man in the blue room next door emerged from their respective rooms at the same time, clad only in their dressing gowns – she as modestly as anyone could ask, for her candlewick gown covered her from neck to ankles. He, however, was wearing a towelling robe that seemed regrettably skimpy, bagging open across a pale chest and revealing far more of his skinny, hairy legs than Ruth thought respectable.

The fact that he was as embarrassed as she was no consolation. In fact, it made things worse, for they both stood on the landing clutching their sponge bags – and, in his case, a razor – dithering in confusion, until Ruth in sheer desperation took the initiative and rushed inside the bathroom as quickly as she could manage, locking the door behind her.

This incident upset her, made her hands shake, and she was still in a ruffled state of mind when she went down to breakfast only to find the same gentleman there before her – he couldn't, she thought disapprovingly, have had much of a wash – sitting at the next table already tackling his Full English Breakfast.

He looked up and nodded at her arrival and she gave an unsmiling jerk of her head in response, embarrassed all over again.

Opposite, by the far wall, sat a stolid, middle-aged couple whom she had not seen before, munching their way through their plates of sausage and bacon and egg; they must be one of the couples who were on the same floor as herself, Ruth thought, for she had met the privileged occupants of the top floor room with its *en-suite* bathroom at dinner the previous night, and they were sitting at the table in the window. Mrs Cornthwaite had introduced them as Valerie and Gordon, but Ruth could envisage no situation in which she would ever wish to call them by their Christian names. She thought Valerie intimidating, with her peroxided hair and nails painted scarlet – both sets, fingers and toes. She had, Ruth thought, hard eyes and an aggressive, meaningless laugh which revealed a quantity of rather prominent teeth. Like Beryl, she was the kind of woman that made her nervous.

Of the young unmarrieds there was no sign, much to her relief. Even thinking about them made her uncomfortable, and she hoped they would have the grace to stay away.

Politely, the two married couples bade her "Good Morning", and she smiled uncomfortably and muttered a wordless greeting in return.

"Isn't this weather incredible?" asked Valerie, in an all-inclusive sort of way.

Ruth took no notice whatsoever, convinced that no one, least of all a woman like Valerie, would wish to address her; but it seemed she was wrong, for on the way out she stopped beside Ruth's table.

"Any plans for today, then?" she asked, with aggressive bonhomie.

Startled, Ruth looked up from her own Full English Breakfast, and swallowed convulsively. Valerie standing two feet away from her was even more intimidating than Valerie at the far side of the room. She was wearing a white sundress with a frill round the top from which rose bare, plump shoulders, and her skirt was at least six inches above the knee. At her age! Ruth averted her eyes. What was the matter with all these people? It seemed that they only required the sun to shine for five minutes before casting modesty and common sense to the four winds.

"Oh, just a chair on the beach," she mumbled in response, once she had collected her wits.

"And very nice, too! That's what it's all about, isn't it – having a lovely restful time, no worry, no fuss. We're off to Land's End, ourselves."

Ruth, watching her go, silently agreed that a lovely restful day was just what she needed. Being here was proving more upsetting, more exhausting altogether, than she had imagined. Today she intended to take it easy – except, perhaps, for a walk up the hill on the far side of the village to see what they had done to the school. Craft Centre, indeed! Whatever next?

Tomorrow, God willing, she would feel stronger – might even be able to go closer to the farm and have a proper look at it – even take a picnic with her to Pedlar's Woods, just as she and Eric used to do in the old days.

But not today. The memory of last night's terror was too much with her. What had come over her she couldn't imagine, but the funny turn had left her wanting only to find a shady spot, hire a deck chair, and sit without moving for the whole of the morning.

Mrs Cornthwaite caught her on the way out.

"Dinner tonight?" she asked.

"I suppose so," Ruth replied, ungraciously. It hadn't been a bad meal the night before, and it was, after all, the easiest option. Cheapest, too. She'd had a look at some of the cafés, and they'd all been overcrowded and overpriced.

"See you later, then," said Mrs Cornthwaite brightly. Her smile disappeared, however, as she returned to the kitchen.

"I don't know who that woman thinks she is," she said snappily to

Arthur, who was slumped at the kitchen table reading a copy of the *Sun*, a cigarette pasted to his lips. "That Ruth Kernow," she added, as Arthur lowered the paper and looked at her without comprehension. "Someone ought to tell her a smile costs nothing."

"It takes all sorts," Arthur said, absently philosophical, returning to his paper.

"And you can put that away and get over to the cash-and-carry," said Beryl.

The household was still asleep when Leo returned, and he assembled the components of breakfast, filling all the available space on the kitchen table with packets of cereal and orange juice and eight bowls and spoons. He was holding a loaf of bread as if unsure what to do with it when Kate put in an appearance.

"My goodness, you're early—"

"You don't know the half of it. I've been for a walk."

"Oh Leo, you are quite disgustingly virtuous! What do you propose to do with that loaf?"

"I was just wondering. There isn't a lot of room on the table."

"Put it on the side, near the toaster, with the butter and the marmalade beside it, then if anyone wants it they can help themselves. Where did you go for your walk?"

"Just up the hill to the clifftop."

"It must have been wonderful. It's going to be another lovely day, isn't it?"

"Glorious. I can't begin to describe how beautiful it is up there. You certainly did us proud, Kate, finding this place for us. It really is incredible."

"Isn't it, though?" Kate turned to look at him earnestly. "Oh Leo, I can't begin to tell you what a relief it was, to find it so suitable in every way. I was terrified you wouldn't like it."

"It's perfect."

"The weather helps, of course. You know, we really should make the most of it in case it turns cold and wet next week."

"I thought that's what we were doing!"

"I was thinking about St Just in Roseland, actually. It really is awfully near, and you said you'd like to see it. We ought to go—"

"Only if it fits in with everyone else's plans."

"Well, it will if we get organised. The girls are keen to look round Truro, so I thought if we made a reasonably early start we could do that first – the cathedral's worth a visit, and I understand there's an interesting museum – then we could go to St Just in time to look at the church and find somewhere to have lunch, and afterwards go on to Pendower Beach for the afternoon. The tide won't be right for swimming before then."

Leo looked amused.

"Yes, Auntie Kate," he said. "What time do we muster?"

"Oh, Lor'!" Dismayed, Kate turned round and faced him, kettle in hand. "I'm being bossy again, aren't I? Oliver's always telling me off about it. I don't mean to be, honestly, Leo. Of course you must do exactly what you want to do. It's simply that such a lot of time is wasted if we're disorganised, don't you agree?"

Leo's reply went unheard, as at that moment the boys erupted into the kitchen both announcing their imminent demise from starvation.

"And the *minute* we've had breakfast, Auntie Kate," said James, helping himself liberally to Rice Krispies, "we're going up to see the kittens. Dad, can we have one to take home? By next Saturday they'll be five weeks old, which is just *about* old enough. Moggity wouldn't mind."

"But I would," Leo said. "And so, I suspect, would your mother."

"She wouldn't," William assured him. "She'd think they were sweet."

"If you imagine," said Leo, "that I propose to drive three hundred miles with you three in the back plus a kitten leaping about—"

"We could get a basket for him."

"I don't think so, James. Think of the poor kitten! How would he – or she – feel to be taken away from his mother so young?"

"He'd have us."

"Well, lucky old him. Something tells me, however, that might not be enough." There was a note of finality in Leo's voice and James said no more; Kate, however, had the definite impression that this was far from the last word that would be heard on this particular subject before the holiday was over.

Her suggested programme for the day, made a little less rigid in the light of Leo's amusement, met with general approval. They would, it was decided, go to Truro first and have a couple of hours there before proceeding to Pendower.

"And since we're discussing plans for the day," Oliver said. "I'd rather like to take my wife out to dinner tonight, if it meets with everyone's approval. One of my more food-conscious patients has recommended a restaurant at St Tudin."

"You don't mind, do you?" Kate asked Lynn anxiously when they had a moment on their own. "Oliver seems awfully keen, and it does seem ages since we went out, just the two of us."

"Good Lord no, don't be daft. Why should we mind?" Lynn said. "We're leaving James with you when we go out fishing tomorrow – you're sure you don't mind about that?"

"Lynn, you know how I feel about small boats. I'll be much happier here."

"Well, then! Fair's fair. You two go out and enjoy yourselves tonight. Leo and I'll do the same before the holiday's over – which is much more of an imposition, because it means leaving you with the boys."

"Have the girls mentioned to you that they want to go to Porthallic again?"

"Lucy did say something—" Lynn's smile died, a faintly harassed expression taking its place. "What do you think, Kate? Leo's not frightfully happy about it, and I confess to being slightly uneasy myself."

"Emma assures me it's all perfectly harmless—"

"Yes, I know." Lynn's quick assent nevertheless left no doubt in Kate's mind that Emma's assurances counted for little. "It's just that Lucy is so young, and we don't know any of these people—"

Kate sighed.

"I'll talk to Emma," she said.

Emma, when talked to, stared at her, open-mouthed.

"Are you saying we *can't go*?"

Kate had run her to earth in the bathroom and now pushed the door closed to ensure a private word.

"Darling, you must see that it's different for Lucy. She's younger than you, for one thing—"

"But it's totally harmless! How's she ever going to grow up if she's never allowed out?"

"It would be different if Uncle Leo and Auntie Lynn had met these people—"

"But we said we'd be there tonight. We promised! Luce'll be devastated if we can't go."

"Maybe another night—"

"*Why*, Mum? I don't get it! There's a fair at Porthallic this week and we said we'd go with the others. It's all arranged! What's wrong with that? Look," she went on, seeing that Kate was irresolute. "They're perfectly nice, ordinary kids like us. Honestly! You'd like them."

"Maybe I would." Kate sighed once more. "I just feel that it would be an awfully good thing if you could stay at home tonight."

"And do what?" Emma asked scornfully. "Play Monopoly? Get real, Mum! It's not as if you're going to be in tonight, after all. We thought you and Dad could give us a lift into Porthallic when you go out to dinner, and pick us up again afterwards. You could take me, even if Lucy can't go. Oh, Mum!" Emma's lips drooped as if, even as she uttered these last words, she saw how impossible such a situation would be. "It's not fair! There's absolutely nothing to do here."

"Well—" Kate was wavering. She thought Emma had a point – that there were few grounds for making the girls stay at home when new friends and a fair beckoned. She trusted her daughter's judgment on these matters, and reckoned that if she said the Porthallic crowd were all right, then they probably were. And she did want everyone to have a lovely holiday – had been worried, right from the first sighting of the farmhouse, that the social scene might be disappointing for the girls.

She sighed yet again.

"I'll talk to Lynn," she said, giving in. "But don't hold your breath. Uncle Leo's worried."

"Thanks, Mum. You're ace," Emma said; diplomatically, she kept her thoughts about Uncle Leo to herself.

The deck chairs, in Ruth's opinion, were ridiculously expensive.

"I'm not wanting to buy it," she said tartly to the youth who took her money.

"Shocking, isn't it?" he said, and grinned, not caring. But he did carry it over to one of the few sheltered spots on the beach where she was likely to be in the shade most of the morning.

She was lucky, she realised. Only just in time. The beach began to fill up almost immediately, and she saw that she would never have achieved such an advantageous position if she'd been only a few minutes later.

Family groups arrived and established little camps all around her. The tide was on its way out, leaving more and more space for children to dig holes, make castles, bury each other, hurl balls and frisbees. Their voices seemed to echo around the beach, representing accents from every corner of the land.

Out in the bay, a speedboat roared up and down, towing water-skiers. Ruth looked at it in pained disapproval. The things people did these days! Why was everyone seeking after speed and sensation? You'd think the beauties of nature would be enough – but no, everything had to be bigger and faster and noisier. And more expensive. Whatever happened to the maxim that the best things in life were free?

Take this beach, for instance. Once it was quiet, with none of this hullabaloo, none of this near-nakedness. Now you might just as well be at Southend for all the peace you could find here.

Are people happier? she asked herself. And assured herself, with gloomy satisfaction, that they were not.

Emma and Lucy trailed round the cathedral with the others, but opted out of the visit to the museum, settling instead for looking around the shops – which, they were both delighted to find, were exactly like the ones they had left behind at home, except for the covered market which had its own attractions. Lucy bought herself a straw hat, sufficiently like Emma's to be acceptable, and in the market Emma splashed out on a feather boa for the simple reason that she liked it. They were both in high spirits, for it had been agreed, albeit with reluctance on Leo's part, that they could go into Porthallic that night.

"And I should jolly well think so," Emma said to Lucy. "You ought to be thankful my parents are so sensible."

"Oh, I am," breathed Lucy, conscious that blame for any restriction on their movements would rightly have been laid at her door.

The size of the party had necessitated two cars, and Emma and Lucy travelled with Kate and Oliver. They had lunch in the garden of a pub near St Just, and after a suitable interval to allow their food to sink and the tide to cover the fine, wrinkled sand of Pendower, they went for a swim.

The general beauty of the countryside and the romantic nature of the coastal inlets triggered many a flight of fancy to enliven the journey home.

"I bet our cove was just as romantic as any other," Emma said. "I bet there was a farmer's daughter once, who was in love with a pirate—"

Kate joined in with enthusiasm.

"And she used to watch and wait for the sight of the Jolly Roger on the horizon—"

"And her croo-el father imprisoned her and took away her telescope and wouldn't let her have anything to do with this absolutely brilliant pirate who looked just like Tom Cruise—"

"Until," broke in Oliver, "he realised the booze cupboard was getting low and it was time some friendly neighbourhood buccaneer brought him some French brandy. So he sent a telegram saying 'Come at once Stop attitude changed Stop bring Napoleon brandy – don't stop—' "

"Your turn, Luce," Emma said.

"And they lived happily ever after," Lucy said at last, not able to think of anything funny. Then she was struck by inspiration. "Only she made the pirate take off the handkerchief thingy he wore round his head because she said it wasn't trendy any more."

"*Plus ça change*," Oliver said. "That's women for you. No self-respecting pirate is safe."

Kate, laughing, looked at him and thought that he looked years younger than when they had arrived. She was glad they were going out to dinner by themselves. Perhaps it would be easy to talk again, to get close to him the way it used to be.

Later that evening, the girls were dropped in the village with strict instructions to be there beside the quay not a minute after eleven o'clock when they would be picked up again.

The Neptune Cavern, where they had all arranged to meet, was a little less crowded than it had been on the previous occasion, but the gang was there in full force and welcomed them with varying degrees of warmth.

Emma, pointedly, didn't look at Jacko, but chatted instead to Stig as if her life depended on it. She felt angry with herself for being shy; she wasn't used to it – hadn't intended it, but here she was, not daring to look at him. Even so, without knowing quite how it happened, once they arrived at the fair she found herself sharing a bumper car ride with him.

It had come about almost by accident. She just happened to be standing next to him at the time.

"Come on, if you dare," he'd said, grinning at her over his shoulder; so of course, she had gone with him and somehow by the end of the ride the shyness had evaporated and she was feeling herself once more.

The fair was nothing, really; no more than a scruffy conglomeration of run-down attractions and stalls – but that was hardly the point. They were having fun. Sophie treated everyone to another go – Stig and Sophie in one car, Polly and Jaffa in another, Eddy and Lucy in yet another. They bumped and screamed and yelled with laughter, and it seemed no time at all until the blaring music stopped and the siren sounded, marking the end of their time.

"One more go," screamed Sophie, waving a ten-pound note at the swarthy young man who was in charge.

"We can't let her—" said Emma urgently, reaching for her own purse, but Jacko told her quietly to put it away.

"Her folks are loaded," he said.

"Even so—"

"You're the independent sort?"

"Aren't you?"

Jacko smiled but said nothing, continuing to look loftily amused as if the question was naive beyond belief – as if nothing in this world could compromise his independence, even having a girl pay for his ride on the bumper cars.

The mock aggression, the laughter, seemed to cement the group into an even tighter band once the ride was over, the shortcomings of the fair becoming the subject of hysterical amusement as Stig and Eddy, feigning terror, rode on the creaking merry-go-round designed for smaller children, causing its custodian to swear at them and stop the ride in order to throw them off. They would frighten the little kids, he said – which was, in itself, a matter for almost helpless mirth as they stumbled away to try their luck rolling pennies and throwing rings. Eddy won a small furry animal in a repulsive shade of lime-green, which he promptly gave to Lucy. Even though Lucy laughed and made fun of it with the others, Emma could tell she was thrilled.

Jacko won nothing – was, in fact, spectacularly unsuccessful at almost everything. The others teased him, but even so, in a strange way it was increasingly clear to Emma that they looked up to him. As time went on, it occurred to her that he was more an onlooker than a participant in all the juvenile fun, a kind of still centre amid all the shrieking and laughter, making the other boys seem hyperactive – almost frenetic in their efforts to be the life and soul of the party. He spoke seldom, but listened to the repartee with an air of inscrutable amusement, smoking his inevitable cigarette, a little taller than the others, pale and thin and oddly dressed. The gear he had chosen for this night at the fair was a tropical-weight jacket and trousers in cream-coloured linen, made apparently many years before to judge by their disreputable condition. Their original owner had clearly been a much broader man, for the jacket drooped limply and the trousers were held up by a multicoloured Indian silk scarf. Beneath this, he wore a collarless black shirt. Emma thought he looked bizarre, but oddly distinguished.

He declined to go on the Chair-o-Plane, though, which gave Emma the courage to do the same. She'd always hated the things and knew perfectly well that Lucy was of the same mind; however Lucy was intent on impressing Eddy and took her seat beside him, smiling nervously.

"You don't have to, Luce," Emma called out, but Lucy just laughed and hung on to the front bar tighter than ever.

Jacko and Emma stood together and watched them as the chairs gathered speed and were flung out horizontally as the music played.

"No power on earth would get me up there," Emma said.

"What?" Jacko bent towards her, struggling to hear.

"I said – oh, never mind!" She shrugged and smiled and gave up the struggle.

Jacko took her arm and led her away to a spot where the music was marginally less deafening. At a little distance, he pulled her down to sit beside him on the grass.

"I suppose this is all kids' stuff to you," he said.

Emma looked at him, frowning a little, not knowing if he was serious, or if he was making fun of her.

"Why should it be?" she said.

Smiling his down-turned, secret smile, he delicately picked a cigarette out of a packet.

"Well," he said between puffs as he lit it. "I get the feeling you regard us as a crowd of country bumpkins."

"I don't! I absolutely don't!" Emma was quick to deny it, but underneath there was a distinct feeling of satisfaction that she had given this impression, that she, too, had seemed cool. "Why should I?"

"Well," he said again, looking at her with sly amusement, "you're the city girl, aren't you? The girl who's seen it all, done it all—"

"Hardly! I think it's all great down here. Everyone's been so nice."

"In our quaint, bucolic way."

Emma laughed.

"Stop taking the mickey," she said. "And tell me – what were you doing on the beach the other day?"

The question coincided with a sudden blare of music from the roller coaster and was lost. Jacko leant closer.

"Sorry – what was that?"

Emma repeated the question. Still he frowned uncomprehendingly, and this time put an arm round her shoulders and bent his head down towards her so that his hair swung against her cheek.

"Say again?"

Emma was conscious of a strange sensation in her chest, making breathing difficult. She lifted her face and once more, her mouth close to his ear, she put the question.

"I asked what you were doing on the beach that day?"

He looked down at her and gave his enigmatic smile, still holding her.

103

"That'd be telling."

"It looked as if you were up to no good."

"What, me? Perish the thought."

They were close, his eyes only inches away from hers. They were amazing, she thought. Like the eyes of a lion, only sort of flecked with green and fringed with thick dark lashes. She swallowed and managed to smile.

"We thought you might be smugglers."

He grinned enigmatically at that, but said nothing, moving his head away from hers, but keeping the arm around her shoulder. The others had finished their Chair-o-Plane ride and were now approaching them over the grass, Lucy looking pale but triumphant.

"We think we've exhausted the possibilities," said Eddy. "Let's go back to the Cavern, shall we?"

"Who's for some candyfloss first?" Sophie asked. "Come on – my treat."

"No, you can't," Emma said. "You keep on paying for things. It's not right."

She was, by this time, feeling quite passionate about it. She had taken to Sophie from the first. She was friendly and sparky and lively, much nicer than Karen who was podgy and had a discontented mouth painted a dark wine-red. But this business of allowing her to pay for so much of their entertainment went against the grain.

Everyone, including Sophie, howled her down.

"Honestly, I *want* to pay," Sophie said. "I've got plenty of dosh, honestly. Don't give it a thought! I can easily get some more tomorrow."

"Mummy gives her everything she wants," Jacko explained. "Compensating because she's the child of a broken home. Isn't that right, Sophie?"

"Absolutely. And as it all belongs to my shitty stepfather, I look on it as my sacred duty to get through as much as I can, just to spite him, until the bastard's bankrupt. Then, perhaps, my mother'll see the light and go back to Dad. Till then, I shall just spend, spend, spend."

"And we shall do our best to help her," said Stig.

Emma's eyes briefly met Lucy's. Both were equally shocked at this revelation, though Emma managed to keep her face expressionless.

Children from broken homes were, of course, ten a penny; half the boys and girls in her form at school had parents who were divorced, and varying degrees of bitterness were no novelty to either of the girls. There was, however, something unusually chilling about the unhappiness implicit in Sophie's statement of intent, and Emma was aware of a sudden feeling of benevolence regarding her own parents who, though far from perfect, could undoubtedly be a lot worse.

The restaurant, set back from the road in a building that had once been a coaching inn, was subdued and expensive, with pink tablecloths and menus the size of the average tabloid newspaper containing a plethora of descriptive material; not a sauce that was not lightly whipped, not a vegetable untouched by the dew.

"I'll 'ave the mooshy peas," Oliver said in an undertone to Kate as he scanned the fare on offer.

She giggled. "Shut up! Don't disgrace me."

"Absolutely everything is served with a garnish of wild mushrooms – but everything! They must have cornered the market."

"Just choose, Oliver," Kate entreated.

In view of the fact that they were so near the coast, they chose a fishy menu – oysters, followed by brill – and had no cause to regret either.

"This is a nice place," Kate said. "Lynn and Leo must come here."

"It's a bit precious, but the food's good, I'll admit."

"It's been a good day. Emma was sweet, wasn't she?"

"You know," Oliver said, "there was a cousin of my mother's who was, in the normal course of events, so rude and impossible that if on any occasion she behaved like a normal decent human being everyone remarked how wonderful she'd been."

"Emma's not a bit like that!"

"I'll remind you of that when we get home and life returns to normal. She's been very amenable since we arrived down here, I'll admit."

"I always knew Cornwall would exert a beneficent influence."

"Maybe you're right." Oliver sipped his wine, then put down the glass with great care. "Even on me," he said, not looking at her. "I haven't been easy to get on with lately. I'm sorry."

"You've been a bit . . ." Kate hesitated. "A bit sort of semi-detached, I admit. Not entirely here."

"I suppose that sums it up."

"Is there something wrong at work? Oh, I know you're terribly busy, but then you always have been. Is it the fund-holding business that's worrying you?"

Oliver shook his head.

"Not really. I'm not entirely happy about it, as you well know, mainly for ideological reasons, but we're coping. My trouble is more . . ." he paused and looked down, as if not sure how to go on.

"What is it, Oliver?" Kate asked at last.

He shrugged his shoulders, giving a rueful, self-mocking laugh.

"Call it a midlife crisis," he said. "After all, it's one of life's little luxuries that the headshrinkers allow us to indulge in these days. A generation or two ago such things didn't exist."

"Like premenstrual tension."

"And postnatal depression."

"And the need to be counselled for everything."

Pensively, Oliver moved his glass to the right and to the left and to the right again. Kate watched it closely as if the movement was an experiment that would prove some scientific law hitherto undreamed of.

"I suppose a general sort of malaise best describes it. I'll get over it."

"My fault?" Kate posed the question anxiously. He looked up and quirked a grin at her before looking down again.

"No, no. Of course not. Why should you always think you're to blame for everything?"

Kate pondered the question.

"I don't really know," she said at last. "Maybe because I usually am. Anyway – is the holiday being good for whatever you want to call it?"

He looked up at her then, and smiled.

"Yes. I think it is."

"I wish I could help."

"You can. You do. I'm an ungrateful bastard, aren't I? Life shouldn't seem so – so savourless; yet middle age seems to be a time for appraisal and reassessment. I'm not alone, I'm very much aware of that. One of my patients said in similar circumstances that he'd pressed all the buttons labelled 'education' and 'ambition' and 'marriage' and 'pleasure' only to find that the lift was broken and he wasn't going anywhere."

Kate stared at him.

"That's an awful thing to say, Oliver! Of course you're going somewhere. Your work is terribly valuable, for one thing, never mind what you mean to us – the family."

"Yes."

The monosyllable sounded bleak, as if, thought Kate, the family was part of the problem – yet one more burden to weigh him down.

"I wish you hadn't taken on this mental health thing," she said. "Surely it just makes extra work."

"Yes," Oliver said again. "But it's fascinating, Kate. I don't mind doing it."

"It's not as if you get any help from Anna."

"Don't get on to that particular hobbyhorse!"

He looked up at her with momentary annoyance. He'd managed to avoid the thought of Anna all day; had enjoyed the light-hearted hours spent with the family, telling himself that this was what was real, the rest only a chimera. Now here was Kate bringing it all back, renewing the longing to see her, to touch her. The annoyance spilled over to include himself. He was, after all, the one at fault.

He forced himself to smile, reaching across the table to take her hand.

"I'm sorry, darling. I didn't mean to snap."

"Didn't you?" Kate removed her hand and went on eating her fish, thinking how tasteless it had suddenly become, angry with herself for bringing Anna into the conversation. It was always the same, somehow. It seemed as if the very mention of her name poisoned the air between them, forcing her to say and do things that were both stupid and reckless. She felt now as if she were poised on some kind of precipice, about to throw herself over, knowing the dangers but incapable of prudence. "You say this malaise thing isn't my fault, that I'm too quick to take the blame for everything, but tell me – why do I get the feeling that I can't do anything to please you these days?"

"That's not true, and not justified. I've apologised for being abstracted recently – isn't that enough?" He poked at his fish dispiritedly, and sighed. "Look, don't pick a quarrel, Kate. You said yourself this has been a good day."

"Yes." She had eaten enough, and put her knife and fork, neatly aligned, on her plate. She looked up at him with a sympathetic, professional smile, hands clasped on the table in front of her. "All right, then, Dr Sheridan. Let's talk about this midlife crisis of yours that's causing such problems. What do you propose to do about it?"

He looked at her and said nothing for a few moments. Then he gave a grunt of laughter and shook his head.

"Grow out of it, I suppose. What else is there to do?"

"You do still love your wife, I take it?"

He took her hand again.

"Very much."

She dropped the professional tone and looked at him, biting her lip.

"Then why haven't you made love to me for so long?" she said at last. "Do you know how long it is?"

"Hey!" Oliver looked over his shoulder, but they were in the right place for secrets. High-backed settles separated each table from the others.

"It was after Brian's birthday party, three months ago almost to the day. And then you were plastered!"

"I was not!"

"Well, almost. Is that because of this midlife crisis, too?"

The velvet-jacketed gentleman they had identified as Mine Genial Host swam into view and replenished their wine glasses.

"Everything to your satisfaction, sir? Madam?"

"Lovely!" Kate smiled at him, wishing him further.

"We take a particular pride in our fish."

"It was delicious. Thank you."

He whisked away the plates and once more presented the menus.

"The strawberries are particularly good this evening but I can also recommend the peach and caramel brulé with apricot sauce. It's quite delicious."

"We'll browse a little, if you don't mind," Oliver said. Adding, once they were alone, "We can't quarrel while we're eating food that costs this much." He gave her a comic look of admonition that was meant to make her smile. It succeeded, but only just. "Come on, darling," he said. "Call a truce while we eat our brulé."

"How did you know I was going to choose that?"

"Because you always do!"

"In that case, I'll have the raspberry and rose petal pancakes."

"Hey!" Oliver was still striving for a light note. "You're trying to shock me out of it."

She looked back at him, wishing she didn't love him quite so much.

"I can try," she said.

"I shall never be able to thank your mum enough for talking mine into letting us go," Lucy said, already in bed when Emma came back from the bathroom.

"The old folks are pretty cool," Emma said.

"It was lovely, wasn't it? Hey, Em—" Lucy sat up a little, resting on one elbow. "Do you think they'll really come and swim off our beach tomorrow?"

"They said they would, didn't they? Well, Eddy did, anyway." She frowned, remembering the way Jacko had refused to commit himself. He would if he could, he said.

"Oh, I so hope they do." She sank back again and looked up at the ceiling, a blissful smile on her face. Emma watched her with a touch of cynicism.

Of all of them, she hadn't taken to Eddy. She couldn't explain it, couldn't in any way put her finger on why this should be, except that he seemed very pleased with himself. But then, so did Jacko – so why did she like one and not the other? It seemed a bit hard if a chance likeness to Jason Donovan was the only answer.

"His name's Adrian," she said as she wriggled out of her trousers.

"What? Who?" Lucy raised her head once more to look at her uncomprehendingly.

"Jacko. That's his real name. Adrian Jackman. Isn't it awful?"

Lucy considered the matter.

"Oh, I don't know. It's rather nice. Sort of – sort of – well, nice."

"I think it sounds pansyish."

Lucy hesitated a moment.

"I still think he's a bit weird."

"He's different," Emma said as she got into bed. "He's got hidden depths."

Lucy giggled.

"Well, I hope there aren't any killer sharks in them," she said. "'Night, Em."

"'Night, Luce. I say—" A thought struck Emma and she raised herself on one elbow. "That Karen! Didn't she look awful when she ate the candyfloss and got that foul lipstick smeared all over her face? I thought she was an awful pain."

"Do shut up, Em," Lucy said distantly. "I'm praying."

And I bet I know what for, Emma thought.

Oliver stood beside the open window, taking his last look at the sea before going to bed. It had become something of a ritual since coming here, as if he found the sight of it soothing and conducive to sleep. Or, Kate wondered, was he brooding over his own troubles, as, according to his own testimony, he had been doing for weeks. She wondered, as she had wondered every other night, what he was thinking.

"It's magic." He turned from the window to look at her. "Come and see. The moon's making a path on the water."

"I saw it," she said, her voice soft. "Why don't you come here?"

For a moment he didn't move, then he came to her and lay down beside her, taking her in his arms.

"I'm not plastered now," he said with a breath of laughter, kissing her gently.

"I know." She touched his face, stroking his cheek, his nose, his hair. "I do love you, darling. I'm sorry you're not happy. I didn't mean to be unsympathetic—"

"Shh." He kissed her again, less gently, and passion flared between them, consuming them as it had done so many times before, the excitement not lessened by familiarity. But afterwards, while Oliver slept, Kate lay awake

She felt out of her depth. She hadn't lied – she did feel sympathy for him; she knew the feeling too well herself. In fact, this feeling of letdown, a dissatisfaction with life, had been what had driven her to arrange this holiday in the first place. But did it really account for the bleak, noncommunication that had been going on for weeks?

It was purely physical, she attempted to assure herself. He'd been working too hard, needed a holiday. Two weeks' rest would put him right.

It really was foolish to go on worrying.

6

"Auntie Kate."

James, chin cupped in his hand and elbow resting on the draining board, looked up at her as she rinsed out their swimming things in the kitchen sink.

"Yes, James?"

"I don't think you've met Mr and Mrs Barstow, have you?"

Kate looked mystified.

"Who might they be?"

James sighed, mildly exasperated.

"We *told* you. They're Paul and Daniel's grandma and grandpa. And they're very nice people. Much nicer," he added after a short pause, "than Paul and Daniel."

"I thought you liked them."

"Wills does. I think they're a bit . . ." he hesitated again, searching for the right word, "bouncy," he finished.

"Like Tigger?" Kate suggested. James nodded enthusiastically.

"Just like Tigger," he agreed. "Only noisier. Of course," he went on, "Wills is a bit Tiggerish himself, so I s'pose that's why he likes them."

"You're probably right," agreed Kate. "I gather they live up the lane somewhere."

"You know the farm?" James said. "Where the kittens are?"

Yes, Kate told him. She did know the farm, and she did happen to have heard of the kittens.

"Well, they've got a house sort of near it. It used to be a barn, but now it's not. Mrs Barstow used to live here when she was a little girl and then she got married and went away and lived somewhere foreign, and now she's old she's come back again."

"That's very nice for her," Kate said.

She went to hang his trunks and her swimsuit on the line outside, and James trailed after her.

"Do you know what Mrs Barstow reminds me of, Auntie Kate? She's like a bird. Sort of beaky, with feathers sticking up on her head, only it's not feathers, it's hair."

"Like a hoopoe?" Kate suggested, trying to keep up her end of the conversation. James shook his head.

"Not quite so sticky-up as a hoopoe. More like a skylark, I think."

"I can't wait to meet her! What's Mr Barstow like?"

James frowned, thinking deeply.

"Not a bird," he said at last. "More like a dog. One of those little, whiskery ones that are so old their whiskers are going white – there's one called Jock that lives down our road at home. That's what he's like."

"They sound an interesting pair."

"I saw him when I was looking at the kittens yesterday, after tea. Paul and Daniel and William were there too, but they ran off and then there was only me and Mr Barstow. We talked about fleas," he added after a moment's pause.

"Really? Is he an expert?"

One behind the other they trailed back to the kitchen again.

"Not exactly. It was just that the Penroses' dog has got lots of them, but Mr Barstow said that we didn't have to worry about them hopping on to us because dog fleas would rather live on dogs than humans. D'you think that's true, Auntie Kate?"

"Yes. I seem to have heard that myself."

"I bet," James said, after a little thought, "that's because we wash too much. A flea wouldn't find us so interesting."

"For which I'm thankful, aren't you?"

"I suppose so." James looked far from certain. "What are we going to do this afternoon, Auntie Kate?"

"What would you like to do?"

James bit his lips and frowned as he considered the question.

"What I'd really and truly like to do," he said, thinking how nice it was to be without William for once who never bothered to consult his wishes, "is to go to the butterfly farm we passed yesterday. It's not very far away. And I don't expect it costs very much," he added hopefully.

"That sounds a good idea. Right now, would you like a drink and a biscuit? Something tells me it's time for elevenses."

James consulted the watch he had been given for his seventh birthday. It looked enormous on his stick-like wrist. "So it is," he agreed. "Why did the others go off so early, if they're not going on the boat until twelve?"

"They wanted to look round Porthallic – do a bit of shopping and so on. Lucy and Emma have both got long lists of people to send cards to."

"Girls are like that," agreed James.

"Well, what about this drink? Are you ready for one?"

"Yes, please. Ribena, please." He looked without enthusiasm at the packet of ginger biscuits that Kate produced. "Why don't we have Jammy Dodgers?" he asked. "That's what Mrs Penrose gave us."

"Well, bully for Mrs Penrose. I'm afraid this is all we have."

"Never mind," James said kindly, after a short and, Kate felt, reproachful silence.

He drank his Ribena and ate the biscuit sitting on the back step, joined by Kate with a mug of coffee.

"Auntie Kate," he said, looking at her with an earnest expression. "Did you know that the red admiral can lay a hundred eggs a day?"

Kate confessed that she had hitherto been ignorant of this fact.

"And do you know, they taste things with their feet?"

"Do they? My goodness, that doesn't sound much like fun, does it? It wouldn't do for me."

James laughed at that, his solemn little face suddenly blazing with life.

"Good thing they don't wear shoes," he said, adding, after a little thought, "'specially ones like Emma wears."

"I'd rather like to see a red admiral in a pair of Doc Martens, wouldn't you?"

James grunted with amusement, but had already progressed to other matters.

"D'you know, Auntie Kate, birds have the *greatest difficulty* in catching butterflies, 'cos they fly so fast?"

"My goodness, you do know a lot about them!"

"I got it from my *Child's Guide to the Hedgerows*."

"You'll be able to explain everything to me when we go to the butterfly farm this afternoon, then. I don't know my cabbage whites from my painted ladies."

James turned to look at her with an air of astonished superiority, but was distracted by the approach of a fly that had come perilously close to his ginger biscuit, thus reminding him of yet another interesting piece of information.

"I say, Auntie Kate, did you know that flies have a sort of tube to suck up food with?"

"You'd better eat your biscuit quickly so they don't suck up any of that." She shuddered delicately as he crammed the lot into his mouth. "I didn't mean *that* quickly."

He gulped and swallowed.

"Auntie Kate," he said, a little indistinctly. "Can I go up to the farm and see the kittens again? Mrs Penrose said I could, any time I wanted to."

"Well—" Kate considered the matter. It was so long since she had been responsible for a seven year old that she felt unsure what was allowed and what was not. However, after due thought, she came to the conclusion that no harm could come to him between Porthlenter and Brook Farm. Besides, it wouldn't be the first time he'd made the journey up the lane. The kittens were proving more of a draw than the sea and the cliffs and the beach combined.

"I'm not a bother to her," James assured her, wide-eyed in his earnestness. "The kittens are in the barn. Another barn," he added, in case she was wondering. "Not the barn where the Barstows live."

"OK, then. But don't be long. And don't go off anywhere else. Or with anyone else."

"I won't," he assured her, getting up and dusting crumbs from his T-shirted chest. He set off for the gate but turned round just before he got to the cattle grid. "I say," he shouted, "is it Dad's day for doing supper?"

"We're having a barbecue. I hope they bring back lots and lots of mackerel, don't you?"

He looked uncertain.

"Will I like them?"

"You'll love them!"

"I expect I will," he said, after a moment's serious consideration, and taking to his heels, tore up the lane as if unable to wait another moment.

Kate smiled and wished, not for the first time, that she'd managed to produce a boy. Not that she was in the least dissatisfied with either of her two daughters, or considered that in any way boys were superior to girls. It was just that small boys were rather endearing. Small boys like James, anyway. There was something, she mused, particularly appealing about the back of their necks . . .

She finished her coffee and took the mug and James's glass inside. She was just rinsing them when a shadow falling across the floor accompanied by a knock at the open back door caused her to look up in surprise. A woman was standing there, so tall and bulky that she effectively blocked out the light.

"Hallo – can I help you?" Gathering her wits, Kate moved towards her, wiping her hands.

For a moment the woman said nothing. She looked nervous, Kate thought. Ill-at-ease. Was she selling something? Collecting for charity? A Jehovah's Witness, maybe?

"Can I help you?" she asked again, when nothing further was forthcoming.

The woman's lips moved as if she was trying to formulate words that refused to be spoken.

"I lived here once," she said at last, in a voice that was gruff, without grace of any kind.

"Really? Then you must be looking for the Dawsons. I'm afraid they're not here—"

"I don't know them. They must have come long after. I was born here. I lived here as a child. I haven't seen it since I was fifteen."

"How interesting!" Kate smiled at her warmly. "I'm fascinated by the place. Do come in! I expect you'd like to see the way it is now."

Her social instincts were asserting themselves, perhaps even more strongly than usual simply because this woman was herself so lacking in charm, so clearly a member of the working classes. Her clothes, her big, plastic shoulder bag, her greying, badly cut hair – even the heavy features seemed to shout the fact aloud.

"I can't remember – 'twas a long time ago—" Tentatively the woman stepped over the threshold, looking about her.

"It must have changed a lot since you knew it, then. It's been totally modernised. You're welcome to have a look round, if you like. We're only renting the place for a couple of weeks, but I'm sure the Dawsons wouldn't mind and I'd love to know something of the house's history."

For a second the woman hesitated. Her head seemed to retract into her shoulders as she considered the matter. Like a tortoise, Kate thought, only huge and ungainly and wearing clothes from Oxfam instead of a nice shiny shell. Immediately she felt compunction at the unkind comparison. The poor thing was tired and hot. Her hair was stuck to her forehead, the coarse skin shiny with sweat. Crimplene trousers and a long-sleeved nylon tunic blouse patterned in shades of red was hardly the most suitable gear for walking in this weather.

She seemed to waver a little as if undecided, then with a jerky, sideways motion she crossed the threshold, looking about her.

"Have you walked a long way?" Kate asked her. "Let me get you a drink."

"No. There ent no need." Again there was that strange, retracting movement, as if the least she had to do with the present occupants of this house the better. "I didn't mean to bother you."

"It's no bother, really. Wouldn't you like to sit down for a moment?"

"I'm all right." The words came out sharply, but then the woman gave a nervous twitch of her lips – almost a smile – as if aware that she had been ungracious. "Thank you," she said again.

"Let me show you the rest of the house, then," Kate said. "It's a lovely old place, isn't it?"

"Yes." The tone had moderated. Softened, even. "I always loved it. I remembered that, all right. 'Tis just that . . ." Her words dwindled into silence, and Kate leapt in to fill the breach.

"Your family farmed the land, I suppose."

"Oh, yes." She frowned, as if in disapproval. "I can see it ent a farm any more."

"No. The Dawsons live in London. They let it out during the season, but Mrs Dawson told me they love it so, they come down as often as they can. They'll be here the week after next, when we've gone. My name is Kate Sheridan, by the way." Kate held out her hand and the woman took it briefly. Her hand was large and flabby. It was, Kate thought, like shaking hands with a Dover sole. "And you are . . .?" she asked brightly, conscious that she had, for some reason, moved into an almost professional mode. This woman might not have marital difficulties – indeed, Kate had automatically noted that there was no wedding ring on her finger – but there was something about her manner that shouted aloud the presence of inadequacy of some kind.

"The name's Kernow," the woman said abruptly. "Ruth Kernow."

"Kernow! That's the old name for Cornwall, isn't it?" The woman stared at her without speaking, and Kate rushed on to fill the gap. "I'm glad to meet you, Miss Kernow. I'm sure there must have been a lot of changes here. This kitchen, for instance . . ."

For a moment or two the stranger looked about her, saying nothing, but then the words seemed to burst from her in a nervous torrent as if, having suddenly remembered the way it was, she was in a hurry to describe it before the memory faded.

"'Twas in two parts, see. There was a wall down the middle – just here where this wall juts out. There was a scullery through there where we did the washing. This kitchen was where we sat. We didn't use the rest of the house much. Here was where the range was and it was always warm. My father had his chair just here – always here, beside the range. A Windsor chair. In the evenings he'd read Dickens to us, and *Pilgrim's Progress*, and, of course, the Bible."

Kate was nodding and smiling, picturing this scene of cosy, old-world domesticity, somehow given more substance by the Cornish accent which, unremarked at first, had become more and more obvious, as if this, too, was something unlearned but now remembered.

"It had probably been much the same way for centuries. How old would you say it is?"

Her visitor ignored the question.

"My father wasn't an educated man," she said. "Only self-educated, you might say. Though he'd been brought up on the land, he loved to read and wanted us to love it, too. He was a hard man," she added after a brief pause, her low voice trembling a little. "Not easy." She paused a moment, staring at the spot where she had indicated his chair stood, her mouth half-open. Kate was conscious of a sudden frisson of nerves as if some supernatural force had caused the man to materialise – as if the woman could see her father there, even though the sight was denied to others. She stood stock-still, her eyes staring, then she moved and the

119

moment was over. She looked about her again, the memories obviously crowding back.

"There was a dresser over there where you've got the washing machine and all those built-in cupboards."

"I don't imagine you had many of those—"

"No one did. Not then."

"Farm kitchens have a lovely atmosphere."

"There wasn't even a tap at the sink. Just a pump, and a tap outside. The girls at school thought you were nobody if you didn't have running water."

"Really? My goodness—" Kate shook her head, trying to imagine managing without it, and failing utterly. "Do come and see the rest," she said.

If she had hoped for illuminating glimpses into the past, she was disappointed, for though she asked questions, her visitor was monosyllabic in reply. She either knew little of its more distant past or was wrapped up in her own memories. What comments she made tended to be derogatory. She looked with disfavour at the half-finished jigsaw puzzle on a side table and the open book that lay across the arm of an easy chair in the large sitting room, as if deploring the fact that this room was actually being used and not kept swept and garnished for weddings and funerals as undoubtedly it had been in her day. There was, she said, more furniture. More clutter. She'd never cared much for clutter, herself. And why carpets? Even rugs on top of carpets? There were perfectly good boards underneath.

"Perhaps because it's cosier?" Kate suggested, at which Ruth gave a cynical bark of laughter. People didn't like the polishing, she said. They were afraid of hard work. Her mother, now, she took pride in her polishing and taught Ruth to do the same.

The tour was quickly over, for she seemed to have no wish to linger over any part of the house. She appeared sardonically amused over the two bathrooms.

"Thass two more than we had," she said. "We had a tin bath in the kitchen, and for the rest we went outside."

"Well," said Kate, feeling that to mention the downstairs shower room would merely confirm present-day decadence beyond hope of any redemption, "you've got to admit this is at least more convenient."

But Ruth's lips were set, her eyes were cold and she was admitting nothing of the kind. Nothing, she seemed to imply, had been improved, and there was much that she could criticise if she so chose.

"My family lived here for five generations," she said, as she preceded Kate down the stairs.

"Five generations! That would take you back to – when? The early nineteenth century, I imagine. Late eighteenth maybe. My daughter's fascinated by stories of smugglers and wreckers—"

"Fairy tales," Ruth said repressively. "This family was always God-fearing—"

"Oh, she'll be so disappointed. No skeletons in the cupboard then?"

They were at the bottom of the stairs by this time. Kate turned casually as she spoke, and saw that her visitor, hand clenched on the newel post, seemed suddenly to freeze as if struck by a sudden pain. Slowly she lifted her head and looked at Kate, her expression fixed, her eyes like two black pinpoints, the hand clasping the newel post rigid, with veins standing out like cords. Her face was deathly pale, the colour of putty.

Kate took a step towards her.

"Is something wrong?" she asked. "Don't you feel well?"

There was no answer from Ruth. Then slowly she seemed to relax, her arm falling to her side.

"No," she said. Her voice was husky, as if creaking with lack of use, and she coughed to clear her throat. "Five generations," she said again.

"What a pity you had to leave," Kate said, talking brightly, sociable to the end. "Was there no one to take over?"

"No one," she said, and repeated the words hollowly. "No one."

"Well—" With a hand on her arm, Kate shepherded her back to the kitchen. "You have your memories, and living in such a beautiful place they must be happy ones. I'm lucky that way, too."

"Memories?" Ruth still seemed vaguely disorientated. "Yes, I have them. More and more."

Kate looked at her with continued concern. The woman really did look ill, she thought. The heat, perhaps?

"Do let me give you a drink before you go," she urged. "It's so awfully hot."

"No—"

121

"It's no trouble. I really think it would be a good idea. Come and sit in the kitchen for a bit. Would you like tea or coffee? Or a cold drink?"

"Well—" Ruth wavered a little. A chair was standing against the wall quite close to the door to the hall, and she collapsed heavily into it as if her legs would no longer support her. "I suppose something cold would be nice. Thank you."

"Is orange squash all right? Would you care for a biscuit?" Ruth looked bemused by all the questions, but Kate continued to make bright conversation as she took a glass from a cupboard, went to the fridge, poured the drink. "Are you staying in Porthallic?"

"Yes."

"Are you sure you wouldn't like something to eat?"

"No. No. I never eat between meals." She looked better, Kate noted with relief. Thank God for that! Her mind, as always, had been leaping ahead. Suppose she collapsed? Had a heart attack? Should she phone for an ambulance, or would it be better to throw her into the car and rush her to Truro? But what, then, would she do about James? How long would an ambulance take to get here anyway? "I've got a picnic in this bag to eat in the woods, where it's cool," Ruth continued, looking more normal by the minute. "My brother and me, we used to go there—"

She broke off and turned an apprehensive look towards the door as running footsteps heralded the arrival of James once more.

"Auntie Kate, I wasn't too long, was I? The kittens are *lovely*, and I'm sure it would be all right to take one home—" He stopped, overcome by shyness, as he saw the stranger in the kitchen.

"James, say hallo to Miss Kernow," Kate instructed him. "She used to live in this house when she was a little girl."

"Hallo." James smiled at the stranger who gave him a brief, unsmiling nod. Her eyes were suddenly watchful, her expression guarded; it was the look of one who has reason to be cautious in the presence of small boys.

"James is a naturalist," Kate said, simply to fill a vacuum; there was something vaguely disconcerting about Miss Kernow's large, silent presence which, she recognised, was causing her to babble inanely. "He loves anything that crawls or flies. We're going to the butterfly farm this afternoon."

"My brother was the same." For the first time there was a softness in Ruth's expression – even the hint of a smile. "He loved all wild things. No need of butterfly farms then, we had them all in the hedgerows."

"I've seen quite a lot in the garden," James told her, forgetting to be shy. "There were *two* red admirals there this morning."

"And what James doesn't know about red admirals," said Kate, "isn't worth knowing. Believe me."

It was as if she hadn't spoken.

"Have you seen the silver-washed fritillary?" Ruth asked him. "There used to be plenty this time of the year up in the woods."

"Wow!" James stared at her with awe and astonishment. "Fritillaries! Maybe they're still there."

"They might be. They like the brambles."

"They sound lovely," Kate said. "Are they silver?"

"No, no." Ruth looked at her with a touch of scorn. "A kind of orange."

"With black sort of smudges," James said.

Ruth transferred her gaze to him and was now, without doubt, regarding him with a look that was almost approving.

"You're like my brother," she said. "You know what's what."

"I've got a book."

"He had one, too. And he borrowed more from the library."

"So do I."

She drained her glass and stood up abruptly. "I must go. Thank you for the drink."

"You're most welcome."

For a moment Ruth hesitated.

"It's been strange," she said. "Seeing it again. So changed."

"I'm sure it must have been."

"Which woods?" James asked.

"What?"

"Which woods are the fritillaries in?"

"Pedlar's Woods, of course. Come outside and I'll show you. You can see from the yard."

"Goodbye, Miss Kernow," Kate called.

There was no reply from Ruth who appeared to have no time to waste on social graces. She was pointing to the cluster of trees at the head of the valley.

"That's where they are," she said. "Where they used to be, anyway. Birds, too. Woodpeckers, greybirds, tinks . . ."

"Tinks?" James stared at her, wrinkling his nose. "I've never heard of tinks."

"You wouldn't have, where you come from. They'm Cornish words. 'Tis all coming back to me. Tinks are chaffinches, greybirds are thrushes. Eric knew them all. A lovely boy, he was."

"I like birds, too," James said. "Maybe my dad will take me up there."

But Ruth was not seeing him any more. Another boy was occupying her mind, thin and dark, with girlish features and a tuft at the back of his head. Without a word she turned and walked away, and for a moment James stood and watched her, a little puzzled, as she picked her way over the cattle grid and progressed up the lane.

"She's a funny lady," he said to Kate, going back into the kitchen.

"Yes," said Kate. "I'm rather inclined to agree. I don't think she's very well."

"She didn't say goodbye," said James, and added, more in sorrow than in anger. "I'm afraid that's what Mummy would call bad manners."

Tinks, Ruth was thinking. Greybeards. How it took her back! And there was another word that escaped her – a word that old men like her father and Mr Penrose used for what she and Eric later discovered were really called long-tailed tits. They'd found pictures of them in a book, too, with the proper name written underneath. They'd always called them—

What had they called them? What was that word? She couldn't remember, though somehow the resonances of it echoed in her brain. Perhaps it would come to her, as so many memories had done since she'd arrived here in this place that seemed both familiar and utterly strange. That house, for instance. Everything different. So light, with its pale walls and furnishings, and small rooms knocked together to make big ones, and bedrooms made into bathrooms. Tiled bathrooms – with carpets on the floor, if you please!

She remembered it as dark; no colours, anywhere. There must have been curtains, surely? Yes, of course; but they were dark, too – a browny-reddish colour, lined with black because of the blackout. She could see her mother now, taking them down and sewing in the lining, yards and yards of it, the sewing machine on the kitchen table whirring day after day.

So changed, she thought. Except for the staircase and the hall; for a moment she was conscious of the blackness again – not close, but threatening, hovering and full of menace, just as she had felt it earlier when she was standing there at the bottom of the stairs.

She paused and looked around her, holding her breath as if she might see it, like a cloud; but there was only the blue sky above her, and the high banks on each side, with bees buzzing round the brambles and the unripe blackberries and the dog roses. Her vision cleared. The moment had passed. The sun was shining, not a cloud in sight. There was no blackness, no threat. She moved her head slowly, to one side then the other, then took a deep breath. It was hot and she was tired; tiredness played tricks.

It was strange finding that boy there, too, not really like Eric in looks, but like him in other ways; in the way his face had brightened when he talked about the butterflies, and in a kind of gentleness she thought she could see in him, as if he were a different kind of species from those dreadful boys on the estate at home.

The house might have changed, she thought, but this was the same – this lane, with the low wall that in Cornwall was called a hedge, its grey stones set in the form of chevrons and covered with ferns and brambles. And the gate just here, where the path led across the fields to the stream with a few, spaced trees, as if the wood was beginning slowly before it grew thick and impenetrable. She and Eric had thought it huge as a forest.

And on the other side, the hills all around were just the same, up and down like a green switchback, except for the fields of summer barley, already being harvested, away in the distance. And as she looked at the distant tractor and harvester going about its work, she seemed to hear an echo – a resonance of other harvests. Someone said, once, that tomorrow harvesting would begin in Two-acre field – but no, she couldn't hold on to it, and it was gone.

There were, she saw, no more buildings here than there had been before. Fewer, in fact. There had been an old cowshed here by the lane's edge, already fallen into disuse and now gone altogether. Eric and she had called it their house and had dragged an old stool and a broken chair and a piece of carpet up to it. It had been their special place until they had found Bal.

Bal! Smiling, she lifted her face to the sky, as if in thanksgiving. She'd forgotten Bal, but this, it seemed, was one memory that was allowed her. One day everything would come back to her in the same way. One day it would all be made clear. In God's good time, enlightenment will come, she told herself.

She paused beside the gate as she had done many times before in her youth, and looked back the way she had come – to the farm, its grey-slate roof only partially visible among the trees that surrounded it, and beyond it the sea that she had loved in all its moods.

Her father had owned this field then; who had bought it, she wondered? Probably the Penroses of Brook Farm whose land adjoined – if, of course, there were still Penroses at Brook Farm.

She didn't know and had no intention of calling there to find out, but she felt sure they would still be there, one or other of them. They were strong, the Penroses. The old man had been tall and ruddy-cheeked, his wife a thin woman, but hardy. A good worker. Even her father, always sparing of praise, had said so. And their three sons – John, Robert and Joe – they were hardy, too. They'd been away throughout the war in the Navy, but all had returned safe. She remembered them only as broad, sturdy outlines, with voices that sounded as if they were always shouting against a force ten gale. Vigorous men, the Penroses.

The Penrose parents – surely long gone? – had come regularly to chapel, but the sons only infrequently, at Easter or Harvest Festival. It occurred to her suddenly that one had married, just after the war – John, wasn't it? She shook her head. It might have been. She couldn't remember.

As neighbours, her parents had been asked to the wedding. Her mother had been ill – too ill to go, really, but she had managed it somehow and had seemed strengthened and cheered by it. It had been lovely, she had reported. Four bridesmaids, all in pink, with roses in their hair; Ruth had read all about it afterwards in the *Cornish Guardian* and had longed to have seen it for herself. But her father said there had been strong drink at the reception, which was not what he would have expected of a chapel goer, like Mr Penrose. He'd been disgusted with Mr Grigson, too – the new, young minister who had taken over the chapel from Mr Pavey, and had been seen to toast the newly-weds with a glass of white wine. He'd never felt the same about any of them after that, and he'd assuredly turn in his grave if he thought his land belonged now to the Penroses.

It was, she remembered, about this time that her father had grown disenchanted with the chapel altogether, saying that standards were falling, that it was now too lax, they were deviating from the path laid down by God. So it was goodbye to the singing and the organ and the Anniversaries; and in a way, Ruth thought now without quite understanding why she thought so, it was the beginning of the end.

She could see glimpses of the farm at the top of the lane, but there was no sign of the Penroses; no sign of anyone. No sheep, even, though it was clear they had been in this field not too long ago. There was just the buzzing, humming heat and the scent of honeysuckle, and the springy turf under her feet.

It was a relief to reach the shade of the trees. She didn't like heat, had never liked it or felt her best when she had to endure it, and she was longing to rest. There were rowans beside the stream, and hawthorns, their berries turning red. And hazel trees with kernels already forming. The summer had reached its peak and was preparing itself for the descent into autumn.

There was, she remembered, an outcrop of rock by the stream which had always been a good picnic place. It was probably still there, though the stream itself was a mere trickle compared with the babbling brook she remembered – and there, suddenly, were the rocks, just as they had always been, providing somewhere to sit and a rest for her back. For a moment she stood still, her eyes closed, memories flooding back in such a torrent that they overwhelmed her. Then she lowered herself to the ground.

There was a thrush singing in the hawthorn tree above her head. And at once the teasing question surfaced again; what was it, the name they called the long-tailed tit?

Eric was lying on the grass beside the rock, his arms folded beneath his head.

"Thought we was going to Bal," he said.

Ruth, always the leader despite being the younger of the two, shook her head.

"We'll go there d'reckly," she said. "'Tis better for a picnic here."

"'Spose you'm right." Eric, smiling dreamily at the sky, was prepared to wait. "I d'dearly love Bal," he said after a moment.

"That's 'cos it's a secret." Smiling a little herself, Ruth took from a bag a cloth in which their mother had wrapped two freshly made pasties. "It's ours. No one knows about it but us."

"How do ee know? Someone must've, long ago. Stands to reason."

"Well, no one's said nothing, have they? Said we shouldn't go there, I mean – and they would, if they knew about it."

"You won't never say nothing, will you, Ruthie?" Eric lifted his head to look at her anxiously. "You'll keep it our secret?"

"'Course I will. Who would I tell?"

Satisfied, her brother relaxed once more, watching the fussy flight of a sparrow from one tree to the next.

"I wish I was a bird," he said after a silence. Ruth laughed at him.

"Just so ee could fly? I'll make two wings for ee in sewing."

The rock at her back felt cool and rough through the thin striped cotton of her summer dress. She leaned forward to spread the cloth on a second flat rock that they always used as a table, two dark plaits falling each side of her face.

"'Twould be 'andsome to fly," Eric said longingly. "Can't ee imagine it, Ruthie? Swooping up and down, going just where ee wanted. I tell ee, I'd give anything. Wouldn't you?"

"Sometimes."

She thought of that terrible night when she had lain listening in her bed to the sound of her father's voice raised in righteous anger, and her mother's tears. She would have done anything that night to fly away. Over a month ago it was now, but still she couldn't get it out of her head. Thank goodness it wasn't me who told about Uncle Ben, she had said to herself then, and repeated many times since. For she hadn't told. She hadn't needed to.

Father had come home from Truro market in a white, blazing fury – though he had made some good sales and was, presumably, in a happy enough mood before he had stopped up at Brook Farm to give Walter Penrose and his brother a hand with unloading some lengths of timber.

It was Mrs Penrose who had innocently mentioned the fact that someone in a blue van had nearly 'bout killed one of her hens.

"Goin' some fast, 'e was, up this lane. A hundred miles an hour, sure as I'm 'ere. Now I don't know who 'twas, but I'd be glad for ee to tell un, Thomas, to take more care. Tidn't no speed track up here, and well ee must know it."

Father had known at once it was Uncle Ben. His anger had been awesome, though he hadn't spoken throughout the entire evening except to rap out orders to his wife and family; fetch this – do that – clear the table – and then, eventually: go to bed. There'd been no reading from the Scriptures, no evening prayers. Just a stern admonition not to forget to petition the Almighty on their own account once they were upstairs.

Ruth and Eric, who had scuttled about at his bidding casting nervous glances at him where he sat grim-faced in his chair, were glad to go. When Father was in one of those moods, the further away they could get, the better.

The shouting started the minute they had gone. Ruth had listened, and trembled; then, with her fingers in her ears, had tried to shut it out. She had cried and she had prayed. Eventually she had slept a little, but she woke to the sound of the kind of keening that turned her bones to water.

Eventually she had got out of bed and crept downstairs, partly through curiosity and partly a desire to help. She'd plead for her mother, she thought. Tell Father it wasn't her fault – she had ordered Uncle Ben out of the house. But the sight that met her eyes as she crept down to the kitchen and peeped unseen through the half-open door made her hesitate.

Her mother, sobbing quietly now, was sitting in a chair, her elbows on the kitchen table, her head buried in her hands. Her father, on his knees beside her, was praying aloud.

"Lord, forgive we pray Thee your daughter who is penitent. Forgive her her wilful disobedience and defiance in that she used Thy house to issue an invitation to a cheat and a liar . . ."

"No, no." Her mother lifted her head at this, and was rewarded by a baleful glare before the prayer continued.

"A cheat and a liar and a bearer of false witness," her father intoned, "who has done nothing but undermine my authority from the moment of our marriage, when out of the goodness of my heart and under orders from Thee, I made an honest woman of her when others would have spurned her. Make her see the true character of this wretched man whose only interest is the land she brought to our marriage, freely making a gift of it to the husband who saved her—"

"Stop it, Thomas." Ruth jumped as her mother brought the flat of her hand down on the table with a loud crack. "You tricked me! It was no free gift, and well you know it—"

Undaunted, the prayer went on, but louder, more insistent.

"Forgive her, oh Lord—"

Ruth crept away again. Her mother looked dreadful – pale and miserable and tear-stained, but she had stopped the hysterical crying that had upset her so much and thrown her into such a panic. Things would probably quieten down now.

She wondered, briefly, what land they were talking about. Uncle Ben owned a farm somewhere the other side of Truro, left to him by his father – her grandfather. She had never known her grandparents, but her mother had told her about them. They'd been chapel folk, too.

"Your grandmother was a lovely lady," her mother had said. "Everyone loved her. Musical, she was. She played the organ in chapel."

"What was Grandfather like?" Ruth had asked.

"Quite strict, but he liked a joke." And she had smiled, and looked wistful. "Ben takes after him. Typical farmers, the both of them. Land means everything to them."

The reference to Father being under orders from God to make an honest woman of her was also incomprehensible. Mother was as honest as the day was long! She'd once walked all the way back to Porthallic after doing her shopping there because the butcher had given her too much change.

Ruth couldn't understand any of it, but she had to agree with Eric. A strange kind of sadness had seemed to oppress Porthlenter Farm recently and the thought of soaring away from it, up into the blue, untroubled sky had a definite appeal. Even so, she felt it necessary to affirm her superiority.

"You'm just mad because Father told you off," she now told her brother, full of virtue. "If you'd just do what you'm told—"

"Yeah, yeah!" Eric pulled a face at her. "Hark at Miss Goody Two-shoes. Why should I have to work every minute of the holidays? Other boys don't."

"Other boys don't live on farms. Not most of them. There's always lots of work on a farm. I've been working too, remember. You think I like cleaning that range?"

"Yeah, well." Eric's round face and delicately modelled mouth was set and mulish. "'Tis better than wallowing in all that pig shit. Tell ee what, Ruthie, I just wish the war would go on for years and years, so I'd be called up. Father'd have to let me go then. He couldn't stop me."

"Yes he could. Farmers are reserved. He could say he needed ee to work the farm."

"The Penrose boys are farmers, and they've been gone for years."

"That's 'cos their uncle works there along o' Mr Penrose. 'Tis different for we."

"Well, I'd go anyway. I'd go into the RAF and be a pilot."

"They'm not training any more!" Ruth had read this fact in the paper Father had brought back from Truro, and true or false, she produced it like a trump card, with triumph. "Anyway, 'tis a terrible thing to say you want the war to go on, when everyone prays for peace all the time."

"I don't."

"You do! Every night Father prays for peace, and you say 'Amen'. 'Tis the same as saying you agree."

"I cross my fingers. Like that – look." He sat up and put his hands together in the prayer position, one middle finger crossed over the other.

"That dun't make no difference. God'll strike you down dead."

"Well, He hasn't yet."

"I'll tell Father."

"You won't!" Eric's hand shot out and grasped her arm, so hard that she gave a cry of pain. "You swear not to, or I'll – I'll pinch you black and blue. Say you won't!"

"Leave go my arm then." She looked at him reproachfully, rubbing the place where he had hurt her. It wasn't like Eric to be so violent. "I wouldn't tell on you, you know that. Anyway, you'm just being daft. The war's nearly over now."

"Maybe." Eric stood up and went over to the brook, and picking up a handful of stones, he threw them in with great vigour and venom, one by one.

"And if it wasn't," Ruth said, watching him. "You'm only thirteen. You have to be seventeen for the RAF. 'Tidn't likely to go on another four years just so you can learn to fly. Here – come and have your pasty."

"I don't feel like un." Eric hurled another stone, and another; but both knew this to be sheer bravado. They had both been up at six thirty; both had worked hard. Ruth was ravenously hungry and she knew he had to feel the same – Eric, after all, had endured the added strain of a run-in with Father and a belt across his backside. Trouble like that always made him hungrier than ever, for some reason.

It was only because a raging toothache, endured all week, had finally caused Father to rush off to the dentist in Truro that they were able to get away at all, summer holiday or no summer holiday. Their mother had felt sorry for them and had taken the pasties from the oven and told them to go and have a picnic – just so long as they were back by three. She even took off her watch and gave it to Ruth to make sure. Father, saving petrol, had gone in on the bus that stopped on the main road every hour; he would be back on the one that was due to arrive at three fifteen, and it would take him a good ten minutes to walk to the farm, so it might have seemed more reasonable if she had said a quarter past three. However, they all, without a word being spoken, regarded the margin of error as wise.

It was already long after one o'clock, so for Eric to pretend he wasn't ready for something to eat was, Ruth thought, proper daft. Sure enough, after his token show of defiance, he turned round and came to sit down again, taking the pastie and biting into it with a bitter savagery. "I ain't going to stick around for the old man to shout at me and land me one every five minutes, and that's the truth. And I'll tell you another thing, Ruthie—"

He paused and smiled, and told her no other thing, his troubles forgotten, for a sound – a trilling warble – could be heard from a nearby tree. He cocked his head, rather like a bird himself, all chewing, all breathing suspended.

132

"Hear that?" he whispered. Ruth nodded. "'Tis an ekkymowl," he told her. "I'd know un anywhere."

Ruth, suspended between waking and sleeping, looked up at the blue sky which she could see through the lattice of leaves above her head.

Ekkymowl. She'd remembered it. It had come back to her, that silly name, echoing across the years, just like so much else had done.

She felt young again, and at peace, and for a long time she sat quite still and listened to all the sounds of the woodland, happier than she had been for a long while. The council estate, the fearsome gang of boys, her need to return to them, were all forgotten. A caterpillar inched its way across her hand. Birds came quite close and cocked their heads to look at her. Still she sat without moving.

Ekkymowl, she thought; and smiled with satisfaction.

7

It was time, Kate thought, that she made Mrs Penrose's acquaintance. She was, after all, the virtual custodian of Porthlenter, and it was to her they were to give the key on their departure so that she could organise a thorough clean-up before the arrival of the owners the following week.

Lynn had gone up with the boys on the first day to pay her respects on behalf of all of them, but this afternoon, returning from the butterfly farm with James, she remembered that William and Leo had each eaten two eggs for breakfast and thought that this would be a good opportunity not only to get some more but to make herself known to their nearest neighbour. She drove cautiously into the yard, not wanting to massacre any stray livestock that might be about. As it was, a black and white collie bitch, barking her head off, seemed determined to get under her wheels.

"If that dog's not careful, we'll kill her *and* her fleas," she said savagely, making James laugh.

"That's Jess," he said, showing off his superior knowledge. He scrambled down from the car and bent to embrace the dog, laughing delightedly as she leapt up and licked his face. "Jess is my friend," he added, but looked a little crestfallen as the collie caught sight of an unwary seagull and abandoned all interest in him to chase it off the premises. "Look," he said, pointing down a further track at the far side of the yard. "That's the Barstows' barn down there. Mustn't it be lovely for Paul and Daniel being so near the kittens?"

Kate reflected that she had been right when she guessed that they hadn't heard the last of these seductive animals, but forbore to comment on the fact.

The top part of the stable-type door to the farmhouse kitchen was open, but though Kate knocked and called, there appeared to be no sign of the farmer's wife. The place seemed deserted. No one was in the yard, though there were sacks of feed half-unloaded from the truck that stood outside. There was, Kate thought, a Marie Celeste quality about the scene.

"Perhaps she's gone to see the kittens," James suggested helpfully. "They're only in that barn over there. I'll go and have a look, if you like."

"We could leave it for another day."

"There's Mr Barstow!" James was waving wildly at a man who was making his way towards the farm down the second track. Kate watched his approach with interest and some amusement.

Very, very old, James had said. And like a whiskery dog.

She could see what he meant. Mr Barstow was short and stocky, with iron grey hair and beard, both streaked with silver. Sixtyish? Sixty-fiveish? Around there anyway, but not unattractive. She saw, on closer inspection, that his eyes were a warm shade of brown and his complexion was almost Gallic in its sallowness.

He approached them, smiling.

"Hi there, James. Come to see the kittens again?"

"Hallo!" James beamed at him, but after a few pleasantries, scampered off, anxious to waste no time in idle chatter. Mr Barstow turned his smile on Kate and held out his hand.

"Colin Barstow," he said. "You must be James's mother—"

"Aunt, actually. I'm Kate Sheridan. He's my sister's son."

"How do you do? I'm very glad to meet you. My wife and I owe you and your family a considerable debt of gratitude. We were just about at the end of our tether when William came along to befriend Paul and Daniel."

"William was delighted to meet them."

"We've been meaning to come down and say hallo to you all."

"Please do! Any time. We'd be glad to see you."

"Were you looking for Mrs Penrose?"

"Yes, I was. I wanted some eggs, but she doesn't seem to be around."

"She can't be far away, not with the door open like that. I think John's working in that field across the other side of the road at the end of the lane. She might have taken him some tea."

"I'll come back another day. It isn't really important."

"I'm sure she'll be back in a few moments. I certainly hope so, because I've been entrusted to get some cream for dinner tonight. Look – I'm going for a swim in a little while, so I'll be going past your house. Serena – my wife – and I usually have a dip in the afternoon if the tide's right, but she's taken the boys off to Truro today to see some friends. I was left in peace to finish some work."

"Oh? I somehow gained the impression you'd retired."

"Semi," he said. "I was an engineer and still do a bit of consultancy. I have a report to write, but I've done enough for today, so if Mrs Penrose is back I could get the eggs and drop them in for you." He grinned, suddenly and delightfully. "That's not very well expressed, is it? Deliver them, I should say."

"Well . . ." Kate hesitated for only a second. "If you're sure it's no trouble. I can always send one of the boys up—"

"No, really. I'll be glad to. How many – a dozen?"

"That'll be fine. I must give you the money." She began to root about in her bag, but he waved his hand dismissively.

"Cash on delivery," he said. "I'll see you later."

There was still no sign of life by the time Kate managed to induce James to leave the kittens – which were, she had to admit, totally enchanting. On their return to Porthlenter, she was engaged in wrestling with the lock on the back door which had remained intractable from the first moment of arrival when she heard the telephone ringing from inside, causing her to redouble her efforts. Caroline, she thought immediately. Or Rose. Something was wrong, there was an emergency. Please, please, she begged silently, keep going – don't stop ringing.

She felt differently when she found it was Anna at the end of the line.

"Kate?" The cool, crisp tones were instantly recognisable. "May I speak to Oliver, please?"

"I'm afraid he's not here, Anna." Kate was equally impersonal, equally business-like. "He's having a day's fishing. What's happened? Is there some kind of emergency?"

"Not exactly." There was a moment's pause, as if for thought. "I just need to speak to him – ask his advice. Get him to ring me, will you?"

No "please", Kate thought, bristling. No "sorry to disturb his holiday".

"Is this important?" she asked. "You must know as much as anyone how Oliver needs to unwind. It seems a bit of a shame to—"

"It is rather important, Kate. To me, anyway." Another short pause, and a distinct change of tone from brisk efficiency to the merest hint of sly innuendo. "And to Oliver too, I think you'll find. There are decisions that have to be made within the next week that could affect us all. I really must insist on speaking to him. When do you expect him back?"

"I really have no idea." Kate was deliberately vague. *Insist*, indeed! How dared she? What gave her the right to insist on anything?

"I'm not taking late surgery this evening, so I'll be at home after five thirty. He can ring me there." Another, almost imperceptible change of tone suggesting – what? Some kind of conspiracy? "I – think you'll find he has the number."

"What is all this, Anna? What decisions are you talking about?" Another pause.

"I'd really rather discuss it with Oliver, if you don't mind. Goodbye, Kate. I must go. As always, I'm frightfully busy."

As always, thought Kate as she slammed the receiver down. Never – *never* – has anyone set my teeth on edge like that woman does!

She wished now that she hadn't asked any questions at all – she wouldn't then have had to suffer the ignominy of Anna's refusal to answer. Still, she could hardly be blamed for doing so. She had, after all, acted as an unpaid secretary-cum-receptionist for years, as had most doctors' wives, and usually people were quite happy to explain to her their business with her husband. Anna, however, always had this ability to make her feel excluded, superfluous to requirements, a total outsider – one who was too dim to be bothering her pretty little head about the important questions that confronted her husband and his colleagues in their daily work.

"You look awfully cross, Auntie Kate," James remarked cautiously, watching her bang about the kitchen, putting on the kettle for tea, setting mugs on a tray to take out into the garden, wrenching a plastic container open to take out the half of a fruit cake that still remained.

Kate looked at him with compunction.

138

"Not with you, darling," she said. "Just that nasty lady on the phone who seems determined to spoil Uncle Oliver's holiday."

It was a moment later that she realised she wasn't only cross, but apprehensive. There had been something unspoken in the conversation, something that hinted—

Was Anna the cause of Oliver's crisis?

"I think you'll find he has the number," she had said in that purring kind of voice. Well, of course Oliver had the number, just as he had the home number of all his colleagues. Why had she said it like that, as if it carried some significance beyond the normal? And what did she mean when she said that the decisions would affect them all? Did she mean all the doctors, or – no, no, she couldn't have meant that!

But just as a housewife whose eyes, having focused on a speck of dirt, suddenly realises there is more dust – whole coats of it – in places she hasn't noticed for ages, Kate remembered, uneasily, other times and occasions. That party where he had dropped her off at home before driving Anna back to her flat in Kensington. He'd taken an incredibly long time to do it, she remembered now. Delayed by traffic, he'd said. A bumper-to-bumper jam, all the way down the A4 as far as the Hogarth roundabout.

She had been too sleepy to query it then, and too busy to think of it the following morning. Bumper-to-bumper traffic as far as the Hogarth roundabout was a daily occurrence – but at that hour of the night? Why hadn't the strangeness of it struck her at the time?

Then there was that weekend he'd gone to that Mental Health conference in Cambridge. He hadn't mentioned that Anna was going too, and it was only by chance that she had discovered this was, indeed, the case. It had been a last minute decision on her part, Oliver had said easily, and he'd quite forgotten to mention it. It wasn't really important, was it?

At the time she had thought it wasn't – but now she wondered. And what about the numerous times he'd been called out at night, lately? She had put it down to Anna's laziness; now she still put it down to Anna, but doubted that it had anything to do with laziness; and suddenly she wasn't uneasy any more. She was frightened.

Was Oliver in love with Anna? Suddenly it seemed more than likely. The evidence had been under her nose all the time and this talk of a midlife crisis was simply an attempt on Oliver's part to rationalise an extramarital affair. Everything now seemed crystal clear.

"Here's Mr Barstow," James called; and it took a great effort for her to look up and to smile and to act normally.

"How kind," she said, as she saw the two egg boxes in his hand. "How much do I owe you?" She was embarrassingly conscious that her hands were unsteady as she picked the coins out of her purse.

"We're just going to have some tea and cake," James said. "It's brilliant cake, Mr Barstow. My mum made it and we brought it down with us. You can have some, if you like. He can, can't he, Auntie Kate?"

"Yes. Yes, of course." Kate gathered herself together. "Do stay for a cup of tea, Mr Barstow."

"Colin, please."

"Colin, then. But I forgot – you were on your way to the beach."

He was looking at her in a way that made her self-conscious. She could feel his concentrated attention as if he sensed her unhappiness and wanted to help.

"Actually, that cake does look awfully tempting. I can go to the beach later. There's no hurry."

"Bring another mug for Mr Barstow, James," she said; adding in Colin's direction. "Do come through. I thought we'd have this on the terrace."

Having issued the invitation, James now hesitated, biting his lip.

"The thing is, Auntie Kate, I've just remembered that *Deputy Dawg* is starting in five minutes. So can I take mine inside and have it while I watch telly?"

"If you swear not to get crumbs on the carpet—"

"I won't, I promise."

Kids! Kate thought with bitter amusement as he went off. The very last thing she wanted was to be forced to make polite conversation with a total stranger. Her mind was too troubled, too full of wriggling worms of suspicion – still, there was no getting out of it now. James had set the scene for a tête a tête, and she had no alternative but to go through with it.

She smiled at her visitor. "Have you lived here long?" she asked brightly.

They'd lived for years in the West Indies, Colin Barstow told her, on some obscure little island that still, astonishingly, belonged to Britain. He'd met his wife at university in Birmingham, but Serena had been born and brought up in Porthallic and they had always planned to retire to Cornwall.

"Actually, we found the barn some years ago," he said. "The Penroses were anxious to be shot of it, so we bought it and camped in it over the years when we came home from leave, doing it up bit by bit. We're rather proud of the result. You must come up and see it."

"That would be lovely." Kate was using her social voice, aware that he was still looking at her attentively, and she was careful not to meet his eye as she dispensed tea and cut the cake. "How long are the boys going to be staying with you?"

"Just another couple of weeks. Our daughter's been in hospital – a hysterectomy – so we're giving her a bit of a break."

"I'm sure she's grateful. They're at a demanding age, aren't they? Though which age isn't demanding? I'd be interested to know. One seems to pass from crisis to crisis."

She felt a little more relaxed now. It was doing her good, she thought, to be forced to make an effort – and it had to be admitted that Colin Barstow was very easy to converse with. They talked easily of children, of retirement, of life in Cornwall; of Serena's talent for art, and the acceptance of some of her pictures for sale at the Craft Centre.

"Have you been there yet?" Colin asked her. "It's an interesting place. There's every imaginable local craft on show."

"I'll make a point of going to it," she said.

"It was once the local school. It seems a pity, doesn't it, to see these villages lose their amenities? The school, the cottage hospital, and so on. Yet it has to be admitted that larger, better-equipped schools give the children more of a start in life. My wife began her education there, of course, but she was one of the lucky ones. She went on to Truro High."

At the word "hospital", however, Kate's mind had wandered. Hospitals meant doctors, and doctors meant Anna. She became aware that a silence had lengthened, and pulled herself together rapidly.

"My daughter and her cousin have made friends with a few young people who are at school in Truro now."

She wondered if her voice sounded strange. He seemed to be looking at her in rather an odd way. With an effort she smiled at him, picking up the pot to pour more tea.

"Do help yourself to another piece of cake," she said, her mind squirrelling away in every direction as if searching for a suitable topic to take his attention away from her. With relief, she thought she had found one.

"I do so envy your wife," she said brightly. "Having a talent for painting, I mean. I've always thought it must be a wonderful hobby – total relaxation, I imagine."

"Serena's always found it so. Oh, she doesn't pretend to be Royal Academy material! She went to art college for a while when she was young, but soon found she didn't have what it took to get to the top. That put her off trying altogether, but since we've been home she's taken it up again and it's a great source of pleasure to her. And of course, she's absolutely thrilled to be able to sell her pictures."

"I should think so!"

"It's the fun of doing it that's the most important thing, though—"

"My mother's the same. Apparently she'd always had this longing to paint, but she did nothing about it until my father died, and then she went to art classes and surprised us all. She's on a course at the moment, learning how to throw pots. In Provence."

She gave a breathless laugh, which even to her own ears sounded mildly hysterical. How long, she wondered, was she going to be able to sustain all this chit-chat? She wished he would go away, so that she could concentrate on her misery and doubt.

She looked at him and saw that his eyes were on her, warm and attentive and rather puzzled.

"And what about you?" he asked. "Did you inherit her artistic tendencies?"

"I'm afraid not." And whether it was his essential kindness or the benevolent interest with which he regarded her that was her downfall she couldn't tell; Kate only knew that suddenly, without any warning, her eyes filled with tears and she was forced to look away from him. "I'm no use to man or beast," she said.

"What absolute rubbish!" He spoke bracingly, but not without sympathy; and at that moment they heard the sound of a car and the slamming of doors. The fishing party had returned.

It had been a good day, and they'd caught a lot of mackerel. More tea was produced, introductions made; Lynn and the children came outside to join Kate and Colin on the terrace, but after a brief greeting Oliver and Leo stayed in the kitchen, saying that since they were all fishy anyway, they would clean and gut the fish and have a shower before attempting to mix in civilised society.

With the fish ready for the barbecue, Oliver luxuriated in a hot bath, feeling calm and happy. He was tired, but not in the wound-up, nerve-jangling way he had been in London. He felt more relaxed and at ease with himself than he had been for some time. Everything, it seemed, had conspired to make life in London more and more impossible; all the new paperwork, the increased workload. Anna. How, now he came to think of it, had he found the energy for Anna and for all the attendant deceptions? What a ridiculous way to live! He would have no more of it.

Out there, in the boat, his problems had seemed more manageable, cut down to size. Suddenly, reeling in the fish, feeling the breeze and the warmth of the sun on his face, he had felt whole for the first time since leaving London, as if his spirit had once again been drawn back into his earthly body.

Cap'n Tamblyn had taken them down towards Falmouth and the Carrick Roads, which provided scenery for them to enjoy as well as fish to catch. In fact, he thought, heaving himself out of the bath, there hadn't been one sour note in the entire day.

For some time, as they chugged towards home, he and Leo had left the fishing to Lynn and the children and had sat in the shadow of the wheel-house talking in a way they hadn't talked before, about life and aspirations and growing older. Though he hadn't been specific about it, it seemed that Leo, too, was facing some major decision – somewhat to Oliver's surprise, for he had thought that since the takeover his future was settled.

He hadn't confided much, but he had said that Lynn was so far in ignorance of his dilemma. Well, they'd sort it out between them, he felt certain. Theirs was a good partnership, and they were good people.

With a feeling of wellbeing, he wrapped a towel round himself and emerged into the bedroom to find Kate sitting on the end of the bed waiting for him.

143

"Hallo, darling. Had a good day?" he said, beginning to dry himself. "We had a wonderful time. It was calm as a millpond – I'm sure it would have been calm enough for you, even. The kids enjoyed it, I think. Emma was a joy! Sweet and funny and enthusiastic, just like she used to be. Not a trace of the world-weary little horror we see so often."

He buried his head in the towel and rubbed his dark hair vigorously. There were, Kate knew, traces of silver around his temples, but they weren't particularly noticeable.

She looked at him with painful, loving familiarity. He was in as good shape as the first time she'd seen him – no extra flesh, his belly still flat, broad shoulders tapering down to a slim waist.

"I sent a postcard to Caroline while we were in Porthallic," he said indistinctly. "A view of the bay. Let her know we're thinking of her. I expect it'll take ages to get to her. We ought to give a ring tonight, maybe."

Kate gave no comment. She crossed her arms over her stomach and hunched her shoulders, trying to contain the pain.

"Are you all right?" he asked, as he emerged from the towel, suddenly aware of her silence. He looked at her anxiously. "Is something wrong, Kate? You're not feeling ill, are you?"

She returned his look for a moment, still silent.

"You had a phone call," she said, at last.

"Oh?" There was, she thought, a touch of wariness in his expression. Or was that her imagination at work again?

"Anna. She wants you to ring her back."

"Oh," he said again, but with a different inflection. Throwing the towel aside, he turned his back on her and went over to get fresh clothes out of the chest. "Did she say what it was about?"

"No, she didn't. Except that it was about some decision that would affect us all."

"Really? I wonder what that could be."

"I can't imagine."

"You sound as if she got your back up."

"I got the distinct impression that she meant to."

"Why would she do that?" He spoke casually, still with his back towards her.

"You tell me!"

144

He pulled on clean underpants and with the shirt in his hand came over to sit beside her, putting his other arm around her shoulders.

"There's nothing to tell."

"She said there was a decision she had to make. A decision that would affect us all."

"Curiouser and curiouser." He bent and kissed her. "I'll give her a call later and see what it's all about." He stood up and put on the shirt. "It's Tuesday, isn't it? That means it's her early night. I'll have to ring her at home."

"That's what she said. She said you'd know the number."

"Yes, I think I've got it in my little black book." He spoke lightly and casually, but he was conscious of annoyance. What was Anna thinking of? Kate wasn't a fool. She would know that there was no possible reason for any of the doctors to be disturbed while on holiday – and it certainly sounded, judging from Kate's manner, as if she had been less than tactful. "Did you see all the fish?" he asked, resolutely changing the subject. "We did well, didn't we?"

Kate wanted to press him further, wanted to demand answers – to ask him flat out if he had lied to her about the late calls and the conference, and if there was anything between him and Anna. She found she didn't dare.

"Yes," she said tonelessly. "Yes, you did awfully well."

And with that, she pushed herself off the bed and left the room.

The aroma of barbecued mackerel filled the garden.

"And probably the surrounding countryside for miles around," said Lynn, light-heartedly. "Let's hope it discourages the midges. Can we get run in for air-pollution?"

"There ought to be chips," William said. "It isn't done to have fish and French bread."

"Oh dear – does it offend your sensibilities?" Affectionately Lynn ruffled his hair. "It looked particularly nice French bread, I thought, when I saw it in the bakery. Never mind. All the more for the rest of us."

"I didn't say I wouldn't have it—"

"Just shut up, Wills, and set the table," Lucy said, dumping down a bundle of knives and forks. "I'm just going to get the plates."

145

Oliver's attention was momentarily diverted from his duties at the barbecue.

"And glasses. And those two bottles of wine on the kitchen table."

"I'll get those," Lynn said. "There's a bowl of salad as well."

"Not salad *again*! We've had salad every single day."

"It's good for you, James," said Kate, appearing through the French windows with the bowl in her hands. "Makes you big and strong. Gives you rosy cheeks."

"Why? Why doesn't it give you green cheeks?"

"Ask Uncle Oliver. He's our resident expert on such matters."

"I expect Mr Barstow would know, too. I like him. He's nice, isn't he, Auntie Kate? I'm glad he's coming."

He wasn't, Kate knew, so glad about Paul and Daniel. It was Lynn who had invited the Barstows *en masse*, having met Colin over the teacups and taken to him as warmly as James appeared to have done. For herself, she wasn't at all sure she was ready to see him again. She felt she'd made a fool of herself and would have preferred a little more time to have elapsed before confronting him; in fact, she would prefer more time to elapse before she had to confront anyone. She felt disorientated, unable to concentrate. Even making the salad, she'd forgotten half the ingredients and had begun taking it outside before she realised it.

What she felt like doing was going to bed and howling. She'd noticed Lynn looking at her oddly once or twice, but Oliver, together with Leo, was busy with the barbecue and full of jokes and bonhomie as if his day in the open air had agreed with him; or, she corrected herself, as if he'd been delighted to hear that Anna had phoned.

The telephone, on its table in the hall, seemed to Kate each time she passed it to look twice as obvious as usual, like a crouched, malignant toad waiting in malicious glee for Oliver to make his return call. He hadn't done so yet, to the best of her knowledge, and she would have known, because there was no other phone in the house, and she had been part of the constant traffic that had taken place for the past hour. No doubt he was waiting for privacy.

Earlier, they had all, including Emma, spoken to Caroline. She had sounded on top of the world. She was having a marvellous time, she said, and she had met, actually, a rather super guy. Such news tended to set a few warning bells jangling, if only faintly, but at least it meant that she was happy.

The Barstows arrived, and, since no one had yet met Serena, introductions effected. In spite of her preoccupations, Kate was amused to see that she did, indeed, have a fluffy crest of dark hair and a sharp little nose; James's description, she felt, had been perspicacious. There was something birdlike, too, in the way she tipped her head this way and that as she listened to the conversation from all sides. And she chirped a lot. A great talker, was Serena Barstow – loving, it was soon made clear, to hold the floor. She was, however, vivacious and amusing and full of information about the area and Kate, for one, was perfectly content to sit back and listen. She felt limp with tiredness, unable to make any effort.

William, Paul and Daniel were leaping around the barbecue, getting in everyone's way, until firmly told by Leo to go away until the food was ready.

Serena, holding court at the table, glass of wine in hand, was talking about the Craft Centre.

"She sold another watercolour today," Colin announced. "She'll keep me in luxury yet!"

"It was only a little one," Serena said, with becoming modesty.

"Never mind the width, feel the quality—"

"Can you paint kittens?" James asked.

"Grub up," yelled Leo.

"I can't think when I've had a meal I've enjoyed more," Colin said, some time later. "My compliments to the chef. Chefs," he corrected himself, raising his glass first to Leo, then Oliver.

"It was *scrumptious*," William said, mopping up his plate with bread. "I didn't know if I was going to like mackerel, but I do."

"It's almost but not quite my favourite thing," said Paul. "Best of all I like curry."

"Ugh!" Daniel made vomiting noises until firmly quelled by his grandfather. "Well, I *hate* curry!" he went on defiantly. "It's all yukky and it makes steam come out the top of your head."

"You could have mackerel curry, Paul, and then you'd have your two best things," suggested William. "Mum, can you have mackerel curry? Wow," he added, not waiting for an answer, "I'm absolutely full up and ready to bust. What's for afters?"

"One thing about dear William," remarked Kate. "You can always rely on him to add just that little touch of refinement to any family gathering."

"Indeed," said Lynn, "we have often remarked on it."

William, unconcerned, put the last piece of bread in his mouth.

"You're jolly lucky to have me. There's never much left when I'm around."

"You mean we're able to economise on bin liners?"

"St William," said Emma. "Patron saint of dustmen."

"Lynn, we feed him far too well, do you realise that?" Leo assumed an anxious look. "He has altogether too much energy."

Oliver, who was sitting next to his nephew, frowned judiciously, and taking hold of William's chin tilted his head so that he could look into his eyes.

"Hm," he said thoughtfully. "As I thought. An advanced case of over-stimulation."

"Gerroff, Uncle Oliver!"

"My advice," Oliver continued solemnly, "would be to cut down on the ice cream and chocolate. Or we could, perhaps, introduce some kind of tranquilliser into his Coco Pops—"

"Uncle *Oliver!* Just because you oldies just want to sit around all day—"

"Hey! Who took you fishing, may I ask?"

"Well, what are we going to do tomorrow?"

There was a general groan.

"William, give us a break, there's a good boy. There's fruit if anyone wants it—"

The boys took their bananas into the sitting room where a James Bond film was showing on television. A moment's appreciative silence ensued as peace fell.

"Do you remember," said Lynn, "how when Lucy was first born I said I would never, never be the kind of mother who sits her children down in front of the television to be entertained?"

"Distinctly," Kate said. "How long did it take?"

"Oh, about six months—"

"Now, come on!" Leo protested at this travesty of their domestic life. "You know we've always tried to give them constructive things to do."

All that sticky-backed plastic, Emma thought, hiding a smile.

"You've got to admit, Leo, the peace is wonderful," Oliver said.

"I've thanked God for the telly every day of the past two weeks," Serena said piously. "What life would have been like without it, I can't imagine."

"That reminds me," said Kate. "I haven't had time to tell you about my visitor. She lived here in this house when there were no amenities at all, not even running water, and came back to have a look at it."

She had, during the course of the meal, come to the conclusion that inviting the Barstows had been an excellent idea. With Serena at the table, only a minimal effort was required by the other participants at the meal. Now, however, it occurred to her that Serena might possibly be acquainted with Ruth Kernow, since she had lived in the village as a child.

Serena's eyes widened as Kate described her.

"Ruth *who*?" she asked.

"Kernow."

Serena continued to look alertly interested.

"I wonder—" she began, exchanging a look with Colin. "I did know a Ruth who used to live here, but her name wasn't Kernow."

"She could have married," said Lynn.

Serena shook her head.

"Somehow I doubt it."

In view of her previous loquacity, Kate thought her manner strangely secretive.

"Is there some mystery?" she asked. "I must say, she seemed very odd. I thought she was going to pass out on me at one stage. She looked as if she'd seen a ghost."

"*Did* she?"

Serena was leaning forward, her nut-brown, beaky face tipped sideways, eyes snapping with interest.

"Serena—" Colin began, a warning note in his voice.

"The boys are watching telly – they can't hear anything. And these two girls are far too old to get hysterical."

"I wouldn't bank on it," said Lynn uneasily, wondering what was coming next.

"Serena, I really don't think this is the time—"

"Nonsense, Colin! There's nothing like a ghost story after dinner, especially in a setting like this."

"Oh, tell us – *please*," Emma begged. "I always knew there was something strange about this house. At least, I always thought there ought to be."

"Actually, I can't guarantee the ghost, but there's no doubt whatsoever that a murder took place here – when was it? Just after the war – 1947 it must have been, just after I left school. A family called Teague were living here – father and mother, a son called Eric and a daughter called Ruth. One morning the father and mother were both found dead from shotgun wounds. Ruth was unhurt, but was found on the stairs holding the body of her mother in her arms. She was totally traumatised. She couldn't give any account of what happened – couldn't speak at all, in fact. Of Eric there was no sign at all, either then, or later."

"Did he do it?" Lynn asked.

"It was assumed so, but he was never brought to trial because they never found him. There was a nationwide hunt, as you can imagine. It was a nine days' wonder for Porthallic, I can tell you – well, more than nine days! It kept everyone in gossip for the rest of the year, and it's still talked about to this day."

"Where?" asked Lucy. "I mean, where in the house did it happen?"

"In the hall. The mother was—"

"That's enough, Serena," Colin said, his voice sharp. Noises indicated that the boys had abandoned the film and their peace was over. Scuffles and shouts and the simulated sounds of aeroplanes heralded their arrival back on the terrace.

"Yes – I think I'd rather the boys didn't know," said Leo, equally firmly.

"Oh, I agree," Serena said readily. "We haven't said a word to Paul and Daniel."

"What haven't you said a word about?" asked Paul, erupting through the French windows.

"About going to Funlands," Colin said smoothly. "It's a theme park," he explained to the others. "These two have been agitating about it for ages. I can't spare the time for a day or two, but would your boys like to come with us when we go?"

"Yeah – wow – whoopee!" With the exception of James, who had gone to stand close to Lynn on his return from the kitchen, the boys all leapt and shrieked with approval.

"It's brill," Paul assured William. "We went once last year—"

"*Quietly*, Paul," begged Serena, putting a hand to her head. "Colin, I really think it's time we took the boys home."

Kate saw Oliver steal a surreptitious glance at his watch. He's wondering when everyone's going to stop tramping through the hall, she thought. He's getting impatient.

"What are we going to do tomorrow?" William asked once the others had gone amid profuse thanks and expressions of esteem.

"I think tomorrow's activities should be Kate's choice, as she missed out on today," said Leo.

Kate protested vigorously.

"I didn't miss out at all. James and I had a lovely day. Still, given the choice, all I want to do really is flop around here. Does anyone mind?"

"I think that sounds rather blissful," Leo said.

"So do I," Lucy agreed. "Our friends might come," she said, by way of explanation.

"And they might not!" Emma sounded pessimistic. "Still, I don't mind having a swim and a sunbathe – all *right*, Dad – I'll plaster myself with Factor 15. Don't fuss."

"A quiet day suits me fine," said Lynn. "We don't need to shop. Do you realise," she added, "that our first week is already half over? We've only got ten days left."

William put a reassuring arm around her.

"Never mind, Mum," he said. "You can fit an awful lot into ten days. Dad – I say, *Dad* – when can we go water-skiing?"

It was after eleven when Oliver phoned Anna. Kate had gone to bed, leaving him downstairs. Now that there was a bit of peace, he said as everyone had drifted upstairs to their respective rooms, he'd make that call.

She waited for him to come upstairs feeling strangely disembodied. Perhaps it was the wine, or perhaps it was a kind of defence mechanism, preventing her thoughts from driving her crazy.

The house was very quiet now, the silence broken only by the sound of the sea and the odd creak and groan as the timbers settled. At least, that's what she thought it was. Perhaps, in view of Serena's story, it could be a ghost – except, presumably, that ghosts were silent.

Briefly, she remembered Ruth Kernow's strange, fixed look as she had stared at the nonexistent chair in the kitchen. Could her visitor really be the daughter Serena had mentioned? And would she have agreed to rent the house quite so enthusiastically if she had known its history?

She put it from her mind. They were here now, and had paid a lot for the privilege. The house was everything that Mrs Dawson had promised: comfortable, spacious, well-equipped, close to the beach. It was unrealistic to expect a place of such age to have no history.

She was, in any case, too preoccupied to care. It was the living she feared, not the dead. What could Anna be saying? Whatever it was, she seemed to be taking a long time about it.

She heard the door open quietly, as if Oliver hoped she would be asleep.

"Well?" she said, out of the semidarkness. "What did she want?"

For a moment he didn't answer, but just began undressing without a word.

"Brian's decided to retire altogether," he said at last. "I suppose it wasn't totally unexpected. God, it's hot, isn't it?" Stripped to his underpants, he went and leaned out of the window.

"What was the momentous decision?"

"What?" He straightened up and looked towards the bed. "Oh – they've offered Anna the job at the Centre on a permanent basis, and she wanted to know if I thought she should take it or if she should accept a hospital appointment in Liverpool. It's something she applied for some time ago when she thought this was just temporary."

"What did you advise?"

Oliver turned back to the window again.

"It's up to her. I'm not making her decisions for her."

"Why did she say it would affect us all?"

"All of us in the firm, I suppose." She could see his profile turned towards the sea, but darkness obscured his expression. She heard him sigh as at last he turned and came towards her. "It affects us inasmuch as any change in personnel affects us. I shall miss old Brian. We've been together for a long time."

"It's no more than that?" Kate said, after a moment.

"No." He stretched out on the bed beside her. "No more than that."

She wanted to believe him. If he'd turned to her – held her and kissed her as he had done the night before, if all her doubts and fears could have been submerged and drowned in passion, then, perhaps, she would have been convinced. But he just lay there for a while staring up at the ceiling, then sighed again and turned away from her; and she felt sure of nothing.

Anna's voice had had a distinct edge to it. She'd expected him to ring earlier, she said, and had seemed cynically amused by his talk of mackerel and barbecues and the need to wait until the house was quiet, as if she suspected him of making excuses.

"They want a decision before Wednesday of next week," she said. "Oliver, what am I to do? What about us? Are we going anywhere? Do you want me to stay?"

"It's your career, Anna. Your life. You must choose."

"That's not fair! Do you want me to go? Because if you don't, you can tell me to stay and I will. But there are conditions. I'm not going to spend my life being the other woman, Oliver. I mean that. I'm fed up with spending weekends alone and snatching time with you whenever you can be spared from home. It's all or nothing if I stay. I've got to make that clear."

"You've every right to."

"Well? What shall I tell them?"

"Anna—" he took a breath. "Anna, I've never let you think for one moment that I'd break up my marriage. I'm sorry."

It was only after a long pause that he heard her voice again, the bitterness coming loud and clear over the wire.

"Then I'll go to Liverpool." She gave a short laugh. "I suppose I should be thankful that you've been forced to state your intentions at last."

"Anna, don't! You mean a lot to me—"

"But not as much as your wife, even though you cheated on her. You men are a pretty despicable lot, aren't you?"

"I can't argue with that."

"Oh, Oliver!" Her mood, it seemed, had changed between one breath and the next. Now she sounded infinitely sad, close to tears. "I can't believe it's really over."

She still had the power to affect him, was still able to reach out over the miles and turn his resolve to water.

"Nor can I," he said. "But there it is."

"Think about it, Oliver. You haven't had time to weigh everything up. I won't say anything about the job yet. Think about it properly. Think about all we've been to each other – oh, you've never criticised Kate to me, I know, but you wouldn't have turned to me if you'd been happy – if you hadn't felt there was something missing from your life—"

"Maybe not. Even so—"

"Think about it," she urged again. "Ring me again in a day or two. Goodnight, my darling."

She had put down the phone without waiting for any more, and he had stood for a while, the receiver still in his hand, not able to move. Even after he had replaced it, he felt unable to go upstairs to where he knew Kate waited for him. Instead he went outside, out to the garden, and through the arched gateway, down to the cliff path. For a moment or two he watched the waves creaming on the beach, then returned to the house, locked the doors, and slowly went upstairs to bed.

"What's that noise?" Lucy asked out of the darkness.

"The sea," Emma said shortly, almost asleep.

"No, not *that* noise. There was a kind of bang."

"Someone shutting a door, I expect. Go to sleep, Luce."

"I can't!" Nevertheless, Lucy was silent for a moment. Then she sighed. "I've sort of gone off this house, haven't you, Em?"

Emma sighed too, recognising that she was not going to be allowed to sleep just yet.

"Why?" she asked. "Because of the murder?"

"I wish that Serena woman hadn't told us."

"It is a bit creepy," Emma admitted. "Still, it wasn't just here, was it? And it was ages ago. Look on it as history."

"Do you think the house might be haunted?"

In spite of her bold front, Emma felt a frisson of fear – a reaction which she recognised as irrational, given that she had seen the house's potential from the beginning. Had even, in fact, rather hoped for ghosts. However, her protective instincts made her suppress any such thought.

"No," she said stoutly. "I've never heard anything more stupid. Go to sleep, Lucy. Think of nice things, like Eddy coming over to the beach tomorrow."

"Suppose he doesn't," Lucy said, in a small voice.

Lying beside Kate in the darkness, Oliver cursed himself for his weakness. He should have spoken firmly, left no room for doubt. One quick yank and it would have been over, like pulling a tooth out, with nothing left to do but recover from it. Now it was still open-ended, still needed his final word.

Oh, what was he thinking of? He'd made his decision – made it last Sunday in Porthallic when he hadn't given in to the temptation to phone her; had renewed it last night when he made love to Kate, and again today on the fishing boat when everything had seemed clear and straightforward and back to normal. Was he really so weak that just the sound of her voice would send him into this kind of turmoil?

He was, at that moment, horribly afraid that he might be.

8

"The funny thing about a heat wave," said Lynn, "is that I always get complacent and start thinking that this is what it's going to be like for ever and ever."

Kate laughed. "I know exactly what you mean. One begins to believe that the British climate has at last pulled itself together and realises how it ought to behave. But it won't of course."

"I shan't complain as long as it lasts until Saturday week."

They were in their favourite spot, under the umbrella on the beach. Another game of cricket was in progress, with Leo being bowled at, very slowly, by Daniel. Paul and William were fielding – Paul, at this instant, looking pleased with himself, having held a difficult catch which had dismissed William from the crease not five minutes before.

James had avoided this activity, and was currently with Oliver, fossicking around the rocks. Lucy and Emma were still at the house, preparing themselves for the possibility of being joined by their friends – preparations which, for reasons that remained obscure to their mothers, involved trying on each other's bikinis as well as the use of quantities of depilatory cream on legs and underarms, and the application of waterproof mascara, purchased the day before in Porthallic's Minimarket.

"Kate," said Lynn tentatively, breaking the silence. "I can't help wondering. There's nothing wrong, is there?"

Kate, who had been looking at the distant, absorbed figures of her husband and nephew, questioning whether a son might have prevented Oliver's malaise – made him feel, perhaps, less the victim of a monstrous regiment of women – dismissed this notion at once, with vigour.

157

"Of course not! What makes you think there might be?"

"I just thought you seemed a bit – I don't know! Quieter than usual, I suppose."

Kate hesitated and for a moment was tempted to confide, but it took less than a second to reject the idea. She didn't want to put her fears into words; it would give the situation a shape and substance it didn't possess. In any event, this morning she had felt happier and almost certain that she had jumped to all the wrong conclusions. Of course Anna's decision would affect Oliver, that went without saying. And as for the rest, it was all circumstantial evidence, capable of being interpreted in an innocent way – as, indeed, she had done until yesterday's phone call had awoken suspicions.

Oliver, this morning, had seemed perfectly normal; had brought her a cup of tea in bed and had chatted for a while – not about Anna, but about Ruth Kernow. Except that according to Serena, she wasn't called Kernow at all, but some other name that for the moment escaped her. Teague, that was it.

It was the trauma part that had interested Oliver. It was, he said, a dissociative syndrome of the kind he was particularly interested in. A dissociative syndrome, he explained, seeing her incomprehension, was caused by hysteria and could affect any sensory function. It could cause deafness or blindness or – as in Ruth Kernow's case – loss of speech and memory.

"She didn't want to remember," he went on. "So she didn't. Easy as that."

"Does this sort of thing last long?"

Oliver shrugged his shoulders.

"Not usually. Not nowadays. There are drugs that can deal with it. But then? In – what was it? 1947? I honestly don't know. Much depends on the severity of the stress that caused the condition in the first place – the degree of gruesomeness, and so on – and how quickly and in what way she was treated. I don't imagine that psychiatric institutions of the forties were as enlightened as they are now. Then, of course, the personality of the girl herself is important. Was she a stable sort of person? Or was she inclined to be hysterical at the best of times?" He frowned into space for a moment or two, then turned his attention back to Kate. "How did she seem to you, forty-odd years on?"

Kate thought about it, sipping her tea.

"Odd's the word," she said at last. "Definitely odd. Shy and abrupt and yet – I don't know! Aggressive, I suppose. She made all sorts of snide remarks about how much better everything was when they had oil lamps and no taps and no carpets. Not to mention an outside loo."

"Well, she's clearly got her memory back now – for some things, anyway."

"Ye-es." Kate assented, but doubtfully. "You know," she went on after a moment. "Now you mention it, I'm not at all sure that she did remember it all. I mean, not before she actually came inside. She looked around as if the place was totally strange, and then she seemed to get quite excited, and out it all came – how the dresser was here, and the kitchen range was there, and Father's chair just there. Now I come to think about it, it was as if it was all coming back to her as she spoke. Might it happen like that?"

"It's possible, I suppose. Every case is different. I wonder if she was ever able to remember the murder in detail."

"Heaven knows – but I'll tell you something else. Didn't Serena Barstow say that the bodies were found in the hall? Well, it was just at the bottom of the stairs that she seemed to freak out—"

"In what way?"

"Well, she was pale to start with, but she went even paler, and her eyes looked really strange. For a moment it seemed that she couldn't speak or move or anything. I honestly thought she was about to have a heart attack."

"But she recovered. Obviously."

"Yes. I sat her down in the kitchen and gave her a drink. And then James came in and they started talking about butterflies and birds and things, and she seemed back to normal. Or at least, as normal as she had ever been. As I said, she was a bit of a weirdo."

"Hmm." Pensively, Oliver ruffled the hair on the back of his head. "Interesting, isn't it? Perhaps it all flooded back there and then, and hit her for six." He was silent for a moment or two, frowning, lost in thought. "If she turns up again, shout for me," he said at last.

"I hope she doesn't!"

He got up, took a turn round the room, stood looking out of the window for a moment, then came back to sit on the bed beside her.

"It occurs to me," he said. "Apropos of what I said about being a stable character, that maybe she wasn't. I mean, she had a brother who killed his own parents."

"Allegedly," said Kate.

"Why did he disappear, if he was innocent?"

"The same person who killed his parents could have killed him and thrown him over the cliff. Or something," she added, seeing his sceptical expression.

"His body would have turned up eventually. All I'm saying is that killing your parents seems to imply a less than well-adjusted home life, don't you agree?"

"So?"

"So I shouldn't let her in the house again if you're on your own."

Kate put her cup down on the bedside table and looked at him without speaking for a moment.

"I'm beginning to wish we'd never come anywhere near this damned house," she said.

"Nonsense!" Oliver put his arm around her and held her close. "It's a gorgeous place and you were very clever to find it."

It was that warmth she remembered now, looking at him over the expanse of the beach, before focusing on Lynn once more.

"I'm fine," she assured her. "Really. Just incredibly – I don't know! Relaxed. Spaced out."

"As long as that's all – I mean, if any of us is getting on your nerves, it'd be better to say—"

"You're not, I promise. Are we getting on yours?"

"Of course not. Well—" Lynn hesitated a moment. "Leo worries about Lucy. About this set she and Emma are running around with." She looked at Kate apologetically. "We're just not as used to this sort of thing as you are."

Kate looked sympathetic.

"Honestly, I don't think there's any cause to worry. I do know how you feel, though – but hopefully we'll see them for ourselves this morning. I hope they come."

Lynn gave a short laugh.

"I don't know how Lucy will bear it if they don't," she said.

160

* * *

The garden on the opposite side of the house from the terrace was always shady during the afternoon because of the large sycamore tree set in the angle of the macrocarpa hedge, and it was here that the adults tended to laze away an hour or two after lunch – chatting or reading or sleeping, or a mixture of all three.

Emma and Lucy were usually happy to do much the same, but today, far from happy, they had a great deal to talk about and had their heads together at some distance from the others.

"I knew they wouldn't come," said Lucy, her face stark with misery.

"They might still—"

"No they won't. The tide's all wrong for swimming now. D'you think we'd be allowed to go into Porthallic tonight, to the Cavern?"

"I don't want to!" Emma was on her dignity. "To hell with them!"

"But maybe they had a reason—"

"They probably went over to Sophie's place. Jacko said they've got a wonderful pool, halfway down the cliff."

"But they *said* they'd come!"

"I bet it was that Karen that persuaded them not to. I could tell she hated me. Every time Jacko so much as *looked* at me, she spat nails."

"I'm sure Eddy likes Sophie."

"They all like Sophie! You can't blame them, really. She's pretty, she's good fun, and she splashes all that money around."

"Wasn't it *awful*, what she said—"

William looked across at them, wondering if they could be persuaded to do something. Climb a few rocks, or play Monopoly. Anything at all. But even he could see this was a lost cause.

"Girls don't half *talk*," he said disgustedly to James, venting his rage by hurling a ball against the side of the house, catching it and hurling it again, over and over. "It's not fair! I thought we were going water-skiing. Dad *said*—"

"He said *one day*. Anyway," James pointed out, with justification, "it's low tide."

"Yes, but we could still *go*—"

"Let's go and see the kittens."

"I'm getting bored with them."

"I'm not! Anyway, you might see Paul and Daniel."

William thought this over as he continued to throw and catch. "OK," he said after a few moments. "Might as well. Come on then. We're going to the FARM," he bellowed towards the recumbent figures of his parents, causing Lynn to stir and groan and subside again.

They met Paul and Daniel coming down the lane as they were going up. Paul had a coiled length of rope held over one shoulder in a casual, professional way.

"We were coming to fetch you," Paul said. He was a thin, bespectacled, scholarly looking child whose looks belied a formidable energy and a brain that was a hotbed of insurrection. "We've thought of a brilliant game up at the mine."

"Which mine?" William, having been harangued at some length about the dangers of such places, was cautious.

"The one on the cliff, of course. We're going to tie this rope round a tree and climb down it. They say the hole goes down for miles, right under the sea."

James felt slightly sick, and was relieved when William, none too happy at the idea of going underground himself, immediately vetoed the idea.

"We're not allowed," he said. Paul looked scornful.

"So what? Nor are we."

"I've got a better idea," William went on. James wondered what it could be. Looking rather anxiously at William, he could tell that really he had no suggestion to offer and that he was thinking furiously.

"You're just scared," jeered Paul.

"I am not!" William clenched his fists and stuck his jaw out. Seeing it James's heart sank. It was that sort of look that had got them both into trouble on numerous other occasions.

"We could go to the wood," he said tentatively.

Paul greeted this with even more scorn.

"That's boring!"

"No, it's not. Not if we do my idea." William had cheered up and James could see that, in the nick of time, he had thought of an alternative way of passing the afternoon. "We could tie your rope to a tree up there and play Tarzan. Swinging from tree to tree."

"*Yeah!*" Daniel said, swooping around with his arms uplifted to

162

demonstrate the action. "Wicked! Come on, Paul – this'll be great." There was something about the alacrity with which he adopted William's suggestion that appeared to James to suggest that going down a hole into a tunnel under the sea hadn't exactly appealed to him, either.

For a moment Paul considered the options. Then he shrugged his shoulders.

"OK," he said. "I don't care. If that's what you want. I just thought we could do something really exciting for a change."

On the way up the lane, however, he seemed to warm to the idea and started to bellow the Tarzan call, joining Daniel in his swooping activities.

James, smaller than any of them, doubted his ability to do any swinging from tree to tree. Still, nothing was worse than being left behind – and who could tell? He might see the silver-washed fritillaries that funny old woman was talking about. He mentioned their possible presence to the other boys, but wished he hadn't when they just made fun of him. Paul put on a silly voice and pretended to be a mad professor leaping after imaginary butterflies, a joke which caused William and Daniel to roll about with hysterical laughter. Well, to be honest, it *was* rather funny, and James couldn't help laughing a bit too, but at the same time, it did nothing to make him feel more comfortable in their company.

Once in the wood, he found he'd been quite justified in thinking the tree-swinging business would be beyond him; his arms weren't long enough, for one thing – and for another, he was just plain scared. William helped him up to hold on to one of the branches from which he was expected to launch himself at the rope which Paul had tied to the branch of a nearby tree, but having got up he was incapable of moving. The ground seemed impossibly distant and his grip on the branch decidedly insecure; he found he could do nothing but hang there, eyes bulging in panic, until he was helped down again.

"He can't help it – he's only seven," William told the others, but conscious of their scorn and not, this time, seeing anything at all funny in Daniel's falsetto rendering of "Rockabye Baby", James announced that he was going to look for the butterflies.

"You're not supposed to go off on your own," said William.

James walked off, saying nothing.

"I'll tell Mum," William warned him loudly. "We're supposed to stay together."

"I don't care—" James turned his head to shout his defiance over his shoulder.

For a moment William stood watching him, biting his lip.

"Let him go, Wills," Paul called from above. "He's weedy, him and his butterflies."

Divided loyalties made William hesitate a moment longer, but he could see that Paul had a point. James *was* weedy – there was no denying it. Anyway, he couldn't wait to try swinging from that rope himself. He knew he'd be good at it. Probably a lot better, even, than Paul.

"Shove off, then," he yelled. "See if we care."

James, plodding down the woodland path, could hear their yells and crashes for some time, but at last he was out of earshot as the wood closed in on him. He didn't mind. Now, he felt, he was among friends.

Ruth emerged from the Minimarket clutching a plastic bag containing a packet of sandwiches and a small carton of orange juice. She hadn't made up her mind if she would walk over the cliffs on the other side of the village or have another morning on the beach, but when she saw the bus waiting in the square, her mind was made up for her.

She would take it as far as Sproull's Corner, she decided, just as she used to do sometimes when the weather was too bad to walk home from school over the cliffs. There was a path into the wood right opposite the bus stop. It had been lovely, she thought, sitting there yesterday beside the brook, quite the best time of the holiday so far, with the gentle birdsong and the cool, cool shade, and only her own thoughts for company. It had brought back happy memories, and might do again.

I ought to come back here to live, she thought, as the bus took her round the twisted lanes with their intermittent views of hills and ocean. I could find a little cottage miles from anywhere, where I didn't have to talk to people – after all, I've got a bit of money still. I can do what I like. I ought not to live in a town. I never liked towns. Except, maybe, Truro, with its wide, cobbled street, and the narrow lanes around the cathedral.

For a moment or two the thought of moving seemed a possibility. She'd managed to arrange the holiday, hadn't she? Anything, now, seemed possible. In her heart, however, she knew it would never happen. She might complain about the estate, might long for somewhere better, but when it came to the point the thought of rousing herself to look for somewhere else to live filled her with panic.

There was nothing to stop her dreaming, though. When she was a child, going to Truro had been a treat, infrequent and anticipated with pleasure and excitement. She'd dreamed then of going there to school one day. Some of the girls from wealthier families went to the Junior School when they were eight years old, many of them boarding, but she knew that for her the exam she would take at eleven represented her only chance. She didn't care much about the educational opportunities this would give her; it was the uniform that appealed. She had longed to wear the brown tunic and gold blouse that all the girls wore, cherishing the belief that a school uniform would make her look more like other people, less of a misfit – but, to her great disappointment, she never got the chance to see if she would be proved right.

The day she heard she'd failed the exam she'd come to the woods to get over the disappointment, and on this day, close to half a century later, she found the wood as soothing as ever, the damp, earthy smell of it comforting in its familiarity. Nothing here had changed. A broad path divided into two narrow ones, the left fork meandering off into the depth of the wood, the right leading to the brook, little more than ditch just here, almost overgrown with brambles and water mint and wild celery. She picked her way beside it, following its course until she came to the clearing and the rocks, where she sat down as she had done the day before.

There were dragonflies darting over the diminished trickle of water, and squirrels rustling the leaves of the trees. Eric, for all his love of wild things, didn't care for squirrels. They were vermin, he said, that ate young birds and tore their nests to pieces. It was, perhaps, the one thing that he and his father agreed on, though Ruth had never felt comfortable when Father had shot them, along with the rabbits that ravaged the fields. At least a rabbit made a tasty pie. You could forget, when your teeth sank into Mother's pastry and its savoury filling, the small, free, furry creature it once had been, but nobody ate squirrel except gypsies, so killing them seemed a wicked waste, a wanton act of vandalism.

Her thoughts ranged back and forth. Before I go back, I must have a look at Truro, she mused. All she'd seen of it on her day of arrival was the station, and the hill out of town, which had looked much the same.

The town itself would have changed. Bound to have done. New roads, new shops, new car parks. All the old places would have gone – that funny little shoe shop by the cathedral, run by the two elderly sisters; they must have died long ago. And the Ladies and Gents Outfitters in Boscawen Street, with the money whizzing about on little rails overhead. And the hardware shop. You didn't often see hardware shops like that any more. Were nails still sold there by the pound, she wondered?

They'd almost forgotten the nails. Thora had needed to go to Truro to see a doctor at the City Hospital. A specialist. The old GP in Porthallic, Dr Crabtree, had X-rayed her at the cottage hospital and when he had seen the results had looked grave and said that a second opinion was necessary – had insisted on it, in fact. And so they had toiled up the hill from the bus stop and they had waited and waited for what seemed hours before at last she was called into the specialist's presence. And in the end, it all turned out to be a lot of fuss about nothing. She was just fine, she told Ruth gaily when she emerged from the consulting room. Father had been quite right when he'd said Dr Crabtree was getting past it, didn't know what he was talking about.

"But at least we've had a chance to see the town again," she'd said. "Come on now, Ruthie. We mustn't waste any more time."

They'd bought a length of material for Ruth's anniversary dress and some matching thread and braid, and some Amami shampoo for Mother because she had decided that soap wasn't doing her hair any good. They'd gone into Smith's and bought a new account book that Father wanted for the milk records, and a book on beetles for Eric. The pictures in it were good, but the words were too long. He wouldn't know what half of them meant. Ruth knew by this time that she had only ever had an outside chance of going on to Truro High, but for Eric it had never been considered. He was always at the bottom of his class and no one, least of all himself, had thought him capable of doing other than staying at school in Porthallic and leaving at the earliest possible moment.

He'd be pleased to think they'd bought him a present. She couldn't help wondering how Mother was going to explain it to Father, though, or account for the expenditure of an extra sixpence.

They'd called into the post office for stamps and were just going towards the Town Quay to catch the three o'clock bus home when they remembered the nails and for a moment turned and clutched each other with the horror of what might have been.

"Someone up there's looking after us," Mother had said, laughing and casting her eyes to heaven.

Ruth was shocked, as if her mother had been guilty of blasphemy. Of *course* Someone Up There was looking after them! That's what they were told all the time. What they all believed.

"Not a sparrow falls," she said reprovingly, loosening herself from her mother's grasp.

She had noticed before on these occasions that her mother tended to behave like a child let out of school. Today she had seemed even more excited and giggly. Anyone would think she was no older than Ruth was herself. She was certainly no bigger. Now twelve, Ruth was of equal height and sometimes wondered if there was anything she could do to stop herself getting any taller.

There was no doubt, however, that Father would have been furious if the nails had been forgotten, and Ruth felt as thankful as her mother that they'd remembered them in time.

They retraced their steps and went back towards River Street; and it was there, just as they were about to cross the road, that they saw Uncle Ben for the first time since the terrible row. He'd stopped coming to chapel and had never visited again. Mother never spoke of him, and Ruth hoped fervently that she had forgotten all about him.

He was crossing the road too, but in the other direction, coming towards them, looking over his right shoulder at the oncoming traffic. He was quite oblivious of their presence. Ruth glanced fearfully at her mother. She had come to a halt on the kerb, not moving, and had turned pale; but when Ruth took her arm and tried to propel her away so that the confrontation would not take place, she shook her off and stood her ground, waiting for the moment when Ben would look up and see her.

"Thora!" He was almost upon them when it happened. He reached out his two hands and held her by the shoulders, smiling in disbelief. "Oh, 'tis you, my 'andsome!"

"Yes, Ben. 'Tis me."

"Are ee all right?"

"Well—" she seemed to hesitate, and glanced at Ruth. Then she smiled. "I'm fine. And you? Are you all right?"

"Why wouldn't I be? I ent married to that miserable, bloody—"

"Stop that, Ben."

For a moment, brother and sister looked at each other, not speaking. Then pulling her away from the kerb where other pedestrians were forced to surge around them, Ben grinned and enfolded her in a bear hug.

"Thora, my love – come and have a cup o' tea," he urged.

"Ben, we can't! We've got to get home."

At this Ben appeared to register Ruth's presence for the first time.

"Well, our Ruthie," he said, smiling at her. "You've grown a big girl."

Ruth looked at him coldly, not returning the smile.

"We'll miss the bus," she said. "It goes at four."

"There's another at five."

"'Tidn't no use, Ben," her mother said regretfully. "I must go – I'll be in trouble, else."

"'Tis over a year, Thora. Can't ee spare me five minutes? I won't say nothing 'bout Thomas, I swear—"

"Better not, Ben." She glanced over her shoulder towards Ruth once more. "No, better not. Just tell me you'm well and everything's fine—"

"Everything's *not* fine! Ent I cut off from my little sister?"

"'Twon't be for ever. There'll come a time—"

"I know, I know! In the sweet by-and-by, I s'pose!" He gave a sardonic kind of smile and shook his head, but then as he spoke the smile died and he hesitated for a moment, biting his lip. "Don't know if I should tell ee this—"

"Tell me what?"

He was silent for a moment longer, then seemed to make up his mind.

"Ken was back last week," he said. "Ken Pawley. Askin' for ee."

"Ken?" Ruth saw her mother's lips frame the word, but no sound emerged from them. Her colour had returned while she was talking to her brother, but Ruth watched it drain away again, leaving her pale and more gaunt than ever. "Back? For good? He's left Australia?"

"Thass right. He joined the Air Force out there. He said he was sick o' they wide open spaces with nothing but sheep, and he hoped they'd send him home to England, but he got sent to the Middle East instead. He was there all through the war till now, but then they sent him to Scotland. That's where he is now, doing training or some such, and he came home on leave to see his old mother last week. He said it was some good to feel good Cornish earth under his feet again."

"Did you tell—?"

"No. I never said a word, but Thora—" Ben glanced at Ruth, and pulled his sister closer. "He d' know, though. Someone else told him."

"Everything?" Ruth, straining to hear, could only just catch the word.

"Everything. Don't be surprised if 'e comes looking for ee."

"He mustn't!" Thora clutched Ben's arm, and in her agitation she spoke louder so that there was no longer any need for Ruth to strain to hear. "Tell him, Ben! Tell him 'twill be the death of me if he comes to Porthlenter."

"I'll tell him." Ben patted her arm soothingly. "I'll tell him – don't worry, pet."

Ruth saw her mother's expression return to its state of harassed normality, saw her exhale slowly.

"Is – is he married?" she asked at last.

"No, still single. He's the same handsome, silver-tongued devil he always was – full of fight and teasy as a snake; you don't 'alf pick 'em, Thora. I'll tell ee that!"

"Ssh!" She glanced swiftly at Ruth. "We must go now, Ben, or we'll miss that bus for sure. Take care of yourself."

"You too, my 'andsome." He looked down at her with concern. "Are ee eating right? You'm some thin, maid."

"I'm all right."

"Well, see you are. Take care of her, Ruthie – she's the only mother ee'll ever 'ave."

"I know," Ruth said, staring at him balefully. He looked at her for a moment, then gave a breath of despairing laughter, shaking his head. "Oh, Ruthie," he said.

"We must go, Ben—"

"Listen – there's something else. I'm gettin' wed myself next month, to Betty Cox over to Tregony. Lovely girl, she is. One in a million. I was trying to figure out some way to let ee know. Will the old devil let ee come to the wedding?"

"I don't suppose so."

For a moment or two they looked at each other in sadness and resignation.

"Well," Ben said at last. "I wish 'twas different, but there 'tis. I mustn't make it harder for ee than needs be. I just wish we could see more of each other, or talk on the phone. You ought to have a phone, Thora, living where you do."

"He won't hear of it, Ben."

Ben laughed.

"I never thought he would, the mean old bugger. 'Bye, Ruthie. Don't think too bad of your uncle – here, take this shillun to buy yourself some sweeties."

Afterwards Eric had said she must have been proper mazed, but she hadn't regretted her reply. It had been, she thought, the only fitting one after that awful thing he'd called her father. She had drawn herself up and stuck her chin in the air, looking at her uncle with open distaste, as if he were a bad smell.

"I wouldn't take it if you went on your knees," she said.

Mother had pulled her away angrily. They caught the bus by the skin of their teeth and sat, side by side, all the way to Sproull's Corner, without saying a word. All Mother's excitement and happiness had gone, in fact she turned her face away from Ruth and stared out of the window from the beginning of the journey to its end, even reaching into her handbag to get out a handkerchief with which she dabbed at her eyes. That's what Uncle Ben does to her, Ruth thought. He makes her cry. He made her cry the last time, and now he's done it again.

It wasn't until they were walking down the lane towards Porthlenter that her mother spoke.

"You shouldn't have behaved like that to Uncle Ben, Ruthie," she said. "It was rude when he was only being kind and generous."

"*He's* the rude one! We shouldn't have spoken to him at all!"

170

"He is my brother. Suppose someone said you weren't to speak to Eric—"

"They wouldn't! It's not the same! Eric wouldn't try to get me away from my children – and anyway, what about the awful things he says about Father?"

"Ruthie—" Mother said, as if she were going to explain or protest some more, but then she fell silent and didn't complete the sentence. "Don't tell your father, Ruthie," she said.

"I didn't before, did I?"

Ruth ate her sandwiches and drank her orange juice. Her memories had been upsetting ones, memories that made her heart beat faster – yet in another way they pleased her by their very clarity. Bit by bit it seemed that all was coming clear. Just wait, she told herself. Watch and pray. Enlightenment will come.

She liked the sound of the phrase, and said it aloud. "Watch and pray. Enlightenment will come."

What came, in the short term, was James. She had dozed a little but had been woken by a wasp buzzing close beside her ear and was engaged in batting it away when his small figure dressed in blue shorts and a Jurassic Park T-shirt appeared on the path in front of her. He stood still and regarded her with cautious friendliness.

"Hallo," he said. "I've been looking for the silver-washed fritillaries."

Ruth had been enjoying her solitude and was in no mood for small boys.

"Well, I ent seen none here," she said shortly.

"You said they liked brambles. I've seen lots of brambles, but no silver-washed fritillaries."

"That's not my fault."

Her voice was impatient and abrupt, and James looked at her in some astonishment. Grown-ups, in his experience, were not usually gratuitously rude.

"I didn't say it was," he pointed out distantly.

He turned to go back the way he had come, but even as he did so his eye fell upon another clump of brambles on which a butterfly was resting. He stopped and examined it closely.

"What's that?" he asked, the question directed at himself rather than Ruth. The butterfly seemed quite content to submit to his scrutiny and obligingly kept still. "I don't reckernize it," he said after crouching, hands on knees, to give it his full attention. He hesitated for a moment, then looked over his shoulder towards Ruth as if wondering if it was worth attempting to address her again. Curiosity won the day. "Do you reckernize it?" he asked, raising his voice a little.

Ruth looked at him. She'd been startled, scarcely more than half-awake, when he had first appeared, and at first sight she hadn't realised he was the boy she had spoken to the day before, the boy who was staying at Porthlenter. Now she knew him, and she saw there was no harm in him – anyone could see that. He was gentle and soft-spoken, full of curiosity about the countryside, like Eric had been. Almost before she knew it, she was levering herself up and going over to peer at the butterfly with him. It was speckled brown, with a single dot at the tip of each wing.

"That's what they call a wall butterfly," she said, and was filled with pleasure that the name had occurred to her so easily. Enlightenment will come, she thought.

"Why 'wall'?"

"Because it likes to rest on walls, I suppose."

"It isn't on one now."

"Well, he ent got a wall to rest on. Not here." Her tone was acerbic. "He'd choose it instead of a bush right enough if he had the choice." She gazed at it in silence for a moment, and when she spoke, her voice had softened as if her thoughts had been happy ones. "My brother used to say it looks like un has a waist, with they markings in the middle."

James looked up at her and laughed, revealing his new half-tooth in all its glory, and seeing him, Ruth was conscious of the strangest sensation. As she had seen before, this child was nothing whatever like Eric, and yet there was something – his eyes, maybe? The way he wrinkled his nose when he laughed? Perhaps it was just the fervour of his interest that made him seem so similar. She couldn't tell. She just knew that the icy, rock-hard casing around her heart seemed to melt a little when she looked at him, that he touched her in a way that nothing and nobody had touched her for a long time.

"We could go and look for more, if you want," she said. "Not far from here, there's a place we called Bal. Just that. Bal." She smiled reminiscently. "No one else knew of it. Eric loved it better than anywhere for it was always full of butterflies."

"Can we go there, then?"

For a moment Ruth looked around her, shaking her head.

"Don't know as I can find it," she said.

"We could always try," said James.

The car arrived just as Emma and Lucy had decided, in desperation, to go for a walk. Somewhere different, they thought. Somewhere in the opposite direction to Porthallic. Fortunately they were still thinking about it when they heard the sound of it bumping over the cattle grid, and with hope renewed, they rushed round from the side garden to the yard where it had come to rest.

Oliver had roused himself to go inside to make a mid-afternoon pot of tea. He saw the car through the kitchen window as he filled the kettle, and watching it come to a halt, he pursed his lips in a soundless whistle. It was a long, low, sleek Mercedes, brand new and top of the range, and so bowled over was he by the sight of it that it took all of five seconds for him to realise that the woman driving it was worth at least a similar whistle, too.

She had the looks as well as the glamour and poise of a model, with her ash blonde hair coiled on top of her head and falling in small, wispy tendrils round her face. She wore a white, minimal suntop, and white pants that looked, to Oliver's appreciative eye, as if they had been painted on, her slenderness accentuated by the heavy gold belt that was slung low over her hips.

A slightly smaller, mini-edition of this vision of loveliness had emerged from the other side of the car, to be fallen on by Emma and Lucy.

He went out to join the party and introduce himself.

"Hi!" The woman accompanied her greeting with a wide, white smile. Her eyes, he noted, were a dazzling shade of deep blue. Well, he thought, amused at himself. They would be, wouldn't they?

"I'm Suzi Renshaw, Sophie's mother," she said. "Our daughters are friends. We just came over to see if we could kidnap these two – take them back to the house for a swim and some supper. The rest of the gang are coming, too."

"That sounds wonderful—"

"We can go, can't we Dad?" He had seldom seen Emma looking more enthusiastic about anything.

"I don't see why not," he said. "But come round and meet the others, Mrs Renshaw—"

"Oh, do call me Suzi, please!"

"Suzi. They're all in somnolent postures in the garden."

Even as he led her round he had a mental picture of Kate as he had seen her five minutes before. She had been half-asleep, clad in shorts and her Friends of the Earth T-shirt. Whilst perfectly respectable, he had to admit that her usually high sartorial standards had been allowed to slip a little – as why should they not on this kind of occasion? Still, no matter what the justification, something warned him that she would not be best pleased to have this glamorous stranger descend upon her unawares without so much as a chance to run a comb through her hair. There seemed, however, little he could do except shepherd Suzi through the hedge and usher her into the presence of Kate and Lynn and Leo – all of whom were showing signs of having heard their approach and were making efforts to look alert and welcoming.

"This is Suzi Renshaw," he said. "Suzi, this is Kate, my wife; Lynn, her sister; Leo, Lynn's husband."

"Hallo! Oh, please don't let me disturb you," Suzi cried at the sight of them. "You all look so comfortable!"

It was Leo who rallied first. He had leapt smartly to his feet, and was taking her hand, smiling, blinking a little as if dazzled by her beauty. Oliver was inwardly amused. Even Leo, he thought. Even he.

"It's time we were disturbed," he said. "We're all being quite revoltingly idle – we've decided to blame the Cornish air."

"It's said to be relaxing," Suzi said, smiling back and opening her blue eyes wide.

Kate, having stood to greet her, collapsed back into her chair and patted the one vacated by Oliver.

"Then do relax just here," she said, with her usual warmth. Oliver, looking at her, felt a sudden rush of affection. She might hate being caught like this, but still her first concern was to make the unexpected guest feel welcome and at ease.

"Well, thank you. Just for a moment," Suzi said. "As I was saying to your husband, I've really come to sweep your girls away. Apparently there was some arrangement for the crowd to come over here to swim this morning, but for various reasons it all fell through. Now it seems that with the tide out, they've decided to swim in our pool – oh, here are the girls! This is my daughter, Sophie. Come along, darling. Come and be introduced so that these people can see that you're a thoroughly fine, upstanding member of society."

"Well, I do my best," Sophie said, dimpling at them with great charm.

Introductions were made once more, acknowledged by Sophie with consummate poise.

"Emma and Lucy can come, can't they, Mrs Sheridan?" she asked when they were over.

Kate smiled at her, liking her air of assurance, her good manners, her pretty face. How fortunate, she thought – how *very* fortunate that this was the kind of girl that Emma had chanced to meet. Surely she would allay all of Leo's fears about this new set of friends.

"Well, I'm only responsible for Emma," she said. "But I don't see any reason why not."

"I should say not!" said Emma.

Lynn and Leo professed themselves equally agreeable.

"What time and where shall we pick them up?" asked Leo.

Suzi waved away such considerations.

"There's no need! Really! We're visiting friends for dinner tonight in St Tudin, so Gerald and I can drop them off on our way – about eightish? They'll have had supper."

"They'll probably need more," laughed Sophie. "The boys cook it on the barbecue, and half of it always goes up in smoke."

Lynn, looking at Lucy, saw that she was alight with joy and excitement. She's so vulnerable, she thought with a sudden pang. So on the verge of everything. Please God let her have a lovely time.

"It's kind of you to come out of your way like this," she said to Suzi.

"Not at all. Sophie wanted Lucy and Emma particularly."

"I was about to make tea," Oliver said. "Won't you stay and have a cup?"

"I won't, thank you. The rest of the gang may well have arrived by now, so the sooner I get these girls back, the better."

They stood in the yard and waved them off, Leo and Oliver vying to see who could give the most help when it came to backing and turning.

"Wow!" Kate said softly, when they had disappeared up the lane. "Glam, or *what*?"

"She doesn't look old enough to have a daughter of Sophie's age," said Leo. "She must have been a child bride."

"I have never," said Lynn, "been more conscious of looking like a sack tied round the middle!"

"Darling, you don't—" Leo hastened to reassure her.

"Darling, in this dress I *do*! But it's so cool and comfy, it comes out summer after summer."

"You don't look nearly such a fright as I do," Kate assured her. "This is the third day I've worn this top, and I knew I was pushing it. Honestly, isn't that like life?"

"Let's face it, ducky," said Lynn. "If we were dressed by the combined talents of Versace and Yves St Laurent, we wouldn't look like that in a million years."

"Actually, I've always thought that T-shirt had a kind of *je ne sais quoi*," Oliver said.

"Shut up and make tea," said Kate.

James thought he had never met an old lady quite so strange as Miss Kernow. One moment she was nice to him, the next she was biting his head off. For no reason! That was the worst of it. He'd only asked if she was going to walk home past Porthlenter because then she could come for tea, but she'd rounded on him and said didn't he think she'd walked enough? Did he imagine she could trail around after him all afternoon and then climb that cliff path? She asked him, "What do you think they have buses for?"

"To ride in, I s'pose," he'd answered sullenly.

"I'm not as young as I used to be," she said crossly, as if that was his fault, too.

Well, who was? Privately James thought this a silly thing to say, but he said nothing because she really had been very nice to him earlier, telling him, among other things, all about how she and her brother had collected glow-worms when they were little and put them in paper cages so that they could see the light shining through. You hardly ever saw them these days, she said. Like lots of other things, they were rare and growing rarer.

"I've seen them in Greece," James told her, but she seemed not to have heard him.

"Nothing's the same any more," she said. "Everything's changed. No, you won't see glow-worms these days."

He opened his mouth to say well, you still did in Greece, so there; but then he closed it again. Sometimes it was hard to remember that she was an old lady, the way she spoke.

Still, she had gone on and on looking for this Bal place, or whatever she called it, in a most un-old-ladyish way, peering through bushes, pulling branches aside, pushing her way through thick undergrowth that most people of any age would have avoided at all costs. The wood climbed up a steep hill, and they'd puffed and panted, on and on, up a place were there was a kind of wall of stones, only it wasn't a wall that anyone had made, the stones just sort of grew there. He had thought this might slow her down, but no, up she went to where the rhododendron bushes grew thickly. She didn't seem to care a bit about getting her hair caught on twigs, or tearing her blouse.

"I know it's around here somewhere," she said. "Things have got so overgrown."

"It doesn't really matter," James began, being by this time rather bored with the search. She took not the slightest bit of notice of him.

"You'll see butterflies there, all right, if only we can find it."

And at last, lagging behind and wishing he was at home having tea, James heard her give a triumphant shout.

"Come along, Eric – come and see! It was here, all the time."

"I'm James," James said, ducking under a low branch to join her. She was too excited to take any notice, however, being engaged in pushing her way through the huge, towering rhododendrons. There was no path here and James's legs were badly stung by a clump of nettles. He gave a yelp, but Ruth, looking around, smiling with pleasure, gave him short shrift. He ought to mind where he put his silly feet, she told him – adding that there were plenty of dock leaves to put on the stings.

They were in a still and silent glade, encircled with thick bushes and trees, in its centre a deep declivity.

"Look," she said. "There's the oak tree. Still there. Still the same. Our house."

It grew close to the edge of the dell, not straight up, but slanted, and it was like a sort of house, James could see, for the branches hung right down to the ground, almost like a curtain. She crouched down and holding a branch to one side, looked into the bare secret place close to the trunk. James looked in it, too, and thought it would be a jolly good place to hide if ever it should so happen that he was around this area when playing hide-and-seek.

For a moment he thought that she was going to creep inside and hide now, but she just peered at it for a little while, and then turned to stare down into the dell that was close by the side of it. This was lined with bracken and brambles. Down the bottom of it was a drift of dead leaves and what looked like a pile of rocks, all overgrown with ivy and other creepers.

James wasn't much interested in the dell, though, for she'd been right about the butterflies. Forgetting his stinging legs, he stared in astonished delight at the clumps of a tall, pink flower around which danced scores of the creatures.

"Wow, there are thousands!" There was awe in his voice as he approached them. They were, he saw, mostly brimstones, but he recognised a silver fritillary and several large whites, as well as one he was almost sure was a speckled wood. He held out a hand, inviting one of them – any of them – to alight for further study. "Wow," he breathed again, very softly, as one of the brimstones duly obliged.

It had all been worth it, then. All the scratches and the tedious searching.

"This is *brill*," he said, half to himself and half to Ruth.

"What?"

Her voice sounded strange, and he looked over his shoulder to where she stood, massive and motionless, her shoulders rigid as she stared down into the dell. He looked down, too, but there was nothing special to see, only the leaves and the creepers.

"This place," he said. "It's great."

She lifted her eyes and looked at him then, and he saw that her face had gone funny; kind of pale and flabby. Her eyes were staring and her mouth was moving as if she was chewing something, and as he watched her she sank to the ground quite slowly, as if her legs had collapsed under her, and covered her face with her hands. For a moment he stared at her in consternation, biting his lip, then hesitantly he went over to stand beside her.

"Are you all right?" he asked her awkwardly.

She didn't answer. She was making a funny, whimpering noise, like a baby. He felt frightened.

"Are you ill? Shall I go and find someone?" he asked.

She lifted her head, took her hands away from her face, and looked at him. At least, she looked in his direction, but her eyes still looked strange, as if she couldn't see things clearly. Her face looked better, though. Put together properly instead of being all crumpled and strange, but still she didn't seem able to speak.

"Shall I?" he persisted. "I know!" He'd remembered the sling bag out of which she had produced an apple during the course of the afternoon. "Have something to eat. You'll feel better then."

For a few moments she looked at him in silence, then she shook her head. She was breathing in a strange way, as if she had been running. Slowly, holding on to the trunk of a tree, she stood up and without a word, turned to go back the way they had come.

James followed behind, dodging the branches that, regardless, she allowed to swing back in his face. He wasn't enjoying himself any more; in fact, he had been frightened by her illness and had stopped enjoying himself quite a long time ago. Except for the butterflies, of course. They'd been brill. But all he wanted now was to be out of the wood and in the sunshine again. It seemed to take them a long time to get back to the main path, but when at last they reached it, she pointed downhill to the left.

"You'll come out at the farm if you go that way," she said.

"Are you better now?" James asked her, politely.

"Oh, yes. Better now." She looked at him, blinking a little as if waking from sleep, then turning in the other direction she began to walk, very slowly, away from him.

For a moment he watched her.

"Thanks for showing me the butterflies," he called after her. But she made no sign, and he had no idea if she had heard him or not.

He took the direction she had indicated, and sure enough, the path

179

came out on the lane that led to Porthlenter, just below Brook Farm, and there was Jess, the collie bitch, lolloping towards him and barking a joyful welcome, leaping up to lick his face. In an excess of relief at this exhibition of normality, James hugged her and suffered the licks gladly, and it seemed only natural that, almost as a reflex action, he found himself turning towards the farm instead of Porthlenter, just to have a quick look at the kittens while he was so near. The thought of their softness and their little pink mouths made him feel comfortable and safe once more. However, before he reached the barn he saw William coming down the track from the Barstows' house. He had taken off his shirt and was swinging it in a circle – until he saw his brother, whereupon he rushed towards him and started swinging it round James's head instead, which excited Jess all over again.

"Where the hell did you go? We looked everywhere, you stupid little twit—"

"Stop it! Gerroff! I was in the wood. I told you."

"You *know* we're supposed to stay together, you bloody idiot—"

"I was all right. Anyway, you told me to go."

"I didn't mean for ever. I haven't been able to go home for tea, just because of you. They'd have *killed* me!"

Fending off William and his flailing shirt, James looked at his watch and was startled to see the time.

"Are we going to get it, then, Wills?" he asked, anxiously.

"We will if you tell them we didn't stay together. Listen, if you say a word, I'm going to zap your stick insects and then I'm going to zap you."

"I won't say anything, Wills. Honest."

William stopped flailing him with the shirt and looked at him through narrowed eyes.

"You better hadn't, matey, that's all. You just better hadn't."

"And you won't touch my stick insects?"

"That," William said, turning to swagger off towards home, "depends *entirely* on you."

Ruth, tired but otherwise recovered from her ordeal in the wood, was eating shepherd's pie and peas. As always after one of her funny turns, she felt excessively tired, but almost euphoric in a strangely remote kind of way. It hadn't, in fact, been quite as bad as sometimes, which she put down to the presence of the boy. Eric? No, not Eric. Some other name, but she couldn't quite remember what.

On the other hand, perhaps the fact that she'd remembered her pill that morning had helped. She didn't always. She didn't really believe in all this pill-taking, whatever the doctor said, but maybe there was something in it after all. She'd take another before she went to bed, just in case.

Lying in bed, earlier than usual because she was so very tired, she thought over the events of the day. The bus ride, the picnic in the wood, the butterfly hunt with the boy, finding Bal. She relived it all, feeling no horror now, not remembering why it should have come upon her like that when she was least expecting it. Until that moment when the darkness had swamped her she had been feeling happy and excited at finding Bal after all, and looking just the same, too, just when she was about to give up the whole idea.

Eric had loved it so. He had loved the enclosed security of it, and the feeling that no one else in the whole world knew about it. Long ago people must have known, of course. They both realised that. But no one went anywhere near it in the 1940s – and not now, apparently.

Bal. They'd seen the name in some old book about Cornwall. Bal was the old Cornish name for a mine, and the girls that worked there were called bal-maidens.

She thought of herself as a bal-maiden, but not a maiden of any old bal. Just this one. Just their place. She'd loved it, too, almost as much as Eric, and it seemed incomprehensible that, standing there, she should have been so swamped by that feeling of – what? How could she describe it?

She felt a chill of fear as the appropriate word came to her. Evil. That's what it was; that's what she had been aware of. Evil, plain and simple. But why? She had remembered so much during the past few days; why couldn't she remember the reason for this?

The thought troubled and teased her, making her uneasy and preventing sleep, much as she longed for it. But then, suddenly, she thought of the boy and at once felt calmer. Eric, she thought – no, no, not Eric. James. He was such a good boy, nothing like those others. He hadn't mocked her, but had been concerned and had tried to help.

Earlier he had talked to her, one enthusiast to another, seeking her knowledge, asking her opinion. She had caught him looking at her gravely from time to time as if he were puzzled by her; well, she'd lost the art of talking to children, if she ever had it. She was a bit sharp sometimes, perhaps, but even so he had seemed to want her company – had known she didn't mean anything by it.

A good boy, she thought again. She had made a point of mentioning him in her prayers that night. It was, she felt, the least she could do. He was so very like Eric.

"You should have seen it," Lucy said. "It was fabulous – just like a house in Hollywood, wasn't it, Em?"

William refused to be impressed.

"How would you know? You've never been to Hollywood."

"I've seen pictures, dope!"

Emma appealed to her mother.

"It was sort of like a Spanish thingummy – you know, Mum. What do they call it?"

"Hacienda?" offered Kate.

"That's right. A hacienda. Buena Vista – that's the name of it. It's right on top of the cliff, with kind of terraces going down and steps cut out of the rock leading down from one to the other—"

"And flowers and shrubs and rockery stuff on each side." Lucy joined in with enthusiasm. "And a bar—"

"On the steps?"

"Shut *up*, Wills! The bar was by the pool – honestly, it was fabulous, wasn't it, Em?"

"Brilliant," said Emma. "You ought to see it, Mum."

"I'd like to," admitted Kate. "So you had a good time?"

"Fantastic! You should see Sophie's room! She's got everything – computer, TV, hi-fi, and *masses* of clothes—"

"Honestly, she's so lucky—"

"I gather," Oliver said dryly, "that the Renshaws aren't short of a bob or two."

"What's her father like?" Lynn asked.

"Mr Renshaw's her stepfather. Her name's Gregory, and her real dad lives in America." Emma and Lucy exchanged glances. "He's OK, I suppose," Emma went on, judiciously keeping to herself Sophie's opinion of her mother's lately acquired husband. "Not that we saw much of him. He just said hallo, and then went off inside the house to work. Sophie says he's always working."

"At what, may one ask?"

Emma shrugged and pulled another face.

"Something to do with financing things," she said vaguely. "Whatever it is, he does it by computer."

"Finance, eh?" Oliver raised his eyebrows. "Sounds as if you and he would have a lot in common, Leo."

"Sure. I'm getting the Merc and the pool next week."

"Well, dismiss any thoughts of trading me in for a newer model," Lynn said. "I'm here to stay, buster."

They were an affectionate family, but even she was surprised at the fervour with which Lucy flung her arms around her at this statement.

"You better had be," Lucy said, holding her tight. "I'd ever so much rather be us."

She felt happy having seen Eddy. He had promised her that he would definitely be coming over on his bike the following morning, and explained that he'd wanted to come that day, but the Minimarket, where he worked in the afternoons stocking shelves, had sent an SOS asking if he could go in the morning as well as the girl on the second check-out had gone sick.

Emma, on hearing this, had asked Jacko if he worked, too, but he hadn't answered directly – just smiled and exhaled a thin trickle of smoke.

"In my own peculiar way," he said lazily after a long pause, as if the subject had needed consideration.

"Doing what?" Emma asked.

"What comes naturally," he had infuriatingly replied, and had refused to be drawn further. Not that Emma had pursued the point. If he wanted to play silly childish games to make himself appear mysterious, she thought, then let him. Who cared what he did, anyway?

Well, she did, was the answer to that, but she wasn't about to admit it. She was definitely in awe of him, if the truth were known, which was something else she didn't want to admit. It wasn't her style, being in awe of people. Especially boys. Still, Jacko wasn't like the usual run.

He read books and knew what was going on in the world and had original views about things, which she found refreshing. All the kids she knew were anti-government and he was no different, but his opinions didn't sound second-hand, as if they were shaped entirely from satirical shows seen on TV. He'd sounded serious and reasoned, as if he'd thought things through and come to his own conclusions.

What, she wondered, did he do with himself when he wasn't hanging around with the others? She'd thought of sounding Eddy out, but didn't want to appear that interested, so was forced to fall back on her own imagination. Maybe, she thought, she hadn't been so wide of the mark when she suggested to Lucy that he had been waiting on the beach for a consignment of drugs. It seemed, now she knew him better, just the reckless, anarchic kind of thing he might do.

He looked awful in the cut-off jeans he wore for swimming – he was so long and thin and pale. Not a bit like Eddy, who, she had to admit had a physique anyone could admire, or even like the others who were unremarkable, but perfectly OK. The funny thing was, though, that nobody appeared to think the worse of him, or attempt to take the mickey out of him like they did to the others. No one even seemed to notice it. When people made jokes, they always looked at him for approval, checking to see if he found them funny. On one occasion Stig told a racist joke. He looked pleased with himself during the telling, clearly expecting people to fall about with laughter at the end of it, but when he saw the expression on Jacko's face he went bright pink and was very quiet for a long time afterwards.

In spite of the weirdness, her father might like Jacko, Emma thought – except for the smoking, of course. She'd had another go at it herself, lying beside the pool, but still, regrettably, didn't like it at all.

Jacko had laughed at the faces she pulled, lying close beside her – but kindly, almost affectionately, picking up a hank of her hair and using the ends to make a kind of brush to tickle her nose with.

She was almost sure he liked her. She didn't know why he'd refused to come over to their beach with Eddy the following day. He had given no reason, just smiled his aloof kind of smile and said that he had things to do.

They'd had a great time, though. They tried to do synchronised swimming and had laughed so much that they had to get out of the water before they drowned; and they'd danced a bit to some of Sophie's tapes, and sung the lyrics in joyful unison. And in spite of what Sophie had said, the barbecue had been amazing, the whole fabulous afternoon one that Emma would remember for ages and ages. Probably for ever.

The house itself was ten miles the far side of Porthallic, down a lane just as narrow as the one leading to Porthlenter, but more difficult to negotiate because it twisted so much. Coming down it, they'd come face to face with an incredibly ancient Vauxhall, with no room for either of them to pass. The Vauxhall, with an even more incredibly ancient pair of wrinklies in its front seats, had stubbonly held its ground, although Mrs Renshaw had scowled and sworn at it, using language that in Emma and Lucy's experience, mothers didn't use. Not habitually, anyway, and not in front of their children, and especially not when wrinklies were involved.

Emma couldn't see what the fuss was all about, since she would only have needed to back a few yards to reach a place where the lane had been made wider for this very purpose. Eventually Mrs Renshaw was forced to recognise this, too, and she backed up a little, not only allowing the Vauxhall to pass but helping it on its way with an unmistakably rude gesture. Emma and Lucy exchanged looks and bit their lips, suppressing giggles. When recounting their visit afterwards, by tacit consent neither of them mentioned the incident, even when their parents had agreed in conversation about Mrs Renshaw's sweetness and charm and beauty and glamour and everything else. As Emma said to Lucy afterwards, what they didn't know wouldn't hurt them.

In any case, it wasn't Mrs Renshaw who was important. Nor Mr Renshaw. He was one of those tall, narrow-faced, bald men with a high-domed forehead; snooty-looking, in Emma's view, but undoubtedly elegant, wearing clothes that looked as if they were brand new and came from one of those expensive little arcades that run between Jermyn Street and Piccadilly. She and Clare had explored in that direction one Saturday earlier in the year and had spent a considerable amount of time looking in shop windows and saying "*Wow* – a hundred and twenty pounds for a *shirt*! Who'd be crazy enough to buy that?" Now she felt she knew. Mr Renshaw would.

No, it was Sophie who was the important one, the impression given by both her mother and stepfather being that they would do anything to keep her happy. Thinking over the events of the day, as she always did before she went to sleep, Emma recognised that there might be some advantages to be gained from having divorced parents. Apparently Sophie's dad was also loaded, so she was the beneficiary of a sort of generosity contest.

Undoubtedly, the whole Renshaw experience had been interesting and terrific fun; a glimpse of another world. But on reflection she was at one with Lucy. She wouldn't want to change places.

9

Ruth was dozing in her deck chair. She'd managed to get the same shady spot as before; and as before, families had settled themselves nearby. She could hear the rush of the waves as they threw themselves on the beach and pulled back again, and the voices of the children growing distant, echoing a little as she drifted into semiconsciousness.

It must be the unaccustomed amount of food that made her so somnolent, she thought. All these full English breakfasts, when normally she ate a piece of toast and nothing more.

"You've got a big frame, dear," Mrs Cornthwaite had said at breakfast when, in an expansive moment, Ruth had mentioned the matter. "You want to keep your strength up."

"I'm quite strong enough, thank you," Ruth had responded tartly.

"Well, I must say you look it, dear." Mrs Cornthwaite's voice was studiously impersonal, but Ruth had the distinct feeling that the implications of this remark were far from kind and she made the strange, defensive movement of her head that had become a habit with her. "Did you have a good night, then?" Mrs Cornthwaite went on.

The ablutions of the man in the next room, whom she now knew to be called George Farthing, a carpet fitter from Leeds, were still an acute embarrassment to her. She had waited until she knew he was well out of the way before venturing to the bathroom this morning, which meant that she was the last to leave the dining room, leaving herself wide open to these conversational overtures as the breakfast tables were cleared. But at least she didn't make her bed these days. Doreen, Beryl's plump assistant she had seen on the first day, had gently told her to leave everything to her.

"It is your holiday, after all," she'd said.

Ruth liked Doreen better than anyone she'd met all the time she'd been away. She did not, however, at all enjoy talking to Mrs Cornthwaite and answered her in the usual gruff monosyllables.

Beryl paused in her labours to leer roguishly in Ruth's direction.

"You should have been up earlier," she said. "Your boyfriend was saying he was off to St Ives for the day. 'All on your own?' I said to him. 'Yes,' he says. 'A bit of company would be nice,' he says." She shook her head waggishly. "I'm afraid you missed your chance there, Ruth. You could have had a nice day out."

Ruth stared at her, shocked. Boyfriend? Had the woman lost all sense of decency?

"If – if you mean Mr Farthing—"

Beryl Cornthwaite laughed.

"Only a joke, dear! You know me! Don't take it to heart." She moved off down the room. "Wouldn't blame you, though. You want to make the most of your chances, Ruth – a nice steady man like that. Only two more nights left and he'll be gone and there'll be another old lady moving into his room – oops, hark at me!" She pulled a face indicative of guilt and repentance. "Shouldn't have said that, should I! *Another* old lady! I didn't mean it, dear. I don't suppose you think of yourself as old. Nor should you! You're as young as you feel, I always say."

Ruth greeted this without expression, still too shaken by the suggestion that she could ever regard Mr Farthing as a boyfriend to take it in. The woman was a fool, she thought, with her dyed hair and her made-up face, and her worldly, grubby little mind.

Mr Cornthwaite was as bad; worse, perhaps. His jokes were at best incomprehensible, at worst disgusting. Unable to feel easy with them, she took comfort in despising them, and she despised Valerie too, for all her friendliness, for the way she shrieked with mirth at their slightest word.

Night after night, sitting at her table in the dining room, listening to the inane banter, Ruth could only feel disaste for them all; but here, on the beach, with the sound of the sea soothing her to the brink of sleep, the present with all its irritations receded and blurred and merged into the past so that she was no longer old, but strong and youthful, able to run and jump and climb.

Not that she ever found much pleasure in being young. Far from it. She had grown too fast, and long before she was twelve she was quite well aware that no matter how fine her anniversary frock might be, or any other frock come to that, she still looked gawky and hideous. "The image of her Dad," people would say, as if this was something she was expected to welcome. There were, she felt, many things about her father to respect – even admire, but his looks were not one of them.

She recognised that he was changing, growing more strict, more fierce; darker in his soul, somehow, and bitter, his strong face set in a scowl as if he could taste and smell all the sin in the world and could find nothing to be glad about, anywhere. In his presence she was silent, careful to do or say nothing to anger him. Oh, why, she often asked herself, couldn't she have taken after her mother? It wasn't fair that Eric should have inherited her good looks.

Other children made fun of her. Nettie Parsons had bumped into her at the school gate one day at home time. She had thought nothing of it then, in fact she'd felt quite pleased, because Nettie had seemed genuinely concerned for her and had apologised and reached to put a friendly arm around her shoulders. It was in the newsagent's shop where she'd gone to buy her father's copy of the local paper on the way home that the kindly proprietor had taken the label off her back. "Beware – Giant Madwoman at Large", it read. She'd walked all through the square, and Fore Street, with that pinned to her back, no doubt with half the population of Porthallic sniggering and pointing scornful fingers.

Then there was the business with Elsie Polglaze, when she'd been putting books away in the cupboard and was hidden by the open door.

"Where's Ruth Teague?" Miss Faraday had asked, coming into the classroom and finding she was not in her seat.

Ruth had looked round the cupboard door to announce her presence, but not before Elsie Polglaze had whispered to Jean Borlase in a voice everyone could hear:

"Up the fields, scaring crows."

The entire class had collapsed in giggles, and although Miss Faraday had reproved them and had managed not to smile, Ruth felt quite certain that she'd been equally amused.

But it wasn't these personal humiliations alone that made her feel awkward about going into Porthallic, forcing her to rush to and from school with her head lowered, performing any errands as quickly as possible. She dreaded being drawn into conversation by acquaintances of her mother; but still they stopped her.

"How is she, dear?" they asked her. "She was looking proper wisht last Sunday."

"She's all right," Ruth always said in reply.

It was what her mother told her, and what she wanted to believe; but even Ruth couldn't help noticing that she seemed more gaunt and tired with every passing week.

Father began praying nightly and at length for her health to be restored; or rather, praying that his wife should be given the strength of mind to pull herself together. Unless it was a matter of a cut or a sprain or a broken limb for which there was evidence he could see with his own eyes, or a rash which might denote measles or some other childish ailment, he was of the opinion that illness was largely a matter of will. *He* was never ill, after all. And why wasn't he ill? Because he wouldn't allow it, that was why. Mind over matter. He had a healthy mind in a healthy body, and no time at all for doctors.

Especially did he have no time for Dr Crabtree, the village doctor, who was a rotund, good-humoured man who should have retired long before, but who stayed at his post during the war owing to a shortage of younger men. He was, Father said, a godless pagan who patronised the Anchor too much for his own good or the good of his patients.

But there was, as well, another reason why Father didn't like him, which Nettie Parsons took pleasure in imparting to Ruth one day in the playground.

Dr Crabtree, she whispered slyly, had stopped Ruth's father one day in the village and questioned him about certain bruises he had noticed on Eric's legs.

"True as I'm here, Doctor was that worried. He couldn't see my mum, but she was inside our front room with the window open 'cos it was a hot day, and she heard every word. 'Twas like he'd been beaten, Doctor said. Is that right, Ruth? Does your father beat you both? Does he pull down your pants and put you across his knee—"

"No! No he doesn't! Shut up, it isn't true."

But it was, of course. At least, partly true. Father didn't hit her – at

190

least, he hadn't for a while now – but Eric came in for a whacking quite often.

She never heard what the outcome was of Dr Crabtree's intervention – what explanation Father had given, or if he had bothered to give any at all. It was far more likely that he sent Dr Crabtree about his business with a flea in his ear. However, it explained why he forbade his family to have anything to do with the doctor, and why Ruth was reluctant to stop when one day he drew up beside her in his car when she was on her way to school.

"Hey – young Ruthie," he called to her. "Come here a moment. I want a word."

She threw a hunted glance over her shoulder, as if expecting her father to materialise and call her to account for disobeying him.

"Well, don't just stand there! Come here, child."

Reluctantly she walked over to the car, stooping down to peer at the doctor through the window. She neither smiled nor greeted him.

"Anyone would think I was going to clap you in irons, girl," the doctor said. "I only wanted to ask after your mother."

"What about her?" Ruth's voice was sullen.

"I gave her a letter to a consultant in Truro. I was expecting her to come and see me afterwards."

"There weren't nothing wrong. I know, 'cos I went with her, and she said."

"Is that so?" Dr Crabtree was frowning, as if he suspected her of lying, and Ruth reacted with indignation.

"Yes, it is. That's what she told me."

"Did she, indeed?" For a moment he looked at her, chewing his lip, his brows drawn together. He leaned towards her a little, resting his arm on the open window. "That wasn't what the specialist said in his letter to me. She needs help, Ruthie. Tell me honestly, how does she seem to you?"

For a moment Ruth hesitated, disarmed in spite of herself. His voice was kind and seemed to express a genuine concern. Then she remembered all her father had said.

"She's all right." Somehow it seemed the loyal thing to say. Family solidarity demanded it. Anyway, Mother *was* all right. Didn't she say so often enough?

The doctor still seemed unconvinced.

"Will you give her a message?" he asked. "Tell her to come and see me." Ruth stared back at him without speaking. "It's important," he said forcibly. "It's all right, child – I know your father's opinion of me, but I'm not at all confident that your mother's as well as you think. If she needs help then we must all try to give it to her. Now, do what I said, there's a good girl. Tell her to come to the surgery. Urgently. Will you do that?"

Ruth nodded and stepped back as he went on his way. He means well, she thought. He's a kind man. He only wants to help. And then: but like Father says, he gets paid by the number of patients he treats. And Mother says she's fine. She's just thin because she works hard and can't shake off the fever she had last winter.

So she said nothing, and only a week or two afterwards, Dr Crabtree, coming home from visiting a patient late at night in bad weather, had swerved to avoid an American soldier on a motorbike. The car had overturned and the doctor had been killed outright. It was a great loss to the village, everyone said. He'd been a good man and would be difficult to replace.

Indeed, for a while it proved impossible to find any replacement at all and everyone who was sick had to go to Tregony to be treated. It was only after a few months that a new doctor arrived who was older, even, than Dr Crabtree. Nobody took to him.

"That Dr Kenway, he'm got a face on him like a poor lemon," Mrs Penrose said, cornering Ruth one day when she was walking down the lane. "And true as I'm 'ere, every ailment you mention, he d'have it before ee. If you've got a bad back, then he'd have one just the same. If 'tis the flu, then blow me if he ent just going down with it. Oh, he'm a poor, weak creature – you never saw the likes of un. He'm like Ludlow's dog; he'd lean agen the wall to bark."

Dr Kenway showed none of Dr Crabtree's tendencies towards taking a convivial pint at the Anchor, but in spite of this he was shown the cold shoulder by the chapelgoers for poor, weak creature though he might be, he quickly made it plain that he had no time for the hypocritical kind of piety that allowed Walter Borlase, builder and decorator and pillar of the community, to take the collection at chapel – even, on occasions, lead in prayer – while refusing to carry out necessary repairs

192

on the row of tumbledown cottages he owned. Children, he pointed out in a much publicised confrontation in the village square, were being brought up in damp conditions with a polluted water supply. What sort of Christianity was that? How could Mr Borlase defend it? For himself, he had no time for it.

Mr Borlase quoted – or rather, misquoted – him to anyone who would listen. The new doctor, he said, had no time for Christianity. He'd said so himself. Admitted it, just as if he was proud of it. An out-and-out atheist, that's what Dr Kenway was, and as such unfit to treat the pious, chapelgoing folk of Porthallic.

But then, Mother didn't need treatment, Ruth reminded herself frequently. That doctor in Truro had said so, hadn't he? And Mother herself said she would pick up once the better weather came; there were days, even now, when she seemed back to normal. Days when she seemed as full of energy as before.

It had been a day like that when Ruth and Eric had seen the stranger. At breakfast, before they had left for school, Mother had been bright, even cheerful.

Father seemed in a good mood.

"Glad to see you'm pulling yourself together," he said approvingly as she put a plate of porridge in front of him.

"I do try, Thomas," she said.

He made no reply to that, but his expression said that she would do well to try a little harder.

It was one of those grey, mist-shrouded days that typify a Cornish winter. Rain was falling in a relentless curtain. Breakfast, as always, was eaten accompanied by the wireless news, better now than in the early days of the war. Ruth had stopped listening to it in any detail, it all seemed so remote and had been going on, it seemed, for as long as she could remember; but certain things caught her attention and made her think that Eric's chances of joining the RAF were now less likely than ever. The Germans seemed to be losing a lot of U-boats, and the Allied forces were doing well in Italy. There were Americans all over the place; not in Porthallic itself, but along the coast and in various other parts of Cornwall. Preparing for the Second Front, people said.

Because of the weather, she and Eric caught the bus to school that day. The quickest way to the bus stop at Sproull's Corner was through

Pedlar's Woods, but it had been raining for days and the woodland path was a quagmire, which meant that they had to take the longer route up the lane and past Brook Farm. And since, by the time lessons ended, it was raining harder than ever, they came home the same way.

Halfway down the lane, bent against the rain that was blowing in their faces, they met a man coming towards them. He was a stranger to them, but he stopped as he drew level and asked them if they were the children from Porthlenter.

Darkness was falling, but they could see enough to know that he was wearing a uniform of some kind; RAF, Ruth thought, until she got closer when she saw that it wasn't quite the usual colour but was slightly darker. His shoulders were hunched against the rain, and his hands sunk deep in his pockets.

"Yes," Ruth said. "Are you looking for my father?"

"No." The stranger was quick to deny it. "I was just wondering." He looked at Eric. "You're Eric, are you? Eric Teague?"

"Thass right." Eric sounded startled, as if he thought he was about to be accused of something. "Why?"

The man said nothing, but just went on staring at him, peering closer through the gathering dark.

"Not very big for fourteen, are you?"

"I shan't be fourteen till April," Eric said defensively, as if three months would make all the difference.

"Come on, Eric." Ruth didn't like the way the man was staring. He had a funny way of speaking, too – kind of drawly, in his nose. She took her brother's arm and pulled him with her as she began walking down the lane again. "Come on, do. We'm like drowned rats here."

Eric did what she told him and the man said nothing, but when she looked round, she could see him through the mist and the murk still standing there, the pale oval of his face turned towards them.

"He's mazed, whoever he is," she said to Eric. "Standing there getting soaked."

"He'm from Australia," Eric said.

"How do ee know?"

"Didn't ee see the uniform? Thass Australian Air Force."

Ruth believed him. It was the kind of thing Eric noticed. His reading was slow, but anything to do with flying he recognised at once.

"What do you think he was doing here, Ruthie?" Eric asked.

Ruth pulled down her mouth and shook her head.

"How should I know?"

But she did know, all the same. This must be the man that Uncle Ben talked about, that time in Truro. The man who was back from Australia. The man whose name made her mother turn pale. The man who'd been asking about her and had been told everything.

It was Eric this time who caused the storm to be unleashed. Innocently, of course. Immediately on getting home from school he'd had his chores to do and there had been no chance to ask about the stranger they had seen. It wasn't until they were all sitting over their tea with the oil lamps lit and the fire glowing red in the kitchen range that he thought to mention the matter.

"We ent never seen un before, had us, Ruthie?" he said. "He was in the RAAF. The Royal Australian Air Force," he explained, seeing his father's sudden stare, the sharpening of interest.

"What are ee talking of, boy?" Thomas Teague's voice was dangerously quiet.

"Just some chap they saw in the village." Thora had got to her feet and was moving dishes quite unnecessarily. "More stew, Thomas?"

"Not in the village," said Eric. "It were just down the lane. He were coming up when we was coming down, like he'd been here, at the farm."

"Well, he hadn't!" Thora spoke sharply, causing him to look at her in surprise.

"I only said it looked like it—"

Thomas Teague had stopped eating the good rich hotpot made from the meat of one of their own sheep, and was looking at his wife, his eyes narrowed with suspicion.

"Thora?" he said, his voice chilling.

Thora shook her head distractedly.

"I'll tell ee later, Thomas," she said quietly. "We can't talk about it now."

"Was this man who I think he is?"

"How should I know what you think?" She looked at him squarely, then backed down in the face of his furious stare. "Yes, then. 'Twas Ken Pawley."

"You let that man in here? Into my house?"

"No. Well—" she corrected herself. "Only just inside the kitchen. It was raining cats and dogs—"

"And you let him in? When no one else was here?"

"Nothing happened, Thomas! We just talked, and I told him to go."

Father slapped the flat of his hand down so hard on the table that all the dishes jumped and Ruth's heart lurched in dread. Whoever the man was, she knew instinctively that he was all mixed up with Uncle Ben, and that he threatened the status quo and for that reason, frightened as she was by him, she was on her father's side. She didn't want him to get angry, though. Not really angry, like he sometimes did.

Fearfully she looked at his face and saw that it had taken on that terrible greyish, carved-out-of-granite look that meant the worst. His eyes were staring, the creases between nose and mouth more marked than ever, his full mouth turned down in a snarl.

"Don't, Thomas," her mother said softly. "You're upsetting yourself over nothing. Like I said, nothing happened, and I told him never to come here again."

"You – let – him – in!" The words were emphasised with more bangs on the table. "Take this food away! I've no appetite for un, and that's the truth. 'Tis the Bread of Heaven we need now."

"I shall not take it away." Ruth saw that her mother had turned pale and was holding tight to the edge of the table. "It's wartime, Thomas, and we can't waste good food! The children are hungry and must have their tea, even if you don't want yours."

"Don't you dare defy me!"

"'Tis all right, Mother – I don't want it," said Eric, fearfully.

"Eat it, Eric. You, too, Ruthie."

But both children were looking at their father, not moving, not breathing. He, with his eyes fixed on his wife and his face contorted with fury, was rising to his feet, coming round to her side of the table. He gripped her arm, pulled her up from her chair and threw her to her knees.

"Pray," he thundered. "Pray for forgiveness, you faithless whore. Yea, though your sins be as scarlet—"

But Thora had slipped to the floor, unconscious, and was beyond praying for anything.

"See to your mother," Thomas Teague snarled in Ruth's direction and strode from the room without another word or a backward glance.

Ruth scrambled sobbing from her chair and rushed to get water and a cloth, and it crossed her mind, as she bathed her mother's forehead, that it was an awful pity that the day had ended like this when she'd seemed so bright that morning. So much better.

Now she was pale as death, and her poor face was like that of an old, old woman.

"Hallo, Miss Kernow."

Ruth's eyes flew open at the sound of her name. James was standing beside her deck chair, looking at her with a tentative smile on his face. So real had her dream of the past been to her that it took her a moment to feel her way back to the present.

"Oh, it's you—" she said, sounding bewildered.

"You weren't asleep, were you? 'Cos I'm sorry if I woke you."

"No. I never sleep in the day." She sounded indignant, James thought, as if he had accused her of doing something bad. "I was just resting my eyes, that's all. What are you doing here?"

"I'm with my brother and my dad and my Uncle Oliver. They're doing water-skiing – well, William is. Look, there he is." James pointed towards the sea where a couple of small boats were zooming across the bay. "He's the one out there that's sort of bent double. He's not actually very good at it yet, but it's the first time he's tried it. I expect," he added with a kind of resigned bitterness which yet had a note of pride in it, "that he'll be jolly good at it soon. Dad and Uncle Oliver are going to have a go in a minute."

"What about you?" Ruth, gathering her wits, realised that she was quite pleased to see the boy, and her question was couched in unusually affable tones.

"I don't want a go," James confided. "I know I'd never be able to stand up straight, and the boat goes awfully fast. I've been exploring. You see those rocks over there? Well, halfway up them there are some pools with some wiggly things in them. Do you know what they are?"

"I might do," Ruth said cautiously.

"They're not very high up, if you want a look at them."

She sighed.

"I've paid for this chair, young man, and I'm going to sit in it," she said, folding her lips together determinedly ignoring the pleading look in his eyes. She found it difficult, however. Oh, how like Eric he was! It was his eyes, she concluded. That kind of innocent, intent look in them. Anyone would think she was the fount of all knowledge – which was ridiculous, of course, but highly flattering. "Oh, all right, Eric," she said at last, heaving herself out of the chair. "I suppose I might as well have a look."

"I'm James," said James.

"What?" She stared at him.

"I'm James," he repeated. "Not Eric. You keep calling me Eric."

"That's silly." She glared at him as if the mistake was his. "I shan't come with you if you're going to be silly."

She stumped off towards the rocks, however, leaving James to follow her, frowning. There was no doubt about it, he thought. She was a very funny lady.

Short though Emma's acquaintance with Eddy had been, she guessed that he would succeed in charming both her aunt and mother, and she was not proved wrong. From the moment he had propped his bike in the yard and come into the kitchen, employing a shy version of his sweet, boyish smile, he had been a rip-roaring success, confirming her belief that he was the kind of boy who would always appeal to parents. Maybe, she thought, that's why she didn't like him much. It was all too much of an act. Jacko, of course, put on an act of a different kind, but at least it was one designed to please himself and his own generation, not curry favour with the adults.

She'd turned down the offer to go water-skiing with the boys or shopping with her mother in favour of staying on Porthlenter beach, but at the last moment she changed her mind and ran out into the yard where Kate was already in the car.

"I thought you wanted to swim," Kate said.

"Don't you want me to come with you?"

"Yes, of course, you know I do! I'm just surprised, that's all."

"I don't think Lucy wants me around."

"Really? I thought you were all friends together."

"Well, we are in a way."

"Eddy seems nice."

"He's OK." This judgment was delivered in a way that appeared to say the exact opposite, and Kate glanced sideways at her daughter.

"Don't you like him, Em?"

Emma shrugged her shoulders, pursed her lips, but in the end had no more to offer.

"He's OK," she said again, and Kate pressed her no further.

"I thought we could look into the Craft Centre before we went to the shop," she said. "Sheer curiosity on my part! I want to see what Serena Barstow's watercolours are like."

"I'm not keen on watercolours," said Emma. "They're so wishy-washy."

"They don't have to be."

"Well, I don't like them, anyway. Mum—" Emma hesitated a moment before continuing. "Mum, talking about Mrs Barstow – what about that murder? Doesn't it make you feel a bit peculiar every time you go upstairs?"

"No." Kate's voice was brisk. "Not at all. I haven't given it another thought. Why? Does it bother you very much?"

"No – o." Emma's reply was long-drawn-out and less than convincing. "I mean, I suppose it does in a way, but most of the time there's too much else to think about. Lucy's the same. She was more worried about it than I was at first, but at the moment I don't think she's got any room in her head for anything but Eddy."

"Good thing," Kate said. They drove on in silence for a few minutes. "After all," she went on, continuing with the subject, "I don't suppose there's an old house – a *really* old house – in the entire country where someone hasn't died at one time or another. It's no big deal."

"They weren't murdered, though, were they?"

"Well, no. Not usually, one imagines. Even so—"

"You'd think that somehow we'd have felt the vibes when we went into the house, wouldn't you?"

"No. I don't believe in that sort of thing."

"You're always saying our house has a happy atmosphere. If one house can be happy, why shouldn't another be spooky?"

"Because it quite obviously isn't, that's why. Anyway, it was all a long time ago. Ancient history."

"Only forty-seven years."

"Before I was born," Kate said, and Emma laughed.

"OK – then it *is* ancient history," she said. "Stone Age stuff."

The place that had once been the school but was now the Craft Centre was a grey stone building up a steep hill a few yards from the village street. Over the doors, set in the lintels, could faintly be seen the words "Boys", "Girls", and "Mixed Infants". Kate parked the car in what had been the playground and stood looking at it, a nostalgic light in her eye.

"It seems a shame, doesn't it?" she said. "I always think a school is the heart of a village."

"I bet the kids were glad to be bussed to somewhere more civilised," Emma said. "I bet it was a poxy little school."

Whether it was or not, it had certainly changed now. Every conceivable form of art and craft was on sale there, from walking sticks with carved handles to magnificent oil paintings, the only apparent criterion being the standard of work and the fact that it was carried out by artists and craftsmen resident in Cornwall.

Emma found herself immediately attracted to an array of pottery, but Kate wandered over to the pictures, slowly circling the walls as she looked for Serena's offerings.

"Here they are," she called softly to Emma when she had discovered them. Emma abandoned the pottery and went over to join her, and for a few moments they looked in silence.

"You say first," Emma said, after a moment.

"Well . . ." Kate hesitated. "They're very delicate."

"Mum, they're *awful*! The twee-est of the twee! If you want that sort of thing, why not take a photograph?"

"Someone likes them. She's sold several, after all."

"Well, I think they're the pits. Now these," Emma said, wasting no more time on Serena but moving on to a row of collages, "are something else. Look, Mum. These are *great* – all swirly and colourful."

But Kate lingered, reading the typewritten notice beside Serena's paintings which gave details of her life and career.

"She studied at the Slade," she said.

Emma remained unimpressed.

200

"She ought to sue them," she said. "Look, Mum. Do come and see these."

Kate moved along the gallery and looked at the collages that had attracted Emma's attention. They were composed of shells, pebbles, seaweed, pieces of net, fragments of the green glass used for fishermen's floats, feathers – everything, in fact, that could be picked up on a beach and used to make a pattern.

"Yes, they are good, aren't they?" she said. "Clever, too, because it would be easy to go over the top with a thing like that and make it really naff, but those designs are great. Really original."

"The longer you look, the more you see," Emma said. "I love that one with the feathers fanning out—"

"So do I. So would Dad. I might even buy one to take back and give him for his birthday next month – it would go really well in his office. Can you see the price anywhere?"

"There's one of those framed cards here. It says . . ."

Emma fell silent, staring at it, her mouth open with surprise.

"What is it?" Kate asked.

"*Jacko* did them," Emma said. Adding faintly: "Gosh!"

"Jacko? The boy you met? Didn't he tell you?" Dumbly Emma shook her head. "What does it say?" Kate went on. "Move over, let me see it."

These collages, read the card, *were composed by Adrian Jackman, aged sixteen, who lives in Porthallic and is a pupil at Truro School. All the material used in them was found on local beaches. This year Adrian was the winner of the Trelyon Trophy for Fine Art which is awarded annually to the most promising art student under the age of eighteen, resident in Cornwall.*

"Gosh," Emma said again, impressed beyond words, as much by the fact that Jacko had said nothing at all about this as by the work itself, good though that was. No wonder he seemed so different from the others. Was it possible to imagine Eddy or Stig or Jaffa producing anything remotely like this? Or herself, come to that. Standing before it, recognising the artistry and the maturity, she felt positively humble – not an emotion with which she was at all familiar.

Her mother was going on about the price. She'd found a ticket, attached to the last collage in the row, and felt that thirty pounds was really very reasonable – but which one did Emma think she should choose? The feathery one was lovely, but maybe the colours weren't quite as striking as some of the others—

"They're all lovely," Emma said, bemused, thinking that so many things were now explained – like, what Jacko was doing on the beach when they first saw him, and why he said he worked, doing what came naturally. She couldn't understand why he should be so cagey about this talent, though. She'd want to shout it from the housetops if she were able to create such marvellous designs.

Beneath all, she was conscious of relief. Idiot, she told herself. Of *course* she'd never really thought he was a drug smuggler!

"They're brilliant," she said again, very softly.

For the first time since their arrival, there were massed clouds on the horizon and the early evening was still and sultry as if a storm might be brewing.

Kate happily agreed to Oliver's suggestion that they should go for a walk, certain now this holiday was fulfilling all her hopes. She'd been mad to read so much into the Anna business. For the last few days, no husband could have been more loving or more relaxed.

They took the path beside the beach which led away from the Porthallic cliffs towards the headland that sheltered the bay on the far side. After a few yards, the path turned inland through head-high bracken and stunted trees, then climbed steeply uphill to a stile.

"This'd better be worth it," she panted, pausing for breath halfway up.

"It will be, I promise," Oliver said, and she found, reaching the top, that he was right, for from this vantage point they could see the whole cove spread out before them, with Porthlenter down in the valley below. For a while they sat on top of the stile side by side and looked at it in wondering silence.

"You run out of words, don't you?" she said at last.

"There can't be a more beautiful place," Oliver agreed. "Only man is vile."

Kate nudged him in the ribs with her elbow.

"Speak for yourself."

"I was thinking of the murder, actually. It seems so utterly incongruous in this kind of setting."

"*Don't* think about it, Oliver. Let's pretend it never happened. I got the feeling from Emma this morning that the girls are still upset by it."

Oliver looked down at her, frowning a little.

"It doesn't intrigue you at all? You wouldn't like to know what really happened?"

"Well, we're not going to, are we? Not after all this time. So it seems a bit pointless to dwell on it."

"I'm fascinated by the medical aspect," Oliver said after a pause. "It's such an extreme example of that kind of trauma. I'd love to talk to that woman who came to the house. Or failing that, find out what else Serena Barstow can remember about it. Shall we drop in and see them?"

"Honestly, you're like a dog worrying a bone when you get your mind set on something."

"Well, shall we? They were most pressing that we should go up and see the house."

"I don't think Leo or Lynn took to Serena much. They were pretty fed up about her mentioning the murder in front of the girls. It was a bit unnecessary, after all."

"We can go on our own. They don't have to come if they don't want to."

Kate continued to look dubious.

"You mean, just drop in?"

"We could phone first. All right then, *I'll* phone! See if we can go after supper. OK?"

"OK," said Kate. "You know," she added after a moment, as having recovered from the hill they went on their way. "This holiday is really working awfully well, isn't it? I mean, you're getting on with Leo, aren't you?"

"Very well. And the kids are happy."

"Lynn was delighted with Lucy's boyfriend, so let's hope Leo's mind is set at rest. I can't think what he imagines they get up to—"

"Can't you?"

"Well, no! I'm not being naive, Oliver. I recognise perfectly well what *can* go on, but I also recognise that both Emma and Lucy are sensible and know the dangers. Emma, anyway. Dammit, you're the one who's spelled it all out for her. Drink, drugs, smoking, underage sex – she could probably go on *Mastermind* with the whole thing as her specialised subject!"

"I hope you're right."

"I'm sure I am. Let's face it, young people are always going to want to congregate together and you can't keep them wrapped in cotton wool. If Eddy and Jacko are examples of the types they've met, it seems to me we've been let off lightly. From what Em tells me, all this particular crowd does is talk and scream with laughter. And drink quantities of coffee, of course."

"It's a relief to me that Lynn liked this Eddy bloke, though," Oliver said. "It takes a bit of the responsibility off our Em."

But Kate had stopped listening. She was, once more, enraptured by the view.

"What are we doing in London, Oliver?" she asked him. "Look at it! We must be mad! Give it all up and come down here."

Oliver raised an eyebrow in her direction.

"Are you sure?" he asked her. "It's an awful long way from Marks and Spencer's."

Kate, on reflection, was glad to have the opportunity to present herself and Oliver to the Barstows as a happily married couple, thus dispelling the impression of neuroticism that she must have left with Colin after her display on Tuesday.

Nothing would please them more, he told Oliver on the phone, than to see the Sheridans – adding that if they came around eight thirty, he would make sure that the boys would be out of the way.

They were greeted by Serena, volubly welcoming as she ushered them inside the converted barn that they had made their home, the only evidence of Colin being a firm voice off-stage telling the boys to settle down and be quiet.

"I know it's rather early for them to be in bed," Serena said, "but quite honestly, by this time of night we've had enough. Believe me, I am totally amazed by women of sixty and more who want to have babies. I mean, nature knows what it's about, don't you agree?"

Without a pause to see if they did or not, she drew them over to the window.

"Now, what do you think of our lovely view?" she asked them. "Isn't it heaven?"

"It's glorious! Oliver and I were only saying—"

"I suppose it's not the most practical place on earth for two pensioners – it is rather remote, but we've never been used to close neighbours, and we do love it so. I can't begin to tell you the number of times when we were in some far-flung outpost that I had a mental vision of just such a place as this, and it seems quite unbelievable sometimes that we're actually living here . . ."

And so on, and so on. Kate and Oliver stood, and later sat, and smiled and assented to it all, until Colin put in an appearance and Serena was forced to keep silence while he consulted their preferences regarding drinks.

She had spent the day painting, she told them, had had a marvellous time, and had two more pictures now to take to the gallery.

Kate, worried that she was about to be asked point-blank if she had yet had time to visit the Craft Centre, an assent to which question would surely demand some kind of comment on Serena's offerings, began, almost hysterically, to talk about the boys and their doings. This prompted a monologue from Serena which went on so long that Oliver began to wonder how best to introduce the subject of the murder, or if the entire evening would pass without a chance to mention it at all. He need not have worried. It was clear that Porthlenter Farm and the Teague murder were inextricably linked in Serena's mind and it wasn't long before she returned to it, as if she found the subject irresistible.

"You can just imagine what a bombshell it was," she said. "I mean Porthallic was such a quiet place. Nothing ever happened – and then, suddenly, we had a double murder on our hands!"

"Yes, it must—"

"You see, I was here all the time the investigation was going on, and of course, knowing the people involved, I found it totally fascinating and followed the whole thing in tremendous detail." Indeed, her sharp little face, vivid at the best of times, had lit up still further at the remembrance of it. "I was about the same age as Eric Teague and a little older than Ruth."

"Were you at school with them?" Oliver asked. "What was she like as a child?"

Serena narrowed her eyes.

"Peculiar," she said emphatically. "Definitely peculiar. I was only at school with them when I was very young. I went to board at Truro High when I was eight – but of course I still saw them around the village, and at chapel, too. My family were regular attenders. It's not surprising that Ruth and Eric were odd. Their father was a horrible man – one of those religious maniacs that gives Christianity a bad name. He was sickeningly sanctimonious, but a harsh, cruel sort of person underneath it all. Of course, now one can see that the children should have been objects of our compassion, but you know what children are! In those days they were social outcasts."

Oliver was giving her his full attention.

"So Ruth probably was a little unbalanced even before the trauma she went through—"

"My dear, they were *all* unbalanced – every man jack of them! Well—" she appeared to think better of this statement. "Mrs Teague – Thora – was quite a sweet woman, but she couldn't say boo to a goose!"

"What was Eric like?" Kate asked.

"Ah, Eric!" Serena's eyes gleamed. "It came out in the papers that Eric wasn't Thomas Teague's son at all, but the result of a love affair between Thora and a wild sort of chap from Truro called Ken Pawley. He had a bit of a brush with the law and went off to Australia to make his fortune – well, that was the idea, apparently, but of course he did no such thing. He just went from sheep station to sheep station – what do they call those sort of people?"

"Jackaroo?" Colin suggested.

"That was it. He had no idea of the state of affairs back home – or so Ben, Thora's brother said, and he was probably right because the wretch never wrote to give his address, so no one could get in touch with him – not Thora, nor his mother, or anyone. So there was no way of telling him that Thora was expecting his child, and eventually she married Thomas Teague just to give the baby a name."

"Poor woman!" Kate looked horrified on Thora's behalf. "Didn't she know what Teague was like?"

"She was probably under pressure from her own family," Colin said. "Anything was better in those days than having a child out of wedlock."

"One wonders why Teague would want to marry her anyway, if she

206

was carrying someone else's baby," Oliver said.

"Ah—" Serena raised a finger. "Now that's a very good point. This was something else that came out afterwards. Thora had been left some land by her grandfather, near Truro, close to the farm owned by her family, the farm that was later taken over by her brother Ben. He, by the way, was rather a nice chap. Cheerful. Liked a joke. He used to come over to the chapel sometimes just to see his sister, though it was a long way for him to come. Teague, you see, had forbidden him the house."

"Why on earth?"

"Because of this land business. They'd had dreadful rows about it. Ben wanted Thora to sell it to him. It made more sense for him to have it because it was part of his farm, really, and much too far away for Teague to make use of. What you must understand is that land, to the Cornish, is like money in the bank. It probably gives rise to more family quarrels than anything else in the whole world. Why, even in my own family—"

"Perhaps we'd better leave your family out of it," murmured Colin amusedly, getting up to refill glasses.

"Very wise," agreed Serena. "Well, this land near to Ben's farm – it wasn't much good for agricultural land, but Ben apparently wanted to buy it to build cottages for his farm workers. There was nowhere else suitable nearby. But Teague wouldn't let him have it even though he couldn't use it himself."

"But if it belonged to Thora, surely it was nothing to do with—"

"She signed it over to Teague." Serena rushed on, not letting Kate finish. "There was a rumour that he tricked her – got her to sign a paper that she thought was for something quite different, but no one knows for sure. I certainly wouldn't put it past him. What everyone *did* know was that there was a move at some time before the war for that bit of land to be bought for a council estate. It was really quite near the city, you see, and would have been convenient. However, it all fell through – shelved because of the slump in the thirties; and then, of course, there was the war and no building went on at all, but it's my guess that Teague thought that eventually the land would be valuable. That's why he wouldn't let Ben have it, and that's why he married Thora in the first place. To get his hands on the land."

She sat back, triumphant, the point proved beyond reasonable doubt.

"Go on about the children," Kate urged. "I got the impression from what Ruth told me the other day that life at Porthlenter Farm was extraordinarily basic."

"Oh, it was. Other people had electricity and water and the telephone laid on, but not them. Eric had friends, but Ruth never did – and she was never allowed to do things that other girls of her age did, like going to dances or to the pictures. Poor girl, she had a dreadful life. She looked just like her father – big and gawky and plain as a pikestaff. No one ever went to the house. I remember seeing her in the village just before the murder. I'd just left school at that time and was at a bit of a loose end, hanging around Porthallic, wondering what I wanted to do with my life. I bumped into her in a shop and not having seen her for a while, I simply didn't recognise her. She looked nearer fifty than fifteen, with dowdy clothes and her hair scragged back.

"Eric was different – quite nice looking. Small, but he had a round, appealing sort of face. By that time he was beginning to rebel. He had friends in the village, and went drinking with them at the Anchor. They all said he wasn't there the night of the murder, though."

"So they couldn't give him an alibi?" Oliver was following the story intently.

"No – but anyway it was thought the murder took place well after closing time, so an alibi wouldn't have helped. Eric's best friend was a chap called Jim Polglaze, and he reckoned that the last time he'd seen Eric at the Anchor was about two or three nights before, when he'd seemed particularly quiet—"

"Depressed?" Oliver asked quickly.

"No. Not depressed at all – quite the reverse. Jim said he seemed to be suppressing some kind of excitement."

"Don't forget," Colin said dryly, "that this was high drama, and Porthallic played it to the hilt. It simply wasn't enough that Eric merely went in for a quiet pint, drank it and left. He had to be hiding something. Elation, depression – who knew or cared, so long as it was sufficiently sensational?"

"It wasn't like that," Serena said indignantly. "I was here at the time, remember, and you weren't. Jim Polglaze said that Eric was terrified of his father – as everyone at the time thought Teague to be – and that he was always moaning about the terrible time he had at home. But he said that on the last occasion Eric visited the Anchor, he seemed elated about something. I've got a copy of the local paper of the time, somewhere. I'll go and find it."

She got up immediately and bustled from the room, leaving Colin to smile at them a little apologetically.

"You can imagine what a stir it all caused," he said. "I hope you don't mind—"

"Not at all. It's fascinating," Oliver assured him. "As a matter of fact, I've been doing a study—"

He got no further before Serena was back, triumphantly bearing two old and yellowed copies of the *Western Morning News*, which she handed to Kate.

"That's definitely the woman who came to the house," Kate said, indicating the photograph of Ruth in a family group which appeared on the front page of the earlier copy. "Even so many years on, there's no mistaking her. My goodness, Teague looks a brute, doesn't he?" She passed the paper over to Oliver, who studied it with equal attention.

"Eric looks a harmless enough sort of chap," Oliver said. "Not that that means anything – "

"He was harmless, I always thought," Serena said. "He wasn't very bright, though. He was a – a . . ." she hesitated, "a kind of child of nature. He knew all about birds and wild things and was always wandering about the fields and the seashore."

"Why would he have killed his mother?" Kate asked. She had taken back the paper from Oliver and was looking at the photographs once more. "From what you say, it sounds as if Thomas Teague had been asking for it for years, but what did Eric have against poor Thora?"

"Oh, didn't I say? She was ill, and there was some talk of a mercy killing," Serena said. "She was suffering from cancer of the stomach, and it was said she was in terrible pain. The post-mortem established she wouldn't have lasted more than a few weeks anyway. Maybe less."

"How horrible! The poor woman—"

"No wonder the girl was traumatised." Kate shuddered. "It's enough to traumatise anyone. I can see why it had Porthallic buzzing."

"No one ever saw hide nor hair of Eric again. Some thought he must have been killed too. Others that he made a getaway to some foreign country, perhaps by boat. To me that didn't make much sense, though I'm at a loss to offer any other explanation. He'd never been anywhere but Porthallic. He didn't have any contacts to help him – didn't speak a foreign language. One imagines he would have stuck out like a sore thumb wherever he went."

"Who was looking after Thora?" Oliver asked.

"Well, Ruth. There was no one else."

"I meant medically—"

"That I don't know." Serena sounded regretful at this lamentable gap in her knowledge. "Not, I think, the village doctor. I believe he said as much." Rapidly she scanned the newspaper reports, trying to find the relevant passage.

"Weren't there ever any other suspects?" Oliver asked.

"Well, Ben was questioned – because of the land business, I suppose – but they couldn't get anything to stick because he had an alibi. His wife had had a baby that evening and he'd been to the hospital to see her and had gone out to wet the baby's head with friends afterwards. The police tried to say that he'd had time to dash to Porthlenter Farm between one and the other, but they soon realised it was impossible.

"And then there was Ken Pawley. He'd been back in England, you see. He'd come over with the RAAF, and got himself demobbed here, apparently meaning to stay. Someone advanced the unlikely theory that he'd shot the lot of them in some kind of jealous fury, but that was found to be not only unlikely, but absolutely impossible. It seems he'd decided to go back to Australia after all and had signed on as crew on some merchant ship that had actually left the country the day before the murders took place."

"Who actually found the – the bodies?" Kate asked.

"The postman, about mid-morning the following day. Teague had a shotgun. Someone had taken it from the cupboard in the hall where it was kept and had shot Teague and Thora. Ruth was discovered unhurt, but as I told you, she was totally traumatised and quite useless as a witness."

"What about fingerprints?"

"Apparently the entire family had handled the gun at one time or another. There were prints all over the barrel and the stock. And Ruth had moved it when she stepped over it to take hold of her mother. It was all reported in the papers. Take them with you, if you'd like to read them at leisure."

"Oh, I don't think—" Kate began, but already Oliver had reached for them.

"Thanks," he said. "I'd be interested. I'll bring them back tomorrow."

"No hurry," Serena assured him. "Though I would like them back eventually. By the way, there was something else that was never explained. You'll read about it in the paper. The Penroses – not the ones that are there now, but John's father and mother – heard a car or van going hell for leather up the lane away from Porthlenter late on the night before the murders were discovered. They didn't see it, and it was never identified, but it caused a great deal of speculation at the time."

"And Ruth?" Oliver asked. "What happened to her after she was found?"

"She was put away in the asylum. In Bodmin. It tipped her right over the edge, you see. No one's heard anything of her for years – until now, that is. I imagine she must have recovered by this time, otherwise she'd still be in some kind of institution, wouldn't she?"

"Not necessarily," said Oliver. "These days there's such a thing as Care in the Community. I imagine you've heard of it."

"Yes, of course." Serena gave a small, uncomfortable laugh. "But people are looked after, aren't they? Kept tabs on?"

"Well . . ." Oliver appeared to hesitate a little. Then he smiled at her. "Let's say that's the plan," he said.

"Why didn't you tell me?" Emma asked Jacko. They were sitting next to each other at a long, corner table, their heads close together.

"I didn't think you'd be interested."

"Of course I'm interested! They're fabulous. You only kept quiet so I'd go on wondering what you were doing on the beach."

He grinned at her, blowing out a trickle of smoke.

"Had you going there, didn't I?"

"I didn't know what to think."

"But now I've been given Mummy's seal of approval?"

"Don't be horrible! She bought one for my dad's birthday, so you ought to be nice."

"I'll remember to touch my cap when I meet her. Except I don't wear a cap."

"I bet you've sold a lot, haven't you?"

"Some." Jacko grinned again. "It's not a bad little earner, for a holiday job. Sure beats looking after the deck chairs like Jaffa, or stacking shelves, like Eddy."

"Don't pretend not to care," Emma said. "You must know they're good. You're an artist. You won a prize."

"Not for those things. The prize was for a picture I painted." He stubbed out his cigarette, not smiling now. "Mummy wouldn't at *all* approve of that," he said. "Nor you, probably."

Emma hesitated. The curtain of black hair was falling forward, hiding much of his face so that his expression was unreadable.

"I'd like to see it, all the same," she said.

He pushed the hair behind his ears, then turned to look at her, so intently that she felt sure she was turning red. Then he smiled.

"One day," he said.

Oliver was sitting up in bed, engrossed in the report of the Porthlenter Farm Murders, as the papers called them.

Kate, removing her make-up at the dressing table, looked at him in the mirror.

"You're a ghoul," she said.

"Mm? Nonsense! It's fascinating," Oliver replied, and went on reading.

Mrs Agnes Penrose, described as a close neighbour, having retired to bed at ten thirty, had been awoken, the report said, by a car passing her house, coming from the direction of Porthlenter Farm. She had no idea who had been driving it, and could not supply a description of it, but at the time she had assumed, since it had been going so fast, that it was Thora Teague's brother, since he always drove at speed. "I had occasion to complain about this before," Mrs Penrose stated.

Ruth Teague (15), daughter of the murdered couple, had been discovered in a distressed state, huddled on the stairs, her clothes bloodstained, cradling her dead mother in her arms. So far she had been unable to be questioned by the police about events at the farm, or her brother's movements that night.

By the following week, the second paper reported, the police had dismissed the report of the car as of no significance to the case. "A distressing increase in poaching activities has recently been reported in this area," said the report, "and it is thought that this vehicle may have been involved." The driver was asked to come forward since he might have seen something that would prove valuable to the police enquiry.

"Murdered Farmer Not Eric's Father", ran the main headline. And underneath: "Natural Son of Childhood Sweetheart Still Missing".

The search continues for Eric Teague, wanted for the brutal murder of Thomas and Thora Teague. In a new and shocking development, it has now been revealed by Mrs Ada Pawley, of Railway Cottages, St Cadwin, that the runaway was not Thomas Teague's son but was the love child of her son, Kenneth Pawley (38).

"Kenneth," said Mrs Pawley, "knew nothing of his son's birth until he returned to Cornwall. He is a good, responsible man who would have liked to acknowledge his son, but was begged to keep away from the family by Mrs Teague herself."

Kenneth Pawley, who emigrated to Australia in 1929, joined the Royal Australian Air Force and was posted to North Africa where he spent much of the war, returning to England in December 1943. He sailed for Australia on 10th August, 1946, two days before the murder of Thomas and Thora Teague.

A police spokesman has told this paper that there are several leads that are being followed in the hunt for Eric Teague, and they are confident that his present whereabouts will be discovered shortly.

Oliver learned no more about Thora Teague's medical condition. The postmortem had established that she had been suffering from an advanced case of stomach cancer which probably would have killed her in a matter of weeks, but Dr Richard Kenway, General Practitioner, was reported as saying that she had never presented herself at his surgery for treatment, and neither had any other member of the Teague family.

Who, then, had treated her? She would have needed help, needed pain relief of the most effective kind. This seemed, to him, to be as much a mystery as anything else; a question he yearned to have answered.

But only one among others. He was also curious about Ruth

Teague's amnesia. What had been its duration? Had she ever been able to remember the happenings of that night? What was her state of mind now? He saw the possibility of a further paper on the subject; the whole question could hardly tie in more appropriately with his interest in psychosomatic illness and the records he was already keeping.

"You're quite sure that Ruth didn't give you any hint about where she was staying?" he asked now, putting the paper down.

"I told you – no, she didn't! She just said Porthallic, that's all. Do forget it, Oliver. You're just being morbid."

"I expect I'll have to. I can hardly go knocking on all the doors of every hotel and guest house in Porthallic asking for her. You can't actually blame her for changing her name, can you?"

"I suppose not." Kate sighed, for clearly Oliver was not about to follow her wishes in the matter and leave the subject alone. "I can't imagine why she came back," she said after a moment. "I mean, why would she? You'd think she'd just want to forget."

"Maybe that's the whole point. Don't you see, Kate? She did forget, didn't she? Maybe it all stayed forgotten, and she wanted to come back to try to remember it."

"Well, I wish you'd forget." Kate climbed into bed beside him. "You're on holiday, not following up some case history."

"I know." Oliver smiled at her, folded the paper and put it on the table beside him. "Sorry darling. You've got to admit it's intriguing though."

"You don't think it's a touch ghoulish to dwell on it like this?"

For a moment he didn't speak, but pulled her into his arms and rubbed his cheek against her hair. "I'm not dwelling on it. Well, not unduly, anyway. I just can't help wondering—"

"About Ruth's state of mind?"

"That, and other things. What happened to Eric? Whose was the car the Penroses heard belting up the lane late that night?"

She laughed and reached to kiss him.

"And who, may I ask, fancies himself as Porthallic's reply to Hercule Poirot? You really think it's possible to find answers after all these years?"

"At least it exercises ze leetle grey cells—"

"Well, if it makes you happy—"

He pulled her towards him.

"You know what would really make me happy?" he asked.

For a moment she hesitated, looking into his eyes. She put her arms round his neck and kissed him again.

"I've got a fair idea," she said.

It rained in the night. Kate slept after they had made sweet, light-hearted love, but woke again when the curtains gusted inwards and the windows rattled a little.

She could smell the rain on the heat-soaked garden and had a sudden fantasy of all growing things lifting leaves and petals and shoots in weary thanksgiving for the water that had been denied them for so long; and felt guilty at her relief when, after only a short time, the breeze died and the rain stopped. She got out of bed and went to the window, to see that the sky was clear again and thick with stars. The air felt fresher, though. Was it the beginning of the end of the heat wave? Surely their luck must run out soon. They'd already had just about the entire summer's quota of sunshine in a single week.

She found, when she returned to bed, that without any warning at all the spectre of Anna had raised its head again. Ridiculous, she told herself, bearing in mind Oliver's loving attitude towards her these past two days; suddenly she was hearing again Anna's proprietary voice and remembering Oliver's strangeness after he had spoken to her the other night.

Night-time fears, she told herself. She'd always been a prey to them. Why now should she feel uneasy again, when earlier she had been quite sure that if there ever had been anything between Oliver and Anna, then it was a transient, insubstantial thing, over already – no more, probably, than a touch of mental infidelity? And who, she thought, was she to cast the first stone on that score? About five years ago she had found herself strongly attracted to one of her clients. Naturally, she had done nothing about it since it would have been, apart from anything else, a gross breach of professional ethics; however, she could not deny the fact that she had looked forward to his visits and that there had been a kind of added ingredient in the counselling sessions, making them more lively and exciting than any that had gone before and surprisingly enjoyable, given their serious content.

So even if her suspicions were justified, and they probably weren't, it was not something to be blown out of proportion. Why, then, couldn't she forget them?

She could see the time on the little illuminated clock beside the bed. Three fifteen. Everyone, she told herself bracingly, had doubts at three fifteen in the morning. She willed herself to relax and managed to regain some of the calm she had been able to achieve over the past days. Oliver, she reminded herself, had been sweet and funny and tender that night. What more did she expect from the poor man?

Already there was the faint sound of seagulls gearing up to greet the day. If she didn't go off soon, she thought wearily, there would be no chance of any more sleep that night. Should she get up and make tea? At home she would have done so without a second's thought. Here, however, she found herself strangely reluctant to go downstairs. She wasn't scared, surely? What about her reassuring little homily, delivered to Emma only yesterday?

Of course she wasn't scared! She had always prided herself on being severely practical, and had no belief in psychic phenomena. The dead, in her view, stayed dead, and had no power to hurt the living. Even so, she found herself unwilling to swop the security of the marital bed for the stairs and the hall where such awful things had happened.

You're mad, she thought. Soft in the head. A total idiot. But nevertheless she resigned herself to a tealess vigil.

10

The sky lightened and the gulls grew more insistent; then, suddenly, it was morning. Maybe, after all, she'd managed an hour or two's sleep.

"I had a lousy night," she nevertheless grumbled to Oliver, ready to be comforted.

"Poor darling! Never mind – you needn't do anything particularly energetic today."

She hadn't done anything particularly energetic for days, Kate reflected. Well, she was on holiday, after all. Maybe she might even catch another hour, if she put her mind to it.

In the room at the end of the passage, Lucy and Emma slumbered on, oblivious of the gulls, but eventually they too awoke. And, as always these days, their social life was the overriding topic of conversation.

The following Wednesday was Sophie's birthday, and she had invited them to her party. As the birthday fell during the summer holiday, the party had become a kind of tradition, the girls had been told. For the past three years the Renshaws had organised a fabulous evening, with music supplied by a *wicked* group from Truro, and truly brilliant food, and fireworks, and everyone staying the night – the girls in the house and the boys outside in the garden in a big tent hired for the purpose.

"It's all terribly proper," Sophie had told them. "Absolutely no chance of any bonking, you can tell your mum and dad." (Lucy visibly blenched at the very thought.) "Everyone stays, because it goes on late and parents don't want to turn out. You simply must come! Shall I get my mother to phone?"

"I'll see what they say," Emma had replied cautiously.

She felt fairly sure that her own parents would have no objection, having met Mrs Renshaw and apparently been charmed by her, but instinct told her that Leo and Lynn would be less than ecstatic about the arrangements, however proper. And if they kicked up a fuss, they could ruin things for her as well as Lucy. A bit of ground preparation, she felt, would be advisable.

"We won't say anything until after tonight," she said to Lucy now. "We don't want anyone saying we're going out too much and how about a lovely family evening playing Scrabble, do we?"

"Why should anyone stop us going out tonight?" Lucy asked. Emma raised her head from the pillow to give her an exasperated stare.

"You know why not," she said. "You should do, anyway. It's your bloody father who makes all the objections. Why doesn't he chill out?"

"Don't talk about him like that!" Lucy glared back, full of indignation; then the fight went out of her, and she dropped her head back on the pillow. "You don't really think they'll stop us going to the Cavern tonight, do you? They can't! Eddy's playing again."

"I wish he'd learn a few more songs," Emma said.

"He knows *lots* of songs!"

"Why does he play the same old things, over and over, then? Honestly, if I hear 'Yellow Submarine' once more—"

"That's what people like. They request it – you know they do. They like to sing along."

"And 'Scarborough Fair'! Honestly, Luce! Those songs are history."

"People like them," Lucy repeated stubbornly.

"You wouldn't care if he sang 'I'm a Little Teapot'!" Emma turned on her side and looked at her cousin with amusement. "You've really got it bad, haven't you? Has he kissed you yet?"

Lucy blushed.

"Not exactly," she said, which made Emma laugh.

"Come on, Luce! Not exactly? What do you mean 'not exactly'? It's something you do or not do."

Lucy hesitated and refused to meet her eyes.

"Well, no, then. Has Jacko?"

"I don't want him to. We're not like that." It was Emma's turn to assume an air of insouciance. "We're just sort of friends. Mates – you know?"

"Oh," said Lucy. For a moment the old sense of inferiority took over, the feeling that whatever Emma did must be right. Should she, then, just be mates with Eddy without wanting to be kissed by him? Was that the in thing? The cool thing? Then she sighed. It was no good wondering – she simply couldn't help it. The fact was that she wanted it very, very much.

At breakfast there was the usual discussion of plans for the day. William was desperate to go water-skiing once more, and both Oliver and Leo were inclined to back him up.

"I wouldn't mind a go myself," Lynn said. "We used to be quite good at it, didn't we, Kate? Remember that summer of the German students—?"

"How could I forget? What were their names?"

"Mine was Kurt—"

"And mine was – what was it? Can't remember. Weren't they divine, though?"

"Order, order." Oliver rapped on the table with his knife. "Riveting though this is, it's not adding a lot to today's discussion. Shall we *all* go water-skiing?"

Emma and Lucy exchanged a look.

"Well, we're all for going to Porthallic," Lucy said. "But not to do water-skiing."

"In fact," added Emma, "we sort of arranged to meet the gang at the harbour."

"Again?" Leo asked.

"Why not?" Lucy's voice was defensive and Leo looked at her uncertainly.

"Well," he said, "I suppose we feel it would be rather nice if we could do something as a family, for a change."

Lucy and Emma exchanged glances again and raised eyes to heaven.

"Get real, Dad," said Lucy. "Emma and I aren't exactly thrilled at the idea of playing on the beach with the boys. Our sandcastle days are over."

"I wasn't suggesting that!"

"Well, we promised to meet the others. And before you make any other objections, we've absolutely got to go to the Cavern tonight, haven't we, Em? You don't mind, do you, Mum?"

Lynn looked at her daughter, recognising the difference that a single week had wrought in her. She was more assertive, more sure of herself, more knowing. Was that Emma's influence? Or Eddy's? Both, she suspected.

Leo was looking at her too, and he also saw the changes. Who could avoid it? He felt harassed and vaguely miserable, recognising that a crucial, enjoyable phase of his family's life was gone for good. Despite Kate and Oliver's calm acceptance of their daughter's social life, his every instinct warned him that for Lucy to spend so much time at Neptune's Cavern was neither wise nor healthy – yet it had to be admitted that so far she had come to no harm. Sophie Renshaw had proved to be charming and he had also been impressed by Eddy's good manners and open, friendly manner. If these two were representative of the girls' new friends, then surely he could have no objection? Boyfriends were, he supposed, bound to become part of their lives from here on, so perhaps it was just as well to begin with one as innocuous as Eddy appeared to be.

However, he tried one last throw.

"Why don't you ask everyone over here?" he said. "Just so we could get to know all of them. We could have a party – a barbecue. You'd like that, wouldn't you?" He appealed to Lynn and the others. "That would be all right, wouldn't it? I could go and get some stuff—"

"Not tonight, Dad. Eddy's playing!"

"Anyway, I thought we were going out to dinner tonight," Lynn reminded her husband, breaking his somewhat crestfallen silence. "We can drop the girls off on our way and pick them up again later, like Kate and Oliver did the other night."

Leo felt a sense of powerlessness. There was nothing he could do, nothing he could say. Everything had been arranged without any kind of consultation, any reference to his opinion.

"Well, then, it's water-skiing for the rest of us, is it?" he said rather stiffly after a few minutes' silence during which he reproved himself for being unnecessarily touchy. No one *meant* to slight him or dismiss his opinions as if they were worthless, he knew that, really. And probably they were right – there was no harm in the girls' activities.

"Not for me," said James.

220

"Of *course* not for you, weed," said William with immense scorn, under his breath.

Lynn looked at Kate.

"What do you think?" she asked her. "On second thoughts, I'd just as soon stay here, then James can stay too. So many years on, I feel it might be better to rest on my laurels as far as the skiing is concerned. You go, though."

"I'm not keen, to be honest. Maybe the three of us could take a walk."

"I could show you the wood where the butterflies are," James said, then bit his lip, remembering his sin in going off on his own, and William's threat of reprisals should he utter a word. "It's not far from the farm," he added hastily. "We played there the other day. William and Paul and Daniel and me."

To his relief no one questioned him further, even when, later that morning after the others had gone to Porthallic, he led his mother and aunt up the lane, across the field and into the wood. Jess, the collie, joined them as they skirted the farm, and she and James ran ahead together.

"He's happy now," Lynn said, smiling. "Heaven knows where he gets this obsession with the furred and feathered world."

"Remember those bloody rabbits?" Kate was laughing. "We pestered like mad until we had them, and it took us about three days to realise that neither of us wanted to clean them out."

"They were sweet, though. There was a grey one I was particularly fond of—"

"Fluffy. That's what you called him. Such originality!"

"You were beastly about that!"

"Well, I wanted to call him something more dashing."

"Thumper, as I recall. Not, if I may say so, any more original."

"Then there was one called Violet and another called Primrose. Whatever happened to them?"

"We gave them to that girl with the squint. Christine Something. They moved from Birmingham – you remember. They bought that white house on the corner."

James, out of earshot, looked back at them while he waited for Jess to finish investigating a rabbit hole. He could see they were laughing together, engrossed in conversation, and felt a wholly masculine astonishment at the way they never seemed to run out of things to talk about. Should he show them Bal? Always supposing, of course, he could find it, which he probably couldn't.

He would love to see it again and have a proper look at the butterflies this time. He'd hardly had a chance before, with Miss Kernow getting ill and everything. Maybe, he thought, leaping along behind Jess once more, he could sit the others down by the stones, where he had found Miss Kernow having her rest, and have a little explore by himself; and *then*, if he did happen to find Bal again, he could come back to them and say "Come and see what I've found," and take them to it.

He practised saying it as he went on, relishing the idea of having a secret of his own. William was always having secrets and teasing him about it, and in his view, having one of his own made a pleasant change. Maybe, after all, he wouldn't tell anyone – though on the other hand, a secret wasn't much fun unless someone else knew you had one and was keen to find out what it was.

It was something he would have to think about.

"We're getting awfully lazy, aren't we?" Kate said, resting her head against the stone and closing her eyes. "I was thinking this morning that I needed more exercise. Still, I did have a lousy night."

Lynn, sitting up with her arms around her knees, was peering into the wood for a sight of James. A flash of red T-shirt showed he was not far away.

"Don't get lost, James," she called.

"No, I won't." His voice was cheerful and confident, and she relaxed a little.

"At least he has the dog with him," said Kate.

"One hears such awful things—"

"I know. Even so—"

"James," Lynn raised her voice again. "Stay where we can hear you."

"I'm here!" Boy and dog bounded out of the wood together. "I'm only a little way away, looking for butterflies. Silver-washed fritillaries," he added, in Kate's direction. "Like the old lady said."

"So she did. He means that Ruth woman," Kate said when he had gone again. "Apropos of which, Oliver has really got his teeth into the mystery."

Lynn pulled a face indicative of distaste.

"I can't bear to think of it."

"It's the woman's mental state that interests him – whether she ever remembered what happened and how it affected her in the long term. He's doing this study—"

"I know. You said."

"Serena Barstow lent him a couple of newspapers that reported the whole thing in full."

"I don't want to see them. Really, I don't. Maybe I'm avoiding facing reality, but I just don't care. If I start thinking too much about it, it'll just spoil my holiday and I don't want that, because so far it's been just great."

"OK, OK," Kate laughed a little. "I'm not keen on rehashing it myself."

"So far Lucy seems unaffected by it, and I'd like it to stay that way. I could have strangled that wretched Serena when she trotted the whole story out the other night!"

"I suppose it was only natural. Fortunately Lucy's preoccupations are elsewhere, I gather."

"Eddy?" Lynn laughed ruefully. "I think you're right."

"I don't suppose he's a lot worse than Kurt."

"And that's supposed to relieve my anxieties? You must be joking! Do you think," she added after a moment, "that our parents worried about us as much as we worry about our girls?"

Kate laughed and shook her head.

"No, I don't. It never entered their heads that we could be doing anything they didn't approve of. And we didn't, really, did we? I think we must have been a bit retarded. The swinging sixties passed without trace as far as we were concerned."

Lynn laughed.

"Speak for yourself. I had my moments."

"The thing was," Kate went on, pursuing her own thoughts, "we cared terribly what the parents thought, didn't we? We really wanted to please them." She sighed. "Sometimes I think our girls couldn't care less what we think."

"Oh, that's not true!"

"Isn't it? You know," Kate went on, "it struck me the other day that we – you and I – were conditioned to please people, to do what looked good in the eyes of the world at large. Anyway, trying to please people and worrying that I don't come up to scratch is what I seem to have spent my life doing. I know I irritate Oliver. He's always accusing me of fussing about nothing, and caring too much what people think. Take this job with Relate—"

"You enjoy it!"

"Do I?" Kate considered the matter. "Well, yes, I do, most of the time. You wouldn't be any good at it if you didn't. But what I'm getting at is that I went into it mainly because I thought people would approve of me, and think it a worthy cause – a suitable occupation for a doctor's wife."

"But you *like* it, so what does it matter?"

"I just feel it throws a distressing light on my character in this feminist age."

"You're an idiot!"

"Very likely. But do I kind of wish I'd yearned to be something totally unsuitable like – oh, I don't know! A tattooist, or a fortune-teller. Something totally dotty, that I could insist on doing just to show my independence. Here comes James again. Very pleased with himself, by the look of things."

"Mum, Mum," James was calling as he ran out of the wood. Leaping around him, tongue lolling, Jess was joining in his excitement. "Mum," James shouted again. "Come and see what I've found."

Saturday. Changeover day – and Rest-a-While Guest House in turmoil, with everyone leaving except Valerie and Gordon. And Ruth, of course. There had been a group photograph taken after dinner the night before, with everyone smiling – everyone, that is, with the exception of Ruth who felt threatened by the occasion but couldn't think how to get out of it – and with Beryl herself sitting in the front smiling more than anyone else and holding a printed notice which read: A Jolly Rest-a-While Party. Ruth had hated every minute of it, and had resolved, there and then, that if the process was repeated the following Friday night, she would take care not to be present.

224

Newcomers would be arriving later in the day. Doreen had already stripped the sheets from the beds by breakfast time, while Beryl had been transformed into a different woman, harassed and tight-lipped, bustling with speed about the dining room, casting plates on tables as if dealing cards. Arthur, meanwhile, busied himself with handling the money.

In spite of her relief at seeing the last of George Farthing, Ruth sat and ate her breakfast in silence as the departing couple from the first floor front made noisy farewells and pressed their address on Valerie and Gordon. She hoped they would depart without attempting to involve her in any way. At least Mr Farthing had removed himself without fuss, as, some days before, had the young unmarried couple. As well they might, Ruth thought grimly. Their presence had been a continuing embarrassment to her.

Valerie stopped on her way to the door to have a friendly word. She meant well, Ruth had by this time conceded, but she still made her feel uncomfortable. It was the look of her – the gloss and the shininess and those red nails.

"Wonder who'll be joining us tonight," she said. "Hope it's someone nice. Someone with a bit of life to them, eh?"

Ruth, buttering toast, twitched her lips in what she thought was a smile, but made no further reply. A little peace was all she asked.

It came to her, as she sat alone in the dining room after their departure drinking a final cup of tea, that this might be a good day for going to Truro, what with one week's visitors leaving and the next not yet come, and by the time she had finished the tea, her plans were made. She would catch the nine thirty bus.

Leo had come to the conclusion during the course of the day that he could not put off talking to Lynn about their future any longer. Keeping it to himself was driving him crazy; they'd never had secrets from each other. And in any case, it was essential that she had time to think things over before the end of the holiday, and after tonight there would only be six days left; not long, in all conscience, for her to give the matter serious consideration.

Tonight, then. It had to be done, but he couldn't avoid a feeling of apprehension.

* * *

Truro had changed up to a point, as Ruth knew it would have done. The Red Lion had gone, the shops had new fronts and there were hanging baskets of flowers everywhere. Otherwise it was much as she remembered it. There were still cobblestones in Boscawen Street, and the narrow streets around the cathedral were just the same; and the cathedral itself.

She sat on a seat in the open space in front of it to eat her sandwiches, and stayed there once they were finished to look at the passers-by. Wouldn't it be funny if she should see Uncle Ben, she thought. Bump into him by chance, just as she had done all those years ago with her mother, the time when she had first heard Ken Pawley's name. She found herself looking closely at strangers, just in case, though really she couldn't imagine how he might look now. He'd be old, of course. In his eighties. She probably wouldn't recognise him any more.

Hedgerow Farm was where he had lived, not far from town. She had never visited it, but had heard about it from her mother who had grown up there. Sitting in the sunshine, so many years later, she wondered if the farm still existed. Maybe it didn't. Maybe Ben didn't, either.

She had heard nothing from him for years. For a while he had tried to keep in touch – had made enquiries about her, or so she had been told. And then – how many years later? She frowned, trying to place the incident in some kind of timescale, but finding it impossible to do so – there had been some fuss about land.

Bristol, she thought triumphantly. That's where she'd been. They'd moved her from Bodmin to Exeter, and then to Bristol. So many hospitals, so many institutions, it was quite a triumph to remember this so clearly. She had still been ill, still unable to deal with everyday matters. A doctor, a kind man with rimless glasses, had explained everything carefully to her. All the property was hers now, he had said; but would she ever want to go back and live there? He thought not. Better far to put the farm on the market, and accept her uncle's offer for the land in Truro.

The same doctor said she should change her name, too, saying it would help to put the past behind her. He'd suggested Kernow, because Kernow meant Cornwall where she came from. She had agreed, rather listlessly. It was as good a name as any other.

The doctor was given authority to act on her behalf, and after the deals had gone through she had been able to pay for specialist treatment, better care, and still have some left to live on. It had seemed a lot then; it was no more than pocket money now. But what did that matter? She spent very little, needed very little. She'd be entirely happy, she reflected now, if it weren't for her unpleasant neighbours. She had her freedom. There was really nothing else she could wish for.

Except memory. Swiftly she corrected herself – there was, of course, that. She wanted to remember everything about the past. Not just snapshots, bits here and there, but everything. Sometimes she thought of her head as a receptacle for a tangle of threads of different colours. What she wanted to do was to straighten them all out, roll them in neat balls, put them away in a drawer. Another doctor had said, long ago, that she would never be happy until she had done so, and she knew he was right. Didn't it say in the Bible that the truth shall make you free?

This doctor had assured her that hypnosis would do the trick. The thought had terrified her. Hypnosis smacked of necromancy, of magic, of everything evil and forbidden; still she went through with it, even though she was racked with guilt. It did no good.

"You're fighting it," the doctor had said. "Just relax, Ruth. We're on your side."

Maybe they were – but what, in the end, had all that expensive specialist treatment done for her except run through much of her money? Very little. It might, she sometimes thought, have been better if they'd allowed her to stay in that blank, mindless oblivion that had been, in its way, so comfortable and undemanding, instead of allowing her to reach this halfway stage where she could barely tell which was memory and which delusion. Still, they left her alone these days, except for handing out the tablets which they still insisted were necessary. Not that she took the wretched things every day, not by a long chalk. Half the time she forgot them, and then had to throw them away before Hannah noticed and asked questions.

A woman with a small dog came to sit on the seat beside her, and Ruth, drawn back to the present by the snuffling of the dog and by the foolish baby talk with which the woman addressed it, got to her feet and walked away down Pydar Street towards the bus station. She might as well go back to Porthallic, she thought. She'd seen enough. There'd never, really, been much chance of seeing Uncle Ben, and it was foolish of her even to think she might have done. And if she did, what would they have to say to each other? Too much time had passed. He would want to ask too many unanswerable questions.

It was strange, really, how few people from the past she had seen and recognised. Only Nettie Parsons, changed from a mean-faced, spiteful little girl into a mean-faced, spiteful old woman. She'd caught sight of her on the quay one day, but had taken care to turn her back and keep well away from her. Then there was the woman in the gift shop next door to the Minimarket. Ruth, seeing her through the window, was almost sure that she was Mary Tredinnick who'd been a pretty little thing all those years ago, but was now grey and shapeless. She wasn't, however, interested enough to find out for sure, and having no need of gift shops, she merely passed it by. Apart from these two sightings, there had been no one she recognised.

And then, climbing on the small bus in Truro, she saw a man she knew. He was older and fatter and had lost most of his hair, but there was no mistaking him. She had no idea what his name was or why he prompted such an immediate feeling of terror. She just knew that she was frightened of him – had always been frightened of him. She might have thought him forgotten; had certainly never spoken or thought of him all these years. All the same, she knew now that the idea of him – the revulsion and the fear – had always been there, somewhere below the surface.

He had always been excessively pale, she knew – pale and fat-faced, with big, tombstone teeth and a tongue that was too much in evidence, as if his mouth was too small to hold it; and though he was looking down towards the hat he held on his knees, she also knew that his eyes were pale, too, and pink-rimmed, with sparse, stunted lashes.

Who was he, to cause this terror? She knew him so well.

His remaining hair was plastered, strand by strand across his head. That, too, had always been pale in colour, she remembered, and lank and lifeless. His skin had looked slippery, like plastic. Like – her mind was scurrying hither and thither in panic at the sight of him – like white rubber gloves. Like the underside of a fish. Like something that had crawled out from under a stone.

Who was he?

For one moment she wavered, clutching on to the handrail, and almost stepped down to the pavement again. Her heart was beating very fast and her head was swimming.

"All right, my love?" The conductor was behind her, putting a hand under her elbow to help her into the bus. Dumbly she allowed herself to be helped, and without looking at the man in the front she walked blindly to a seat a few rows behind him, collapsing heavily into it.

Who was he? There were a few minutes to wait before the bus started, and she spent them staring out of the window, not seeing anything outside, not able to think clearly. Who? Who? she asked herself.

They were some miles out of Truro when the bus stopped to pick up a woman and a child, and as if the jolt of the engine had triggered a similar jolt to her thought processes, she remembered. Eli Dowrick.

She felt sick; could not stand the airlessness and the heat and the proximity to him any more, and without hesitation she blundered to the front of the bus.

"We'm not at Porthallic yet, my 'andsome," the driver said, but she waved away his words.

"I'm getting off," she said.

Eli Dowrick. She had always hated him, even when she was small – had always shuddered at the look of him and the smell of him. Had always, for some reason, seen something evil in him – both him and his mother. She sank down on a bank beside the road, her pounding heart recovering its normal beat and her breathing returning to normal. The Lord must have meant her to catch that bus, she told herself. She was meant to remember the Dowricks. They were a part of the jigsaw, essential to the whole.

She had known them as long as she could remember, for they had both been regular attenders at chapel until the time when everything changed. Old Mrs Dowrick was little more than layers of old clothes, malicious eyes, and clawlike, dirt-ingrained hands that reached out to pluck at the children as they passed her, forcing them to stop and asking questions. Had they been good? Did they remember their prayers? Did they help their mothers?

Her son, Eli, was, to Ruth, two pale, sausage-like hands that passed along the collection plate. She tried not to look at his face for she thought him the most repulsive man she had ever known, with his unnatural skin and slobbery mouth, for ever fixed in a meaningless smile. It was, however, a revulsion she could never admit to anyone but Eric, for it was mixed with a feeling of guilt. Eli Dowrick was, according to her father, a good man – almost a saint. Touched, anyway, with saintliness, for it was said that he was able to heal all kinds of diseases that the medical profession had given up for lost, merely by the laying on of those hateful hands and by wild transports of prayer.

Her father had always seemed to regard him with a strange subservience which she didn't understand. She asked her mother about it once, and she had laughed and said something about flattery oiling the wheels of friendship; and certainly, Eli Dowrick laid on the flattery, thick as cream. To hear him speak, Thomas Teague was the best thing that had happened to Cornwall since John Wesley.

When all else seemed to fail, her father had called him in to attend her mother. As before, some days were better than others, and these her father attributed solely to Eli's powers. On the bad days, he blamed his wife for not making an effort.

"'Tis lack of faith, Thora, that's what 'tis. Eli can't do nothing without it. What does it say in the Good Book? 'Thy faith has made thee whole'. If our Saviour couldn't work without faith, how can His servants manage?"

Ruth, remembering, could see again the derisive, bitterly amused look her mother turned on him.

Thora did her chores slowly now, dragging herself around the kitchen to cook. A woman from Sproull's Corner came in once a week to do the washing – an extravagance, in Thomas Teague's eyes, of which he constantly reminded his wife. Ruth cleaned the house and did the ironing. Somehow they managed.

Eric had been clouted when he asked his father, shouldn't they call for a real doctor?

"I ent got no time for you, you faithless little worm!" Thomas had flung the words at him with scorn and loathing. "I might have known you'd show your weakness. When have ee done anything else? 'Tis said, be strong in the Lord, not run from Him the moment we'm put to the test."

"Tidn't Father being put to no test," Eric said sullenly to his sister afterwards. "'Tis Mother who'm suffering."

"Father won't let Dr Kenway near."

"They'm saying in the village she'll die for sure if she don't get treatment."

Ruth knew what they were saying in the village, and the guilt she felt on the subject was more than she could bear – far greater than the guilt she felt for disliking Eli Dowrick. It was something she would never be able to share, not even with Eric.

She had never passed on Dr Crabtree's message. She understood now that he had known how bad her mother was, how bad it was going to be. She knew now that the doctor had only wanted to help, but she'd said nothing, and then he'd been killed and there seemed no point even in thinking of it. Now, however, she found it impossible to put it out of her mind as, powerless and inadequate, she watched her mother's bouts of pain with anguished eyes.

"That Dr Kenway," she said one day when her mother was slumped at the kitchen table. "People say he's not so bad. We should ask him to come."

Thora, her body wasted and her skin almost transparent, had shaken her head.

"It'd be no good, Ruthie. Your father won't have him in the house. Besides, there's nothing he can do."

"You don't know that."

"Oh, yes, I do. Remember that time we went to Truro? I knew then."

"But you said—"

"I know what I said. I – I couldn't face the truth. Dr Crabtree had taken X-rays up the cottage hospital and sent them to the specialist. He told me then." She paused and gasped a little as the pain washed over her. "He said – he said I could have an operation, but there wasn't much hope."

"You should have had it!"

Thora shook her head slowly.

"Call me mazed, but I've always been feared of the knife. I thought I'd rather die clean, in my own home, not messed about in an operating theatre. 'Tis the pain that's taken me by surprise. I didn't—" she gasped again, closing her eyes against the agony that gripped her. "I couldn't imagine the pain," she said at last.

"Maybe the doctor could give you something for it."

"Tidn't no use. Your father wouldn't leave him come."

"Why not, if he could help? He can't mean you to suffer like this."

"'Tis God's punishment." Her voice was so low that Ruth had to bend closer to hear it. "'Tis because of my sin."

"What sin, Mother? You'm no more sinful than the rest."

Thora opened her eyes so that she looked straight into Ruth's, and she opened her lips, too, as if she would speak. But then she closed them again.

"I think 'tis gone for the moment," she whispered after a while. She seemed to wait and listen as if for the sound of the pain's return, then pressed her hands down on the table and got to her feet with difficulty.

She didn't move, however, but stood looking at Ruth, frowning and biting her lip as if in indecision. Then she appeared to make up her mind.

"Ruthie—" she began. "Listen to me. When I'm gone—"

"*Don't*, Mother!"

"No, listen. 'Tis important. That Eli Dowrick. Your father's got plans—"

"What?" Bewildered, Ruth stared at her.

"Have nothing to do with him, Ruthie. He'm an evil man, no matter what people say."

"What do you mean?"

Thora closed her eyes as if the effort to speak was almost too much, then opened them again.

"Your father thinks he'd do for you. Be a good match."

"*What?*" Ruth recoiled in horror. "Oh, no! I hate un, Mother! I couldn't bear un. Anyway, I'm too young."

"That's what I told un. She'm just a girl, I said, not yet left school."

"What did he say?"

"He said . . ." Thora drew a deep breath as if talking was an effort. "He said you were big for your age. And strong. And that Eli would wait."

"He's horrible," Ruth said, shuddering. " 'Tisn't just the way he looks, though I hate that worse than poison. 'Tis the way he talks."

"I know. He'm smooth as butter and talks to God like He should think Himself favoured, but underneath he cares for no one. No one but Eli Dowrick."

"Why does Father think so much of him?"

Thora laughed, without mirth.

"They're two of a kind, Ruthie. Just be warned."

"Why should Eli—?" She broke off and her mother looked at her with love and with pity. She knew what she had been about to say. Why should even Eli want to marry someone as ugly as me?

"The farm will be yours one day," she said. "It'll never be left to Eric." Then she said it again, more desperately than ever. "Be warned, Ruth."

The evening was cloudy once more and a fresh breeze had sprung up.

"It's almost a relief," Kate said, giving the boys their bacon and eggs and beans on toast at the kitchen table. There was a Western on television, and they were anxious to eat quickly before it started.

She had plans for something simple but a little more celebratory for herself and Oliver; not for any real reason, but just because it had been a lovely, friendly sort of day and at the end of it they were alone together. Happily alone. Two salmon steaks lay waiting in the fridge, and she was contemplating making Hollandaise sauce, looking thoughtfully into space and wondering if it was worth the bother and deciding, just as Oliver came into the kitchen with Serena's newspapers in his hand, that it was.

"Do you intend to read these?" he asked. "Or shall I nip up to the Barstows with them now, before they're thrown away by mistake? I've got time before supper, haven't I?"

"Sure." Kate spoke absently. Having made up her mind, she was rooting in the cupboard for a bottle of wine vinegar which she felt sure she had seen somewhere among the items of food left by the previous tenants. "Ah, there it is," she said triumphantly, reaching into the depths for the bottle. "To tell you the truth, I'll be glad to get the wretched things out of the house before any of the children see them. You won't stop for a drink though, will you, darling? Don't even cross the threshold, or Serena will have you pinned to the wall for the next hour. This isn't going to be long."

"Straight there and back," Oliver promised.

Kate was humming to herself as she took an egg and butter from the fridge, amused because here she was, on holiday, but taking pains in the kitchen just as she did at home and really rather enjoying it. It made a change from the rather more slapdash meals they had eaten over the past few days.

She was just separating the yolk from the white of egg when the phone rang. Not quite so eager to answer it this time, she pulled a face and waited until the operation was completed before going to answer the summons.

"Hallo?"

"Is that Mrs Sheridan?"

Good English, but unmistakably foreign. Male. Totally unfamiliar. With both Caroline and Rose currently on the Continent, Kate's mind immediately went into its usual tailspin of panic and foreboding.

"Yes," she said breathlessly. "Who's that?"

"It's Patrice Colbert. You remember, perhaps, we met in Bruges? When I was so unfortunately taken ill with the heart attack?"

"Bruges?" Kate was bewildered. She'd been to Bruges once in her life, roughly twenty-five years ago on a school trip, and could remember little about it.

"In the foyer of the Hôtel des Trois Rois. You and your husband were so kind. Never shall I forget."

"I'm – I'm sorry. You must have the wrong number."

"*Non, non.* I think not. This is the number for Dr Sheridan, yes?"

"Yes, but—"

"May I then speak to him?"

"I'm afraid he's not here at the moment. How did you get this number, anyway?"

"I ring his surgery in London, they give it to me. When do you return here, Mrs Sheridan?"

"A week today. Look, I don't understand."

"Ah, *quelle dommage!* Myself, I go back to Paris next Wednesday. I wished so much to entertain you both to dinner at my hotel – some small recompense, you understand, for the quick action that perhaps saved my life? Another time, perhaps. You will please give my good wishes to your husband. Tell him a – how do you say? – a by-pass operation was required, but I am progressing well and am sorry we are

234

not meeting again. Goodbye, Mrs Sheridan."

"Wait—"

But he had gone. Kate put the phone down slowly, her mind clear now, and highly active. At some time over the past months, clearly Oliver had been in Bruges – and with a woman, since this unknown Frenchman seemed to be under the impression that he was accompanied by his wife. When, and in whose company, had Oliver been to Bruges? And why Bruges? The answer occurred to her at once: it must have been the time that he and Anna were supposed to be in Cambridge. What could have been easier? Ferry from Felixstowe to Zeebrugge, maybe; or perhaps there was a handy local airport. "Progressing well", the Frenchman had said. Not quite better yet, it seemed – so the dates would appear to fit.

She felt wild, hysterical laughter welling in her chest. The adulterer's nightmare, she thought. Some unexpected emergency, shattering his anonymity – some cry of "is there a doctor in the house?" American doctors, she had heard, had taken to ignoring such a cry for fear of litigation; better for Oliver if he had done the same. But he never would. Not Oliver. He would have been there on the instant, anxious to help. With his wife.

Let us not forget his wife, she thought grimly, feeling now no compulsion to laugh, but only a slow, burning anger. No doubt she was equally ready to help, equally skilled.

So there was the proof. She had been right the first time, and the mountain really existed, bearing no resemblance to a molehill at all.

She sat down heavily at the table, staring at the bottle of wine vinegar and the bowl and the butter. She had no use for them any more. She couldn't move or think or do anything but sit and wait.

Oliver, true to his word, had returned the newspaper, had managed to nip in the bud Serena's attempt to tell him about the murder all over again, and had come straight home. He was thinking of Anna as he walked back down the lane. He hadn't phoned her yet, but would put it off no longer. At the first opportunity, he resolved that he would tell her, without equivocation, that she should go to Liverpool – that they had no future together. Surely she must see that? She had seemed to make it clear at the beginning that serious commitment was the last thing that interested her. Why on earth had she changed now?

He'd behaved badly; OK, he admitted it, and was sorry for it, but it must also be said that Anna hadn't been entirely guiltless in the matter. It was she who had made the first move, his the culpable weakness that had responded to it. Now the madness was over he was overwhelmed at his own stupidity. Imagine living with Anna – living *up* to Anna! All that crisp efficiency, morning, noon and night.

What had he been thinking of? The question made his head reel, made him feel weak with relief that the madness had, apparently, left him. To put his marriage in jeopardy – to risk Kate and the children and the way of life that had grown around him, fitting him like a second skin; to think of leaving the house, of starting up somewhere completely new, of attempting to make some kind of division of the spoils of nineteen years – how could he even have contemplated it?

Thank God no hint of it had reached Kate! With luck he could put this whole thing behind him, forget it ever happened, put it down to experience.

She was so innocent, so unsuspecting. He experienced a rush of gratitude and of love for her as he stepped over the cattle grid and made for the back door. Of course she had faults; who hadn't? In his eyes, at this moment, they merely served to make her appear more lovable.

He knew something had happened the moment he saw her. Gone was the bustling, happily occupied woman he had left ten minutes before. She looked older, her face strangely set and rigid, her eyes cold as she looked at him.

"Tell me about Bruges," she said.

In the end, Leo couldn't say anything. Not in the restaurant. It had been such a long time since they'd been out to dinner in that sort of place, just by themselves; a quick hamburger or a pizza with the children had been more the thing for longer than he cared to remember. It seemed a shame to spoil the event.

And Lynn was looking so lovely and so carefree that he couldn't bear to risk upsetting her. Anyway, she was so full of chat about her and Magda's plans for the shop that he hardly had the chance to say anything. They were planning to expand, to start selling CDs – classical, not pop – and to stock cards. Good, artistic ones. He'd heard most of it before but allowed her to tell him all over again, even though he realised it wasn't perhaps the kindest thing to do, allowing her to run on like that when none of the plans might come to fruition; or at least, that she might have no part of them, even if they did. However, he temporised when she reminded him that he had said there was something he wanted to discuss.

"Maybe later," he said, and she had pressed no further. She thought she knew what he had on his mind. His mother hadn't been too well lately and he'd been worried about her ability to continue to look after herself. Was he going to suggest building a granny flat? Or – much worse – inviting her to live with them? Neither was an attractive proposition, for his mother was critical of the children and of Lynn herself, and had made it quite clear from the first time of meeting that in her opinion, her one and only son could and should have done a great deal better for himself. Lynn knew herself well enough to realise that if and when the worst came to the worst, she would probably bow to whatever solution Leo had in mind, but in her usual *laissez-faire* way felt that the longer discussion of it could be postponed, the better it would be.

They arrived home, having picked up Emma and Lucy en route, to find that Kate and Oliver had apparently decided to have an early night and were nowhere to be seen.

"Come for a stroll on the beach," Leo said, once the girls, too, had gone to bed. "There's a clear sky now and it looks wonderful with the moon on the water."

Lynn laughed at him as she took his arm.

"You old romantic, you!"

Romance was the last thing on his mind. He had suddenly come to the conclusion that he couldn't bear to keep his secret for one more night.

He was silent however, as they walked along the beach. The moon was shining on the water like a searchlight, making it almost as light as day.

"It's been a lovely evening, Leo," Lynn said and was about to add "We must do it more often" when Leo halted in his tracks and pulled her round to face him.

"Darling, we really must talk," he said.

"OK." Lynn's heart sank a little. "It sounds a bit ominous," she said.

"Yes – well . . . look, let's sit on that rock." He fussed a little, making sure she was comfortable. "It's kind of difficult knowing where to start."

"That bad?" Lynn turned to look at him. She saw his frown and heard him draw a deep breath.

"It's just that . . ." he hesitated. "I've been offered another job, Lynn."

"Really?" She sounded cautiously pleased. "Is that so terrible? It means promotion, I take it?"

"No. No, it doesn't actually – nothing like that. It's not with Reitz-Keppel. Lynn, I don't think you're going to like this."

"Why?" Her smile died and she looked wary. "What is it, Leo? And *where* is it?"

"North Devon."

"North Devon." She repeated the words expressionlessly, thinking immediately of the bookshop and the plans that she and Magda had made and her excitement at the thought of putting them into practice when she arrived back home. Not to mention the house, and the near impossibility of selling it, and her reluctance to do so, even if they could. "What's the job, Leo?"

"This is the bit you're not going to like." Leo paused, biting the inside of his cheek. "Look, you know those boys from the Home I took on that holiday to the Lake District last year?"

"The young offenders?"

"They weren't young offenders. Not exactly. Just difficult kids from broken homes."

"What are you trying to tell me, Leo?"

"You remember it was run by the Hockridge Trust?"

Lynn nodded, waiting and watchful and full of apprehension.

"Well, one of the Trust's social workers who came on the trip approached me on behalf of the board of governors. They've been left a pretty hefty bequest by some benefactor and they're enlarging the size and scope of the home. They wondered if I'd be interested in running it."

For a moment Lynn looked at him without speaking.

"And you are," she said at last.

"The money's not good—"

"Surprise, surprise!"

"There's a house in the grounds that's part of the package."

"Leo, for God's sake, what are you *thinking* of?"

"Hear me out, Lynn. I know this must come as a shock."

"You can say that again! What about the children's schools? And my job? And the house! We can't sell the house. You know that. Nothing's selling."

"The market's picking up – but anyway, we don't need to sell it. We can keep it and rent it out for enough to pay the mortgage so that we'll always have it when we want it. As for the children – well, they'll adapt. Greer – the headmaster – assures me that the schools in Barnstaple are perfectly acceptable."

"Never mind that they're happy and doing well where they are! Leo, have you really thought this through? What's wrong with Reitz-Keppel, for heaven's sake? Remember how relieved we were when they renewed your contract and we knew your job was safe? You were pleased enough with them then."

"Well yes – in a way—"

"What do you mean, in a way? Of *course* you were!"

"I don't know, Lynn. I was glad to have a job, of course, but the longer the uncertainty went on, the more I began to feel I'd welcome a change of direction. My heart's not really in finance. It never has been. I began to think that perhaps I'd be able to retrain, as a teacher or a social worker. That's what I'm most suited for."

"But you haven't retrained have you? Why should they want you to run a place like that?"

"Because they know me and they know that I've got the good of the boys at heart. Also they know I'm good at financial management. I'd be the administrator – Greer and the other staff run the academic side. Lynn, I really did get on awfully well with those boys. It seems such a worthwhile sort of thing."

"And what about the rest of us?" Lynn asked after a moment. "Will it be worthwhile for us?" Her mind couldn't seem to encompass it – the rooting up and moving and the changing of schools – and her job. What about that? "Have you thought," she went on, "about the effect on the children if they're constantly in the society of social misfits? My God –

you worry about Lucy spending her evenings in a café drinking coffee – have you thought of what effect these inadequates might have on our children? On Lucy, particularly? She needs the society of teenage hooligans like a hole in the head."

Leo sighed with exasperation, running a hand through his hair.

"It wouldn't be like that, Lynn. Honestly. Of course I've thought it over, and I know there are serious things we have to consider. That's why I wanted to talk it over with you. We've got to agree about this. I'm not taking the job if you're not one hundred per cent behind it. As for your job . . ." He paused and Lynn waited. "They say there'll be one for you if you want it. Think, darling – we could run the place together! Make it a real home for the boys. Isn't that something worth doing?"

Lynn looked at the sea with its silver path and said nothing.

"Just think it over in a positive kind of way," Leo went on after a moment. "I know it's a bombshell, but it could be fun, you know." He smiled at her persuasively. "Working together, spending more time together."

Still she looked at the sea, not speaking.

"It's really a very beautiful part of the country, North Devon," Leo said.

Lynn laughed, unamused.

"You do choose your moments, don't you?" she said, bitterly. "I was enjoying this holiday up to now."

"I know. I'm sorry. But the thing is, darling, I thought that if you were at all in favour, we could stop off on our way back, just to have a look at the place, see what you think of it. It wouldn't mean much of a detour."

"I don't know," she said. She got to her feet. "I don't know about anything. Come on, let's go back. I don't want to talk about this any more until I've had time to think."

She walked swiftly away, straight-backed, leaving Leo to stumble after her through the sand. Breathing heavily, he caught up with her and took her arm, pulling her to a halt.

"Lynn, it really wouldn't be as bad as you think," he said.

"Leave it for now, Leo. Do you mind?"

"Anything you say." He held her shoulders as if trying to read her expression, then pulled her close, his arms tight around her. She remained stiff and unresponsive, however, and after a few moments he let her go again. "Don't decide now, darling," he said. "Just sleep on it."

"Sleep on it?" she echoed disbelievingly. "Sleep, did you say?"

And without another word, she turned to go back to the house.

11

"The trouble with grown-ups," William said, pouring a generous measure of Shreddies into a bowl and on the floor, "is that on holiday they go all weak and feeble and want to sleep all the time."

James looked at him, chewing meditatively.

"You went water-skiing," he pointed out, after due thought. "Twice."

"Yeah!" The memory of it brightened William's eyes. "It was brill. I want to go again. Next time I *know* I'll be able to do it properly."

"Uncle Oliver's pretty good, isn't he? For someone old, I mean."

"He'd done it before, when he was young."

"I didn't know they did it in the olden days," said James.

"'Course they did. Even Mum did. Listen, James, *you* ask if they'll take us again today. It's always me who asks for things, so they'll take more notice if it's you for a change."

"But I don't want to go! I wanted to show Dad the woods. Hey, I know this really, really brill place—"

"Bet it's not as good as the hide-out we've made."

"But this is secret—"

"Hey, look what I did! I can balance a Shreddie on my nose and throw it up and catch it in my mouth. Bet you can't!"

"Don't you want to know where this secret is?"

"I bet it's a poxy secret. I bet everyone knows about it. Look – I've done it again. Bet you can't."

"Dogs can. With biscuits."

"They can't!"

"They can."

"Bet you."

"Well, some dogs can. There's that King Charles spaniel that belongs to that man with the green gate up our road. The man showed me."

"We can go to the woods with Paul and Daniel right now," William said, abandoning the subject. "They've made a new hide-out."

James showed no enthusiasm for this exploit and continued to eat his breakfast in silence. It was just like life, he thought, that when he had a secret nobody wanted to know about it. He absolutely, definitely, wasn't going to show Bal to Paul and Daniel. He had decided, regretfully, that he disliked Paul and Daniel. They'd teased him right from the first day they'd come across each other on the beach, but he'd tried very hard to laugh at it, making a pretence of not minding, but the truth was he was getting fed up with it. Really, *really* fed up. Sometimes he could think of suitable answers to their taunts, but it was nearly always after they'd gone away. Or else they didn't listen. They didn't listen to William much, either, but he was as noisy and bouncy as they were and didn't care if people took any notice of him or not. His view was, if they missed his jokes or didn't understand them, that was their bad luck. James would like to have been like that, but had grown resigned to the fact that he wasn't, and never would be.

"When I've finished breakfast, I'm going to see the kittens," he said.

"You can do what you like. *I'm* going to see Paul and Daniel."

William had lost interest in the kittens, which was something that James regretted bitterly. He was the only one that cared about them now, which meant that any chance of being able to take one home was reduced by half. More than half. William had a way of going on and on about things he wanted that chipped away at any adult resistance, not often but sometimes resulting in total capitulation. Without his backing, James knew the battle was all but lost.

It was probably lost anyway. His father, who had just come into the kitchen, looked glum and pasty and kind of deflated. He wasn't often in a bad mood, but this was the way he looked when he was. He greeted them, grunted instructions to clear up after themselves, and seeming disinclined for further conversation, concentrated on filling the kettle to make tea.

"Why are you so grumpy this morning?" William asked.

Leo hastily denied the accusation.

"No one's grumpy! People are entitled to be monosyllabic at breakfast time."

"What's mono-whatsit?" James asked.

William flicked a Shreddie in his direction.

"Syllabic, moron. It means saying words of one syllable. It's self-explaining."

"Explanatory," said Leo.

William, his mouth full of food, chose to ignore this.

"Aren't you two getting up?" he asked when at last he could speak. "Honestly! What time do you call this?"

Leo consulted the kitchen clock with a jaundiced eye.

"I call it nine fifteen," he said. "What time do you call it?"

"Time you got up."

"We propose to take it easy today. You'll have to help. Clean up after yourselves when you've finished." William pulled a face, unseen by his father who had looked round to greet Oliver who, tousled and bleary-eyed, had appeared in the kitchen doorway. "Hi!" Leo said. "You look about as good as I feel. Bad night?"

Oliver grunted something noncommittal; then remembering that Lynn and Leo had been out the previous evening, roused himself to be a little more sociable.

"Did you like the restaurant?" he asked.

"Yes. Fine." Leo's tone, however, was unenthusiastic. "The food was a bit too rich for my taste, to be honest," he went on, seeing Oliver's mildly questioning expression. "Neither of us slept well. You two were pretty early to bed, weren't you? Not a sign of you when we got home last night."

"No." Oliver did not elaborate, not even wanting to think of the interminable evening he and Kate had spent; the silences, the bursts of anger, the explanations, the misery of it all – combined with too much alcohol which seemed a good idea at the time, but was now proving otherwise.

Leo yawned widely and scratched the back of his head, while Oliver leaned against the kitchen unit with his eyes closed, waiting for the kettle to boil.

"There," Leo said, pushing two mugs in his direction. "You take these. There's enough in the pot for two more."

245

William watched them go, one after the other, a look of derision on his face.

"Pathetic or *what*?" he demanded. "And what about the water-skiing? You didn't ask."

"It wouldn't have been any good. They weren't in the mood."

"You could have mentioned it, just casually. Put it into their minds, sort of thing. You never know, it might have cheered them up. I suppose I'll have to ask, as always."

"Well, it's you that wants to go."

"Only 'cos you're as pathetic as they are. Come on! Let's go to the farm."

"We haven't cleared up. Dad said—"

"We'll do it when we get back. Anyway, serves them right for being lazy."

"You haven't washed."

"I had a bath last night. How can you get dirty, just lying in bed? It's daft, washing in the morning. Are you coming or not?"

"OK," said James, sliding off his chair with a brief, guilty glance at their dirty cereal bowls, still on the table. "Wait for me." His voice grew more shrill as William headed out of the back door. The bowls were forgotten and abandoned. "Wills, *wait* for me! Don't be mean. *Wait*!"

Kate was the next to appear. She had rinsed her face in cold water and dragged a comb through her hair; had pulled on cotton trousers and a striped, sleeveless top. Still she felt only half-alive, unready to face the day.

She made more tea, and slumped down at the kitchen table with her hands circling the mug, staring at the wall. Thus it was that Lynn discovered her.

"God, you look awful!" she said.

In reply, Kate raised her eyebrows and favoured her sister with a sardonic stare. Lynn was wearing a short cotton negligée showing distinct signs of age and decay along its lacy frill, and she looked, in addition, as if neither brush nor comb had been anywhere near her hair.

"I call that a prime example of the pot calling the kettle black."

"Oh, shut up! I've had an awful night."

246

"Join the club."

"I came down for more tea."

"Help yourself. I've just made some."

Lynn poured herself a fresh cup, and took the chair opposite her sister, looking with distaste at the remains of the boys' breakfasts.

"Dirty little beasts," she said. "They might have cleared up." Kate made no comment, and Lynn inspected her more closely. "Are you all right?" Kate's only reply was a shrug. "What's up, Kate?" she asked.

"Nothing."

At this reply, so clearly untrue, Lynn frowned, then reached over and touched Kate's arm.

"Come on," she said softly, giving her a gentle shake. "It's me you're talking to."

Kate looked at her for a moment, then sighed heavily.

"Would you believe it," she asked, "if I told you that last night I discovered Oliver has been having an affair?"

"With Anna Vincent?"

"*There!*" Kate's eyes flew open wide. "They always say the wife's the last to know."

Lynn hastily disclaimed any prior knowledge.

"I didn't know anything at all, honestly. It's just that there was something in the way you spoke about her that made me think you suspected her – but I never thought – I mean, I thought she might be making a play for Oliver, not that he reciprocated."

"Oh, he reciprocated, believe me! You're right – I did suspect something, but I managed to persuade myself that I was overreacting. As usual. He's always accusing me of it."

"But you weren't?"

"Not in the least. I discovered last night that he took her over to Bruges for the night, when they went to that conference in Cambridge."

"He told you?"

Kate gave a brief, despairing little laugh.

"Not exactly," she said. "I have to admit there was an element of farce about the way it came to light." She explained about the unknown, grateful Frenchman who had discovered Oliver's holiday whereabouts.

Lynn looked astonished.

"The surgery should never have given his phone number, surely?"

"No, of course not. His bad luck. I can't imagine why they did, but it would never surprise me if Anna had a hand in it. Sanctioned it, in some way, just so that the whole thing was blown wide open. I've always thought she was devious and manipulative."

"What does Oliver say?"

Kate sighed again.

"About Anna? Oh, that it happened. It was a momentary madness, he says. Put it down to the male menopause. It never happened before and won't again, and he regrets it bitterly. And so on, and so on."

"I'm sure that's true, Kate."

"Very likely. It's hurt me, though. I can't dismiss it lightly."

"Of course not!"

"Be thankful you have someone as loyal and single-minded as Leo."

Lynn's sigh turned into a laugh, as despairing as Kate's had been.

"Believe me," she said, "being married to Leo isn't without its pitfalls. Wait till I tell you about the bombshell he dropped last night. He only wants to resign from Reitz-Keppel, would you believe?"

"Really?" Kate looked astonished. "Has he been offered something better?"

"It depends," Lynn said, a note of bitterness in her voice, "on your definition of the word 'better'. He seems to see it that way, but the more I think of it, the more it seems infinitely worse to me. More, you might say, like a fate worse than death."

Kate listened to the account of Leo's intentions with growing astonishment, tinged with horror.

"Deprived boys?" she said, when Lynn had come to the end. "God, how awful! After all you've been through! Just when you thought all your troubles were over! Oh Lynn, what are you going to do?"

Contrarily, Lynn began to defend her husband.

"You can understand it, I suppose. He says he only went into commerce because his parents were so keen on it. He's never really liked it. He wants to do something worthwhile, something with young people. He feels he'd be good at it, and he would, of course."

Kate bit her lip and said nothing, though she had her own thoughts about this. That Leo's heart was in the right place, there was no question; she couldn't help wondering, however, if he were sufficiently au fait with modern trends and modern youth to make a success of an enterprise such as this. Perhaps it didn't matter, she told herself. Perhaps love of erring humanity was the important thing.

"And he says there's a job for me, too," Lynn continued, after a pause. "He's all excited at the thought that we'll be working together." She paused again, and sighed. "How can I condemn him for that? He has such good intentions."

"What about your own children? What sort of a life will they have?"

"I know, I know! I keep thinking of that ghastly friend of Auntie Grace's – the one we used to say filled the house with mentally retarded, single-parent, lesbian lepers. Everyone said how marvellous, what a saint she was, and all the time her own children were quietly going to the devil all around her. Heaven knows, Kate, I try to do my bit for various charities, but it's my own children that concern me most."

"Well, of course! They're bound to. And oh, Lynn, what about your lovely house?"

"And garden. I know, I know. I love that place – leaving it doesn't bear thinking about. A house goes with the job, so we wouldn't need to sell, Leo says. We could let it and keep it for our old age – as if that's any comfort! By that time it'll be too big for us. And what tenants would keep up a garden of that size? It will have turned into a jungle by then." She paused for another sigh. "Then there's my job," she said quietly, more miserable than ever. "The shop. Magda and I had so many plans. I was really fired up about it."

"I'm not sure that wives are expected to put their own desires and interests completely on one side."

"No?" Lynn gave a hopeless little laugh. "But if I love Leo, can I really expect him to give up this chance to do something he really longs for? I'm ashamed of myself for even wanting to try. He could end up hating me – and after all, it's he who brings home the bacon. The shop pays so little, it's hardly more than a hobby. On the other hand . . ." She paused, miserably gazing into space.

"On the other hand?" Kate prompted.

"All this togetherness! I don't know if I can take it. I love going off to the shop – the feeling that this is something of my own, something I'm good at, miles removed from the house and the children and domesticity. Well, it's Magda's really, of course, but you know what I mean. Still—" she smiled ruefully, "I know what Rose would say."

" 'Stand By Your Man'?"

"What else?" The sisters were silent as they contemplated this. It was Kate who spoke first.

"I wonder if she would?" she said thoughtfully. "I know it was the principle she followed all her married life, but ever since Daddy died she seems to have blossomed in all kinds of directions. When you think about it, he was a bit of a male chauvinist on the quiet, wasn't he? He dictated what they did and how they lived."

"But she went along with it. They were happy."

"Maybe she could have been happier. I mean, look at her now! No sooner does she get the chance than she's off perfecting all kinds of skills and interests we didn't even know she had. Daddy never wanted to go anywhere exciting, never wanted to go further than Cornwall, but she's found she loves travelling. She's been abroad three times already this year. Who's to say that he wouldn't have liked it, too, if she'd insisted on it? It certainly wouldn't have killed him to indulge her once in a while.

"*And* she's learned to drive – taken to it like a duck to water. Why didn't she do that when she was young? I'll tell you why! Because Daddy persuaded her that she had no need to and wouldn't be very good at it. And what about this holiday? To be honest, I was a bit hurt when she said she couldn't come. I thought she'd welcome it – would be thrilled with the offer, but no! She preferred to go off with Amy, doing her own thing, throwing her pots. She's probably had family holidays up to here! Maybe she's regretting that she spent so many years not following her own inclinations."

Lynn looked at her sister in astonishment.

"What are you trying to say? You're not suggesting she was unhappy, surely? She was devastated when Daddy died. She's made an effort to stand on her own feet and build a new life, that's all."

"Maybe." Kate reached to pour herself yet another cup of tea. "And maybe not. I know they were happy, and that they loved each other, but we don't really know what it cost her to defer to Daddy's wishes all the time, do we? After all, you can love people without approving of everything they do."

"Like you love Oliver?"

"Oh, Lynn!" Kate put the teapot down on the table with a thump. "What am I to do?" She pressed her hand to her mouth and after a minute, got up to tear a sheet from a roll of kitchen paper that hung beside the sink, using it to wipe her eyes. Lynn got up too, and put her arms around her.

"Don't cry, love. I'm a pig to burden you with all of my problems when you've got so much to worry about. But it'll work out. I'm sure it will."

"Are you?" Kate gave a despairing laugh that was half a sob. "All I wanted," she said after a moment, "was a lovely family holiday. Now look at us!"

"Maybe it's this place. This house. Unhappy vibes. That horrible murder."

"You can't blame the house for Anna Vincent, or for Leo's tender conscience."

"No, of course not! I wasn't serious. It's a gorgeous house. The perfect place for a holiday."

They looked at each other and burst into laughter, heavily tinged with hysteria. The holiday, so carefully planned, had taken an unexpected and unwelcome turn, there was no denying the fact. Still, Kate reminded herself as the laughter died and she dabbed her eyes with the kitchen paper once more, for the children's sake they'd have to make an effort to put a good face on what was left of it.

"You know what I think?" she said, after a few moments spent doing some desultory clearing up. "You and Leo should take off and go to see this place while you're down here. It can't be that far."

"He thought we could go on the way home."

"With all the children? Much better to go without them, just the two of you. And the sooner the better. After all, you might find that the reality is better than you think; or Leo might find it's much worse than *he* imagines. Either way, it's better than sitting here brooding about it."

Lynn thought this over.

"Maybe you're right," she said. "But I don't like to bother you with the children. Not now, when you've got so much else on your mind."

"For heaven's sake!" Briskly, with something of a return to her usual form, Kate squeezed washing-up liquid into the bowl. "That'll be no problem. In fact it will be a good thing. Give Oliver and me something to think about, besides Anna."

Lynn bit her lip and looked with sympathy and in silence at her sister's back view.

"You know something, Kate?" she said at last. "You're going to have to forget, as well as forgive."

For a while Kate said nothing, getting on with washing the few items as if she had nothing else on her mind. Then she paused, her hands motionless in the soapy water, her head bent.

"I'm not at all sure I'm going to be able to do either," she said.

Ruth was pleased with the change of personnel at Rest-a-While. Only one of the new couples seemed what she termed Mrs Cornthwaite's type. They were quickly taken under Valerie's and Gordon's respective wings, even to the extent of moving to share their table, from which screams of mirth had emanated all through dinner.

The other newcomers were more restrained. So far. Things could change, of course, as they became more accustomed to the place, but last night and this morning they had appeared to greet Beryl's attempts at humour with suspicion, talking only to each other in sibilant whispers – or, in the case of the elderly lady placed in the room lately vacated by George Farthing, not talking at all. Even so, Ruth had not passed a peaceful night. She had been shocked and upset by the sight of Eli Dowrick after all these years; but more than that, he seemed to have opened a door to memories and emotions that had long remained hidden. It was what she wanted, of course. The very thing she had come in search of. But it did not make for restful sleep, despite the fact that she had taken one of her pills. Instead, she found herself reliving the past in a strangely removed, insulated kind of way, as if it were a film that unrolled in slow motion before her eyes, and she, the viewer, was wrapped in cotton wool.

Guilt. With an unusual flight of imagination, Ruth saw it in those days as a sea mist, seeping into the house through every crack and fissure, bringing misery and desperation and hopelessness. She felt guilty. Her mother felt guilty. (What sin had she committed? Ruth asked herself the question constantly, but her mother didn't speak of the matter again, and she couldn't bring herself to ask.) Even Eric felt guilty, for the only way he could cope with his mother's illness was to get out of the house and leave it behind, and she knew he despised himself for it. He and Ruth were not so close now, which added to her feeling of despair. She no longer knew how he spent his time, who his associates were. She'd heard he visited the Anchor with old school friends, and knew that he hung about the square with them, eyeing the girls. He'd lost interest in the wild creatures he had loved so much and had become secretive and sly. But who, really, could blame him for saying nothing about his doings? No matter what he did, it was wrong. Father was more savage than ever in his disapproval, more wrapped up in his joyless, denying religion. He didn't hit Eric any more, though; just treated him as if he were less than the dust, beneath his notice.

Events had moved on, in the world and in Porthallic. Others had, in September, celebrated the end of the war in the Far East, but though thanks had been given, in the Teague household there was no gaiety, any more than there had been earlier in the year on VE Day. On both occasions there had been dancing on the quay, but dancing was wicked and Ruth was forbidden to go. She didn't mind – had, in fact, not wanted to go. Why should she? She had no girlfriend to sit with on the harbour wall, no boyfriend to ask her to dance. Anyway, she wouldn't have known how to go about it. She was ugly and awkward and had no wish to lay herself open to the derision she knew she would meet with if she presented herself there in her strange clothes, which were all too tight now that she had grown so much.

Closer to home, Mr Pavey, the pastor at the chapel, had been replaced by a Mr Grigson – a much younger man with a different style of stewardship altogether and one that Thomas Teague despised. Services became calmer, less engrossed with hell and damnation and Mr Grigson spoke more than Mr Pavey had ever done about redemption and God's love. He even consented to marry a couple who had conceived a child out of wedlock.

A Youth Club was formed and each month a dance was held – attended, if you please, by Mr Grigson himself, who was known to draw raffle prizes in aid of club funds. It was even said – by Mrs Hunkin of the newsagent's, who should know – that the Grigsons took a Sunday paper.

Thomas was incensed. After several months of angry criticism and of attempts to rally support among the more rabid members of the congregation, among which the Dowricks were the foremost, he formed a breakaway group with himself as the regular preacher. Mr Borlase, another supporter, allowed the use of an old disused warehouse on the quay for the meeting, generously paying for chairs that were going cheap in Truro market.

Ruth regretted the move. She missed the chapel service, particularly the organ music and the lusty singing. Now Mrs Borlase played the piano, very slowly, always choosing the drearier hymns, to the accompaniment of which the gathered handful of souls droned tunelessly and without joy. The sermons were longer, too, and the extempore prayers seemed to go on for ever, with many members of the group taking it upon themselves to add their own particular supplications. Eli Dowrick never failed to get to his feet, and once up, was likely to stay there for a long time, his voice impassioned, raising passion in others, until he had many among the congregation moaning and sobbing in penitence for their sins. But not Ruth. She still thought him slimy and repellent, and shuddered as she suffered his handshake.

It was seldom that her mother was well enough to come to the weekly meeting of the Brethren.

"Not that I care," she confided to Ruth. "Your father's gone too far. God doesn't demand this of us."

"But you think He demands you to suffer!"

Thora had said nothing to that; had had no energy to reply, as a wave of pain had bent her double and drained her of her ability to speak, or even think.

Eli Dowrick still came to the house to lay those horrible hands on her and drone and shout in prayer. He was a carpenter (an occupation not without significance for Thomas Teague and his followers. Was not Our Lord a carpenter?). He was employed by Mr Borlase and lived in a hamlet called Tregrath which was linked to Sproull's Corner by a narrow lane, one of a network of narrow lanes. It wasn't far from Porthlenter, if you took the path through Pedlar's Woods. He nearly always came that way when he came to the farm, slipping through the kitchen door like a pale shadow, making no sound.

One night Ruth was alone in the kitchen, sitting at the table, trying to write a composition for school next day. She had no imagination and hated compositions; it took all of her concentration to string sentences together, which perhaps was why she failed to hear Eli enter the house. Without warning of any kind, she felt the icy touch of his fingers on the back of her neck and leapt up in fear and revulsion, overturning the ink bottle on the chenille cloth that covered the table.

"Look what you've done! You startled me," she said, her voice trembling as she tried to mop up the ink with an inadequate piece of blotting paper. "Why do you creep around so?"

He hadn't answered; just stood smiling at her in that way of his, his stretched lips red in his pale, pale face, reaching out to touch her again as soon as she straightened up, this time on the straining front of her school blouse.

Her father had come into the room at that point and she had looked round guiltily, as if it were she who had sinned, she who had invited his touch, instead of shaking with the horror of it. She had expected a shout of anger, but instead he, too, was smiling.

"Getting friendly, then?" he said, silkily. There was, she thought, a strange light in his eye as if what he had witnessed had given him pleasure. "That's good, Ruth, that's good. God's meant you for each other."

"No—"

His smile died and his eyes grew hard.

"I know what's best, girl." He spoke quietly, not shouting as he so often did, but in a way that Ruth found equally chilling. "We've prayed about it, Eli and me. It's meant, I tell you."

"I'll – I'll take the cloth."

Clumsily she gathered up her books and put them on one side, then pulled the cloth from the table and took it to the sink, not looking at the men. By the time she had pumped the water to rinse it, they had gone upstairs to her mother's room. She could hear Eli's voice, hear it take on the hysterical note that meant it was raised in prayer.

Mother was right, she thought. He was wicked and hateful, all his piety a sham. Why didn't others see it as she did? And she shuddered again as she remembered his hands and the feel of those fat, white fingers on her neck, her breast. Like slugs, she thought.

* * *

255

Emma, looking round the door of her parents' bedroom, discovered her father staring moodily out of the window.

"I've been looking for you," she said, coming inside. "Are you OK? Where is everybody?"

Oliver turned and smiled at his daughter, grateful for the evidence that someone, somewhere, was at least marginally interested in his continued existence.

"Mum and Lynn have gone for a walk. The boys have gone to the farm. Leo's gone to church. How about you? Are you OK? Did you two girls enjoy yourselves last night?"

"Yes, it was great. Dad—" She hesitated, looking at him sideways. "I wanted to talk to you about something really, really important. I'm a deputation."

"Oh?" Oliver went to sit down on the bed and patted the space beside him, inviting her beside him. "Come on, then. Sit and tell."

"It's about Sophie," Emma sat beside him. "Well, about her party. On Wednesday." She launched into an explanation; told him about the band, the fireworks, the desperate need to stay all night. "Do you think," she finished, "that you could get Auntie Lynn and Uncle Leo to agree to it? You know what they're like!"

Oliver scratched his chin thoughtfully. He wasn't, at first flush, madly keen on the idea himself. They didn't really know these people, after all. On the other hand, kids did, increasingly, seem to sleep over at each other's houses, and no harm had yet befallen his precious daughter.

"We'd have to talk it over," he said.

"But you are on our side, aren't you? You'll talk them into it? Sophie said she'd get her mum to phone."

Oliver seized on this with relief.

"Good idea," he said. "Get her to phone. Put it on a more official basis."

"But you're not *totally* against it?"

The sight of her anxious, pleading face reminded him so much of Kate that it was almost a physical pain.

"Not totally," he said. "I'll do what I can."

Emma threw her arms around his neck.

"Thanks, Dad. You're a star," she said.

"No promises, mind."

She little knew, he reflected ruefully as she left the room, the frailty of his authority at this moment. It was quite likely that if he supported the plan, Kate and the others would be all the more vigorous in their opposition to it. He'd come face to face with Leo just before he set off for church and knew by the almost imperceptible chill in his manner that he had heard the news of his transgressions and had been shocked. If ever, he thought, any *persona* was *non grata* . . .

He wandered to the window and looked outside, both hands braced on the sill. It was as lovely as ever out there, but this morning he could draw no comfort from it. He'd been a fool; would, if he could, call back every moment of the past three months and live it all differently: be a better husband, a stronger character.

That, however, wasn't possible. So what else *could* he do but say he was sorry – that he'd been wrong, that it would never happen again? Show by his behaviour that he wanted to put the past behind him?

Nothing, he thought. There was nothing more. But he wasn't altogether surprised that Kate didn't seem to think it enough.

That afternoon, Jacko took Emma to see his prize-winning picture. She did not underestimate the importance of this; it elevated her, she thought, to a very special kind of status.

Eddy and Lucy and the others were having canoe races just off the quay, with Lucy flushed and excited and screaming with laughter at every word Eddy uttered. Emma called to her that she was leaving with Jacko, but felt she might just as well not have bothered, for Lucy barely registered the information. She was, Emma thought with almost as much disapproval as Leo would have felt, getting a bit silly. It was all going to her head.

Jacko, she found, lived in quite a large house high up above the village. He had never talked much about his family, but Emma had gleaned that his father was a solicitor and worked in Truro and his mother was involved in good works. He spoke of them with casual, deprecatory tolerance. There was a brother and a sister, but neither lived at home.

He was smoking the usual cigarette as they approached the house, but she was amused to see that though it was far from finished, he ground it under his heel before going up to the garden at the back, which, even higher than the house, offered a wonderful view of Porthallic Bay. It was an action which put him in a slightly different light; made him seem normal – a little less than superhero, but more likeable, more reachable.

They discovered Mr and Mrs Jackman in the garden with their feet up, reading the Sunday papers. They were both fair-headed and rather plump, and bore no resemblance to their son.

"I'm supposed to be like my grandfather," Jacko said when Emma commented on this. They were on their way upstairs to his room at the time. "He was a bit of a wild man. A devil with the women, so I'm told." He turned round and grinned at her over his shoulder. He looked nice when he smiled, she thought, not replying to this. He didn't do it very often.

She had expected an untidy room; well, most people had untidy rooms, didn't they? But instead it was almost clinically neat, with books on shelves and the duvet hanging straight. There were none of the usual posters on the midnight-blue walls, either – just the picture at the foot of the bed, so big that it might almost have been a mural.

"Wow," she said softly, getting the full impact and not knowing what else to say.

"Don't go any closer," he told her. "Look at it from the door. I called it 'The Flip Side'," he added.

" 'The Flip Side'?" She glanced at him sideways, at a loss, not understanding the title. It was a modern painting, not representational in any way. The colours were sepulchral, and at first sight the picture made no sense to her. A woman's face, the mouth open in a scream – of fright? Of despair? – was in surreal juxtaposition with a shape that could be a shattered boat, while elsewhere a derelict building collapsed in a pile of bricks.

"Don't you get it?" Jacko asked.

"Tell me."

"It's Cornwall."

"*Cornwall?*" She echoed the word, staring at the picture, with a touch of anxiety. She had so wanted to like it, to approve what he was trying to say, but was finding it more difficult than she expected. "It's – it's very striking," she said weakly at last. "Really well done."

"You don't like it, do you?"

"Yes, I do. It's just that – well, it's bit gloomy, isn't it? I'd never thought of Cornwall as that."

"No? You thought it was all cream teas and smugglers and picturesque crap like Porthallic?" He gave a short, derisive laugh. "You're the same as all the others. This is the side of it tourists don't see." He was looking at her with a twisted smile, a satirical glint in his eye. "Cornwall's just a theme park to you, isn't it? It's du Maurier country, or Betjeman country, or Poldark country. But you're wrong. It's *our* country – a real place with real people and real problems."

"I know that!" She thought of her fantasies about dashing pirates and romantic smugglers and felt guilty. "I see what you mean, though. What – what's the woman screaming for?"

"Help," Jacko said simply. "Work, housing. Oh, I suppose you can't be blamed for thinking of Cornwall the way you do. After all, it's the picture the Tourist Board likes to put out, but this is the real Cornwall. Who wants to know about poverty and massive unemployment?"

"Yes, but . . ." Emma looked at the picture again, biting her lip. Oh, she *did* want to like it! "You've only painted one side of it, too. You haven't made it look at all – well – attractive. I mean, where's the – the beauty?" She spoke diffidently, as if it were a dirty word.

"Beauty!" He snorted derisively.

"Is unemployment really worse here than anywhere else?"

"It's always been bad here. Why do you think John Wesley made such an impact in these parts? Because the people were poor as church mice, that's why. It's no better now. There aren't any tin mines any more and the china clay industry isn't what it was. Fishing's suffering because of all the bloody EEC regulations. This may look a pretty-pretty sort of place and so it is, in parts – but take a look at the mining country. You never saw any place more bleak."

Emma turned to the picture again, seeing now the point of its grimness.

"I do see what you mean," she said slowly. "It really is good. Depressing, though."

Jacko looked quite cheerful at this.

"It should be," he said. "That's just what it's meant to be. A depressing picture of Depression."

"Thanks for showing it to me, anyway."

"That's OK." He held the door as if to usher her out but for a moment she stood her ground.

"Are you going to study art when you leave school?"

He shrugged his thin shoulders.

"Maybe. Or maybe not. Sometimes I think I want to be a journalist."

Emma looked at him. The strange picture had done nothing to reduce his stature in her eyes, but had merely pointed up the difference between him and the others. She felt more awe-struck than ever, more certain that he was going to amount to something.

"Will you come to London?" she asked, and he shrugged again.

"Maybe. I dunno. I've got to do A levels first."

"Well, if you do . . ." The words hung in the air and she did not add to them. She knew in her heart that she wouldn't see him again once she left Porthallic. Even if he came to London, he would have forgotten her, moved on. It seemed infinitely sad, but she managed to smile.

"I can't wait to get on with it all, can you?" she said.

"With A levels?"

"No, with life, idiot."

He took her by the shoulders and kissed her.

"You'll be OK," he said.

They had another barbecue that night; and they all, Oliver thought, deserved a medal of some sort, because in spite of everything, the adults had contrived to make it a normal, cheerful evening. And if the jollity was a little strained, none of the children appeared to notice.

Emma didn't overestimate the importance of Jacko's kiss. It had been brief and casual and almost meaningless. She'd known better; but even so, she felt it underlined their special relationship – the relationship that had prompted him to show her the picture – and she felt happy. The subject of Sophie's party arose over the sausages, and she exchanged a relieved glance with Lucy at the ease with which they obtained approval for it. It was true that Mrs Renshaw had phoned and put in an earnest plea on their behalf, but even so, Emma couldn't believe that Uncle Leo agreed so easily without uttering all the usual useless, superfluous words of caution. It was almost possible to believe that his mind was on something else; except that as far as Emma could see, his mind never seemed anywhere but on the dangers that might beset Lucy.

It was after the children had gone to bed that Kate raised the subject of Leo's proposed job.

"Did Lynn tell you what I said, Leo?" she asked him. "You ought to go and have a look at the place on your own, without the children. Why don't you? Have a night away. We don't mind, do we, Oliver?"

"Not a bit."

"It does sound quite a good idea, Leo," said Lynn. "What about Wednesday, when the girls will be away as well. Would that be OK, Kate? Then at least you won't have them to worry about."

"It's very good of you," Leo said. "I'll give the Trust a call tomorrow to see if it suits them, and if they agree, we'll accept your offer – but only on one condition. We'll take the kids out for the day somewhere tomorrow, so that you two can have a day on your own. Fair's fair."

"Oh, honestly, you needn't bother," Kate demurred, not looking at Oliver.

Later, upstairs, they prepared for bed in silence. Oliver, emerging from their bathroom, looked at Kate as she creamed her face. She could see him in the mirror, standing awkwardly beside the bed, but she gave no sign and the silence lengthened.

"Kate, I'm so sorry," he said softly at last. "You will forgive me, won't you? It's not going to go on like this?"

Kate took a long time to answer.

"I don't know," she said at last, concentrating on wiping her hands on a tissue. "I don't know what I'm going to do. What I'm capable of doing. You've got to give me time."

"Let's for goodness sake take the offer of a day to ourselves. Go off somewhere – some place we haven't been before. You'd like that."

Another long pause elapsed. Then she sighed.

"I would have liked it," she said. "Now I'm not so sure. I can't think what we'd talk about."

"That's nonsense—"

"No, it's not." She turned and looked at him miserably. "She's there, between us, Oliver. I can't just put it all to one side. I'm sorry, but that's the way I feel." Oliver greeted this with silence. There was no sound but the hiss and the drag of the waves from the shore beyond the open window, and the cry of some night bird. Kate turned back to the mirror, picked up a hairbrush.

"We'll see," she said.

"I'll be that glad when she's gone," Beryl Cornthwaite said to her husband, returning to the kitchen with a pile of dirty plates after supper on Sunday night. "Five more days! I don't know how I'm going to stand it. I swear she's bats! Never ought to be allowed out."

Arthur Cornthwaite turned the page of the sports section and changed his half-smoked cigarette from one side of his mouth to the other.

"Know what she's doing now?" Beryl went on. "She's just sitting in there on her own, talking to herself. Having quite a conversation, she is. Never a smile or a word to a living soul, but she'll rabbit on when there's no one there. She's bats, I'm telling you. Well, it's supposed to be the first sign, isn't it? Talking to yourself."

"Ought to be locked up," Arthur said absently, turning another page.

"She really gets on my nerves," Beryl said. "She's just got worse and worse. Heaven alone knows what she'll be like by Friday night. Go on, Arthur. You go and clear the rest away, then you can have a look for yourself."

But when, at last, Arthur put the paper aside and did as he was told, Ruth had gone. She had experienced a sudden urge to walk up the cliff path and look down on Porthlenter once more.

It was a perfect evening for a walk. Clouds had threatened rain during the day, but none had fallen and now there was a cloudless sky and only the lightest of summer breezes.

Ruth sat for a long time looking down at the house. There was a drift of smoke coming from the far side that was hidden from her, and for a while she thought the whole place must be about to burst into flames. But the smoke diminished and died, and after a bit a woman came round to her side of the house and began to water the flowers, her manner unhurried and casual, proving there was no danger.

And then, at last, she saw what she had been waiting for all along. The boy came to help her, staggering a little to one side with the weight of a bucket of water. He set it down and stood, hands on hips, while the woman replenished the watering can. Faintly the sounds of voices floated up to her on the still air.

She rested her chin on her knees and watched them, a warm glow in her heart such as she could not remember experiencing for years. Beryl Cornthwaite would barely have recognised her, so contented and calm was her expression.

What, Ruth asked herself, did she care for Eli Dowrick? He was of no importance now. Why should she give him a moment's thought, now that Eric had come back.

12

It was Lynn who insisted that they should carry out the plan to give Oliver and Kate a day on their own. They needed space, she said, and it was only right that she and Leo should provide it. They would take the children to Flambards.

Emma and Lucy, who might have been expected to object to anything as uncool as a family outing, were, on the contrary, enthusiastic about the proposed trip. There was nothing else to do, they said. Everyone else was going to be working.

Emma, it was true, did have a brief pang of conscience, remembering Jacko's strictures about theme parks, but this was quickly stifled as she recalled what everyone else had told them about this particular attraction. It was, they said, a great place to spend the day – an 'in' sort of place that shouldn't be missed. So clearly they would be able to enjoy it without any loss of street cred, and squashing up in the back would present no problems at all.

Oliver and Kate, once everyone had gone, were left to get through the day as best they could. By mutual consent they said little of what dominated both their minds. They behaved towards each other with distant politeness, each aware of their separateness, each knowing that whatever the outcome, things could never be quite the same – that the relationship had subtly changed. Whether for good or ill had yet to be established.

Kate said she would walk to Porthallic along the cliff path. They needed milk, she said. And bread. And cereal. Did you ever know anyone eat cereal like those boys? She assured Oliver she was happy to go alone, but thinking that such an expedition might break the icy barrier between them, he insisted on going too.

At the top of the hill they stopped to regain their breath. Kate looked at the view, while Oliver looked at Kate.

"We must talk," he said, seeing the bleakness of her expression.

"Not now. I'm not ready."

"But until we do—"

"Not *now*, Oliver!" She turned and continued walking, not looking at him, and after a moment he followed her.

On the way back he suggested a beer and a sandwich at the Anchor, and was a little surprised when she agreed, though later he thought that her ready assent had only been given because she thought there could be no intimate discussion in such a public place. Instead, Oliver initiated talk of Emma and Caroline; it might, he thought drearily, remind her of all they held in common.

Silence fell after a while – a heavy kind of silence, as if they had come to the end of all such mutual interests and could find nothing else to say. What else was there, really?

In Kate's silence, Oliver could see the subject of Anna gathering weight like a looming storm cloud, and he reached wildly for some uncontroversial gambit to forestall the outburst.

"You know," he said, "I keep thinking about Thora Teague."

"Thora—?" Kate looked momentarily mystified. "Oh, you're on about that again."

"Sorry. I know you're not really interested."

"What, exactly, about Thora Teague?" Kate asked after a moment, as if she, too, thought any subject was preferable to silence.

"Well, I keep wondering who treated her. She had terminal cancer, yet in the paper it said that the local GP had never seen her. It seems inconceivable to me that she had no treatment from anyone at all. Her pain must have been intolerable."

"Yes. Yes, it must have been. Poor soul." Kate, normally the most sensitive of women, spoke absently. Oliver, looking at her, saw that her own pain was too great to allow of any other, just at this moment. He reached out and covered her hand with his.

"Oh darling, I'm so sorry," he said, yet again. "Let's go home, shall we? We must talk and we can't do it here."

"Yes, that's probably a good idea. At least . . ." she hesitated, removing her hand. "I'd actually like to be on my own for a bit," she said. "Do you mind? Is there something you can do?"

"We ought to make the most of today. Surely it would be a good time—"

"I want to be alone!" A touch of anger now; of waspishness, of an end to the pretence of calm.

Oliver looked at her sadly, then sighed and resignedly shrugged his shoulders.

"OK, Greta," he said wearily. "If you want to be alone, then I'll get out of your hair."

He waited for her to ask what he would do with himself, where he proposed to go, but she said nothing. It was enough for her, he thought, that he should disappear for an hour or two. Well, fair enough. That's what he would do.

Since there was shopping to carry, common decency seemed to dictate that he should accompany her back to Porthlenter. The walk was accomplished in near silence, with not even the pretence of the normality that had sustained the previous few hours.

Once home, he considered his options, deciding against the beach. Kate heard the car leave the yard and felt a small but distinctly discernible twinge of conscience. The morning hadn't, after all, been so bad. He was trying so hard to make amends – had, she knew, phoned Anna to tell her it was over. Perhaps she should have seized with more enthusiasm the olive branch he was holding out in her direction. And it was, as he had implied, a good time to talk while the others were out of the way.

She just didn't feel able to, conscience or no conscience. As she had told him, she needed time.

Oliver was not at all sure where he was going, his only object at that moment being to get away from the house. He had a vague idea of exploring the coast westwards; but when, after he had gone a little way along an unfamiliar road, he saw a signpost to Truro via the King Harry Ferry, a sudden thought made him change his mind.

Though for the sake of conversation he had exaggerated his preoccupation with Thora Teague, the matter was certainly one that had occurred to him several times over the past day or two. His curiosity was aroused. The newspaper Serena had given him was the *Western*

Morning News, a paper that served the whole of the south-west. It now occurred to him that there must be a local paper produced simply for this part of Cornwall which might carry a more detailed report of the murder – or perhaps simply a different one which highlighted other aspects of the case. And if so, he reasoned, it was odds on that the public library would have archive copies.

His guess was right; the local papers of that era had been photographed on to microfilm, but coming across the relevant reports after racing through months of parish meetings and court cases and flower shows at breakneck speed, he found they differed very little from the ones he had already read.

It was, he found not surprisingly, a story that ran and ran. He rolled the film on to the next week, and found that by then, sightings of Eric had been reported from various parts of the country, from Liverpool to Penzance, but his exact whereabouts were still a mystery. The driver of the car which passed Brook Farm late at night, now definitely assumed to be a poacher, was asked to come forward as he might be able to give valuable evidence of events at Porthlenter Farm. Benjamin Stansfield (35), brother of Thora Teague, had been dismissed as having nothing to do with the matter.

He found himself no further forward regarding Thora Teague's illness – nor, come to that, Ruth's mental condition. If only he could talk to her! It was maddening, knowing she was so near. Someone, surely, must know where she was staying. But who?

The answer came to him at once. The brother, that's who. Ben – what was his name? Oliver scrolled the reel back. Stansfield. Benjamin Stansfield. After some thought he went to the shelves that housed the telephone directories for the entire country, and found the local one.

He was there; it was as easy as that. At least, there was a B H Stansfield, living at Titchfield Farm, Penlivery, Nr Truro. The address was different from that given in the *Cornish Guardian* of 1946, but that was hardly surprising. Anything could have happened since then.

Should he phone first, to check? Oliver thought about it some more and decided that he wouldn't. He had the afternoon to kill and nothing better to do, after all. He would go out there and try to see Stansfield in person. It didn't sound as if it would mean a long journey.

He asked directions of the librarian when he handed back the reels of film and was assured the drive would take him no longer than fifteen minutes. In fact it took him almost as long again to find the farm which lay along a long, unmade track, open fields on either side of it.

He stopped the car before he reached the yard, pausing for a few moments' thought, preparing what he would say. Kate would think he was crazy, he thought. She'd say he was intruding, overstepping the mark – and who was to say she'd be wrong? On the other hand, he had nothing to lose and might have much to gain.

He put his doubts to one side and walked up to the farm. It was a modern house as farms went; built since the war, anyway, as indeed were the outbuildings and barns that surrounded it. A small, dark woman whom he judged to be in her early thirties came to the door in answer to his knock. She was dressed in shorts and a skimpy T-shirt and was carrying a crying baby – both of which circumstances surprised him, for he had expected someone elderly. He gave her his best smile.

"Good afternoon." He had to raise his voice to be heard over the baby's cries. "It looks as if I've come at an awkward time – and anyway, I think I may have come to the wrong house. I was looking for Mr Benjamin Stansfield—"

"That's right. I'm Alma Stansfield. Ben's my husband."

"Oh!" His shock must have been obvious, for she laughed as she shifted the baby against her shoulder, patting its back in an effort to keep it quiet. "Or is it old Ben you're wanting? Ben's dad? He's up in the top field mending a gate. Where are you parked? If you carry straight on until the track peters out, you'll find him, no trouble. Excuse me – I must go! This little chap thinks he's dying of hunger."

"Give him my apologies." Oliver raised his hand in farewell. "And thanks. Sorry to bother you."

It was, as she had said, no trouble to find Benjamin Stansfield, Senior. He was bending down beside a five-barred gate, hammer and nails in hand, and straightened up with some difficulty as Oliver brought the car to a halt within a few yards of him. He wore a battered hat on his head, the smoke from his pipe keeping at bay the flies and midges that were present in clouds. His shoulders were stooped, but for all that it was easy to see that he had been a fine-looking man and was still vigorous, despite the fact that he was in his eighties.

He looked at Oliver enquiringly.

"Lost, are ee, sir?" he asked.

"Not if you're Ben Stansfield," Oliver said. "How do you do?"

"How do?" Ben's polite reply was cautiously curious. Nothing to do, Oliver thought, but leap straight into it.

"My name is Oliver Sheridan," he said. "I'm staying with my family at Porthlenter—"

"Porthlenter?" Ben frowned, but Oliver saw that the expression in his eyes had sharpened. "I've had nothing to do with Porthlenter for years."

"I know. And I realise it can only bring back unhappy memories. I just wondered if you could tell me where Ruth is staying."

"Ruth?" Ben looked totally bewildered at this. He pushed back his hat and meditatively wiped his brow with a stained handkerchief pulled from his pocket. "Ruth Teague? I ent had nothing to do with her for years, either. I don't even know if she's alive or dead. What's it to you, anyway?"

A mild belligerence had crept into his manner, as if he suspected Oliver of stirring up things best left forgotten. Oliver hastened to smooth him down.

"I just wanted a few words with her. I'm a doctor, you see."

"Bloody doctors," said Ben. In spite of the apparently unfriendly words, he looked mildly amused. "She must have had a basinful of them, poor girl. I've no time for them, myself – you're better off without them, if you ask me." He stuck the pipe back in his mouth and bent to his work once more, chuckling a little to himself. Oliver laughed, too.

"I daresay you're right," he said. "Well, I'm sorry to have bothered you. I just thought Ruth might have contacted you, seeing she's back in Porthallic—"

"What?" Ben reacted at once to that, turning to look at him in astonishment, not smiling any more. "Ruth's back? You didn't tell me that."

"I thought you'd know."

"I told you – I've heard nothing for years. She was in hospital in Bristol, last I heard. That must have been – ooh, going on twenty years. More."

270

"Well, she's in Porthallic now. She came to Porthlenter, and my wife showed her round."

"By Gor – thass a real bombshell." Ben pushed his hat back once more and scratched his head. "But 'tis no surprise she hasn't come near me. She took against me when she was a child. Thought I was trying to get her mother away."

"A pity you didn't."

"Don't you think I've told myself that a million times?" He turned away again, not this time to resume his work. He put his tools down on the ground and leaned against the gate, arms on the top rung. As if lost in sad remembrance, he puffed at his pipe. "A lovely girl, Thora was," he said at last. "Pretty, and sweet-natured. It was the worst day of her life when she married that bastard – and the worst day of mine, too. I knew she was in for trouble." His voice – the frail voice of an old man – shook a little.

With an almost imperceptible movement, not wanting to draw attention to himself unduly, Oliver came closer and leant beside him. On the other side of the gate the peaceful countryside dreamed in the August sunshine, a patchwork of small fields coloured green and brown and gold, and beyond all the distant dazzle of the sea.

"'Twas handsome weather that August," Ben said after a moment. "Hot, like this."

"Did they ever find Eric?" Oliver asked curiously.

Ben shook his head.

"Never." He sucked at his pipe, looked at it in disgust. He tapped it out on the gate and reached for a battered packet of tobacco in his back pocket, filled it once more and tamped down the tobacco with his finger. Oliver watched the whole proceedings, not moving. "He was never no murderer," Ben said at last. "I never believed that."

"What do you think happened to him?"

"I don't know. Not for sure. Poor little bastard," he added, as an afterthought.

"Why?"

"'Twas cruel, the way Teague treated un. Nothing the boy did was right." He sucked at his pipe again. "I got my own thoughts about Eric," he went on, nodding inscrutably. "I think he'd gone away before the murders. No one came forward to say they'd seen him in the days

271

previous, only his friend who said he was in the pub three nights earlier. He seemed happy, he said. Only one reason why Eric should be happy, you ask me. He was going away."

"Where?"

"Australia's my guess."

"With Ken Pawley?"

"Ah, you know about him, eh?" Ben removed his pipe and stared at Oliver. "You know a lot, don't you?"

"Well—" Oliver shrugged. "I've read the newspaper reports. I admit I've become intrigued by it all. Ruth's mental condition most of all. That's my job, among other things."

"She went right over the edge," Ben said. "She always was a strange one – but then, why wouldn't she be, with a father like Teague? At least young Eric was spared that, even though Ken was no great shakes."

"And you really think they went away together? Eric and Ken Pawley?"

"They could have done. Can't say no more. Ken had been meeting him – filling him up with drink, telling him lies about how well he'd been doing down under. I knew that for certain. I met them once in the Globe, in Truro." Ben looked at Oliver and gave a scornful breath of laughter. "Shooting lines, they used to call it. That was Ken Pawley all over. It wasn't what he said when he first came over with the Australian Air Force, I can tell you. Australia was the last place God made then, and he'd had more than enough of it, so he said. 'Twas only when the war was over and this country was struggling to get on its feet again and times were harder than ever that he began thinking the grass was greener back there."

Oliver frowned.

"I can see Eric would want to go with him, given the lousy life he had here, but surely if he had, there would have been a record of it, wouldn't there? He would have needed a passport. The police would have found him."

"Ah, you'd think so." Again Ben nodded. "But you don't know Ken Pawley. He was a crafty devil – a sharp one, always a little bit the wrong side of the law. All this persuading of Eric to go with him was done for his own purposes. He wouldn't have done it, else, that I'd swear to. He didn't give a bugger about having a son. My guess is this

– he had some sharp scheme afoot and he needed Eric to help him carry it out."

"But you've got no proof?"

Ben shook his head.

"No, no proof. 'Tis all guess-work. But don't forget, I knew Ken Pawley since we was tackers together. I knew how his mind worked."

"But surely—" This made no sense to Oliver and he frowned again. "Surely, even so, Eric would have needed a passport. And Pawley would have been questioned afterwards. If he was in the clear because he'd left England before the murders, and if Eric was with him, then why didn't they come clean so that Eric was in the clear, too?"

Ben lifted his shoulders.

"Lord knows! 'Tis just a feeling I have. An instinct. 'Tis possible Ken got Eric to smuggle something back to Australia – or maybe there was no way they could get a permit for him to enter the country and it was part of some kind of illegal plan to get people in, people the Australian Government wouldn't want."

"Why wouldn't they want Eric?"

"He was underage, wasn't he? He would have needed his father's permission – which Teague would never have given, because Eric was cheap labour to him." Ben turned a narrow, knowing look on Oliver. "You don't know him like I did, sir. I'm just saying, any dodge like that would be par for the course where Ken Pawley was concerned. By Gor," he added, shaking his head as if in astonished disbelief at himself. "'Tis many a long year since I've thought of him."

"But I bet it's all as clear to you as if it happened yesterday," Oliver said, artfully encouraging.

"Ah, that it is! The younger generation don't want to know – but then, nor did my dear wife, God rest her soul. 'Twas the day my eldest daughter was born that it happened. Three daughters we had, and then a son, and none of them want to know. Past history, that's what they say. Best forgotten. Well, maybe they're right." He stared in front of him, not speaking for a moment, then sighed and shook his head once more. "It makes sad remembering," he said.

"I'm sorry—"

"You met my daughter-in-law, up at the farm?" Ben brushed aside Oliver's tentative apology. "A good girl, she is. She listens to me, sometimes. Lets me talk. She's his second wife, you know. First one ran off with a sailor."

"She seemed very nice."

"A good girl," Ben said again. "Makes no bones about having me there. The council bought Hedgerow, see, as part of the new Industrial Estate; 'tis all showrooms and warehouses and factories and God knows what now. I didn't mind. 'Twas all too much for me, and I made a tidy sum. It meant young Ben could expand here and build a couple of new barns."

"He must have welcomed that," Oliver said, his dutiful murmur masking an urgent desire to get back to the main subject under discussion.

"Funny thing about Alma," Ben said after a moment. "She puts me in mind of Thora sometimes." He puffed contemplatively at his pipe. "There's something about her smile," he added.

Oliver took the bull by the horns.

"Thora must have suffered a great deal," he said. Ben's face twisted, but he said nothing. He passed a hand over his face, and took out the grimy handkerchief to dab his eyes. Oliver put a hand on his shoulder, filled with compunction. "I'm sorry, Ben. That was tactless. I didn't mean to upset you."

"It still does, you know," Ben said after a moment. "It still does. When I think how that bloody, black-hearted, sanctimonious bastard refused her a doctor—"

"Did he? Is that what he did?"

"She wrote to me, near the end, just to say goodbye. I had no idea, till then, what she was going through. 'Tis all right—" still distressed, he nevertheless waved aside Oliver's attempt to halt the reminiscences. "In a way, 'tis a comfort to talk of it." He blew his nose noisily, and continued with relative calm. "I went over to Porthlenter, even though she asked me not to. I pleaded with him to get a doctor to the house. I knew 'twas too late to save her, but he might have been able to relieve the pain." His voice trembled a little and he bit his lip, breathing hard. "He wouldn't let me near her. My own sister, and her dying, or near enough! She'd been having treatment, he told me. There'd been a laying-on of hands—"

"A *what*?"

"He called in a faith healer. A chap called Eli Dowrick. He went to the chapel and Teague always thought the world of him, though the Lord alone knows why. Thick as thieves they were, the two of them. Dowrick was the worst hypocrite I ever knew – no, that's wrong! They were both as bad as each other. Dowrick was a nasty-looking fellow – an evil, creeping bastard with the kind of smile on his face that curdled your blood. He was one of they – whatd' you call it? Albino? He was supposed to have cured his old mother of shingles and another woman of the palsy, just by the laying-on of hands—"

"For God's sake! They would have cleared up anyway."

"Someone else at the chapel couldn't seem to have a child, but once he'd said his magic words she found she was pregnant."

"That could be coincidence."

"Maybe." Ben gave a snort of laughter. "Or a different sire. I never believed his mumbo-jumbo had anything to do with it." His smile died. "I never could make up my mind if Teague really believed Eli could help her, or if he wanted her to die. There was a rumour going around about him and a young woman who went to the Meeting. He broke away from the chapel, you know, once they got a new parson. He was a good man, this new chap. Grigson, his name was. A real Christian. Stayed there for years, and everyone loved him, but he was too free and easy for Teague, so he set up shop for himself. He wanted the power, see. Wanted to be top dog."

He gave a long and tremulous sigh and smoked his pipe, while Oliver waited.

"Any rate," he said at last. "I tried to get the doctor to her. I called at his house and asked him myself."

"But he didn't go?"

Ben gave a short, derisive laugh.

"Teague was right about one thing. That Porthallic doctor was no good. Kenway, his name was. He was off out to golf when I caught him – said by rights a near relation should have sent for him if he was needed. What am I, then? I says to him. En't I a near relation? In the end he says he'd go out to Porthlenter and see what was going on, but my guess is that Teague turned him away with some cock-and-bull story and Dr Bloody Kenway was only too glad to be spared the trouble. Any rate, he never saw Thora, so he told the papers."

"I can see why your opinion of doctors isn't exactly high!"

"Well—" Ben gave a ghost of a grin sideways, "you'm not all like that, I daresay. I've been lucky; managed to steer clear of the lot of ee. So there it was. Thora only had Eli Dowrick to tend her. I don't know who killed her, but one thing I'm sure of . . ." He paused again, and Oliver continued to wait. "No," he said at last, after a few more puffs on his pipe. He sounded regretful. "No, 'tis wrong to say I'm sure. Tidn't something I could swear to under oath. 'Tis just a feeling . . ."

"What is?" Oliver asked when he said no more.

"That Dowrick knew more than he ever told. My poor Thora," he said after a moment. "By Gor—" He wiped his eyes again. "Tidn't no good, sir. I can't speak of it."

"No – please don't! I'm sorry. Look, can I take you back to the farm? You look as if a cup of tea would do you good."

"No, no, no!" Ben rejected this idea vehemently. "I'll finish the job I set out to do. 'Tis the best medicine, hard work. Besides—" he managed to grin at Oliver. "Tidn't exactly peaceful back at the farm with the new little tacker. He'm a grand chap, all right, but he got a bravish pair of lungs on him."

"He has, indeed." Oliver smiled back, apologetically. "I really am sorry to have upset you. I had no intention of doing so, believe me. I only wanted to ask you about Ruth's whereabouts. Maybe she'll turn up at Porthlenter again."

"Maybe she will. If she does, tell her to look me up. Tell her . . ." he hesitated. "Tell her 'tis time we buried the past."

"I'll do that," Oliver promised. "And thanks for talking to me."

So what had he learned? He thought about all that Ben had said as he drove back along the rutted lane, and found himself more confused than ever, and angry on Thora's behalf. How could any human being have denied her treatment – still less a man who professed to be a Christian? And what about Ben's theory regarding Eric's disappearance? Surely it was unlikely he could have left the country, with or without Ken Pawley's assistance?

On the main road, a thought occurred to him that was so shattering that he almost stalled the car, causing the driver behind him to hoot madly and give a baleful glare as he swung past him.

Suppose Thora Teague had killed first her husband and then herself?

She might have done. She must have hated him and lost all hope for herself.

For several miles this theory occupied his mind and the more he thought about it, the more plausible it became. Had it ever been put forward as a possibility? And if not, why not? It made sense, particularly if one went along with Ben's belief that Eric had left some days before.

Why not? he asked himself again. He had almost reached Sproull's Corner before he saw the flaw. A shotgun was far too long for anyone, least of all a slight woman such as Thora had been, to shoot herself in the chest.

You're not so damned bright, Sheridan, he told himself, but realised that at least in pursuing this theory he had forgotten his own problems which, now that he was almost home, came rushing back to him. In what mood, he wondered, would he find Kate?

She'd tried to sleep – heaven alone knew, she'd hardly slept at all since Saturday evening when she'd answered the telephone and brought her world crashing down about her ears. She felt so tired that she would have welcomed sleeping for a week – but her mind was in a turmoil and it was impossible to relax, despite the welcome peace that lay over Porthlenter.

When, from her chair in the garden, she heard a cheerful hail from Colin Barstow, she felt both irritation and relief, needing company yet feeling unable to cope with it. Even the relief was tempered with caution. He'd caught her in a weak moment on a previous occasion, and she had no intention of letting him do the same again.

"Hallo, there! All alone?" He was smiling as he came across the grass towards her.

"Yes, just temporarily." She'd decided that politeness demanded a friendly response to the visitor; indeed, she was incapable of giving any other. She indicated the chair beside her. "Come and keep me company. They've all gone to Flambards – except Oliver," she felt constrained to add. "He's off exploring. What can I do for you?"

He'd come, it seemed, to ask if tomorrow would be convenient for him to take the boys to Funlands.

"It's good of you. I'm sure they'll be thrilled," Kate said.

"Not at all. It's the least I can do. I've been busy with this report of mine and feel I've been shirking my duties this last week or more. Serena's had the brunt of it as far as our two are concerned. She's taken them to some boating lake over on the north coast this afternoon while I dotted the i's and crossed the t's. We have to do *something* to tire them out!"

Kate found that relief at having company had taken the upper hand, pushing other matters to the back of her mind. Temporarily, anyway. She made tea and brought it out to the garden. Colin was pleasant company, easy to talk to, ignorant of recent events, and their conversation was superficial and without strain. They talked of gardens; of the need to choose carefully when stocking a garden so close to the seashore; of gardening in the tropics and in London.

Impersonal things; yet she knew that he liked her. Had taken to her. His eyes were kind. Watchful. Too watchful, perhaps.

She talked, rather too animatedly, of holidays – of a longing to see the Caribbean, which somehow led to holidays in general, and the approaching end of this holiday in particular.

"Is it back to work for you on Monday?" he asked.

"No, Tuesday. I only work part time."

"With Relate, you said. I'm sure you're awfully good at it."

"Oh?" Kate laughed self-consciously. "I don't know about that. Not bad, I suppose."

"It must be fascinating. And rewarding."

"Well, sometimes. At others, it's deeply depressing, I assure you."

"Yes, I suppose so, human nature being what it is. At least the couples who come to you must have admitted there are problems and feel the need to sort them out. They've taken the first step, which I imagine is important – rather like an alcoholic who can't be helped until he's faced the fact that he has a drink problem. Tell me," he went on. "What is the single thing that contributes most to a marriage break-up, would you say?"

Kate hesitated, conscious of the intensity of his conversational manner, as if the matter in question was the thing that interested him most in all the world. It was, it seemed, natural to him; he brought the same concentration to discussion of the suitability of hydrangeas to the local soil, or his apprehension that mass tourism might have a

278

deleterious effect on Caribbean culture. She had noticed it before, but on this occasion and on this subject it was distinctly unnerving. She managed, however, to reply casually enough.

"I don't know that there is such a thing. Unemployment's a big factor these days, of course, and money problems in general. Bad housing, too. People living on top of each other, different generations, getting on each other's nerves."

"How big a part does infidelity play?"

"Infidelity?" He was making conversation, Kate told herself. There was no way he could know.

"Yes. Affairs. Playing away. Whatever you choose to call it. I read somewhere that contrary to popular belief, the majority of people stay together in spite of it."

Kate sipped her tea, then put her cup down carefully on the table beside her, turning to him with a smile.

"It depends," she said. "Are you ready for more tea?"

"Thank you." Colin passed his cup over and Kate concentrated on filling it. "I ask because not so long ago I became very much involved in that kind of situation," he went on. "Not personally, I hasten to add! It was a couple we'd known for years in the West Indies. They were like family – we were fond of them both. Anyway, to cut a long story short, he found that she had been having an affair for some time, and he confided to me that he felt just as if he had been bereaved. I suppose that's quite typical. I can understand that one might well feel like that."

"Well, yes." Kate spoke hesitantly, with none of her customary briskness. "It's true that there's often a period that can only be described as mourning. Followed often by anger – anger with your partner and anger with his lover. Or her lover, of course," she added hastily.

"What on earth do you counsel people to do in situations like that?" Colin was genuinely interested. "It was the end of everything for this particular couple, and quite frankly, I find it hard to see how you could put something like that behind you. Is it ever really possible?"

"Oh, yes," Kate said after a moment.

"But what do you say to them?"

"We say—" she took a breath, hesitating for a moment. "We say, talk things through. Talk about everything. The – the wronged partner needs to know why and how and what it was like. It's only when the talking has run its course that the affair can be relegated to the past."

"It's true, isn't it, that you don't give direct advice, or apportion blame?"

"That's right. Apportioning blame isn't considered helpful."

"I suppose there are always faults on both sides."

He couldn't know, Kate told herself. There was no way. But she found it impossible, nevertheless, to look at those dark, thoughtful, interested eyes. She was silent for so long, apparently lost for words, that Colin frowned.

"Or aren't there?" he prompted.

"Yes, you're right," she said at last, suddenly becoming aware that the silence had gone on too long. "We usually take the view that both partners have made some kind of contribution to the situation, wittingly or unwittingly." She contrived to laugh. "Hey – I didn't expect to face these sort of questions until Tuesday! Give me a break, Colin. Talk about something else."

He laughed too, and apologised.

"It's too bad of me – sorry! I've never met anyone in your line of business before. I must say I take my hat off to you. I'd probably end up banging heads together."

He left soon after this, with Kate promising that Lynn or Leo would be in touch with him that evening about the next day's promised outing; and when he had gone she sat for a long time without moving.

Knowing the theory was one thing, she thought. Putting it into practice was something other. Wearily, she got up and took the tea tray indoors.

Sproull's Corner. Get off at Sproull's Corner. Walk down through the wood and wait for him to come.

Ruth was unaware that she was muttering the words aloud, and that people on the bus were looking at her, nudging each other, embarrassed or amused according to their nature. She got to her feet some way before the bus arrived at the stop, and stood rocking with its motion until it halted and she was able to stumble to the front.

"All right then, my 'andsome?" It was the same kindly driver that had been on duty on Saturday when she had returned from Truro. He left his seat and helped her down. "Sure this is where you want to go?"

"Sproull's Corner," she said in reply.

"Thass right, my love. This is Sproull's Corner. Mind how you go, now."

For the benefit of the other passengers, he rolled his eyes as he took the wheel again, and some of them laughed; but of this Ruth was unaware as she watched the bus go on down the lane.

When it was out of sight, she turned towards the wood, welcoming the dimness and the damp smell of it which never changed no matter how dry the weather. In winter the path was muddy; she could remember well having to pick her way through the worst of it – edging along a bank here, jumping a section there, to avoid the morass. Now the mud was dried in ridges, the path hard under her feet, and of the little stream beside it there was not even a trickle.

She hesitated as she drew level with the thicket that hid the way to Bal. Should she go there? The pull of it was almost irresistible, but the thought that Eric wouldn't see her there when he came made her decide to go now, at once, to sit by the stones. They could go to Bal afterwards, like they always did. Like they belonged to do. Beryl Corthwaite had said only this morning that she was growing more and more Cornish in her speech the longer she stayed.

("'Tis nothing to be ashamed of," Ruth had snapped in reply, at which Beryl had bridled.

"Well, pardon me, I'm sure," she'd said, flouncing towards the door bearing her tray. "It's a pity when folk can't take a joke.")

How peaceful it was by the stones! She settled down and rested her back against one of the uprights, where she could see the path in both directions. She didn't, after all, know which way he would come, but like this she was sure of seeing him. From time to time she heard a noise, a rustle, which made her think he was about to appear; but no one came.

Her was busy, she thought. He had so much work to do. But he would come, she knew he would. They were so close, so loving, he would want to see her just as much as she wanted to see him.

Her eyes grew heavy and eventually she slept; and though she was annoyed with herself for doing so, she found when she awoke that she felt calm and at peace. She ate her sandwiches, drank her orange juice.

Soon he would come, she felt sure of it. She hadn't missed him. It was usually afternoon before he arrived.

She didn't mind waiting.

13

What do you buy as a birthday present for the girl who has everything?

Emma and Lucy were sorely exercised by this problem and in the end managed to persuade their parents that only a trip to Truro was likely to solve their dilemma. Leo, normally pathologically opposed to shopping in any form, was reminded by Lynn at breakfast that it was also his mother's birthday the day after they were due to arrive home and was therefore prompted to take them into town to do some shopping on his own account – so long as Lynn went as well, to give the benefit of her advice. Once, therefore, the boys had departed with Colin towards Funlands, Kate and Oliver were again left alone.

"It's a conspiracy," Oliver said, with a tentative grin in her direction. "We must talk."

"Hey – that's my line. You wanted to be alone."

"Now I want to talk. It's a recognised fact that it's the first step towards reconciliation."

"Well, let's by all means do it by the book!"

"Don't be flippant!"

"I'm not. Honestly. If there's one thing that's important to me, it's that we should be reconciled. You may find it hard to believe, but I love you. I always did."

"So why turn to Anna? Why risk losing everything?"

Wearily Oliver sat down at the kitchen table, put his head in his hands.

"God knows," he said. "I was flattered, I suppose. It was a touch of excitement in a world that seemed to have gone a bit stale."

"You weren't in love with her?"

He remembered the hand that had trembled as he had handed Anna a sheaf of notes, the quickened heartbeat and dry throat, the sheer bloody *fun* of it at first – the covert glances, the secret meetings. The in jokes, and the conversations made easier because of the intimate knowledge each had of the way the other had spent the day. He'd felt young again, that was the truth of it. No fool, he told himself now, like a middle-aged fool trying to be a teenager.

"Yes, I suppose I was, in a way. But remember what I said the other day about being in love? It's a kind of madness, bearing no relation to reality. It's nothing like what we have."

"What we had," Kate said.

"Kate, *please!*"

She sat down opposite him, and resting her chin on her hand, looked at him sombrely.

"You know," she said after a minute. "I couldn't have borne it if you'd said you weren't in love with her. Either you would have been lying, which I would have hated, or it would have been true, which would have been worse, as if absolutely anyone in the world was an improvement on me, even someone you weren't really attracted to. But *Anna,* Oliver! She's sheer poison."

"Maybe we're two of a kind."

Kate didn't deny it. The thought of physical infidelity was bad enough, but infinitely worse was the thought that he had been close to someone who had, from the beginning, made no attempt to hide her assumption of superiority, or her amused contempt for what she saw as Kate's small, domestic concerns.

"She despises me," Kate said now, in a small voice. "She always has."

"That's nonsense!"

"No, it's not. She thought me petty-minded and bourgeois, preoccupied with domestic affairs and overprotective of the girls. No doubt that was something you felt you could agree with—"

"Never, Kate. We never discussed you."

"No?" Kate got up from the table and moved restlessly around the kitchen, tidying things away, throwing knives into a drawer, as if she found it impossible to keep still. Oliver watched her unhappily.

"Kate, darling – please! Sit down. I'll make you a cup of coffee—"

"I don't want one!" But she sat down, nevertheless, and faced him again across the table. Her eyes were full of tears. "The awful thing is," she said, "that I know she's right. Well, sort of right. I am preoccupied with domestic concerns. When you've got a home and family I don't really see how you can be anything else, not if you do the job properly. As for being overprotective of the girls . . ."

She paused, thinking of Caroline and how she had agonised on her behalf – unnecessarily, as it turned out. She thought, too, of Emma. Surely she had nothing there to reproach herself with? Some would say they'd given her too much freedom. Certainly they'd given her as much as seemed wise – trusted her, without crowding. Which didn't mean that you didn't worry. Anna had no idea what being a parent was like.

"Am I really overprotective, Oliver?"

"She should meet Leo," Oliver said, and for one fleeting moment there was, between them, the old gleam of amusement.

There was a different, less friendly bus driver on duty when once again Ruth took the bus to Sproull's Corner. He looked impatient as he was forced to wait for her to make her way to the front of the bus and far from helping her down, drove off almost before she was safely on the ground. The weather was different, too. It was still hot, but the sky was clouded and the air heavy. There was no sunlight now to filter through the branches overhead and dapple the path.

Ruth was conscious of feeling strange. Her head felt heavy, full of noise and movement, as if she had a swarm of bees inside it. Was she ill? Sickening for something? No – she was just tired, she told herself. She had slept heavily, but her sleep had been troubled by frightening, inconsequential dreams, now half-forgotten. Unrecognised figures loomed at her out of the fog, chasing her towards a cliff where, at their foot, lapped a sea of blood. At one stage she was running through a wood, searching for something, but for what she could not now remember.

She had been disappointed yesterday when the boy hadn't appeared, and had not shaken off the disappointment all evening. This morning, however, though unrefreshed and disinclined to make an effort, she nevertheless knew she would have to return to the wood. Doggedly she plodded down the path towards the stones, sitting down thankfully when she arrived there, closing her eyes almost immediately as if willing the peace of the wood to descend and bring a measure of calm to her troubled spirit.

But the peace did not come. Restlessly she levered herself to her feet and went to Bal, able now to find it without difficulty. She stood for a while on the lip of the dell, staring down at the tangle of brambles and drift of leaves. Today the glade felt shut in and airless. She could hear no birdsong, and there were no butterflies to hover around the hemp agrimony.

There was peace here, though, and stillness and comfort. She wanted to stay, yet she wanted to go, too, in case the boy should come and she should miss him. Perhaps if she stayed just a little while—?

She crawled into the earthy, twiggy space under the cascading branches of the crooked oak tree, and sat with her back against its trunk, closing her eyes, half back in that twilight world between sleeping and waking. She felt calm at last – until, like a print coming into focus, she remembered her dream in all its fearful detail. This time she recognised her enemy. It was Eli Dowrick.

She'd been walking home through the darkening wood one night on her way back from Sproull's Corner, when she met him coming in the opposite direction, returning from a visit to Porthlenter Farm.

She had been up to the little hamlet at the crossroads to deliver a message to Mrs Grose, one of her father's congregation, asking her if she would play the piano on Sunday since Mrs Borlase had been taken poorly. Though young, Eva Grose was a widow whose husband had been killed in an accident on the farm where he worked, since when she had returned to live under the same roof as her mother once more and had resumed many of her former activities. Teaching the piano was one; attending Thomas Teague's meeting was another. Added to this was a new activity: nursing her ailing and querulous mother.

She made Ruth feel bigger and more awkward than ever, for she was a small woman with a neat, round face and smoothly brushed hair. She readily agreed to play the piano in Mrs Borlase's place, looking neither pleased nor displeased at the request. She was not a woman who showed much emotion of any kind, though Ruth had seen her dark eyes glow with intensity during sermons given by her father, particularly at the points where he dwelt on the sins of the flesh or the punishments awaiting wrongdoers. She was, everyone said, a good woman, sorely tried – first the death of her husband, then her mother's illness. She should marry again, people said, but who'd have her with such a difficult mother to tend?

Eli, as always, was moving quietly so that she had little warning of his approach, coming almost face to face with him as she turned a corner in the twisting path. For a moment he stood, his loose lips stretched in a smile that showed his tongue and his teeth. Big and yellow, they were, with wide spaces between them. She took a step to one side to pass him. But he blocked her way.

"Ruth?" Still smiling, ingratiating, he reached out to hold her arm, but she moved away from him. "Now, Ruth," he said chidingly, his voice soft and sweet as honey, as if he were talking to a child. "Don't run away. There's no call to be frightened of me."

"I want to get by." Her voice was breathless and high-pitched.

"But 'tis a lovely evening, maid." He was holding her tighter now, pulling her towards him. She saw the spittle at the corner of his mouth, could smell his breath. "I'll walk back home with ee."

"No – no, I don't want you to!"

"Now, Ruthie!" A note of sternness now, and real strength and determination in the way he clasped her arm with his right hand and took hold of her shoulder with his left. "Remember what your father said. We're to be friends, you and me. Come on, now. A little kiss won't hurt ee."

His mouth was on hers – his wet, disgusting mouth – before she could move, but she was strong and was able to thrust him off balance, sobbing with revulsion. She scrubbed at her lips with the back of her hand as she ran down the path towards home, tripping on tree roots, catching her clothes on branches. Only when she emerged into the field that bordered the lane did she stop, still looking fearfully behind her into the depths of the wood, her breath rasping in her throat.

He hadn't followed her – had made no attempt to do so, but it was some time before she could stop shuddering at the thought of his touch.

She managed to calm herself and had walked home to deliver Mrs Grose's message to her father who was sitting in his usual place beside the range. He nodded in acknowledgement of it.

"Did ee see Eli, coming back?" he said, turning to look at her with a strange kind of smile. For a moment Ruth hesitated. "Well?" her father pressed her.

"Yes, I saw him," she said. "And Father – I don't want him." Her voice was trembling, but there was no mistaking her determination. "He mustn't touch me. You must tell him."

His smile died and he looked at her with narrowed eyes.

"Are ee saying I don't know best?" he asked in his quiet, dangerous voice. "Are ee saying a silly young girl like you wants to tell her own father what's right? Eli's the man for you, maid. Sooner or later you'll be man and wife, and don't ee forget it."

"But I don't want any man! I'm too young."

"Sit there and listen to me." Her father pointed at the chair by the table, and slowly, her eyes on him, she lowered herself into it. "A woman," he said, "is a danger to herself and everyone else." He was still speaking quietly but with grim intensity, his eyes burning with the bigotry that had grown more and more apparent over the years as if it had fed on the power he wielded over his small flock. "Listen to me!" He held up an imperious hand as Ruth made as if to speak. "You'm no different from all young women, even if you don't know it yet." His voice dropped, became ragged. "Women are a seething mass of carnal desires, arousing lust and wickedness in the men around them. They'm only safe when they'm married with a home and family to keep 'em busy."

Ruth saw the deep lines that ran from nose to mouth, his expression of disgust, and she trembled as his voice rose.

"I've seen these modern girls, flaunting themselves, painting their faces, heard 'em talking about education and being as good as a man. I want no truck with it. Don't think I'll let you work in an office!" His face had darkened and he thumped the table with his fist.

"B-but I don't want to work in an office, Father. I'll stay home—"

"Only one reason why girls work in offices and such," he went on, ignoring her. "Tidn't nothing to do with shorthand and typing or keeping accounts. 'Tis to get a man for herself, lure them away from the straight and narrow."

"Oh, Father, it's not always that—"

"You know best, do you? You know best?"

His anger boiling over, he rose from his chair and strode to the sink, above which hung a small mirror. He wrenched it from the wall and brought it over to her.

"Take a look in that," he said harshly, thrusting it under her nose. "What do you see? Eh? Eh?" He took on a mincing, pseudo-genteel tone. "A pretty, pink-and-white little beauty? Ha!" His voice returned to its former harshness. "Or a great gawk of a girl who'll be lucky if a man so much as looks at her? Go on, tell me which. Go on, girl."

"A – A great gawk—" began Ruth tremulously at last, beginning to cry.

He snatched the mirror away from her.

"So don't tell me what man you'll have or not have. I've agreed with Eli. You're a big, strong girl – just the sort he wants to look after him and his mother and have his children. He's got no fancy notions about beauty. All he wants is a workhorse. I'd have thought you'd be grateful, a godly man like him."

"I – I don't like him," Ruth whispered. They sounded such feeble words; there were none she knew that could begin to describe the loathing she felt for him. Her father braced his arms on the table and brought his face close to hers.

"You – don't – like – him?" His face was distorted and she shrank away from him in fear, shaking her head.

A stinging blow made her head ring and she gave a cry, quickly stifled. Her father looked at her in disgust, and returned to his chair.

"You'll like the man God's chosen for you, my girl. Stop snivelling and get upstairs to your mother. She needs you. She's brought up blood again, all over the quilt."

Blood. Sitting in the wood so many years later, Ruth seemed to see it ebbing and flowing like the waves on a beach. She recognised it as part of her nightmare; she had been running from it. Or towards it. She couldn't remember.

Either way, it had been a reality then. She knew that now, and remembered that she had grown accustomed to washing sheets and mopping the floor, while each day saw her mother weaker and more helpless, more wracked with pain. These days she talked more and more of dying, of her wish to die.

"Bleach'd do it," she said to Ruth on that occasion, seeing her swab the floor having added bleach to the water. "Just put the bottle close and leave the rest to me."

But Ruth had clutched the bottle and looked at her in anguish.

"I can't do it, Mother. I can't!"

"But look at me! There ent no hope for me, Ruthie. I can't do anything for myself any more. No strength even to reach the basin."

"Don't ask me, Mother."

It was, in fact, one of Thora's better times. They sometimes descended on her still, giving her momentary peace.

"Do something for me, Ruthie," she said now.

"What?" Ruth was still cautious.

"Bring me some paper and something to write with. I must say goodbye to Ben. You'll post the letter for me, won't you? There'll be a stamp in the drawer, maybe, where your father keeps the milk records."

"Tomorrow morning, when he's out I'll find one."

"Good girl. You can post it when you go to school."

"I'm not going to school any more, Mother. I told you, I've left. Anyway, 'tis summer holidays."

"So 'tis. I'm all at sea!" Thora managed a ghost of a grin. "Prop me up, there's a love, and I'll write the letter. Poor Ben," she added. "He'll be some sad when he hears. Oh, I'd dearly love to see him."

It was only a short letter, less than a page. Ruth found an envelope and addressed it, whisking all evidence out of the way in case her father should take the unlikely step of coming to see his wife. He sometimes, though not always, looked in for a few minutes after he came in from the yard, but unless Eli Dowrick paid a visit he stayed away thereafter and relied on Ruth to see to her needs. It had been days since Thora had been able to come downstairs, though there were times when she moved about her room or on the landing.

"Where's Eric to, Ruth?" she asked now. "He'm not been near me these past two days. He'm all right, ent he?"

"Oh yes, he'm all right." Ruth spoke with some venom. She was jealous and resentful of Eric's friends and his new activities. Once they had been so close. Once he wouldn't have gone anywhere without asking her if she thought he should, or telling her all about it afterwards. Now he was up and off the moment he was at leisure, shutting her out of his life, not telling her anything. "I don't know where he'm to these days. You'd think he'd want to stay with you," she added, as if this was the reason for her annoyance.

"I'm sorry, Ruthie. You'm left to do everything. It's too bad. Still," Thora added after a moment, "don't be too hard on Eric. He'm a soft-hearted soul and it grieves him terrible to see me suffering. You've always been the strong one – and after all, 'tis woman's work, tending the sick."

"Tidn't right," Ruth said sulkily.

"I'm sorry," her mother said again. She was silent for a while and seemed to have lapsed into a light, uneasy sleep, small tics and twitches chasing themselves over her papery cheeks. Then she opened her eyes. "Ruthie – you'll mind what I said about Eli, won't you? About when I'm gone? Don't let your father push you together, or you'll have as bad a life as I have."

"He says – he says I must."

"Well, I say you mustn't! For me – well, I used to think 'twas punishment. Now I don't know. I don't think the Lord would punish me as much as this, no matter if my sins were as scarlet. But never mind about me – you'm at the beginning of your life and I won't have you spoiling the rest of it by tying yourself to that monster. I won't have it!"

And when, Ruth thought miserably, had anything her mother thought been of any account? It was her father's will that prevailed, and always had.

"Why should the Lord want to punish you at all, Mother?" she asked. "You never sinned. You've always been good."

"Oh no, Ruthie. You don't know the truth. It was a long time ago, before – before Eric was born."

"Well, if you repent, then you'm forgiven. That's what the Bible says."

Thora closed her eyes for a moment.

"Trouble is," she said faintly. "I don't know whether I repent or no." She opened them again and looked at Ruth. "Sometimes I do, and sometimes I think—" she hesitated before finishing the sentence. "Sometimes I think, thank God I had *that*! Do you understand, Ruthie?" Bewildered, Ruth shook her head without speaking. "Then I'll tell ee," her mother said at last. "As a warning. Before I was married I fell in love. The man – oh, he wasn't much good really, not much of a

291

man. I know that now, but he was tall and strong and handsome and he was the sun and the moon and the stars to me. I loved him with all my heart, and he said he loved me. I let him . . ." she hesitated, the matter not being one she had ever discussed with her daughter. "I let him have his way," she went on. "And by the time I found I was having his baby he'd gone and I never saw un again until the time he walked into my kitchen a few years back. You remember—"

"I remember," Ruth said. "The man from Australia."

"Ken." Thora was silent for a long time while Ruth, frowning, took in the meaning of what she had been told.

"So Eric . . ." she began, then paused, biting her lip. "Did Father know?" she asked at last.

Thora smiled faintly.

"Oh yes," she said, her voice hesitant and breathy. "He knew. He rescued me from disgrace and humiliation. That's the way he saw it – and I suppose 'tis the way I saw it, too, if I'm to be honest. My father certainly did. My mother was dead by then. She might have had something to say – who knows? 'Twas a convenient way out."

"Yes." Ruth could see that it would be. A baby out of wedlock was still the cause of whispered outrage and ostracism.

"So you see," Thora went on, "I really was a sinner. Your father has never let me forget it." She gave a breath of bitter laughter. "That's why you should never marry a man who sees himself as virtuous, Ruth. He won't see any sin in himself, but he'll never let you forget yours."

"Father's changed so," Ruth said after a moment. "He was always strict, but now—"

"'Tis the power, Ruthie. Having his own meeting. Being able to stand up and preach and tell folks what to do, with them all looking at him and saying 'Amen'. When we went to chapel, 'tis true he was much the same, but then Mr Pavey was the boss, and any power he had was because Mr Pavey said so. Now he'm the boss, and 'tis gone to his head. But Ruthie—" she struggled to sit up a little as if to underline her words. "Don't let him put you off our Heavenly Father, there's a good girl. We'm all sinners, save one. Look at Jesus, not Thomas Teague. Mind what I say now – I'll not have you losing faith."

"I won't, I promise. Mother – does Eric know?"

Thora looked at her daughter and reached out to touch her.

292

"He does," she said. "I told him a few nights back, the last time he came to see me. And do you know? He already knew! He's been seeing Ken – his father. He's a grand chap, he says, full of talk and laughter, just the way I remember him—"

Ruth, in stunned silence, stared at her. Eric knew! He had known this shattering fact for days – weeks, maybe, and he had said nothing to her, though they had always shared secrets, shared everything. It was betrayal, nothing less.

Thora slumped back on her pillows, aware of nothing but her own pain and exhaustion. "I'll sleep now, love. I've worn myself out, talking. No need for you to stay."

For a moment Ruth hesitated. What should she do? Where should she go? It was hard to think clearly with such anger and resentment boiling inside her. She reviewed the alternatives; sit with her father in the kitchen, or go to her comfortless bedroom? The parlour, never used, was an option that simply didn't occur to her.

Since her mother's illness, one of Thomas's flock had donated an old armchair, that was now beside the window. She crossed the room and sat down in it.

"I'll stay here," she said. And to the accompaniment of her mother's troubled breathing and her own bleak despair, she sat and watched the swooping bats and the gathering dark, and the waves that hurled themselves against the far cliff.

"Have you decided what you're going to wear?" Lucy asked.

"Not really." Emma was reaching into the cupboard, bringing out odd, unrelated garments and strewing them on the bed. "I thought maybe this skirt and *this* top, plus the feather boa."

"It'll look great." There was a wistful note in Lucy's voice, for she could think of nothing in her own wardrobe that would strike a similarly fashionable note.

"On the other hand, I did bring this dress, just in case I had a chance to wear it. What do you think? Do you like it?"

"Oh, it's brilliant! But wouldn't your mum mind you wearing it?"

"Why should she?" Emma held the garment up against her. It was black, slinky, the hemline falling in ragged points. "I bought it in Oxfam with my own money."

"Well, it's a bit . . ." Lucy fell silent, not knowing quite how to describe it, but recognising that her own mother would bar it from the house, or at least, from anything other than the dressing-up box. "It's brilliant," she said again, more enviously than ever.

"I'll try them both on and see. Hey—" Emma flung down the dress and held up a brief garment, little more than a frill with narrow shoulder straps. "Do you want to borrow this, Luce?"

"Gosh, *could* I?"

"Why not?" Emma tossed it over. "Try it on. It'd look good with those white pants of yours. I thought I'd wear it myself at first, but then I thought the black one would look better with the skirt."

"Are you going to wear those silver earrings?"

"I thought these, actually." Emma peered into the mirror, holding two long black tassels up to her ears. "What do you think, Luce? Are they a bit OTT?"

"No, they'll look great." Lucy hesitated a moment. "I say, Em, can I borrow the silver ones?"

"Sure." Emma sounded distrait, as if something worrying had occurred to her. She sighed. "I do hope Sophie likes those earrings we bought her. It's not a very original present, is it? I bet she's got thousands of pairs. Maybe we should have bought that belt."

"She's probably got thousands of belts, too."

"I suppose so." Emma sat on the bed amid the clothes and pondered the matter. "Mustn't it be peculiar, having everything you want?" she said. "I can't imagine it, can you?"

Lucy, trying on Emma's proffered top, shook her head as she looked at herself in the mirror.

"Not for a minute," she said. "I can always think of something." And would be able, she reflected, to think of a whole lot more after this association with Emma. She was appalled at the deficiencies of her wardrobe – of her *life!* "She jolly well ought to like the earrings," she went on, returning to the original subject. "They cost enough."

"I don't suppose for one minute she appreciates the value of money." Emma sounded prim and mildly censorious.

"I don't suppose we would if we were as rich as she is," Lucy pointed out. "Oh, I can't *wait* for tomorrow night. Do I look all right in this?"

"Great," Emma assured her. She couldn't help thinking, though, that it was probably just as well that Uncle Leo wouldn't be there to see it.

Lynn and Leo left for North Devon soon after breakfast on Wednesday morning, waved off by the rest of the family. The children had not been told the real reason for this excursion, but believed it to be some kind of early wedding anniversary celebration. Lynn had persuaded Leo that it would be time enough to tell them that their familiar way of life might be coming to an end once the proposal had been thoroughly investigated.

"All I ask," Leo said, without preamble, once they were out on the main road, "is that you look at the whole question with an open mind."

"I've said I will," Lynn replied.

In the intervening days since Leo's revelation, discussion of the matter had been deliberately restricted, partly because of the children's presence, and partly because any such discussion inevitably ended with them agreeing that it was pointless to get heated until they had seen the place for themselves. In spite of which, Lynn had to work very hard not to get heated. She hated the thought of Leo's new job no less now than when it had first been mentioned; more, perhaps. All that togetherness! She felt quite certain that she would find it unbearably suffocating – but how she could ever put this point to her doting, devoted husband, she couldn't think. How did you tell someone you loved and who loved you that you needed, sometimes, space to do your own thing, however trivial?

"We think we've got problems," Kate said to Oliver as they watched them go.

"We're going to sort them out, aren't we?" At this moment, Oliver could spare no thought for Leo's heart-searchings.

Kate, so well-versed in the theory of reconciliations, so ill-prepared to put them into practice on her own account, didn't look at him.

"You tell me," she said, as she walked away.

Oliver would have gone after her, but was interrupted by William who had returned having, as if by way of farewell, performed what looked like a Maori war dance in the wake of his parents' car.

"What are we going to do, Uncle Oliver? Any hope of water-skiiing?"

"None whatsoever," Oliver said. "We'll stay on our beach today. The tide'll be right for a swim in about an hour."

"OK," said William, resignedly. "I expect Paul and Daniel will come down."

"Well, I wish they wouldn't." James joined them, kicking at a stone. "I've had enough of them. I had *more* than enough of them yesterday."

"You and I can go fishing in the pools," said Oliver.

He would, normally, have been pleased at James's delighted acceptance of this suggestion – would, indeed, have made it with pleasure on his own account. He had a soft spot for James and was constantly amused by his solemnity and his thirst for facts.

Not today, however. Today he seriously wondered if he would ever find anything amusing again.

Ruth moved from Bal back to the stones beside the brook so that she had a clear view of the path through the wood; but still he didn't come. She began to get angry. It was always the same, she thought. Everything left to her, while he was out enjoying himself, knowing secrets, not telling her. What had happened to change things like this?

It wasn't right, or fair. She had always loved him. Loved him more than anyone. But he had left her, abandoned her, gone whoring after false gods, made her feel less than nothing.

He needn't think he was going to get away with it. There was always tomorrow.

The party occupied the thoughts of the girls all day, necessitating hair-washing, nail-painting, the application of face packs and slices of cucumber on their eyes, followed by several changes of heart about the clothes they should wear and, as a final touch once they were dressed and ready to go, a puff of Kate's *Ysatis*.

But at last it was time to leave, and Oliver bore them off towards Buena Vista and the night which they both seemed convinced would be the high spot of their lives.

"Who," he asked, bringing the car to a halt outside the house on the cliff, "is the follically-challenged dude in the pink shirt?"

Emma giggled.

"That's Mr Renshaw," she said.

He came over and greeted them in a lordly way, waving expansively towards the house from where the strains of pop music could already be heard.

"Come along, girls, come along – you'll find all the crowd inside," he said. "Can you manage to turn, old boy?" he added in Oliver's direction, thus succeeding in underlining the fact that he had no intention of asking him in for a drink despite the number of parked cars which surely implied that other parents were present. Other adults, anyway, unless the teenagers of Porthallic habitually drove Mercs and Porsches and Jaguars, which seemed unlikely.

"I expect I can manage. Be good, you two. And have a good time."

Mr Renshaw gave a snort of laughter.

"The response to that in my day would have been 'Make up your mind'," he said. "Take no notice of your father," he called jocularly after the girls, already disappearing inside. "You go and enjoy yourselves." He stooped down again to look at Oliver through the car window. "Have no fear, old boy. We'll take good care of them." He slapped his hand down twice on the roof as if in casual dismissal and without a backward glance turned to go inside once more.

You better had, old boy, Oliver said to himself as he reversed and returned up the narrow lane. He found – without good reason, he tried to convince himself – that he had taken an instant dislike to Mr Renshaw.

Once inside, the girls found that it was as much a party for Mr and Mrs Renshaw and their friends as it was for Sophie, though it was true that the usual crowd were there in full force. Emma picked out Jacko immediately. She could see him leaning against the balustrade on the pool terrace below, as always a little detached from the others. As she watched she saw him lift a hand, saw the glow of his cigarette. He was dressed more conventionally than she had ever seen him, in trendy light trousers and a dark shirt which somehow made him seem even older and more sophisticated than usual. Eddy, by contrast, was wearing a violent mauve and red shirt slashed with white that looked several sizes too big and somehow succeeded in making him look exactly what he was, a young and immature teenager dressed up for a party. Maybe someone had given the shirt to him for Christmas, Emma thought charitably. Not even Eddy would surely have chosen it for himself?

The girls went down the stone steps to join the teenagers on the lower level where a five-piece group was belting out dance music. The oldies were on the terrace above, near the bar – looking, Emma thought, if the roars of laughter and the uninhibited behaviour was anything to go by, as if they had been there for some time, drinking freely. Mrs Renshaw – Suzi, as she begged everyone to call her – was dressed in a slinky oyster pink satin sheath with narrow shoulder straps that showed off every curve of her delectable body to perfection.

"She doesn't really look like a mother, does she?" Lucy whispered as they went down the steps. Emma considered this as inane a remark as any she had heard, and forbore to reply to it. Maybe in darkest Worcestershire mothers were all cosy and frumpish, but in London they could be actors or models or anything.

It was a wonderful backdrop for a party. Darkness had not yet fallen, but the clouds that had threatened a storm all day had cleared and stars were beginning to appear in the sky. The sea was an improbable shade of gold. It occurred to Emma that maybe the Renshaws were so rich, they'd managed to get it coloured like that especially for the occasion. Both terraces were ringed with light, the top one, from down below, looking as if it floated in space. Emma felt a *frisson* of excitement at the sight of it; this had to be the most glamorous party that ever was.

Sophie looked glamorous, too, in a kind of gold pleated floaty top and harem pants – maybe the sea had been ordered to match, Emma thought – and was holding court down here just as her mother was doing above. She was busy opening presents and screaming with delight and hugging people. She hugged Emma and Lucy, too, when she opened the box containing the earrings, but Emma could see that in spite of the fact that they really cost a lot more than she and Lucy could afford, still they were pretty poor compared with most of the other birthday gifts – except, perhaps, for the present from Stig, who had given her a mug with her name painted on it of the kind that hung outside every gift shop in Porthallic, price two pounds fifty. Still, he got just as big a scream and a hug as anyone else, so maybe he'd done the sensible thing in buying something commensurate with his means.

Jacko had given her a picture, painted by himself. After Sophie had duly screamed her thanks and put it aside, Emma picked it up and looked at it. It was a seascape, painted from almost this position, with the stone balustrade in the foreground.

"Like it?" Jacko had appeared at her side. "Pretty, isn't it?"

"It's lovely."

"Much better than the other one."

He was being sarcastic, she knew, and she hastened to correct his view of her artistic taste.

"Not better. Different. Easier to understand."

He gave a rather lofty smile at that, but he didn't pursue the matter, and taking the picture he put it down on the table with the other presents. "Come and dance while we can. Before the night's out the oldies will all be down here and there won't be room for the likes of us."

"Who are they all? They don't live here, do they?"

"They're pals of Suzi's, down from London. Mostly showbiz," he added casually, as if he hobnobbed with such people every day of the week and was not at all impressed by them. "Suzi used to be an actress herself, you know."

"Gosh," said Emma, forgetting to be sophisticated.

"I'll tell you something else," he said, pulling her close so that he could whisper in her ear. "You could be in showbiz yourself. You look gorgeous."

"Thank you," she said coolly. "You look pretty good, too."

She had to turn away to hide her grin of sheer, unadulterated bliss. It wouldn't do for him to know that he had just made her the happiest girl in the entire universe, and that this was being, without any doubt at all, the very best night of her life.

"I've got misgivings," Oliver said to Kate when he got back from delivering the girls. "I wish they weren't staying the night."

Kate looked surprised.

"Why? It's what they do these days."

"I know. I just didn't take to Renshaw *père*."

"You liked Renshaw *mère*, all right!"

"So did you, as I recall. She even had old Leo drooling a bit, didn't she?"

"Leo wouldn't look twice at anyone other than Lynn."

Kate was still distant, still unfriendly. He put his hands on her shoulders and turned her to face him.

"Look," he said. "You said yourself we had to talk. Get mad at me. Curse and swear and hit me over the head. Just don't ignore the situation! You've hardly said a word to me all day."

Kate ducked away from him.

"It's no use, Oliver. I can't think of anything except that I'm hurt. That you hurt me. I can't go on saying that over and over again."

"And I can't go on saying I'm sorry. That I never wanted to hurt you. You know that's true."

"Do I? I don't know that I do."

"For God's sake—" He went over to the cupboard where they kept the drink and reached for the whisky; but having taken out the bottle he put it down on the table without opening it. "Maybe I won't have a drink," he said. "Just in case Emma phones and says they want to be picked up tonight after all."

"You really are worried, aren't you?" Kate, jolted out of her own preoccupations, stopped putting the remains of their supper away and looked at him anxiously. "What happened back there?"

"Nothing, really. Just a sort of instinct that this wasn't the usual sort of kids' party."

"Well, they have got beyond the conjurer and Ronald McDonald stage—"

"I didn't mean that. I just got the feeling that it was going to be more adult and sophisticated than we realised. There were a whole load of expensive cars with London numberplates outside."

"That doesn't necessarily mean they were all inside swilling champagne and shooting up—"

"I know that. It's just that . . ." he shook his head. "Oh, forget it. I'm sure they're all right, really. Anyway, Emma's got her head screwed on the right way."

He had, however, succeeded by this time in infecting Kate with his doubts.

"I'm not sure we can say the same for Lucy," she said. "My God, if anything happened to her, Leo will never forgive us."

"I'll never forgive myself—"

"If you feel as strongly as this, you shouldn't have left them there."

"Shouldn't have left them? Are you crazy?" He gave an incredulous laugh. "There were lights and music pouring out, and all their friends inside, not to mention the fact that they've been preparing for it all day! It would have taken a better man than I am to turn around and bring them home."

"Yes, I suppose so. Well, it's pointless worrying. Emma knows she can always phone us if there's any trouble."

She went out of the kitchen to join the boys in the sitting room where they were watching television, and after a few moments, Oliver went, too. He felt, obscurely, a little more hopeful. At least they'd had a conversation consisting of more than three words. It was, he felt, a beginning.

Later, when they had gone silently to bed and Kate had settled down to sleep with her back firmly turned towards him, he acknowledged that there was still a long way to go. Contrary to his usual custom, he found it impossible to sleep. There was simply too much on his mind: guilt, regret, anxiety. Anxiety about the future – his and Kate's; anxiety about Emma and Lucy. Even, to his fury, anxiety about Caroline. Had he been right, making her stay in Germany when she wanted to come home? Sure, she sounded happy now – but what about this super guy she'd mentioned when they'd last spoken? He could be anybody. How the hell did they know who she was mixing with, how she spent her time? Suppose, in her unhappiness, she'd turned to someone totally unsuitable?

He told himself to shut up, to stop behaving like Leo, but it had little effect. Sleep remained elusive.

"I wish," Kate said, her voice coming out of the darkness with a cutting edge, "that you could suffer insomnia quietly! Why do you have to sigh and thresh about like that?"

"Sorry." He turned on his back, forced himself to lie still.

"Are you still worried?" she asked, her tone marginally more sympathetic.

"What do you think? Kate, what's going to happen?" He turned to her and tried to take her in his arms, but she remained rigid and unresponsive. "I couldn't bear it if we didn't get over this."

She sighed.

"I expect we will," she said, dully. "Eventually. People do. You'll have to give me time."

"I'm so sorry—"

"So you keep saying."

He was silent for a while. In spite of the worry over Kate, he could not rid himself of his other worries; namely, Emma and Lucy.

"I keep thinking that maybe I should go out there."

"To the Renshaws?" Kate was sufficiently astonished to lift up her head to look at him. "You can't, Oliver. The girls would be mortified."

"I know. It's just that I can't help wondering—" he left the sentence hanging, and forgetting other troubles, forgetting that for the past two days they had circled round each other, never touching, Kate reached over the expanse of mattress and took hold of his arm.

"What's got into you?" she said, her voice more gentle than it had been for some time. "I'm the one who worries. You're the one who soothes."

"That's right." He laughed ruefully. "I seem to have forgotten my role. It's just that they looked so vulnerable, so heart-breakingly young in their grown-up clothes and dangly earrings. I wanted to grab that smug bastard Renshaw by the throat and yell at him that if he allowed one hair of their heads to be harmed, I'd tear him limb from limb."

Kate made no comment, and the silence between them lengthened.

"I wonder what Anna would have to say about that?" she said at last. "I expect she'd laugh at you for being overprotective."

"What Anna would have to say is a matter of supreme indifference to me," said Oliver. There was silence again from Kate. And then she sighed.

"I can't tell you how I want to believe you," she said.

Emma, watching the fireworks from the top terrace, Jacko's arm around her, felt drunk with excitement and the beauty of it all. Not with anything else. She'd stuck to the non-alcoholic fruit punch, more because she liked it than for any other reason; which was more, she noted, than most of the adults had done. Or many of the teenagers, come to that.

The fireworks, set off from a large raft some way offshore, sent jets of coloured lights soaring into the sky to burst with a crack and come cascading down again, spinning and whirling and flowering in the night sky, criss-crossing like magical searchlights. On their own they

302

would have been intoxicating enough. Seen here, with Jacko, the whole occasion was something she knew she would never forget.

There was a universal sigh of regret when they were over and a few moments of anticlimax, but then the band started up again and people began to dance. There was, as Jacko had predicted, more toing and froing between the two levels now, with the oldies coming down to dance – or trying to. Most of them, Emma thought scornfully, as she gazed down on them, had absolutely no idea – though it had to be admitted that Mrs Renshaw – try though she might, Emma couldn't think of her as Suzi – was jolly good.

"She's a doll, isn't she?" Jacko said.

"Who's the guy she's dancing with?" He was dishy in a rather Hugh Grantish kind of way, Emma thought. He held a champagne bottle in one hand and drank from it as he danced.

Jacko could shed no light on his identity.

"I expect he's one of her actor friends," he said. "Hey – look down there at Mr Renshaw."

Emma looked and saw their host, standing tensely beside the lower balustrade with his back to the sea, arms folded. He was clearly illuminated by one of the torch-shaped lamps, and even at a distance seemed to give an impression of smouldering anger.

"I don't like him awfully, do you?" she said.

"He's a shit," Jacko said forcefully. "Sophie hates him. Look – he's decided to wade in and pull Suzi away from that creep."

"How awful!" Emma's excitement evaporated a little. "There's not going to be a fight or anything, is there?"

"Maybe not. Maybe lover-boy will just get chucked in the pool. It doesn't matter much, because they'll all be in the pool, drunk as skunks, by the end of the night."

But nothing dramatic happened at this juncture. Suzi left the improvised dance floor, laughing immoderately at her husband's annoyance, kissing him and patting him on the head as if he were an engaging small boy, and together they walked away from it, arms around each other. Emma let out a breath of relief. She hated rows and violence and unpleasantness. She had never been used to such things, and on the few occasions she had come across them, they made her feel physically sick. It was the same with Lucy, she knew.

Which reminded her – Lucy! Where was she? She had been standing near when the fireworks started, but she and Eddy had wandered away somewhere and now were nowhere to be seen.

"Did you see where Eddy and Lucy went?" she asked Jacko, but he laughed and shook his head.

"Don't worry about them!"

"But I promised my folks to keep an eye on her."

"They're OK. They're probably dancing."

They weren't, but Stig and Polly were, and when Jacko and Emma joined them Stig organised a ridiculously juvenile game of musical tag that caused so much laughter that Emma rapidly forgot her responsibilities. At last the band took a break and subsided into silence, and Emma, once more, remembered Lucy.

"Where do you think they are?" she asked Jacko; and turning to the others, asked them too. "Did anyone see where Lucy and Eddy got to?"

Stig laughed.

"Have a heart, Emma. Give them a break. They've probably found a nice quiet grotto somewhere."

With warning bells ringing, Emma left the group and went up to the top terrace. The Hugh Grant almost-look-alike was propping up the bar, still drinking champagne, talking in a loud, affected voice about what Ken and Em had to say to him about producing Shakespeare and how Larry would have adored Ken's interpretation of *Henry V*.

"Stupid prick," said Jacko in Emma's ear. She hadn't realised that he had followed her, but felt glad that he had.

"Where can they be?" she said worriedly. "You know the place better than I do."

"They won't thank you for chasing after them."

"Look, Lucy's just a kid! She's not fourteen yet—"

Jacko looked astonished.

"Really? She looks older."

"Well, she's not. And it's not as if she knows her way about. She's led a very sheltered life."

"Haven't we all?"

"I'm serious, Jacko! I'm under strict instructions to look after her. And I don't trust Eddy."

"Eddy's all right." Jacko automatically leapt to his friend's defence, but Emma thought she could detect a slight note of unease in his voice.

Wide French windows opened onto the terrace from the sitting room. Some of the adult guests had retired here from the evening chill, Emma saw as she entered it. One couple, oblivious of anyone else, were half lying on one of the satin-covered sofas, kissing passionately. A handsome, elderly man whom Emma vaguely recognised as having appeared for a time in a soap opera was weaving unsteadily, glass in hand, from one side of the room to another, his eyes fixed on a young girl with legs up to her armpits and a skirt no longer than the average pelmet. Another exotic-looking woman was engaged in telling fortunes while a lone, white-faced, kohl-eyed girl solemnly gyrated in a weird, spaced-out dance for one.

"The lunatics have taken over the asylum," Jacko said derisively, looking at them from the threshold.

"Come on – where might they be?"

As if on cue, a door at the end of the room opened and Sophie came in, looking agitated. Her eyes alighted on Emma with relief.

"I was coming to look for you," she said. "Lucy doesn't seem very well—"

Hurriedly Emma followed her out of the room and along a passage to the front hall. From there they went up the open-tread staircase to an upstairs corridor.

"What's wrong? What's happened?"

"She's been awfully sick – probably eaten something . . ."

"Or drunk something?" Jacko suggested.

Eddy was standing on the wide, upstairs landing looking dishevelled and unlike himself in a way Emma immediately recognised.

"You're high," she said accusingly. "What have you done with Lucy? If you've given her—"

"She's OK! Chill out!" He smiled vaguely and Emma pushed past him, through the door that stood open behind him. Lucy was inside, sitting on the bed, crying helplessly.

Emma went over, and taking her by the shoulders, shook her vigorously.

"What have you been doing, you dope?" she demanded. "Didn't I tell you—" She broke off at the sight of Lucy's woebegone face as her cousin looked up. "Oh, Luce," she said, sitting down beside her on the bed. "What's been going on?" But Lucy's only reply was to cry all the harder.

Outside the door, Jacko was talking softly to Eddy, laughing with him, sharing a joke.

"I feel awful," Lucy groaned at last. "Oh Em, I've been so sick. I think I'm going to die."

"What have you taken, Luce? Tell me," Emma went on, shaking her again.

Jacko appeared in the doorway.

"From what I can gather, it was the booze that made her throw up," he said. "Eddy thought it would be a jolly wheeze to pour rum into her fruit punch. Then he gave her a drag on his cigarette—"

"What sort of cigarette?" Emma asked, immediately suspicious. "Do you mean pot?"

"Can't you smell it?" Jacko asked, amusedly raising an eyebrow.

Emma sniffed.

"Yes, I can, now you mention it. But that smell's downstairs, too. And I don't think it's funny," she added fiercely, seeing the grin on Jacko's face.

"Everybody's doing it," he said. "Just put her to bed. She'll sleep it off. It's no big deal."

"How can you *say* that? I could *kill* Eddy!"

"I just meant . . ." Jacko lifted his shoulders and his hands to heaven in exasperation. "It's no big deal, Emma. I mean, let's face it, she's not going to wake up addicted to crack, is she? She's got to grow up some time. Just put her to bed."

Emma stood up.

"Well, sorry," she said. "I just happen to think it is a big deal. Whatever your moronic friend gave her, he only had one thing in mind – getting her paralytic! I never did trust him as far as I could throw him. Look at her! She's just a kid."

"Well, just be thankful he got too spaced out himself to have his wicked way with her. It could be worse."

"I want to go home," Lucy moaned miserably.

"Well, you can't!" If there was one thing Emma was sure of, it was that. She'd never have any freedom again if this episode ever came to light. She looked around for Sophie. "Where are we supposed to sleep? No one's told us."

Sophie, it seemed, had gone downstairs again to rejoin the party, thankfully shrugging off responsibility now that reinforcements had turned up to look after Lucy.

"The girls usually sleep in the big room at the end of the passage," Jacko said. He went along to look, and came back again. "Yeah, that's it. They've moved in extra beds. Only thing is, Karen and Jaffa have got there before you and they're in one of them. I don't suppose they'll bother you."

"Are you out of your mind?" Emma asked him, forcefully. "Go and chuck them out!"

Jacko looked at her, his eyes suddenly hard and cold. She was aware of a sinking of the heart. He's gone off me, she thought. He only likes people who admire him and tell him how great he is. He doesn't like being told what to do.

"I suggest you chuck them out yourself," he said. He looked at her with his small, superior smile and left her to it.

Beryl Cornthwaite had been annoyed since suppertime, and getting into bed next to Arthur's bulky recumbent form, she was still grumbling.

"You'd think she'd have the courtesy to *say*, wouldn't you? Just not turning up isn't right. I'll have to charge her for it."

"I expect she met a friend," said Arthur.

"Friend? Her?" Beryl snorted derisively. "She hasn't got a friend in the world, for all she says she used to live here. Move over, Arthur, do – you haven't left me an inch. Oh, leave off – I'm too tired!"

"'Night, then." Arthur, always, was easily dissuaded from amorous advances.

"It's not as if," Beryl continued after a moment's silence, "I ever get a thank you from her. A lovely bit of lamb breast it was last night – a bit fatty, but ever so tasty. Honestly, she hardly touched it! Anything wrong, Ruth? I says, and she just stares at me with that peculiar look of hers as if she couldn't understand a word I said. She gets me down, she does, straight. Thank goodness I've only got another two days of it, that's what I say."

"Soon be over," murmured Arthur, pacifically.

"I do my best," Beryl went on querulously. "I try to ring the changes. Not one of my guests can say different. Breast of lamb last night, lasagne tonight, cod tomorrow, chicken pieces Friday. Valerie was only complimenting me tonight. Say what you like, there aren't many places you'd find as much variety."

A faint snore from Arthur was the only reply, and Beryl lapsed into a disgruntled silence. She *was* tired, that was no word of a lie, and who could wonder at it?

Roll on winter, she thought.

Karen and Jaffa had been smoking pot too, and the bedroom was full of its pungent aftermath. They had been in a giggly mood and had laughed helplessly when they looked up to see Emma standing over them like an avenging angel. The giggles had slowly died, however, when they realised she was serious in asking them to leave. They didn't mind having other people in the room, they said. It wouldn't bother them in the slightest.

"It would bother me," she told them. "Find somewhere else." And eventually, her determination had succeeded in persuading them to go and look, very unwillingly, for other accommodation.

It was almost more difficult getting Lucy undressed and into bed. She had been sick once more – fortunately in the bathroom, so it might have been worse – and was still sobbing dismally, her limbs as uncoordinated as if she had been a rag doll; however, this task, too, was accomplished in time, whereupon she lay down and fell instantly asleep.

Emma recognised that Jacko was right; Lucy's troubles were probably more due to liquor than to anything else and she would be all right after a night's sleep. Well, she'd probably have a hangover, but that would serve her right.

That, Emma thought, was hardly the point. The point was that Jacko had cared more about his own ego than about anything else. The fact that Lucy was so young and that she was responsible for her simply hadn't registered with him.

He didn't give a damn for her, that was the truth of it; all he'd liked was her admiration. He was Jacko – the aloof, intelligent, superior Jacko – and no one, she now saw, was allowed to criticise him or tell

308

him what to do. Well, she had news for him. She thought his precious picture was crap, prize or no prize.

Certain crashes and shouts coming from somewhere below the bedroom's open window caused her to draw the curtain aside and look out. She found she had a good view of the bottom terrace where, currently, Mr Renshaw appeared to be having a fight with the Hugh Grant look-alike. One or two other men were getting involved, trying to keep the protagonists apart. Some of the women were screaming; others were laughing.

As she watched, the laughter appeared to become predominant. There were splashes as people jumped or fell or were pushed into the pool. She saw Jacko, standing to one side. She couldn't see his face, but she knew he would be smiling at their folly. I was as wrong about him as Lucy was about Eddy, she thought.

For some time she looked at him; then she let the curtain drop and turned away from the window. She might just as well go to bed, too, she thought. The party was over.

14

After one of the hottest nights of the summer, Thursday's sky was overcast, the sea a flat, metallic silver with hardly a ripple on it.

"They say the hot spell's coming to an end," Kate said. "Storms are forecast for tonight."

It seemed for the moment, hotter than ever, however, with no breeze to stir the branches of the sycamore tree. The boys, joined by Paul and Daniel, were content to sit at the table on the terrace playing Monopoly. Kate, too, was disinclined to stir very far, and it was left to Oliver to drive into Porthallic to buy milk and bread before going on to Buena Vista to pick up the girls.

Lynn and Leo were back in time for lunch. Kate looked searchingly at her sister as they got out of the car, but her expression gave nothing away – which in itself boded ill, Kate thought. If everything had worked out wonderfully well, Lynn would have come bouncing out of the car, grinning all over her face. As it was, both she and Leo remained silent on the subject of the proposed new job, devoting themselves to greeting the boys who leapt upon them as if they'd been absent for six months.

"Are the girls back?" Leo enquired as he came into the house.

"Just. Oliver got back with them about five minutes ago. They went straight upstairs, but no doubt they'll be down in a minute. They're all right," she added, seeing his anxious expression. "Honestly! They seem a bit tired, but what would you expect? I don't suppose they had much sleep."

"Nor did we," Lynn said, in a meaningfully casual kind of voice.

It wasn't until after lunch, however, that Kate learned the full story. She had gone up to the bedroom to fetch a book with which to while

311

away the lazy afternoon hours when Lynn came in after her, shutting the door and leaning against it in a conspiratorial fashion.

"Well?" Kate said.

"Oh, Kate!" For a moment Lynn said no more, letting her expression speak for itself. Then she came closer and sank down on the bed. "It was ghastly. I hated it!"

"Tell all," Kate said, sitting down beside her.

"Well, it's in a beautiful place, I have to admit, at the end of a valley with incredible views, not all that far from Barnstaple. An old manor house. Grey stone. Rather lovely, really."

"And—?" Kate prompted.

"It's pretty obvious why Leo wants to go there. You'd have thought he was Prince Charles the way they hung on his every word. Two of the staff members were with him in the Lake District, and the headmaster knows of him by repute, and they all think he's *wonderful*! If they'd had a red carpet, they would have laid it out, I can tell you. As it was they were all over him, laughing at his jokes and telling him how wonderful his ideas were, generally buttering him up."

"And he went for it in a big way?"

"Well, can you blame him? Anyone would. One of his gripes against Reitz-Keppel is that it's so big and impersonal now and none of the really top brass cares whether you live or die."

"So far," Kate said carefully, "I have to admit that it all sounds wonderful. But I gather it wasn't."

"Kate, I would *die*!" Lynn turned tragic eyes on her sister. "It's so claustrophobic. The headmaster's wife showed me round while the men were talking business – she knows her place, you see, such high-powered conversation wasn't for the likes of us – and she said that all the staff lived on the premises, either in flats at the top of the main house, or in houses around the grounds somewhere. They were all One Happy Family, she said. The wives take it in turns to drive each other into Barnstaple for shopping once a week, and of course there's a rota for the school run—"

"That seems sensible—"

"It's *awful*! Don't you see? You'd hate it too, having to do things by numbers, never feeling free to nip off somewhere on your own. And that's not all! Somewhere between showing me the games room and the

312

dormitories for the most disturbed boys, Gloria – the headmaster's wife – gave me a rundown on the private life of every member of staff – wives, children, lovers, the lot! You wouldn't be able to exchange a reproachful glance without everyone knowing, let alone have a row about anything. And you know Leo said there would be a job for me? Well, there would. Looking after the linen. But as Gloria gaily told me, just to sugar the pill, I'd be a kind of surrogate mother as well, with plenty of Opportunity for Service on my own account." Close to tears, she fell silent, adding after a moment, "I'd die, Kate."

"Have you told Leo?" Kate asked. Lynn shook her head.

"I said I would have to think about it. He loved it so much, I didn't have the heart. He was full of it – couldn't stop talking about it all the way home. Opportunities for Service are just what he wants. Bloody Gloria took us to see the house they were thinking of giving us, and it was a modern, characterless box with a pocket-handkerchief garden, but all Leo went on about was the view and how convenient that there was a utility room. As if I give a stuff about a utility room!"

"Lynn, you've got to tell him how you feel."

"But how can I *do* it to him?"

"He said you'd have to agree."

Lynn gave a bitter laugh.

"I know. I know that's what he said. I was the one who was supposed to keep an open mind, but from the moment we went inside the place you'd think the whole thing was cut and dried, with nothing to talk about at all."

"You've still got to be honest with him. This is your life as well as his. Did you actually see the boys in question?"

"Oh, yes. They were everywhere. They seemed OK – I had nothing against them, poor little sods. I just don't want to be their surrogate mother or have to count their towels."

"Tell him," said Kate urgently.

When Doreen came downstairs and reported to Beryl that Ruth's bed hadn't been slept in, Beryl's main emotion was one of annoyance. What was the wretched woman playing at?

"She could have *said*," she grumbled. "What are we supposed to think? And will she be here for supper tonight, that's what I want to know."

"D'you think she's all right?" Doreen asked, her broad, kindly face creased with worry. "You don't think she could have gone wandering off somewhere? She's been acting ever so strange these last couple of days."

"You can say that again," Beryl agreed; but she was too busy checking the storecupboard to take much account of it, and when Arthur came in from the fishmonger's to say there was no cod but he'd managed to get some rock salmon, the subject of Ruth Kernow went right out of her head. It wasn't until after lunch that Doreen mentioned her again.

"No sign yet," she said. "I hope nothing's happened to her. You read such awful things."

For Beryl, taking a five-minute break with her feet up to relax with the *Sun*, the remark seemed horribly apropos. Even as Doreen spoke she was reading a lurid account of an elderly woman found bludgeoned to death on a building site in Birmingham. She lowered the paper and looked at Doreen.

"You don't think it could have done, do you? Not here! I mean, Birmingham, yes – but not Porthallic. This is a law-abiding sort of place."

Doreen looked dubious.

"I don't know so much about that. There was that poor old man over Truro who went missing. And that pensioner in Newquay, battered half to death for two pounds fifty. Nowhere's safe these days."

"D'you think I should tell the police, then? Arthur. Arthur!" She reached out with her foot and gave Arthur, still at the table and drowsing over his cigarette, a small but painful nudge. "Arthur, what do you think? Should we tell the police about Ruth Kernow? She didn't sleep here last night and there's been no sign of her this morning."

"She's probably found a boyfriend," Arthur said, wheezing at his own wit. For once Beryl failed to laugh.

"Leave off, Arthur. It's not funny. Something might have happened to her."

"It would take a brave man," Arthur said. "The size of her."

Frowning, Beryl took her feet from the footstool and folded the paper, preparing herself for decision-making.

"Maybe we should report it," she said, this conclusion bringing with it a not unpleasurable *frisson* of excitement. "Just to be on the safe side. I mean, you never know, do you? You could do it this afternoon, Arthur."

"There's no cop shop in Porthallic any more," Arthur pointed out, with a touch of triumph.

"You'll have to phone Truro then," said Beryl, undefeated.

James trailed after Leo as he headed in the direction of the sun lounger in the garden.

"Dad, come to the wood with me. I want to show you a place with lots of butterflies. Thousands and thousands."

But Leo had already stretched out next to Oliver, not really listening.

"Later, love," he said. "Teatime? It's a bit hot right now."

"Da-a-ad!"

"Why don't you go with the others? Look – Paul and Daniel have come to collect you."

"I want to go with you!"

"Well, give me an hour, there's a good boy. Your poor old dad feels like a bit of a rest – and I want to talk to Uncle Oliver."

James looked at him disconsolately for a moment, then seeing his cause was hopeless, trailed away again. He didn't want to play with the others. On the other hand, he didn't want to be left on his own. The grown-ups weren't being at all receptive this afternoon. Mum had gone and shut herself up with Auntie Kate, and Dad seemed unusually disinclined to devote himself to his sons' concerns. Even Lucy had told him to shove off. She wasn't, he thought, being nearly as nice down here now that she had Emma as she was when they were at home. On the whole, he rather felt that the holiday had gone on long enough. Maybe he'd get a book to read. On the other hand—

"Wills, wait for *me*," he yelled, suddenly making up his mind and sprinting after the others.

Leo's account of his visit to the Hockridge Centre, as confided to Oliver, differed markedly from Lynn's. The delightful atmosphere, charming surroundings, friendly staff, stimulating challenge were all described in detail. Even the house was reported as being not roomy, exactly, but plenty big enough, with a manageable garden.

"But you and Lynn love your garden," Oliver pointed out. "It's your hobby – a show place. Are you going to be able to bear to leave it?"

"It'll be a wrench, of course, but there would be compensations. We certainly wouldn't have much time for gardening at the Centre. It's more a seven-day-a-week job."

"What does Lynn think of that?"

"She hasn't said much," Leo admitted. "She wants time to think it over."

"Yes," said Oliver, thoughtfully. "Yes, I imagine she does."

Ruth hadn't meant to stay the night at Bal. After a day divided between dreaming and roaming the wood, she finally fell deeply asleep, lulled at last by the quiet. When she woke, it was almost dark and she felt cold. For a while she could not remember where she was or how she got there; but as she lay and listened to the scurryings of small creatures in the undergrowth and the calling of night birds, she remembered. At once a deep feeling of contentment – even euphoria – swept over her. She reached for the cardigan she always carried in her shoulder bag even in the hottest of weather and pulled it on, smiling to herself. She was, she felt, where she should be. Close to Eric.

She had told him, at the first opportunity, exactly what she thought of him for not sharing with her the secret of his parentage, but instead of being properly contrite he had grinned with the same kind of suppressed excitement that once he had kept for the sighting of a strange bird.

"'Tis the best news I ever had, Ruthie, that the old man's no father of mine."

"Well then, why didn't you tell me?"

She'd followed him to the top pasture where he'd gone to herd the cows back to the milking shed, and for a moment he didn't answer, concentrating on thwacking one recalcitrant animal with a switch to get her back on course.

"Ken said 'twas best I kept my mouth shut," he said at last. "Father'd stop me, else, miserable bugger."

"Stop you? Stop you doing what?"

"Meeting Ken, of course. And something else—" he broke off to

316

bring another cow back into line. "If I tell you something, you won't tell, will you?"

"I never tell on you."

"You promise?"

"Yes, I promise." Ruth was getting irritated. "What's the secret?"

Still he hesitated a moment.

"I'm going away," he said at last. She couldn't speak, but turned to him with her mouth open. "I was going to tell ee, Ruth, honest, but I couldn't risk the old man finding out. Ken said—"

"You can't go," Ruth said.

Eric laughed.

"Just watch me."

"What about Mother? 'Twould break her heart and you know it. How could you do it to her, Eric, when she'm so ill?"

Eric, grinning, whacked a cow's backside just for the pleasure of it.

"She knows," he said. " 'You go, son,' she says to me when I told her of it. 'You'll have a better life out there than ever you'll get here,' she says."

"Out where?" Ruth asked, knowing the answer already but dreading to hear it from his own lips.

"Australia, of course. With Ken. He'm a big man out there – owns land and that."

Ruth stared at him dumbly, unable for a moment to say a word.

"You can't go now," she said at last. "Not till after harvest. Father says he'll be starting on Two Acre field next week."

"Well, he'll have to hire someone else, won't un?" Eric chuckled, in the highest of spirits. "What do I care? He'm nothing to me now."

"But there's me, Eric," she said pleadingly, her voice shaking. "Don't go. Don't leave me."

He thwacked the cow again and said nothing, only whistled through his teeth. She looked at him and saw his excitement, his unyielding intent, and knew it was hopeless. Whatever she said, however much she begged him to stay, he was going.

For a few more yards she walked beside him, saying nothing; then without warning she darted through a gap in the hedge and ran away from him, instinctively heading for the place where she always went for comfort. Pedlar's Woods.

317

It had been August, then as now, with cow parsley frothing in the hedges, and patches of late honeysuckle, and the countryside in all its loveliness peaceful under a cloudless sky. There had been no peace in her heart then, however. There, in the privacy of the secret hide-out she had shared with her brother and with him alone, she flung herself down and wept with misery and rage, beating the hard earth with her clenched fists.

When at last the paroxysm of anger was over, she sat up and hugged her knees. She would have to put a stop to it somehow. But how? Should she tell her father? Would it do any good if she did? There'd be an almighty row, and Eric naturally dreaded the anger that would be unleashed just as he had always dreaded it; but who could say that at the end of it, he wouldn't still leave? He had changed. Grown more determined. He even had his mother's blessing, which was perhaps the worst thing of all. With her on my side, Ruth thought, we might have been able to stop him. Without her—

She covered her face and wept again. They would soon be without her for ever – and who would Ruth have then? Only her father, with his implacable determination to marry her off to Eli.

I would rather kill myself, she thought; and she looked up at the branches of the tree above her and thought how easy it would be, if she brought a rope. She could clamber up on one of the lower branches, fix the noose, and jump into a new world where all her troubles would be over.

It seemed, suddenly, the answer to everything. Jesus waited for her; death was nothing to fear. Not like Eli Dowrick. Some deep, primeval instinct made her fear him more than anything she had ever known.

That's what she would do, then. She would wait until her mother had gone before her, and then she would come here and take the same path, the path to glory. How easy, she thought, with gratitude. How easy it was all going to be, to leave this life behind. She would make all the preparations. Find a rope, hide it in the secret place, leave everything ready. And as she rose to go home, she found herself smiling, filled with a feeling of exaltation and power, realising at last that ultimately her destiny lay in her own two hands.

Over the evening meal, she saw Eric looking at her uneasily. She knew he was afraid she would tell, and it made her feel even more

318

powerful and mistress of the situation. Her father went upstairs for a few moments while Ruth cleared the table and washed the dishes, and instead of leaving the house at once, as he had been accustomed to do, Eric carried the used plates to the sink and hovered beside her uncomfortably.

"You ent going to tell, Ruthie, are ee?" he said.

"I promised, didn't I?"

"He couldn't stop me, but he'd have a damn good try." Ruth could sense him looking at her. "Tidn't that I want to leave ee," he added awkwardly.

"No?" She smiled a little as she added hot water from the kettle to the water in the bowl. She didn't believe him. It seemed to her now that he had left a long time ago – that he had never realised how much he meant to her. How without him life wasn't worth living.

He stood for a moment looking at her with dumb misery, not knowing what to say. Then he turned and left. Ruth heard the door bang behind him and without looking round, continued washing the dishes, the small, bitter smile still on her lips.

She realised later that she had not asked him when he was leaving and it was not until the following day that she had the opportunity to do so. He didn't answer directly, just looked secretive and said he didn't know. She didn't believe him. She knew that look – had seen it often enough, for it had been essential to his survival to lie frequently to his father. To the man he had always thought to be his father. He was lying now, she was certain of it. His plans were made. He knew exactly when he was going.

She didn't talk about it to her mother, mainly because Thora seemed to have taken a turn for the worse and was in constant, searing pain, unable to focus on the world outside herself – unable, even, to protest when Eli Dowrick came to lay his useless hands on her yet again and shout aloud for God to remove this devil from her.

Thomas Teague also did his share of petitioning the Almighty in his usual, hectoring way, while Ruth hovered on the landing outside the door, wringing agonised hands. Why couldn't they leave her in peace? she asked herself. Her mother could say her own prayers in her own way. This shouting was only hurting her more.

The men emerged at last, looking solemn and self-important, but she

noticed that no sooner were they walking down the passage away from
the bedroom than they were chatting about everyday affairs, as if the
grim tragedy in the bedroom was of no more importance than
harvesting the barley, or – in Eli's case – putting in a cupboard in Mrs
Ramsey's house over at Threemilecross.

"'Twill take a day or two," he was saying.

"'Tis a bravish step—"

"Ah, but Mr Borlase leaves me take the van, and keep it overnight."

"You should have saved your legs and come over here in it, Eli."

"More than my job's worth, Thomas. 'Tis meant for work, not
pleasure."

Pleasure? Did he regard it as pleasure, this forcing of his unwelcome
attentions on her poor mother?

I hate him, she whispered to herself. I hate him. She couldn't allow
her father to think she would ever marry him. Somehow she would
have to persuade him he needed her to stay at home. If only she could,
then she wouldn't have to kill herself – a solution that grew less
appealing the more she thought about it. And he did need her – that was
no word of a lie. She did all the housework now. Since she'd left
school, he'd said she didn't need the woman to do the washing any
more.

She said nothing then, for after Eli left, Thomas sat at the table and
immersed himself in preparing his sermon for Sunday; but when he sat
back at last, looking satisfied with his efforts, she took her courage in
both hands.

"Father," she said tentatively. "Mother's getting worse, isn't she?"

"What?" He was reluctant to tear his eyes away from the words he
had written. He tapped the page in front of him. "'Tis good stuff here,
Ruth. Inspired. Powerful. Straight from the heart."

"Mother's getting worse," Ruth repeated.

"'Tis God's will." He moved from the table and sat down in his chair
beside the range, easing his body into it, stretching his legs.

"And when she goes," Ruth went on, taking a step towards him,
"you'll need me to tend you and clean the house, like I do now. If I
marry Eli," she went on more urgently, "I'll not be here to look after
you. You'll need me, Father. You know you will." In the face of his
blank stare, she redoubled her efforts at persuasion. "Who'll do the

cooking if I'm not here? And the cleaning? And wash your clothes and make your bed and darn your socks, and look after the hens?" Her voice rose still further. "Who'll do all that, Father?"

Thomas Teague did not often laugh, but he laughed then.

"Need *you*?' he asked. "Need *you*? You'm mazed! I got other plans, girl. I'm a man in my prime, Ruth, with a man's needs—"

He fell silent suddenly, as if he had said more than he intended, and Ruth stared at him.

"You mean you'd get married again? But not at once, Father. Not for some time."

"Go and see to your mother," he said roughly. "I heard her call out."

Ruth looked at him helplessly, but did as she was told. She found her mother groaning; groaning and praying and feebly weeping. She dragged the armchair close to her, and stayed with her all night, not undressing, sleeping only intermittently. Still she rose to get breakfast for her father and Eric, cleaned the kitchen, made beds. It was later, halfway through the morning, feeling more dead than alive herself, that she went downstairs to fetch a bowl of warm water, and brought it upstairs to her bedroom. Hoping to revive herself a little, she stripped off her clothes and began to wash herself.

It was while she was engaged in this that she heard some kind of commotion in the yard outside – a car door slamming, voices raised. Her curiosity aroused, she stopped sponging herself and listened, but by the time she had made herself decent enough to look out of the window, all she could see was an unfamiliar truck disappearing up the lane. It was not until her father stamped into the kitchen at midday that she learned there had been a visit from Uncle Ben.

He was still raging with anger.

"I'll not have un here, stirring up trouble. Years ago, it was, I told un never to come."

"Does Mother know?" Ruth asked.

He paused, his pasty halfway to his lips, and glared at her.

"She does not, and you won't tell her. Like as not, she wouldn't take it in."

Maybe he was right about that, Ruth thought. And maybe not. Though for most of the time her mother was preoccupied with her own suffering, she had flashes of lucidity. Which would grieve her more: to

321

know that her brother had been at the farm within yards of her and yet had not been allowed to see her? Or to think that her letter had had no response from him?

She would think about it, Ruth decided. She still found herself with mixed feelings about Uncle Ben. He had, after all, wanted to take her mother away; even now she could feel the burning rage she had felt then. She looked at Eric, eating his pasty and taking his time about it as if anxious to spin out the brief break. I feel the same now about Eric, she thought miserably. He's going away, and I can't bear it.

Her father was shouting at him, telling him to hurry, telling him there was work to be done, the tractor to be fixed if they were to start harvesting next day as planned. But even after Thomas had stamped out of the kitchen, Eric lingered. Ruth was on her feet, clearing the table, but he caught her arm and pulled her round to face him.

"Ruthie," he whispered. "I've had word. We'm leaving tonight."

She had barely looked at him or spoken to him since he had broken the news of his impending departure, but now she stared at him.

"You can't. There's the harvest – the barley. He'm starting on Two Acre field tomorrow. He just said."

"Let him hire someone else." He stood up, took her by the shoulders. She looked into his face, on a level with her own, and saw that it was still the face she had always loved and protected, still the round, innocent face of a young boy for all he was seventeen and almost a man.

"What'll I do?" she said, blank with misery. "There'll be no one."

"You should leave, too."

"I've got nowhere to go. Don't leave me, Eric."

"I got to go. Even Mother sees that. Listen, Ruthie – he mustn't know, not till I'm gone. He can't bear the sight of me, but he pays me less than he'd pay anyone else, so he'd stop me if he could."

"So would I!"

"No, you wouldn't. I want you to help me. Please! You got to help me, Ruthie."

"I won't! Why should I?"

"Please, Ruthie! 'Tis for the last time. The last thing I'll ask. Listen, I'll be working on that bloody tractor and he'll be in and out of the yard all afternoon. I've left my bag under the bed. When you see your

322

chance, take it up the wood for me. Please!"

He wouldn't relent, Ruth could see. It was all planned, all cut and dried. She ran her tongue over lips that were suddenly dry.

"Up the wood?" she repeated.

"Up to Bal. I'm catching the last bus from Sproull's Corner to Truro, meeting Ken there, then we'm taking the night train to London. I'll pick up the bag on my way. All right? You'll do that? 'Tis only that little 'un I used for school, Ken says he'll buy everything new for me, but if Father sees me carrying it out tonight there'll be questions. He'll hold me up – make me miss the bus. I can't risk it, Ruthie."

Thomas was shouting from the yard, and Eric looked towards the door, then back at Ruth.

"All right?" he said more urgently. "You'll take it up?" He took hold of her and shook her shoulders. "All right, Ruthie?"

"All right," she said.

The girls had gone to the beach thinking that it would be cooler there, but in fact it seemed as airless as anywhere else. Both felt listless, oppressed by the impending storm.

"They said I was looking pale and tired," Lucy said.

"They were right," Emma agreed.

"I don't know what to tell them."

"*Tell* them?" Emma turned an astonished face towards her. "You don't tell them anything, dope. You just keep on saying what we've said already – that we had a lovely time."

"How can you say that?" Lucy began to cry. "Eddy's never going to speak to me again. And I lo-o-ove him."

Emma groaned and looked over her shoulder to see if anyone else was witnessing this exhibition.

"Look," she said, struggling to be sympathetic but finding it difficult in view of her opinion of Eddy. "Put it down to experience. Honestly, he's not worth bothering about. Oh Lor', haven't you got a handkerchief or anything?" She delved into the pocket of her shorts and came up with a used tissue of dubious cleanliness. "Here – take this. Look, Luce, it's just as bad for me. It's all over with me and Jacko."

Lucy blew her nose on the tissue.

"Well, you didn't like him that much, did you?"

323

"I did, as a matter of fact. I thought he was great."

"*Jacko*?" Lucy's surprise was so great that it made her stop crying. "But he was so weird! And anyway, you said you were just mates. You didn't love him like I loved Eddy."

"You didn't—" began Emma, then she sighed. What was the use?

"Look," she said. "I know you feel as if you'll never get over it, but you will. I mean, he behaved like a shit, didn't he? Getting you drunk, and making you smoke pot. And he looked awful in that shirt."

"Jacko looked awful in everything. Especially those swimming trunks. They were *gross*."

"We're not talking about Jacko," Emma said, with dignity. Then she giggled. "They were, weren't they?"

"It's all right for you." Lucy turned the tissue over, looking for a dry place. "You've got Damien when you get home. I won't have anyone." She sniffed miserably.

Emma was beginning to lose patience.

"Surely you can see that you're better off without a nerd like Eddy?" she said. "Anyone with a shred of common sense could see he was a phoney – smarming up to the oldies and singing his old-hat songs. He's probably a train-spotter, as well."

"My mum and dad liked him," said Lucy defiantly, and Emma gave a short, derisive laugh.

"I rest my case," she said.

William and Daniel and Paul, having deserted the Tarzan game for a few days, decided as they pushed and jostled each other playfully up the lane that they would try it again.

"Maybe Jamie-baby has grown enough to have a go," Daniel said nastily. "Come on, let's find the tree."

"We could make a tree-house," Paul said. "We could haul him up with a kind of pulley if he couldn't climb far enough."

James couldn't think, now, why he had come. It was a kind of automatic reaction to want to tag along with William, but even before they'd got as far as the farm he'd realised his mistake.

"I don't want to play with you lot," he said. "I'm only coming as far as the farm, to see the kittens."

"Scaredy cat, scaredy cat," chanted Daniel.

"Oh, let him go if he wants to, him and his kittens," William said. "He still thinks they might let him take one home. What a hope!"

"Well, they might—"

"No they won't."

"You don't know."

"Yes, I do."

They continued the argument at an increasing distance, as William and the others made for the woods and James kept on towards the farm. Only a day and a half left to persuade his mum and dad, he thought sadly. He didn't hold out a lot of hope.

He looked around for Jess as he went into the farmyard, but there was no sign of her; she was probably up in the fields somewhere with Mr Penrose, he thought, chasing rabbits.

The kittens were getting quite big and adventurous now. He'd given them all names. Garfield was his favourite. He (or she) had a white nose and white paws and seemed bolder than the others, more of a comic, always getting stuck in positions he couldn't get out of without help. The others were sweet, too, but it was Garfield he'd take home if he had the choice. They were quite big enough to leave their mother, he felt sure, no matter what Dad said. Tonight he would have another go at trying to persuade them. Meanwhile he contented himself with making them all chase bits of grass and each other's tails.

Even this, however, palled eventually. He stood up and brushed the hay from his shorts and shirt. Still no Jess. He wondered if an hour was up yet and whether he should go home. He looked at his watch; the trouble was, he'd forgotten to look at it when he set out.

Maybe he would go and see the butterflies on his own while he was up near the wood. Something told him Dad wasn't really keen on the idea.

That's what he would do then, he decided, making up his mind. He'd go to Bal.

Ruth hadn't eaten all day, but the lack of food had never even crossed her mind. There had been some orange juice remaining in her bag, and she'd drunk that which had been sustenance enough.

The Rest-a-While Guest House had faded from her memory altogether, though it seemed to her that her mind felt clearer than it had ever been; crystal clear, as if her head had expanded to allow room for all the memories. How right the doctor had been when he said that only when she remembered all would she be happy. How right she had been when she had told herself that she needed only to be still for enlightenment to come.

She had always imagined it would come like a flash of lightning, like St Paul's conversion on the road to Damascus. She had been wrong. It was happening in slow motion, one piece at a time, and she was content that it should be so; calm and relaxed and content. And sleepy. All she wanted to do was sleep – here, in the quiet of Bal. It didn't matter. It seemed that even as she slept, the threads were untangling themselves, forming neat balls. Soon there would be no tangle left.

Enlightenment would come.

She'd found the bag under the bed. It was an old attaché case, a good one, made of leather, used by her mother when she went to school. It still had her name in faded ink inside the lid: Thora Stansfield. Eric had crossed it out and written his own underneath.

Ruth put it on the bed, opened it and looked inside. He hadn't packed much. A pair of pyjamas. A clean shirt, threadbare round the collar and cuffs. His best blue sweater. His brush and comb and toothbrush, and a picture of Mother taken before her marriage that had stood in the parlour. Two books: *Birds of Cornwall*, and the book about beetles she and her mother had bought in Truro, that day they'd met Uncle Ben – the day Mother had seen the specialist and had pretended there was nothing wrong.

Suppose she didn't take the bag up to the wood after all?

He'd go, just the same. Ken would buy him new things. Hadn't he said so? So she'd take it and hide it, just as he'd asked; and when tonight he went out as usual, she'd say she was going out with him, just for a breath of air, and would walk up through the woods with him. It would be her last chance to talk to him, to try to make him change his mind.

It was hopeless, though. She could see that from the start, though she tried to prick Eric's conscience by talking about Mother.

"You could at least wait for her to die," she said as together they went up the lane. "It won't be long."

"But Ken's going now, and he says if I'm going at all, I got to go with him." He looked at Ruth sideways. "Can you keep a secret?" Ruth returned the look, not deigning to reply. "Tidn't easy, see, 'cos you need permits and all that trade," Eric went on. "But Ken's fixed it. He'm the tops, Ruth. He can fix anything he wants."

Ruth looked unimpressed.

"Tidn't fair on Father, not with the harvest to get in."

"Fair on Father?" Eric laughed scornfully at that. "Ent you got it in your head, Ruthie? He ent my father. I slaved my guts out all my life for un with never so much as a thank you, so I don't owe un nothing. Nor do you nor Mother, come to that. 'Tis my guess he can't wait for her to go." He gave her another sideways glance. "I ent told you what I seen t'other night, up the woods."

"What was that, then?" Even in the midst of her misery, there was something in his voice that made her look at him curiously.

"Your precious father," Eric said scornfully. "I seen un with that Eva Grose. Two nights ago – remember? He took his gun and went out after rabbits, so he said. I didn't go to Porthallic that night. I went up through the woods to meet Ken at Sproull's Corner. We went to Truro."

"They'd 've been talking about the meeting—"

Eric laughed again, more scornfully than ever.

"Thass the funniest way of talking I ever saw, maid. I heard rustling, see, and noises, and first I thought 'twas some big animal, so I crept round a bush and there they was, hard at it with their asses bare—"

"Don't talk so dirty. I don't believe you."

Ruth's voice was trembling. She didn't want to believe him, but she knew in her heart that it was true. It was what Father had meant about a man's needs. It was all becoming clear to her. He wanted to get rid of her so that he could marry Mrs Grose the minute Mother was gone. Filthy, filthy men with their filthy, filthy needs. She hated them all.

Her world was crumbling around her ears. She had always known her father to be harsh and opinionated, but she had always believed in his virtue, always managed to persuade herself that he acted from the best of motives, the highest of principles. Didn't he preach, Sunday after Sunday, about the sins of the flesh? Wasn't he the first to denounce the wrongdoings of others, to describe in horrifying detail the punishment that awaited them?

327

"He ent nothing but an old hypocrite, the dirty bugger," Eric said, and she knew it to be the truth. She clutched his arm and pulled him to a halt.

"Don't leave me, Eric," she begged once more. "What'll I do when you'm gone?"

"I'm going, Ruthie. Ent nothing you can say."

He pulled himself free and walked on. It was a beautiful summer's evening; not dark yet, but with the light fading and the air scented with the flowers which only revealed their sweetness once the day was over.

Ruth said no more. There was such pain in her heart that it seemed to flood over and fill her throat so that there was no room for words, and it was in silence they went through the field to the wood and the stream, turning from the marked path to take the way they knew so well to the still heart of the wood and their secret place.

"Did you put the bag down the shaft?"

He didn't wait for her answer, knowing that she would have done. It was where they put everything secret, where they had always put things for as long as he could remember.

Slipping a little on the dry leaves he slithered sideways into the dell, down to the bottom, and Ruth followed after him.

There were branches placed artfully, as if they had fallen off the trees above. Some of them had, but Eric knew the ones to move. He pushed them to one side and lifted the turf until he revealed a square sheet of metal. He'd found it one day beside the road, and had taken it for himself, knowing that it was exactly what they needed to hide the shaft from other prying eyes.

"Been a good friend to us, has Bal," he said, kneeling to reach down into the abandoned shaft. "How deep is un, I wonder? We never did find out, did us? And now I never will." He felt around with his hand. "Where did ee put it to, Ruthie?"

"'Tis there, on the ledge. Where we always put things."

"Damned if I can find it. Why did ee put it in so far?"

"Look in and you'll see it, plain as the nose on your face."

He put his head almost down the shaft.

"Don't know why you—"

Ruth, standing behind him, took a quick breath. Then she pushed with the whole of her strength.

Taken by surprise, totally off balance, he fell at once, but even so managed to grab the slippery edge of the hole with one hand. Ruth, standing above him, saw his terrified face looking up at her, heard his feet scrabbling against the side of the shaft.

"Ruthie, for God's sake—"

"You're not going away, Eric," she said, and stood and watched as his hand lost its purchase on the grass and he fell, screaming, beneath the earth.

It was wonderful being close to him after so many years. She could see the outcrop of rocks, just as it had always been, but nature had taken over and covered good old Bal so that without the rocks she would hardly have known where the opening was to be found.

No one else had found it, that was certain. It had stayed hidden; their Bal, their Place, hiding their secrets just as it had always done.

He would have been happy there, Ruth thought contentedly. He wouldn't have liked Australia. She'd never fancied it, herself. It looked so dried up and bare in pictures, not like Cornwall with its woods and streams.

Yes, he'd always loved this place, this hidden enclosure, this secret dell that hid a further secret that no one seemed to guess at but themselves. Once it might have been busy enough, if the mineshaft was anything to go by. They'd made up stories about the men who worked there – where they had come from, how they must have tramped through the woods. But in fact they had always really believed that it had never been used. It was common knowledge that shafts had been sunk all over this part of the county, and not all of them had been thought productive enough to bother about. If it had ever produced any minerals of any kind, then someone would have known. It would have been marked and mapped, and eventually blocked and fenced and rendered harmless like all the others. Eric always thought that someone had tried to block it up but hadn't done the job very well, so that years later it had opened up again. He could have been right. Such things did happen.

She'd hated that awful, echoing scream that Eric had made. Not a sound had there been after that. She had stayed there beside Bal for some time, and then she had gone home.

"I'm not upset, Father," she said.

"Well, then, get the work done," he said, but not as roughly as he might have done. And still he watched her through narrowed eyes, not able to put his finger on the difference in her.

Not that day, nor the next would he admit to himself what was wrong. This, after all, was his daughter. Eric he had felt able to accuse of any manner of things, for they shared no blood, did not come from the same stock.

Ruth was different. Time and again he looked at her over the next two days. It took a while for him to remember his grandmother who had died when he was no more than eleven or twelve.

That's who she had reminded him of, that first day when he had come home and found nothing done. That strange, unfocused look and the vague movements – it was how the old girl had been before they took her off to Bodmin.

It was hard to admit it, but he felt sure he was right. Ruth was losing her mind.

She had stayed, motionless in the wood, for some time when it came to her that it would, after all, be right to do something for Eric – that it wasn't good enough to let the ivy grow over Bal and the brambles encroach. Her eye fell on the hemp agrimony flowers that Eric had liked so much, because they attracted the butterflies. She would open the shaft, she thought, and pick the flowers and throw some down. For Eric.

It was harder than she had thought. The creepers were tough and cut into her hands and it was very hot. Her head was swimming and all she wanted to do was rest; but some compulsion made her go on, tugging and pulling at the creepers, throwing branches to one side, until the space was cleared. She could hardly believe it when she came to the metal plate and was able to tug it away from the hole so that the shaft lay open before her, just as it had done so long ago.

She stared into its blackness, her heart pounding and her breath sawing in her throat. It was then that she heard a voice.

"Hallo!"

It came from above. She looked up and saw a figure standing above her, and she blinked several times, finding it hard to get it into focus. The voice floated down to her again.

"Hallo, Miss Kernow. What are you doing?"

She blinked again and her vision cleared, and all at once she was filled with joy.

"Eric!" she cried.

"No, *James*," said James, laughing. "You're always forgetting."

But she was scrambling up the side of the dell, not listening to him.

"Oh, Eric, I knew you'd come back," she said.

After a while, Leo went in search of Lynn and met her coming downstairs.

"Let's go for a walk," he said. "Just along the beach a bit. We need to talk."

Lynn, however, had something else on her mind.

"What's up with Lucy?" she asked him. "She's just run into her bedroom and I think she was crying. I tried to follow her but she told me in no uncertain terms to leave her alone."

"Where's Emma? Have they had a row or something?"

"I don't know – oh, there she is!" Emma had walked in through the front door. "What's wrong, Emma? Lucy seems upset."

Emma hesitated, wondering how much to tell.

"It's Eddy," she said at last. "They had a bit of a falling out last night."

"Oh dear!" Lynn looked distressed. "The poor love. These things hurt so."

"She'll be all right," Emma said.

"Maybe I should go—"

"I don't honestly think so."

Lynn continued to worry.

"I can't just leave her. Maybe if I go up and let her know—"

"I think she just wants to be left alone for a bit."

"Well—" Lynn hovered by the door, undecided, weighing priorities. "Perhaps you're right. We're not going to be long, anyway."

Emma held her breath until Lynn and Leo had departed for their walk. Let Lynn go near Lucy now, and heaven alone knew what things she would confide. Though none of what had happened to Lucy could be laid at her door, she felt quite certain that she would get the blame for it and be made to pay the price in one way or another. Like no more parties for the rest of her life, or something.

She went into the sitting room and looked for something to read, but couldn't see anything that attracted her. She felt at a loose end, not able to settle to anything. She wasn't like Lucy, she told herself. She hadn't kidded herself that she'd fallen in love with Jacko, but on the other hand, she had spent an awful lot of time thinking about him, and wondering about what might happen if they ever met again, and now that nothing would happen, ever, she felt strangely sad and hollow, as if the space inside her that had been filled with Jacko was now painfully empty.

She wished like anything that she could have a really good heart to heart with Clare. Speaking of whom, it would really be great to see her again. Had she done all her holiday reading? Or written the essays? She rather hoped not; then they could confer and get down to it together.

Suddenly, home – improbably distant these past days – was beginning to come clear again, while Porthallic, Emma realised, was already fading. She wouldn't actually mind too much when the holiday was over.

"Oliver seems to think I'm rushing you into this," Leo said as they strolled slowly along the beach at the edge of the waves, their feet in the water. "I told him he'd got it all wrong – that we understand each other. Damn it, I'm not about to take any lectures from him on the subject of what makes a good marriage."

"They're going to be all right, he and Kate," Lynn said. "I think so, anyway."

"I hope you're right. Anything else would be a tragedy. Poor Kate! It's a lot for her to forgive."

"She'll do it, though. She's a forgiving sort of person." For a moment Lynn said nothing more, then she glanced at Leo sideways, biting her lip. "How about you?" she said. "Are you a forgiving sort of person?"

He laughed and catching her hand, swung her round to face him.

"Are you about to Confess All? Is there Another?" His smile died as he looked at her expression. "What is it, darling? You are with me on this Hockridge thing, aren't you?"

Lynn took a deep breath.

"No, Leo," she said.

For a moment he stared at her, saying nothing. He looks as if I've slapped him, she thought miserably. As if he would have found a lover preferable to this disappointment. Then he shook his head disbelievingly.

"I don't get this, Lynn. I thought you were as keen as I was."

"You didn't give me a chance to say."

"You got on so well with Gloria."

"What?" Lynn gave a short and incredulous laugh. "If you must know, I thought Gloria was a poisonous woman."

"You didn't like her?" He still couldn't quite take it in.

"I didn't like her – and oh, Leo, I didn't like the prospect of living there. I'm sorry. I'd do anything within my power not to disappoint you, but this isn't within my power. I'd hate it. And I won't give up my lovely home for it."

"But, darling, it's such a worthwhile thing—"

"Not for me."

They looked into each other's eyes. Leo was the first one to look away, still unable to take it in.

"But you're so good with children – such a marvellous home-maker. You could help those boys—"

"I know," Lynn said. "And I don't feel particularly proud of the fact that I don't want to spend my life doing it. But there it is, Leo. I'm not going. I'm sorry."

His plump, good-natured face had fallen into lines of disbelief and disappointment and he looked at her for a few moments longer before turning and continuing his walk. She stood biting her lip, looking at his retreating back view before running and catching him up, putting her hand through his arm.

"I'm truly sorry," she said again.

"That's all right." He spoke crisply, almost impersonally. "I said at the outset that you would have to agree. It would only have worked if we'd gone into it together, with a joint commitment."

"I know you're disappointed."

"I'll get over it."

"Maybe there'll be something else. Something more suitable for all of us."

"Perhaps there will."

"You don't have to stay at Reitz-Keppel if you don't want to. I wouldn't want you to do that."

"Just leave it, Lynn, will you?"

"Oh, Leo." She reached up and kissed him. His implacable expression melted a little, and he put his arms around her and held her for a moment.

"Come on," he said. "Let's go back and see what we can do for poor Lucy. And James might have come looking for me by this time – I did say I'd go to the wood with him. At least I must do the best I can for my own boys."

"You've never done anything else," said Lynn.

James was nowhere to be seen, however.

"I expect they're all up at the farm," Lynn said. "They'll come home when it's teatime."

But William was on his own when he came whistling down the lane, kicking a ball in front of him.

"What have you done with James?" Leo asked him.

"Isn't he home? Gosh, it's hot. I want to go for a swim – come on, Dad. Come for a swim."

Leo appeared not to register this urgent appeal.

"Where is James then? Haven't you been together?"

"He said he was going to the farm. I thought he'd have been back ages ago. Honestly, he's really *flipped* over those kittens."

"I wonder if he's gone to see Mrs Penrose?" Lynn suggested. "She seems to have taken quite a shine to him. Don't worry, Leo. I'm sure he's all right."

"Yes. Still—" Leo stood, undecided, jingling the change in his pocket. "I'll just walk up and see. It's time he came back, anyway."

Kate looked up from her book as he left.

"Did you tell him?" she asked Lynn.

Lynn sighed.

"I told him. I said I couldn't do it."

"Hooray! Bully for you."

"I feel the worst kind of heel. He's upset – and so is Lucy, by the way. Apparently she fell out with Eddy at the party last night."

"Kids," said Kate. "Who'd have 'em?"

But Lynn's attention had wandered and she was looking out of the garden, in the direction of the farm and the woods, an anxious frown on her face.

"I hope James is all right," she said.

15

Leo phoned Lynn from the Barstows. His voice sounded unnaturally calm, as if he were making a great effort not to alarm her.

"There doesn't seem to be any sign of James at the farm, and Mrs Penrose hasn't seen him all afternoon because she's been in Truro," he said. "She's only this minute got back. She suggested I tried here, but the Barstows haven't seen him either. I'm just ringing to let you know I'm going to look for him in the wood. It seems likely that he went there to look for the other boys and somehow managed to get himself lost. Paul and Daniel are going to come with me."

"Shall I send Wills up too?"

"Yes, good idea. Maybe he'll have some idea where James might be. Don't worry. I'm sure he's OK."

"Yes, I'm sure he is," Lynn agreed. At least, she thought as she put the phone down, she wanted to be sure. Of course she was sure! What could possibly have happened to him in a rural place like this? Almost immediately a host of horrifying possibilities presented themselves, of which straying off the path in the wood was far from the worst.

"I expect he's wandered off somewhere, looking for his wretched butterflies," she said as she rejoined the others outside.

"We are sure he went to the wood, are we?" Oliver asked. Lynn shook her head.

"No, not at all. He went up the lane with the other boys, but apparently left them to go and look at the kittens. He could have done anything after that."

"If he'd come back here, you would have seen him," Lucy said. She had come down from her room but had remained subdued and in the background. Everyone had combined in treating her with a brisk and

337

cheerful normality, totally ignoring her red eyes and air of misery – all except William who had greeted his first sight of her with a cry of "What's up with Luce?" but was despatched to join the search party before he could say any more.

"He might not have come down the lane," Oliver said. "He could have taken that path from the farm—" to the cliffs, he was about to say, but managed to prevent himself in time. "Maybe I'll just take a stroll over Porthallic way," he went on casually, finishing his tea and getting to his feet.

It was then that they heard the helicopter, the beat of its engine coming nearer and nearer; in a moment they saw it, too, hovering over the cliffs where they had walked so often. Lynn watched it with her eyes wide with alarm.

"Oh God, you don't think—" she began. "Could he have fallen? Someone could have seen him on the cliff and given the alarm."

"I don't suppose it's anything to do with him – not for one minute," Oliver said firmly. "But I'll go up there and have a look."

"I'll come too," Lynn said.

Oliver looked as if he would like to argue about this, but he restrained himself and they set off together. They were away almost an hour, returning hot and tired having walked all the way to Porthallic.

"Aren't they back yet?" Lynn asked anxiously as she and Oliver reappeared on the terrace. She had managed to convince herself on the way home that she would find James there eating cake and drinking orange squash, just as normal. "I was sure they would be by now. What can have happened?" Distractedly she went round the house to where she had a good view of the countryside to the rear, and she looked once more towards the woods which, to her eyes, seemed suddenly to have taken on a sinister aspect she had never noticed before.

"At least we're sure he hasn't fallen over the cliffs," Oliver said quietly to Kate. "We looked really thoroughly in all the possible places, but there wasn't a sign of him."

"I didn't really think there would be, did you?" Kate looked at him, biting her lip, her brow creased with worry. There was no room in her mind for anything other than James's disappearance. Oliver, Anna – what importance did they have now? "I can't see James going up there on his own – and certainly not without telling someone," she went on.

"Oh, Oliver, what can have happened to him?"

"We mustn't leap to the worst conclusions," Oliver said. "He must surely still be in the wood somewhere. Where are the girls?"

"Gone to join in the hunt. I wanted to go too, but I thought I ought to stay here in case he reappeared from some other direction. Oh – did you find out what the helicopter was all about?"

"The word is they're looking for a holiday-maker, who's gone missing," Oliver reported. "Some elderly woman who was staying in a guest house in Porthallic. It peeled off just before we got there and went further down the coast. I wouldn't have known what they were up to, but I saw Cap'n Tamblyn on the quay, and he seemed remarkably well-informed. Kate . . ." He paused, ruffling the hair on the back of his head.

"What?"

"Oh, nothing. I expect he's just lost his way. I can't help thinking, though, that he might have climbed a tree, and fallen and broken an ankle or something."

"If he has, they're bound to find him. The wood's not that big."

"Big enough. And it looks quite dense in parts." Oliver looked at his watch. "Six o'clock," he said, uneasily. "Four hours he's been gone. I wonder when we call out the big guns?"

"Oh, Eric, I am so very, very glad you've come back," Ruth said.

"I keep *telling* you—"

"Sit down, dear." Ruth lowered herself to the ground and pulled him down beside her. "Sit down and tell me everything you've been doing with yourself. I knew you'd come one day," she went on. "I've waited and waited."

"Have you?" James frowned at her, not understanding. It was jolly nice of her and all that to be so keen on seeing him, but it hadn't occurred to him that they were on those terms. And he wished she wouldn't hold his arm so tightly. He tried to pull it away, but she held it all the tighter and it was really hurting him. "I knew you'd see it wasn't right to go away. Porthlenter's where you belong."

Her eyes looked funny, James thought. Kind of glittery and excited.

"Well, I've got to go soon," he said. "It's nearly teatime and they'll wonder where I am."

"No, no, they won't! You belong with me. You belong here."

He was beginning to feel scared. She seemed so strange, so different. Well, she'd always seemed different from other old ladies he knew, like Grandma Rose and Granny Bryant. They were quite different from each other, but yet in another way they were the same. You knew where you were with them.

Not Miss Kernow, though. Sometimes she was friendly and sensible, and she was certainly interesting because she knew a lot about butterflies and things, but at other times she seemed not at all friendly, and no older than he was himself. And now she seemed really peculiar, not taking in anything he was saying.

He tried to stand up, but she pulled him down beside her again.

"Be a good boy, Eric," she said.

"I'm *not* Eric!" He was close to tears now. "How many more times have I got to tell you? And I must go home."

"This is your home, dear."

"No, it's not. I live in Brascombe. Near Worcester," he added desperately, as she continued to look at him with an expression of mild reproof. "We're going back there the day after tomorrow."

"Back?" Her frown deepened.

"To *Brascombe*, silly." He'd got beyond caring about being polite to old ladies. She didn't deserve it.

"You're going away?"

"We're going home! We don't live here. We just came for a holiday. Let me go." His voice soared with fright and with pain as he struggled in vain to free himself from her iron grip.

"You can't go, dear," she said softly. "I'm not going to let you."

At six thirty Leo phoned the police. They sounded concerned and said they would send a police car to Porthlenter right away, but it was after seven by the time it arrived, bringing two policemen: a sergeant and a constable. The constable looked very young, but the sergeant was thickset with a square, dependable-looking face and greying hair.

It was left to Lynn and Kate to talk to them, for Leo and Oliver had gone back to the wood to make yet another search. It was better, they said, than sitting and waiting – and Oliver still clung to his theory that

340

James could have hurt himself in some remote part of the wood and be unable to get home.

"It's certainly possible," the sergeant said when Lynn advanced this theory. "Likely, even. But I'd be glad if you would give me a full description of James – what he was wearing, and where he was last seen."

Lynn, keeping a tight control on her fears, did as he asked.

"Hasn't a woman also gone missing?" Kate asked, when Lynn had finished giving the necessary information. "We saw the helicopter."

"Yes – yes, that's true," the inspector said. "Though I can't imagine there could be any connection. This woman was a visitor, quite elderly, staying in Porthallic. Apparently she's seemed rather confused these past few days, and the theory is that she's perhaps lost her memory and wandered away."

"What's her name?" Kate asked, gripped by a sudden intuitive feeling of foreboding. Unable to keep still she had risen from the kitchen table to make futile preparations towards an evening meal that she knew no one would want to eat. Now she turned and gripped the back of the chair, waiting for the inspector's answer.

"Ruth Kernow," he told her. Kate stared at him for a moment, frozen-faced.

"Then there's a connection," she said.

Ruth heard voices, calling, coming close. She kept quite still under the sheltering branches of the oak tree, and soon the searchers had moved away – without, it seemed, catching a glimpse of her. Which was how it should be. This place was her secret, hers and Eric's.

She smiled and hugged her trousered knees. She had done the only thing possible, and he would thank her for it in the end.

The sergeant went out to the yard to talk on his mobile phone to unseen colleagues, presumably organising backup, a more thorough search. The constable, a little awkwardly, did his best to reassure Lynn.

"It hasn't really been very long, Mrs Bryant."

"How long does it take for a little boy to be— ?" Lynn didn't complete the sentence. She didn't need to. She buried her face in her hands and Kate moved swiftly to sit down and put her arms around her.

"Bear up, love," she said softly. "Things will swing into action now."

Police cars were parked in the yard of the Penroses' farm, and a minibus arrived full of police personnel. The wood became alive with torches and searchlights. Leo, white-faced, went back to Porthlenter for a while to comfort Lynn who had stayed there in case there was news from elsewhere, but unable to sustain a passive role, he left her with Kate and went once more to join the searchers. There was a flash of lightning over to his right as he hurried up the lane. Not a storm, he thought. Oh God, please, not a storm. But the thunder was rumbling even as he prayed.

Before reaching the farm he saw two torches moving across the field. He hurried to follow them and found that they were held by Oliver and John Penrose, striding purposefully towards the wood once more, accompanied by the dog, Jess, who clearly thought the whole expedition was got up for her benefit. She was dashing here and there, making little sorties into the bushes to sniff down a rabbit hole or chase a field mouse, leaping at them out of the shadow of bushes, her tail waving joyously.

"The whole place is crawling with police. You'd think if he was there, we would have found him," Leo said hopelessly.

"Not necessarily," Oliver was determinedly bracing.

"The wood's bigger than you think," Penrose said. "And it's got very overgrown these last years. Out of hand, you might say." This was no more than stating the obvious, and Leo said nothing. "Tidn't nothing to do with us," he went on a little defensively. "Our land stops at that row of trees. 'Tis all part of the Penglower Estate, and they ent got the cash for foresters and that. There was talk of the National Trust taking over at one time, but there were those who thought . . ." His voice trailed away as if he was struck by the irrelevance of these past controversies.

"Surely you must have played there when you were a boy," Oliver said. "You must know the wood as well as anyone."

"Sixty years ago, maybe, but the fact is I ent been near the place for years, no more than walking through with the wife on a nice Spring Sunday, up to Sproull's Corner. Pretty it is, when the primroses are out."

342

"Where would a boy play, though?" Oliver persisted. "Is there any part of the wood that would be more attractive than another? Aren't there any local boys we could ask?"

"Not now. 'Tis all holiday places up to Sproull's Corner."

"James is keen on butterflies," Leo said. "My wife was with him in the wood the other day, and she said he found a place where there seemed to be lots of them. He wanted them – my wife and her sister – to go with him to see them, but they made some excuse . . ." He fell silent. As I did, he thought, racked with guilt. We were fed up with butterflies. Didn't want to know.

"Wait, now. That rings a bell." Penrose stopped, as if a thought had struck him. "There was one place we used to go when we were little tackers, my brothers and me. There was a pink flower grew there that the butterflies liked. It grew by the side of a kind of dip where we played. We pinched teatrays from the kitchen and slid down on them – there was always dead leaves and bracken there, see, and stuff that made it slippery, and this tall pink flower—"

"Someone's bound to have looked there already," Leo said. But he was unable to prevent a glimmer of hope, and a renewed note of optimism in his voice. "Still, it's worth a try."

"'Twas off the beaten track, like," Penrose said doubtfully. "I just hope I can find it. 'Tis all of sixty years since I was there."

"It's worth looking," Leo said doggedly. "He mentioned butterflies when he asked me—" He couldn't finish the sentence, for the guilt and the panic had rushed back to choke him. If anything has happened to him, the blame is mine, he thought. How on earth can I live with that? I should have gone with him.

"Sixty years is a long time." Beside him, John Penrose ruminated aloud as he trudged along, preparing them all for disappointment. "'Twas hard to find even then."

"Just do your best," said Oliver.

Ruth was feeling thirsty. There was no more orange juice left in the bottle; she'd drunk the last of it a long time ago, but still the thought of leaving the safety of Bal never entered her head.

It was much cooler now than it had been the night before. A breeze had sprung up and no stars were visible through the interlaced branches of the trees. She was engaged in putting on her cardigan once more when she heard the first, distant rumble of thunder, and then, shortly afterwards, there was a flash of lightning that briefly lit up the wood around her, followed by the fat splattering of raindrops on leaves.

She drew the woollen jacket more closely around her. She didn't mind the rain, she told herself. And Eric was all right where he was. In the best place, you could say. Sheltered.

Inspector Baines had arrived in his own car to coordinate the hunt for James, but when the rain began in earnest, conditions were so bad that he conferred with the sergeant about calling it off until morning, or at least waiting until the worst of the rain was over. Even then—

He scanned the sky and looked around him. It was not yet nine o'clock and should still be light at this time of the year, but because of the lowering clouds darkness had set in early and it was hard to imagine a worse night for a search like this. Privately he felt almost sure that the boy was no longer in the wood, if he ever had been.

God alone knew where he was. He could have gone up to the road. There could have been a passing car driven by some marauding pervert and he could be well up the M5 by this time. You could go a long way up the motorway in five hours; more than five hours. No one had seen the boy since just after two o'clock.

The rain was getting worse, had set in, you could say, and looked as if there would be no quick end to it. The wind had become strong and gusty and branches were dipping and swaying. Two of the additional constables in streaming oilskins were making their way back to him.

"It's hopeless, sir," one called as he approached. "You can't see a thing."

"I know." The inspector sighed. It made sense to say wait until morning, but he didn't relish communicating this decision to the father. Imagine the kid being there, somewhere, lost and helpless and frightened, with the thunder and the lightning and the rain beating down like this! He'd got children of his own and needed no diagram to explain to him the thoughts that would be going through Leo Bryant's head. Still, it made no sense to keep the men out in this weather; the visibility was inches rather than yards.

He felt a touch on his shoulder, and turning, he saw Leo.

"Mr Bryant," he shouted, forced to raise his voice to combat the wind and the rain. "I think you'll agree it's only sensible—"

"We've thought of something," Leo shouted back. "At least, Mr Penrose has. He knows the wood, you see – used to play here when he was young—"

"I know! He was here earlier, searching with the team. But, Mr Bryant—"

"He's thought of something," Leo repeated. "A place—"

"God knows if I can find un in this." John Penrose was shaking his head.

"At least we can look. Come on, John – lead on."

Penrose called sharply to Jess. Even her enthusiasm for this unexpected excursion was diminishing with the rain and she was turning for home.

"She'll be a help, maybe," he shouted over his shoulder to Leo and Oliver who followed close behind, together with the two constables. Though convinced that this initiative would be as doomed to failure as all the others, the inspector hadn't the heart to deny them one last throw.

When they reached the stones beside the brook, Penrose paused and looked around him.

"There used to be a path somewhere here, on the right," he said, peering at the closely packed bushes. "'Tis all overgrown."

"Someone's broken through here fairly recently," said the older of the two policemen, who had been a Boy Scout in the distant past and had won badges for Tracking and Woodcraft.

"Some of us, I expect." The young one, though sympathetic, had long lost hope and privately thought they should have called off the search fifteen minutes ago.

Leo pushed past them through the bushes, shouting James's name. Another loud crack of thunder drowned his voice, and tears of rage and frustration mingled with the rain on his face as he pushed on through the undergrowth, heedless of the brambles that scratched and the whippy branches that cut and slashed and the bracken that caused his feet to slide.

"Wait, wait—" Oliver, shouting in his ear, caught his shoulder and pulled him in another direction. "John's going this way." He indicated

345

a rocky bank of natural stone. At the top of it there seemed to be an impenetrable barrier of huge rhododendrons, towering to the sky.

Jess, barking noisily, was up it before any of them, and had disappeared into further undergrowth. The young constable, too, found little difficulty with it, and stood at the top shouting directions to the others, pointing out footholds and handholds and finally hauling them up to join him.

Oliver could only guess at what Leo was thinking, but for himself he couldn't imagine that James would have penetrated so deeply into the wood or overcome so many obstacles. Thankfully, the rain had eased off; had almost stopped. Again Leo shouted James's name, and in the silence that followed his shout, came the sound of Jess's frenzied barking.

Ruth, huddled in the shelter of the oak tree, knew that she was wet and cold, but her mind seemed to have taken her to some other place where these things had no significance. She barely noticed the thunder and the lightning. Lights had come and lights had gone, but none had picked her out, she was too well hidden in the heart of the tree, under the drooping branches. Now, suddenly, she was aware of an animal rustling through the leaves, sniffing excitedly at her legs. Its fur was wet and she pushed it from her. It seemed to dance away, but was back at once, thrusting its black and white muzzle through the leaves and barking.

She hit out at it, harder now, frightened at its persistence. She groped around and picked up a stick, landing a blow across its nose that made it squeal with pain and dance away again. But still the barking went on.

"Jess?" Someone was coming – coming after the dog, closer and closer. A light was shining. More lights.

The branches were pulled aside, and she put her hands up to shield her eyes, cowering back against the trunk of the tree, as a torch was shone directly into her face.

"It's all right," she said wildly, before anyone could speak. "Eric's quite safe."

Leo was crouching, reaching for her and hauling her out before either of the policemen could move.

"Have you got my son? What have you done with him?"

"Wait, sir." The older constable put a firm hand on his shoulder and moved him to one side. "Let me handle this, if you don't mind. Come out, please, madam."

She stood in the light of their torches, old, ugly and bedraggled, her hair hanging lankly on each side of her strangely innocent face. She looked mildly surprised, as if she had no idea why she should be such a centre of attention.

"He's all right, you know," she said.

"Are you Miss Ruth Kernow?" the sergeant asked.

"Teague," she replied. "Ruth Teague."

"*What?*" Oliver had lowered his torch to sweep it around the nearby ground, but at this he lifted it to her face again. "You're Ruth Teague?"

Yes, of course, he could see that she was. She hadn't changed so very much from the girl in the newspaper photographs.

"By Gor!" John Penrose, a little slower to react, sounded even more astonished. "You'm the Teague girl! The girl that—" words failed him, silenced by the weight of all the horror that was associated with the name.

For Leo, her name had no relevance.

"Where's my boy?" he demanded urgently.

"Do you mean Eric?" she asked, bewildered. "Eric's safe. He won't go away now, not ever again."

"It's James we're looking for."

The words burst from Leo, loud and agonised, and he reached out for her again as if he would shake the truth out of her, shake some sense into her head; but then he froze. The rain had lessened and momentarily the wind was silent, and from somewhere below them and to their right a sound came to them. It was the thin, despairing weeping of a frightened child.

"James!" roared Leo, and half falling with the suddenness of the descent into the dell, plunged downwards to its bottom and the hole that still gaped open to the sky.

"She's mad, isn't she?" Lucy said to Emma when at last they had gone to bed. She was sitting up, her arms wrapped around herself, shivering a little, for though she had at first been euphoric with relief that James was found, the horror had finally caught up with her. "She must be mad to do a thing like that. Stark, staring, raving mad."

"It's my worst thing, being shut up in a small place." Emma, too, shuddered at the thought of it. "Poor James! It must have been awful for him, hour after hour, and the darkness and the storm—"

"Shut up, Em! Thinking about it is worse than ghosts."

"But he's all right. That's the only thing that matters."

"She didn't know he would be. She didn't know those tree roots would have grown across the shaft so he'd get caught up in them. She thought she was pushing him down—"

"Try not to think about it," Emma urged her. "She didn't even know it was James. Dad said she was all mixed up and thought he was her brother."

"Well, whoever she thought he was, she still pushed him down the hole. Oh, Em, I shall be so thankful to get home, won't you? I never want to see this place again. Today has been the very worst day of the whole of my life. When I think what nearly happened to James—"

At least it's taken her mind off Eddy, Emma thought. But she felt a little ashamed of this reflection and kept it to herself.

Kate didn't go to bed. Even after James had been carried home, wrapped in Leo's anorak and Oliver's kagool and had been given a mild sedative and, Leo's arm about him, been fed Marmite toast which was his very favourite thing, followed by a Mr Man Yoghurt. Even after he'd turned up his nose at a hot, milky drink and opted, as usual, for Ribena, after which he was tucked up warm in Leo's and Lynn's bed so that his mother could hold him close in the night if the fears should return. Even after it was reported that he was sleeping soundly, apparently none the worse for his ordeal, and Leo had poured stiff drinks for her and for Lynn, supposedly to help them sleep, too. And even after Leo and Lynn had gone upstairs, Leo to sleep in the boys' room. Still she sat and waited for Oliver.

He had gone to Truro in the police car with Ruth Teague. When he'd told them he was a doctor, they'd asked him to go, for Ruth's calm had deserted her once they'd bundled her down to the main path, and for a time she had become hysterical and hard to manage. The inspector had phoned to tell her they'd be bringing Dr Sheridan home the moment Miss Kernow had been handed over to the police surgeon – adding that he was extremely relieved to have him along while they were taking her in. It was a blessing, he said, that there happened to be a doctor handy.

It was after midnight on a day that seemed to have been going on for ever by the time she heard him at the back door and ran to let him in.

He stepped inside the house, and for a moment they looked at each other before, as if at a given signal, falling into each other's arms. Where else would either of them go for comfort?

"Is James all right?" Oliver asked at last.

"Fine. Sleeping soundly, thank God. What about you? You must be exhausted. Was it awful?"

"Awful," he said.

"Can I get you something? You haven't had anything to eat, have you?"

"I had a sandwich at the station." He slumped down at the kitchen table. "I could use a whisky, though."

"I'll get you one." Kate sat down with him at the table while he drank gratefully. "You've been ages," she said. "What's been going on?"

He took another sip of his drink as if considering his answer.

"She talked," he said. "On and on. We were waiting for the police surgeon – he was held up somewhere and there was no one but me to hear. There was no stopping her. It was like breaching a dam – like water, flooding out, swamping everything."

"Did she talk about—?"

"The murders?" He shook his head and gave a rueful laugh. "No, she didn't. Everything but. She talked about her parents and her brother and her terrible, terrible childhood. And about the chapel – on and on about the chapel – and about the sermons her father preached when he set up his own religious group. And someone called Eli Dowrick."

"Who?"

"Some faith-healing nutcase her father got in to cure her mother. She hated him. Still hates him."

"But she didn't say who did it?"

"No. Perhaps she still doesn't know."

"It wasn't the brother?"

"No." Oliver took another swallow of whisky, not meeting her eye. He couldn't tell Kate yet; it was all too close and too horrible. The woman might not have been telling the truth anyway. The police would have to investigate the old mineshaft, see if there were any remains to be found down there.

"Why wasn't this mine place closed off?" Kate asked, and he looked at her with consternation, thinking that she must have read his mind; but he saw she was thinking of James, still shuddering at what he must have endured.

"Apparently nobody knew about it. The inspector said that shafts were drilled all over the place at the beginning of the last century and not all of them were ever developed. He reckons this must have been one of them that somehow was overlooked. It was very well hidden. John Penrose didn't know about it, even though he and his brother used to play there, but fifteen years or so later, Ruth and her brother found it and used it as a kind of secret hidey-hole. She told me about it. There was a sort of shelf, a projection, a little way down, and they kept their treasures there – things they didn't want their father to find out about. Silly, harmless things – books, mainly, as far as Eric was concerned. Picture books of butterflies and birds and a necklace that someone gave her as a present. Her father didn't believe it was right for women to adorn themselves, you see, and told her to throw it away, but she didn't, she hid it down the shaft. And she had a photograph of Ingrid Bergman she cut out of a magazine because she thought she was the most beautiful woman in the world and she liked to look at it."

And Eric's little case. Oliver stopped short at mentioning that. He'd tell her everything later. Not now.

"Funny she remembered so much but stopped short at the murders," Kate said, as he took another sip of his drink.

"I tried to lead her to tell me what she could remember about that night, but she became sly and suspicious and clammed up on me, so I let it go – but as for the rest of it, it was the most chilling thing, Kate. I've never heard anything more soul-destroying – any story more full of hate and despair and misery." He gave a long, shuddering sigh and passed his hand over his face. "Thank God it's over. Thank God we're going home—" he looked at his watch. "Tomorrow," he said. "We're going home tomorrow. Hallelujah!"

"Some holiday," Kate said bitterly. He laughed again, briefly.

"It hasn't exactly been without incident, has it?"

350

"You could say that." They reached out to each other, clasping hands.

"How about something really restful next year?" Oliver said, his eyes holding hers. "Like trekking in the Himalayas or white-water rafting? Oh, Kate," he went on, not waiting for an answer. "Forgive me. Please."

"Do you know what I've been sitting here thinking?" she asked him.

"After nineteen years? I couldn't possibly guess."

"I was thinking—" she hesitated, biting her lip, but smiling, her eyes bright with excitement. "I was thinking – let's have another baby."

"*What?*" He stared at her in horrified astonishment.

"Somehow all the trauma put everything in perspective, and I thought – oh, Oliver, let's do it! It might be a little boy. You'd like that."

"You can't guarantee it."

"So what? We'll have another girl. You'd like that, too."

"We're too old—"

"Rubbish! Some women don't start until they're older than I am."

"Kate, Kate!" He was laughing, wearily shaking his head. "This is no time of night to spring this kind of thing on me." He stood up, pulling her to her feet and into his arms. He held her close, rubbing his cheek against her hair.

Another baby? Another hostage to fortune? After tonight, would he dare? How did anyone dare, ever? The responsibility was awesome. But at least, he thought, this surely meant he could assume Kate's forgiveness. A new beginning? Maybe it wasn't such a bad idea at that.

"I know it's something of a bombshell, but you will think about it, though, won't you?" Kate had pulled away from him a little to look up into his face.

"I blame the corn dolly," he said.

"Promise you'll think about it!"

"OK – I'll think about it. Now, bed – please!"

She reached and kissed him briefly.

"It's as good a start as any other."

"I've got a headache," he said.

She woke early to the sound of the gulls. The rain had stopped and a tentative sun was shining. Raising herself on her elbow, she looked

351

down on the still slumbering Oliver, smiling a small and rueful smile.

I love him, she thought. That's the bottom line. Whether she forgave him now or later was the only point at issue, really; and now seemed a great deal more sensible.

Yesterday had, as she told him, put everything in perspective. Only James's safety had seemed important; James in particular, children in general. That there would be other times, other priorities, she had no doubt; life was like that. It was far too simplistic to think that this incident, horrific as it was, would inform their lives for ever. But last night, for once, had made everything crystal clear.

Crystal clear for Lynn and Leo, too. She grinned to herself as she flopped back on her pillow, thinking of it. Lynn, last night, would have agreed to incarceration at Dotheboys Hall for the rest of her life if it meant she could be sure of getting James back, but it had been Leo who had gone on and on, once James was safe and in bed, about getting him home to his own room in the house he'd lived in all his life, with his friends close by and the school he loved. And of course he could have one of the kittens! Neither he nor Lynn could imagine why they had ever thought it a bad idea. Maybe, Leo had said, he'd be able to buy a basket in town in which to take it home.

Was it really going to be as easy as that? Her smile died as she relived the small boy's horror. What sort of a legacy would it leave? Oliver thought not much, so long as he was encouraged to talk about it as much as he wanted to, and then allowed to forget it. It was Lynn who might suffer more, he thought. Lynn who would have to school herself not to be too possessive, too protective. A hard lesson for her – and for Leo! God, what would Leo be like?

The perils of parenthood are legion, she thought. So why was she suddenly so anxious to embark on it one more time?

No doubt people would say she was mad, having another baby at her age. They'd probably pity Oliver, think she'd pulled a fast one, say it wasn't fair on the girls.

They say, she thought. What say they? Let them say. And she smiled because she had just realised – could it really be for the first time in her life? – that she really didn't care a bit.

Ruth, opening her eyes, saw that the curtains were yellow. And the walls were plain cream, not festooned with rosebuds. Where was she?

Something had happened. Her head felt as if it were filled with cotton wool, just as it always did after she'd been taking those dratted pills; her thoughts were jumbled, but dimly she remembered the cold and the rain and the happiness she had felt because she knew that Eric was safe.

There'd been a dog barking, and people, and then she'd been taken somewhere. A hospital, she thought, because there had been a doctor who had sat with her and listened while she talked. Like they did. And then someone else had come and there'd been an injection, and she had come here and been put to bed.

She must be ill, then, she thought. Perhaps she'd had one of her turns. Or had everything been a dream? The flat in Wandsworth and the horrible boys on the estate and the train journey, and all the things she'd seen and done since she'd been in Porthallic. Maybe none of it was real. Maybe all the time she had been in a home somewhere, having treatment, given injections, doing what she was told, eating and sleeping to order. She couldn't think, couldn't remember.

Her eyelids felt heavy. They seemed to close by themselves and she drifted off into sleep again. Or semi-sleep. She could hear shouting, cries of "Go away! Go away! Don't come near me!" And it was she who was shouting.

The boys, she thought. She was shouting at the boys, down the stairwell, her voice echoing and re-echoing; but then she saw a face and it wasn't the estate boys at all.

She had come in from the beach through the little used front door, meaning to creep upstairs without letting her father hear. The beach had been deserted, quiet and peaceful, the gentle waves turning all colours of the rainbow in the setting sun; and then at last it was dark and only their white, lacy edges could be seen coming further and further up the beach as the tide came in.

She had no idea how long she had stayed on the beach; it was like that these past two days. Sometimes she would sit looking at nothing, and would find that hours had passed without her noticing them. Other times she felt quite normal and went about her duties quite calmly and sensibly. She knew now it was time to go home. She had stayed out a long time; too long, really, for her mother would surely be needing her.

Poor Mother! There was such a weight of sadness in her heart when she thought of the suffering, wraith-like figure she had become that she hardly knew how to bear it.

It was, however, her mother who'd told her to go.

"Get some air, dear," she'd said in the faint, thready voice which was all she could manage these days. "You don't have to stay to see that man if you don't want to."

"Father'll be some mad if I'm not here to make tea for un."

"Leave them make their own tea. They're not helpless."

"But you might want me—"

Thora closed her eyes, let out her breath.

"You'm a good girl, Ruthie," she whispered. "A good daughter to me. But you go out for a breath. Only one thing I want now, and that's an end to it. That's all I pray for."

With infinite caution Ruth lifted the latch on the front door, and opened it. She had forgotten how it creaked. She paused – but there was no help for it; she had to open it, and the noise of it seemed enough to waken the dead. And when at last it was open sufficiently for her to go inside, she looked towards the kitchen door at the end of the passage and her heart lurched in panic. Eli, his pale face gleaming in the half-dark was coming towards her, smiling, stretching out his hands towards her.

Ruth clung to the door knob as if it were some kind of defence against him.

"I thought you'd be gone," she said.

"I was late coming. Had a job to finish over Threemilecross, but I came straight here when 'twas done. I had the van, see—"

"Don't come near me!" Ruth cringed away from him, from the touch of his hand on her face, her body. "Don't you dare touch me."

"And where do you think you've been to?" It was her father, coming down the stairs. "Your mother was calling."

"I went for a walk."

She expected anger, but he seemed strangely muted, and he looked at her with a guarded expression.

"Come to the kitchen then, now you're here."

"I was going up to bed."

354

His ready anger flared.

"Come to the kitchen, I said." He took hold of her arm, pulling her past Eli and into the far room. "Sit down. Eli's here to see you."

"No!"

"You're sick, girl. Sick in the head. Eli's going to lay his hands on you—"

"No. *No!*" Wildly she looked around, tried to get up from the chair where her father had thrown her, but he pushed her down again.

"The Lord will heal you," he shouted.

Ruth was shaking, paralysed with horror, staring from one to the other of the men, yet seeing nothing. It seemed to her that she could see the evil, feel the darkness, coming nearer, extinguishing life and she shrieked, on and on, small piercing shrieks of terror. Her father slapped her, hard, but she kept on screaming.

" 'For rebellion is as the sin of witchcraft,' " he thundered in her face. "First Samuel, Chapter fifteen."

"Thass what 'tis, Thomas," Eli said. "'Tis witchcraft, right enough. We'll have to use force." There was a gleam in his eye as if the prospect was one he relished. "Lay her down, on the floor. See her eyes, Thomas. Wild, they are – wild like she got demons inside her. Witchcraft, that's what 'tis."

Their combined strength overcame her and forced her down. Still she moaned feebly as Eli beseeched the Almighty to help her, writhing with revulsion away from the hands that were placed on her head, on her mouth, on her breast, on her abdomen. But at last, sobbing quietly now, she recognised the futility of struggling and lay still with the passivity of despair. She felt dirty, contaminated, as if she would never be clean again.

"Praise the Lord, the devil's coming out of her," Eli said, sitting back on his heels to rest from his labours.

It was then that they heard the noises from the hall; the bang of a door, a scraping sound. Even Ruth, passively accepting what she was too weak to resist, heard it and struggled to a sitting position, her heart pounding faster than ever. For a moment, until she remembered, she thought it must be Eric. Who else could it be?

Thomas flung open the kitchen door intent on finding out.

"Thora – what—?" Ruth heard the note of surprise in his voice, and

355

heard it sharpen into fear as he spoke again. "Put that down, Thora. Don't be a fool—"

If he said anything more she did not hear it, for the sound of the explosion seemed to fill not only her ears but the room and the whole house; the whole universe. And then there was only silence – a silence which she realised, gradually, was broken by a sobbing, agonised breath.

She stared at Eli; and Eli, shaken for once out of his customary leering composure, stared back at her, his mouth open and his face blank. The first to move, she scrambled to her feet and ran to the door, forced to step over her father's outstretched leg as he lay on the floor of the hall. He was still and silent, blood from a hidden wound already seeping into the narrow strip of carpet that lay underneath him.

The rasping breath was coming from her mother who was leaning, colourless and exhausted, against the side of the staircase, the butt of the shotgun she had taken from the cupboard under the stairs still in her hand, its barrel resting on the floor. She looked up as Ruth went to her.

"I know 'twas a sin," she said. "I did it for you, Ruthie. I did it for you. I found the strength."

Eli had, by this time, appeared in the doorway behind her.

"You killed him!" His voice – not unctuous and honeyed now, nor shouting authoritatively to his God, was shaken with terror. "And you'll burn in hellfire for it for all eternity."

"Then I might as well use both bullets," Thora said. She tried to raise the gun once more, but her strength had gone. "You'm lucky, Eli Dowrick." Her lips were drawn back and her face was full of hatred. "Get out of here. You'd be worth burning for, the pain you've caused me. But you'm not having my daughter. Get out of this house, and never come back. And if you ever show your face here again, or say one word of what's happened tonight, I'll say you shot Thomas. We both will, and be glad to do it, for there's no just punishment for the lie you've lived. Get out, I say."

She made another superhuman effort to lift the shotgun and this time it rose a few inches. Ruth watched it, unable to move. She was conscious that Eli, after one petrified moment had gone like a rush of wind, and dimly she heard the bang of the back door and the noise of a van starting up and careering out of the yard.

"Oh, Mother," she said. They had never touched each other much, never kissed, not since Ruth was small, but now she went and put her arms around Thora, struck afresh by the littleness of her, the insubstantial nature of her body inside the cotton nightdress. She's hardly here at all, she thought. And she did this for me.

The gun clattered down from Thora's hands to the floor, and not knowing what else to do, not thinking of the future, of what must be done, Ruth began to lead her as if to take her upstairs again; and for a few steps, as if all her energy and will had been exhausted, Thora went with her submissively. But then, at the foot of the stairs, one hand on the newel post, she halted.

"No," she said. "I'm not going."

Ruth tightened her grip on her.

"I'll help you, Mother. I'll carry you, if you like. I'm very strong."

For a long time Thora hung on to the post and looked at her without speaking. Her face was worn and shadowed with pain, and there was no flesh on it, the skull beneath the skin more obvious than Ruth had ever noticed before. Still she managed to smile.

"Only one thing you can do for me, Ruthie," she said. "Go get that gun. Your father shot a sick cow the other day. Why should the cow have better treatment than me. Eh? Eh?" She was still smiling – was inviting Ruth to smile in return.

"I can't, Mother."

"Yes, dear, you can," said Thora. "Go along. Get the gun. Do as I tell you. 'Tis the kindest thing. The only thing. Just think – maybe it'll be the hangman's rope, else. Do it for me, Ruthie."

"There, there, there's no need for tears."

Ruth's eyes flew open as she heard the voice. She recognised it. Well, not the speaker, exactly, but she knew the type. It was calm, professionally kind. She had heard a lot of voices like that in her time. They seemed to imply comfort and security and an end to worry. They meant a life free from her tormentors on the estate, and of being harassed to make decisions, and of people like Valerie who expected her to converse. And if they told her what to do and when to do it, then that, too, was a kind of freedom.

"Oh, it's nice to be back," she said.